'This is a must read for anyone who loves to delve into psychological thrillers!' *Linda Strong (Netgalley)*

'A tantalising and taut thriller with more twists and turns than a corkscrew. Red herrings swim all the way through it. An excellent page turner.' *Sally (Goodreads)*

'With brilliant main characters and a wonderful plot, this book is a real page turner. I would highly recommend this book.' *Stephanie Collins (Netgalley)*

'I absolutely adored this book.' *Lu Dex (Netgalley)*

'Great book…keeps you guessing!! If you love twists and turns then this book is for you!' *Diane Merrit (Netgalley)*

'With twists and turns that will wrong-foot you all the way, a dash of dark humour and a strong emotional punch, this is an excellent debut that more than earns its place within the genre.' *S.J.I. Holliday*, author of *Black Wood*

He Will Find You

DIANE JEFFREY

ONE PLACE. MANY STORIES

HQ
An imprint of HarperCollins*Publishers* Ltd
1 London Bridge Street
London SE1 9GF

This paperback edition 2018

First published in Great Britain by
HQ, an imprint of HarperCollins*Publishers* Ltd 2018

Diane Jeffrey asserts the moral right to be
identified as the author of this work.
A catalogue record for this book is
available from the British Library.

ISBN: 978-0-00-831005-9

MIX
Paper from
responsible sources
FSC™ C007454

This book is produced from independently certified FSC™ paper
to ensure responsible forest management.

For more information visit: www.harpercollins.co.uk/green

Typeset by Palimpsest Book Production Ltd, Falkirk, Stirlingshire
Printed and bound in Great Britain by
CPI Group (UK) Ltd, Croydon, CR0 4YY

For my three wonderful children, Benjamin, Amélie
and Elise.
You make my world beautiful.
You don't have to read this book, but if you do, please
wait until you're much older.
I love you,
Mummy xxx

"What the truth is and what we want as the truth are two separate things.

The former sheds light; the latter darkness."

Unknown

Chapter 1

2017

This can't be it, I think, my heart sinking as I see it for the very first time. I pull in to the side of the country lane. Resting my arms over the steering wheel, I lean forwards and study the house through the windscreen. Even from this distance it appears austere. Isolated. Built in cold, dark grey stone, the building dominates the valley from the top of a steep gravel driveway. It is prison-like with its barred sash windows. It must be at least five times the size of the two-bedroom semi my boyfriend – ex-boyfriend – and I bought as our first home ten years ago in Minehead.

I look to the right, observing the lush green grass speckled black and white with sheep, and beyond that the blue-brown water of Lake Grasmere. I'm struck by how incongruous this residence seems against the surrounding countryside. *This isn't the right place.* But a quick glance at the black and white chequered flag on the satnav screen confirms that I have arrived at my destination. Even so, I remain hopeful that the right house might be situated a few metres further along the road until I see the slate sign on the wooden gate. *The Old Vicarage.*

I can't quite believe it. It has taken me nearly eight hours to drive all this way, but I'm here at last. The Old Vicarage, my new home. I've left everything and everyone I know; I've left my whole life behind in Somerset. Here I am, moving to a region I've never visited, into a house I haven't laid eyes on before. This is the start of a new existence for me. It should be exciting, but I feel so scared. Butterflies are hurtling around in my stomach. It's only to be expected, I suppose. This is such a monumental change.

As I get out of the car to open the gate, I notice a mailbox. To my surprise, my name is on it. He has handwritten it on a scrap of white paper and stuck it next to his own name, engraved on the rectangular metal plate. It must have rained since it was added because the ink has run slightly where the Sellotape has come away. I can still make out my name, though. KAITLYN BEST. But even that is about to change.

There is a cattle grid and I'm careful walking over it as I push the gate open. I have to get out of the car again to close the gate once I've driven through it. It's only then that I realise how cold it is outside this evening. Even as I shiver, I can't help but admire the view of the fields and the lake. The daylight is fading fast now, but the scene is breathtaking. I could get used to this place.

But then I turn around and see the house again. It's late Georgian, although it makes me think of a Gothic castle. It's been in his family for years, this place, and I know he loves it. Telling myself it's probably more welcoming inside, I drive up to the house.

I use the heavy knocker to bang on the front door. I wait for several seconds, but there's no sign of anyone moving inside. I step down from the porch and pace up and down in front of the house, looking around me and pushing my hands into my coat pockets for warmth. Creeper covers part of the wall. I imagine in any other season it must look beautiful and detract from the drab colour of the stone, but at this time of the year the web of spindly branches looks dead and bare. There's a light on upstairs. He must be here. I'll try again and then I'll text him.

Am I making a terrible mistake? I wonder, not for the first time. My dad and my elder sister both tried to talk me out of coming here. After all, I've only seen this man once in the past twenty years. I step forwards again and go to grab the knocker, but then I spot a metal handle hanging down to my right and so I pull on it instead. I hear a loud chime sound inside the house. Seconds later, the door opens and he's standing there. Alexander Riley. My heart beats madly. He's smiling and it warms me through. Any doubts I had evaporate as I look up into his handsome face.

'Katie,' he says, sweeping me into his arms and squeezing me so tightly I can hardly breathe. He smells amazing. 'Come in. Welcome.' He releases me, takes my hand and leads me into the house. 'Would you like something to drink?' He doesn't pause for me to answer. 'I hope your drive wasn't too long,' he gushes as we walk side by side through the entrance hall, away from a huge pine staircase leading upstairs.

'Here's the sitting room. Go on through and I'll bring you some tea.' He pushes me gently into a spacious room to the left with high ceilings and a log fire burning at the end of it. 'I'll bring your stuff in from the car later. I'm so glad you're finally here.' And with that, he disappears.

I stand with my back to the fire for a couple of minutes, admiring the built-in bookshelves. Many of them have books on them, but there's more than enough space for some of my paperbacks when I bring up the boxes I've stored at my dad's house.

Feeling exhausted after the journey, I sink into an armchair. I look out of a sash window at the other end of the room. This one has thin wooden bars, too, in keeping with the Georgian period, no doubt. They're supposed to be decorative, I imagine, but I find them disturbing. The windowpanes are black now; night has fallen quickly.

Alex soon comes back carrying a tray with sandwiches, biscuits, a teapot and two mugs. He puts it down on the coffee table. Then he walks over to the sideboard and pours himself a Scotch. Holding the glass in one hand, he puts his arm around me from behind my armchair and, stroking my breasts and then my tummy, he plants a kiss on the top of my head. Then he bends over the coffee table, and from a little bowl on the tray he takes two ice cubes, which chink as he drops them into the amber liquid. He drags a heavy armchair nearer to mine and sits down.

I watch him as he does all this, his blue eyes bright with excitement. Tall with dark curly hair, he's very good-looking. I know he has an incredible, muscular body under those jeans and that sweater. When he smiles, dimples appear in his cheeks. He has an aquiline nose. His sideburns are way too long, but I find this endearing. His face has the healthy glow – even in winter – of someone who spends a lot of time outdoors. I have so many photos of him – I've kept all the photos he sent me in his emails – but none of them really do him justice.

'I'm finding it hard to believe we're finally together,' he says, picking up the teapot and swirling it around. Then he pours tea into a mug that already has a little milk in it. 'Do you take sugar?' he asks.

It seems strange, this question, when we know each other so well. At school, I hardly talked to him. I fancied him like mad, but I kept that a secret from everyone, especially him. Both my sisters had more to do with him than I did back then. But since we reconnected about seven months ago – initially thanks to Facebook – we've exchanged hundreds and hundreds of emails and phone calls. We've spent hours and hours chatting on FaceTime.

We've talked about our respective families in detail. I've never met Alex's children, but he has told me all about them so I feel as if I have. I know that Alex's favourite dish is shepherd's pie and that his favourite dessert is tiramisu. I could tell you his place of birth, his date of birth, his hobbies and interests and his tastes in music. I know so much about his education and career that I could probably write his CV.

He read *Wuthering Heights* when I told him it was the best book I'd ever read and he watched *The Piano* because I told him I loved that film. Once, he sent me a purple silk scarf and another time, I received a pink T-shirt because these are my favourite colours. He knows I adore roses and lilies and he has had bouquets delivered to both my place of work and home. He knows I hate take-offs and landings on planes. He's familiar with my deepest fears and darkest secrets. He could even describe my sexual fantasies.

But he has no idea how I drink my tea. I do take sugar, usually, but I can see that Alex hasn't put any on the tray, so I shake my head.

Alex talks non-stop when he gets excited – I know this from our numerous phone calls – and he babbles away as we eat. He says that tomorrow we'll visit Grasmere. He mentions a famous gingerbread shop, which he says is open almost every day of the year. And he promises to show me William Wordsworth's house and his grave.

I love the idea that this Romantic poet, whose works I studied at school, links my old home to my new home. I've come from Somerset to the Lake District; William Wordsworth did the opposite. He moved from Cumbria to the village of Nether Stowey, which is only about fifty miles from Porlock, where I grew up. And slightly closer to Minehead, where I lived until this morning. Eventually, Wordsworth returned to his roots. He was homesick. I hope I won't be.

I have that familiar nervous feeling in my tummy as I wonder again if I've made the right decision coming here. But it's a bit late to be asking myself that question now. The rain starts to beat down all of a sudden and Alex gets up to pull the thick curtains across the two sets of bay windows. Before sitting back down in his chair, he kisses my cheek, and once again I'm reassured and content.

We chat for ages, although Alex does most of the talking. Even though it can't be that late, I yawn. Alex immediately leaps up and clears away the tray. Then he insists that I stay by the fire while he brings in my things. I protest and get up to help, but he won't hear of it.

'You lost a lot of blood,' he says. 'You're not to take any more risks.'

It wasn't a lot, really, but I'm not going to argue.

The car is packed to the hilt with boxes, suitcases and bags, and it takes him about forty minutes. I feel a bit bad about letting him lug in all my stuff by himself, but I really don't want to go out in the rain. I've had a long drive and it's all too easy to persuade myself I'm only doing what I've been told. So, closing my eyes, I enjoy the heat emanating from the fire.

When he has finished, Alex comes back into the sitting room, combing his wet hair with the fingers of one hand and holding his other hand out to me. He pulls me out of my chair and leads the way upstairs. He has left the boxes and bags in the entrance hall, which he calls 'the vestibule', but he has brought my cases upstairs to the master bedroom, which is similar in size to the entire ground floor of the house I've just moved out of in Somerset.

It's cold up here and I'm almost reluctant to take off my clothes. After taking a shower to warm myself up a bit, I climb into bed naked, next to Alex, who is waiting for me. He makes love to me with just the right mixture of passion and tenderness. This is only the second time I've been to bed with him and I'm surprised at how natural it feels.

He falls asleep with his arms around me. At first, I relax and breathe in time with him, but after a while he starts to snore. I'm cold again and I begin to shiver. I slip out of his embrace and get out of bed. I manage to feel my way to the en suite bathroom and I turn on the light in there. Leaving the door open just enough to see what I'm doing, but hopefully not so much that the light will wake up Alex, I move silently across the carpeted floor of the bedroom to the suitcase that contains my nightwear. I look over my shoulder as I unzip the case, but he doesn't stir.

When I climb back into bed a minute or two later, I'm snug in my fleece pyjamas, but I'm wide awake. I can't get comfortable. The bed is lumpy and the quilt is tucked in tight around my feet, which I hate. For a while, I toss and turn.

After a few minutes, I realise I've disturbed Alex because he turns over and asks, 'Are you all right?'

'I'm fine. Sorry,' I whisper, feeling a pang of guilt for waking him. 'Go back to sleep.'

'Night, princess,' he says into my ear as he rolls towards me and puts his arms around me.

I lie still even though I can feel a spring digging into my lower back. Reminded of the story of *The Princess and The Pea*, I smile wanly in the darkness. Alex's body is like a hot water bottle against me and now I'm sweating slightly. Listening to the rain outside, I wait for sleep to come. It's a long wait.

~

The phone rings, waking me up with a start. It takes me a second or two to remember where I am. By the time I'm fully awake, the ringing has stopped.

I've been dreaming about Louisa, but I can't remember the details. I reach out for Alex, but he's not there. I get out of bed, stretch and walk over to my suitcase to find my slippers and dressing gown. I wonder if he could be in the bathroom, but I don't hear any water running. I open the door anyway and peep inside. Just as I thought, he's not in here. I freshen up a bit, and then I make my way downstairs to find him.

'Alex?' I call out.

I go into the sitting room, where the fire was crackling last night. It's chilly in here this morning, and I wrap my dressing gown around me and knot the belt.

'Alex?'

I walk down the hallway and peep into the kitchen. He's not in here, either. There's a strong smell of coffee, which makes me feel queasy even as my tummy rumbles.

As I'm hunting in the cupboards for teabags and a mug, I catch sight of the note. He has written a message on a Post-it and left it next to the kettle.

Gone training. Back in a bit.
Make yourself at home.
Mi casa es tu casa.
Alexxx.

I'm disappointed, of course I am. But it was nice of him not to wake me. He has left out some bread, butter and jam on the worktop.

As I wait for the kettle to boil, I look out of the window at a large tree in the back garden – I remember Alex telling me there was a damson tree, so this must be it. Its trunk is leaning at an angle that seems to defy gravity, but perhaps it's the visual effect created by the grassy slope. Not far from the tree, there's a swing set, and behind that, a thick wood.

The window bars give me the unnerving impression that I'm being kept prisoner. The rain is lashing down outside and the sky threatens to keep this up for a while. I don't expect we'll be wandering around Grasmere today after all.

The toast pops up and startles me, and this is followed by the telephone ringing again. I'm tempted not to bother answering, but then I think it might be Alex trying to get hold of me. I haven't turned my mobile on yet, I realise, so he would have to use the landline. I run out into the hall, where the sound is coming from, find the phone and pick up the handset.

'Hello?'

There's no answer.

'Hello?' I say again.

Still no answer.

'Alex, is that you?'

I wait for a second, but then there's a beep as if the caller has hung up. I dial 1471. I think I'd recognise Alex's mobile number if it was him. But the last caller's number is withheld. Shrugging, I go back into the kitchen to eat my breakfast.

Sitting at the long wooden table, I feel a bit lost and very alone. To shake off that sensation, I picture Alex and me feeding our children at this table one day. I see myself making cakes with my stepdaughters, whose mother has finally forgiven Alex – for whatever it is she thinks he's done – and let them come to stay with us. I close my eyes and inhale, imagining the mouth-watering smells wafting towards me from the oven and almost hearing the girls' laughter.

I've always wanted lots of children. At least four. Ideally, two boys then two girls. Having kids was a dream that didn't come true for me with Kevin. It wasn't for want of trying. It was the overriding desire to have a baby that killed the passion in our relationship and made it go stale. Looking back, I think it was over long before I left. Or perhaps I'm just telling myself that so I don't feel so bad about walking out on him.

Alex still isn't back when I've showered and got dressed, so I decide to explore the house. On the ground floor, there are several rooms I haven't seen yet. There's another lounge, which also has an open fire, and opposite it, a study. It has alcove built-in wooden cupboards and when I open them, I see they're empty.

As I discover my new home, I keep mentally comparing it with the house Kevin and I lived in, which we've just put on the market. The upstairs bathroom in Minehead would easily fit into either the laundry room or the cloakroom in the Old Vicarage.

Coming back through the hallway, just outside the kitchen, I notice a door near the staircase. I turn the handle, but it's locked. Briefly, I hunt around for a key – on the wall, in the cupboard under the stairs – but then I leave it. I realise the door probably leads to a cellar and I don't want to go down there anyway. I walk on towards the staircase.

Upstairs, there are five bedrooms altogether. Ours is the only one with an en suite bathroom, but there is another bathroom and a separate loo along the landing.

Although the views are better from the master bedroom – you can see Lake Grasmere – I prefer the bedroom at the back of the house, which, like the kitchen below, looks out onto the garden. It's smaller and cosier, with some sort of period fire grate and surround. The walls are painted a warm peach colour, but I notice there are no pictures on them, and it strikes me that I've seen no paintings or photos – not even of Alex's daughters – anywhere in the house.

While I ponder this, I push the last door open wider and step inside. Decorated in pink and lilac, it is a large room with two single beds. Fairies fly around on wall stickers and a giant stuffed cuddly dog lies on a multicoloured rug on the floor.

This must be Poppy and Violet's bedroom. Then a thought pushes its way into my head. Alex's daughters would be too old now for fairies and teddies. Alex's wife walked out on him five years ago and the girls are in their teens now. He said he hadn't seen them for a year. Surely if they'd come to visit a year ago, they wouldn't have wanted to sleep in such a childish environment. They would probably each want their own space at their age anyway.

Briefly, this puzzles me. But then I reason with myself. Alex didn't say the girls had ever come to stay with him before his ex-wife cut off all contact. Maybe they haven't slept at the Old Vicarage since his wife – ex-wife now – left him. That would explain it.

Sitting down on one of the beds, I run my hand over the hearts on the quilt cover. Quite unexpectedly, a chill runs down my spine. I scan the room. It's beautifully decorated. There are toys, games and children's books everywhere. And yet, there's something I don't like about it. I can't quite put my finger on what it is. The sense that someone was very unhappy in here? No, that's not it. Scared more than unhappy. In danger, even. As if something bad once happened in here.

I laugh at my silliness. I've always had an overactive imagination. Julie would have taken it seriously, though. My elder sister is into feng shui and mental wellness. She's reluctant to set foot in Dad's house now on the pretext that it has had negative energy and bad vibes since Mum died. I'll have to invite Julie to stay with us at the Old Vicarage. She'll have the chi flowing, or whatever it is you need to do, in no time.

I decide to start unpacking. Maybe when I've tidied away all my things, I'll feel at home in this house.

Mi casa es tu casa.

Hopefully Alex will be home soon. That will help, too.

Today is the first day of the rest of my life, I say to myself. A completely different life to the one I've had until now.

To: kaitlyn.best@newzmail.co.uk
From: alexanderriley9987@premiernet.co.uk
Sent: Mon, 01 Aug 2016 at 23:34
Subject: KISMET, KATE

Dear Katie,

I was thinking today how lucky I am that you sent me a
friend request on Facebook. You can't imagine how glad I
am that we've reconnected after all this time. And speaking
of Facebook, I was beginning to think I'd never get to see
a photo of you other than with your family and friends on
your wall. Thank you so much for your selfie! You're beautiful!

I love you being part of my day. Thanks to all your emails
and texts, it feels like you're close even though you're so far
away. Plus I like to know what you're doing and where you
are. You're very funny, and you made me laugh out loud
this afternoon when I was in a boring meeting with my
accountant.

Katie, you said this is moving too fast for you and you
feel a bit overwhelmed, but I've never felt a connection like
this before. We've only been in touch again for a month,
but it's as if I've known you for so much longer. Perhaps
it's because of all we have in common. At the same time, I
have this urge to make up for lost time. Two decades! You
understand, don't you?

I don't believe in fate or anything like that. But I do
wonder if things sometimes happen for a reason, and I
think that you coming back into my life at this moment in
time was meant to be! It feels so right. You're the real deal.

You said Kevin was going to the pub with his mates
tomorrow evening. Would you like to FaceTime? I love

hearing your voice on the phone, but it would be even lovelier to see you!

Sorry if I've come on a bit strong this evening. I've been on the single malt! I'll say goodnight now and leave you in peace! You'll be my last thought before I go to bed and my first thought when I wake up. And I'll probably dream about you, too. Hope that's all right with you.

Night,
Alexxx

Chapter 2

I'm desperate to get out of the house, but it doesn't look like we're going to be able to go outside the next morning, either. The rain is still beating down, although, looking out through the bars of our bedroom window, I can see a tiny patch of clear sky over the lake. My mother used to say if there was enough blue to make a pair of trousers for a sailor, the weather would turn out fine. Wishing I'd inherited her optimism as I stare at the sky, I reflect that the seaman in question would have to be fairly small.

I sigh, and Alex pleads with me to get back into bed. He's lying on his back, his hands clasped behind his head. He seems to be appraising my bare body. I kneel on the bed next to him.

'Lie on your tummy,' I order. He doesn't move for a second or two, but then he turns over. I start to knead his shoulders. He groans – in pleasure, I hope, rather than pain, but just in case, I massage his muscles more softly.

'Is this new?' I ask, running my fingers over his right shoulder. 'I haven't seen it before.'

'Is what new? Oh, the tattoo. Well, I had it done before Justin Bieber if that's what you mean.'

'You've lost me.'

'Bastard has the same tat. It's Banksy.'

'I know that,' I say, admiring the artwork inked onto Alex's skin. The picture is of a girl with her hand stretched out towards a red balloon. 'My nephew Oscar is a big fan. We've taken him to Bristol a couple of times to see Banksy's street art and some of his works on display at M Shed.'

'Well, Girl with a Balloon appeared on a wall somewhere in London, not Bristol,' Alex informs me. 'I still haven't decided if I want the caption inked on next to it.'

'What is it?'

'There is always hope,' he says.

I examine it again. The balloon is heart-shaped. It's not clear to me if the girl has let go of the balloon or if she's trying to catch it. Either way, it's out of her reach. Before I can ask Alex any more about it, he jumps out of bed.

'Breakfast in bed,' he says. 'You wait here.'

I'm left for a while to muse on Alex's choice of body art design. I would have thought he'd go for something more athletic, but I'm not sure what exactly. I suppose you wouldn't have the five Olympic rings unless you'd actually competed in an Olympic Games. Or the Nike logo unless they sponsored you. And a slogan like "no pain, no gain" would be a bit trite. But something along those lines. I didn't even know he had a tattoo. I'm surprised at this, although I'd only seen him naked once before coming here, and on that occasion the lights were dimmed.

I allow myself to reminisce about that night. It was four months ago. I close my eyes and can feel myself smiling. I remember Alex stripping off his clothes in a few seconds flat and then climbing into bed. He lay on his back, propped up on his elbows, watching me undress as he waited for me to join him. I'd been amused and turned on by how keen he seemed. Thinking about it now,

15

it's hardly surprising I didn't see the tattoo on the back of his shoulder.

I noticed the scars, though. At the time, I didn't dare ask him about those. Now, I'm burning with curiosity.

Alex comes back into the bedroom, carrying a tray. Smelling the toast, I'm conscious of how hungry I am. I plump the pillows up behind me and sit up straight as he puts the tray down carefully on my lap and gets into bed next to me.

'Don't get too used to this,' he warns, twirling a strand of my red wavy hair between his fingers and then taking a mug from the tray.

At first I don't understand what he's referring to, but then I catch him looking down pointedly at my tummy.

'Lie-ins will soon be nothing more than a distant memory,' he adds. 'Or is the plural lies-in?' He slurps his tea.

'No. You were right first time. Lie-ins.'

'Ask the language expert,' he says. He puts his mug down on the bedside table, and then he starts to fondle one of my breasts. 'And is it my imagination, or have these already got a bit bigger?'

'It's wishful thinking on your part, I'd say,' I reply, mirroring his grin. 'Seeing as we're on the subject of bodies ...' I begin in a more serious voice.

'Ye-es?'

Gently, I take his arm and stroke his wrists. 'Can I ask about your scars?'

'OK,' he says, but then there's an awkward silence and I regret bringing it up. 'Well, it's not a big secret. I was nineteen,' he says eventually. 'I'd left school. I was supposedly on a gap year, but I ran out of money very early on, got dumped by my girlfriend when we were in Australia and came home. I started to hang out with the wrong crowd, we were taking drugs, I got depressed ...'

'Go on,' I say when he pauses.

'Long story short, one evening I decided to end it all. I was a stupid, self-absorbed teenager. I ran a hot bath, got in and slit my wrists.'

I'd only seen scars on his left wrist. I resist the urge to turn over his right arm, particularly as he's holding his mug and I don't want to scald him.

He sees me peering at his other hand, though, and adds, 'Well, my wrist. I did it wrong. Used my right arm. Apparently if you're right-handed, like I am, you should start by slitting your right wrist. That way, you can finish the job off better when you need to swap hands. And I managed to cut into a tendon in my left arm. I was in agony even though I hadn't cut nearly deep enough to kill myself. So, it was a botched job.'

I can hear my own breathing. It has become shallow. I'm uncomfortable talking about his suicide attempt, so I don't say the words that have just wormed their way into my head. *There are more foolproof methods than slitting your wrists.* Nor do I point out that he should have cut vertically rather than across his wrists. How do I even know that? 'I'm so glad it was a botched job,' I say instead, nuzzling in to him as much as I can without upsetting the breakfast tray on my lap or the mug in his hand.

'So am I,' he murmurs, kissing the top of my head.

And then it hits me like a punch to the stomach. If Alex was nineteen, I would have been seventeen. My chest tightens at that thought and I feel nauseous. I have a sudden vision of Alex throwing himself off a cliff and plummeting to his death.

I leap out of bed, making Alex cry out as I cause him to spill his tea. I make it to the bathroom just in time. Seconds later, he is next to me, holding back my hair with one hand and rubbing my back the other as I throw up into the toilet.

'Morning sickness,' he comments wryly when I've finished retching.

It's not, but I don't contradict him.

~

17

The sun comes out in the early afternoon and so Alex drives us the short distance into Grasmere. I'd rather walk, but I don't protest; I'm just happy to get out of the house. There are lots of people out and about. From the car park, it's a short walk to St Oswald's church, where William Wordsworth is buried. We follow the path round to the back of the church, walking on paving stones with people's names and hometowns engraved on them. From a much bigger paving slab, I read aloud the first verse of 'I wandered lonely as a cloud', Wordsworth's most famous poem.

After Alex has shown me the Wordsworth family's tombstones, we go by foot to Dove Cottage, a little further up the road. The sign on the house says *The loveliest spot that man hath ever found*. 'It is really beautiful here,' I say. 'I can see why the area inspired him to write his poetry.'

'He lived in this cottage with his sister, Dorothy,' Alex says informatively. 'They were very close.'

Unbidden, tears well up in my eyes, and I brush them away with my sleeve before Alex can see. I miss Louisa terribly. When we were little, we swore we would live together in the same house, with our husbands. Being without her is like being without a part of myself. Even now, all sorts of things remind me of her. Smells, songs, phrases. Not for the first time, I wonder if one day the void in me can be filled.

By now I'm used to feeling I'm not quite complete, but I feel a very special bond with Alex, similar to the one I once had with my twin sister. Alex and I like the same music, the same activities, the same TV programmes. He often reads my mind, just like Louisa did.

'There's a walk that goes from here to Rydal Mount,' Alex says, interrupting my thoughts. 'That's the house he bought once he became rich and famous.'

'Ooh, can we go and see it?'

'Well, it's about five and a half miles altogether,' Alex says, 'and there's a bit of a hill.'

'I won't break, Alex.'

'Yes, but you're supposed to be taking things easy, the doctor said.'

'She also said it would do me good to walk.'

'It's a bit chilly, though. Wordsworth died because he caught a cold you know,' he says, elbowing me playfully in the ribs.

'That was in 1850,' I say, pleased with myself for remembering the date on the tombstone. 'Anyway, if you show me the way instead of standing around pretending to argue with me, we'll soon warm up climbing that hill you mentioned.'

Alex chuckles. 'Come on, then.'

He takes my hand and leads me along a country lane. He proves himself to be a great guide and he knows a lot about the area, its geography and its history. He points out Helm Crag, whose distinctive peak, according to Alex, has earned it the nickname the Lion and the Lamb. I stare at it, shielding my eyes, but I can't see anything remotely resembling a large feline or a woolly ruminant.

'That sounds more like the name of a pub than of a fell,' I comment, but if Alex hears me, he doesn't respond.

It's a lovely walk and the sun stays with us the whole time. I'm so glad that the weather has brightened up and we weren't stuck in the house all day today like we were yesterday, although after my journey up here, it was great to have a lazy day, too, especially as it was spent mostly in bed with Alex. I look at Alex and he smiles at me. A warm feeling of happiness engulfs me as I beam back.

'This route is part of the Coffin Trail,' Alex announces, a little further up the hill. That wipes the smile off my face for a moment.

'The Coffin Trail?'

'Yes. People used to carry the coffins down this hill to St Oswald's church to bury their dead.'

We continue to walk up the hill and after a while, we arrive at the tiny village of Rydal. A dog barks as we walk around the grounds of Wordsworth's home, and again as we walk away, down the hill. On our left is a large sloping field.

'This is Dora's field,' Alex resumes. 'Dora was Wordsworth's favourite daughter and he was heartbroken when she died.'

'What did she die of?' I ask, intrigued.

He shrugs. 'No idea,' he says. 'He lost all his children. Dora was the only one left but then she died, too. He planted hundreds of daffodils in this field as a memorial to her. It's quite impressive in the spring when the flowers are in bloom.'

A line from the verse I read on the church paving stone echoes in my head.

A host of golden daffodils.

'That's so sad,' I say.

'Yes, it is,' Alex agrees. 'I can't imagine what it must be like for a father to lose his children.'

It crosses my mind that in a way Alex has lost his daughters. For the moment, at least. His ex-wife won't let him see them. I wonder if that's what is going through his head. Then my thoughts turn to my own father. And my mother. It seems to me that it's somehow far worse for a mother to lose a child, but I keep this to myself.

Alex and I sit down on a wooden bench and admire the view over Rydal Water.

'I've got something for you,' Alex says, letting go of my hand and thrusting his hand into the pocket of his jeans. He brings out a small blue jewellery box.

I open it and gasp at the necklace inside. 'Thank you. It's beautiful,' I say. And it is. It's a red heart crystal pendant on a silver chain and I'm instantly reminded of his tattoo.

Alex puts it around my neck and I hold my hair up and bow my head so that he can do up the clasp.

'Maybe you can wear it on the day,' he suggests.

I tilt my head upwards to kiss his lips, suddenly aware that the sun has gone behind a cloud and the air has become cooler since we've been sitting on the bench. Alex must feel me shiver as he suggests we get on with our walk.

I take his hand as we get up from the bench, but he pulls it away to scratch his nose. I turn my head to follow his gaze and see a woman coming down the path towards us, chatting away to her little white dog. I'm not sure what breed it is. I sense Alex hesitate next to me before striding more purposefully up the path. I have to quicken my pace to keep up.

The woman widens her dark oval eyes, which seem to bore into me as she approaches. I think she's about to say something as she opens her large mouth, revealing a rather prominent set of very white teeth. She has short dark brown hair with red highlights, and severely plucked eyebrows, which only serve to heighten the look of shock on her face. She brushes my arm as we pass.

'Do you know her?' I whisper.

'Never seen her before in my life.' He has answered me so loudly that I nudge him, certain that the woman has heard him.

But I can tell something is not quite right. I look at him askance.

He glances over his shoulder. 'I'm just a bit wary of dogs,' he admits in a much quieter voice than before.

This amuses me. That white dog is so small, after all, and Alex is tall and strong, and he doesn't seem to be afraid of much.

Something else I didn't know about him. Perhaps I don't know him quite as well as I thought. This idea makes me a little uneasy, but that feeling is quickly dispelled as I imagine the fun we'll have getting to know each other better.

To: kaitlyn.best@newzmail.co.uk
From: alexanderriley9987@premiernet.co.uk
Sent: Sat, 10 Sept 2016 at 22:56
Subject: SEE YOU!

Dearest Katie,

I'm sorry my replies to your emails have been so brief lately. I've been really busy at work. I promise to make it up to you. Maybe I can do that very soon …

I've got a proposition for you: would you do me the honour of dining with me one evening? I have a supplier in Exeter and he has just brought out a whole new collection of sports clothing, which I'd like to go and see for myself. I'm planning to go down by train next month. If you'd like to meet up, I can time it so it's on a day when you're working at the university. I'd love to meet up with you again after all these years!

Now I know we've been getting kinky in our emails recently (I love it when you talk dirty – you're so hot!) and I know you wanted to try and slow things down a bit, but I assure you that I can be the perfect gentleman and I'll be on my best behaviour. I'm just asking you to let me take you … out for a meal.

If you don't think this is a good idea, please say so. If I walked through the door of a restaurant with you on my arm (or at my side) I would probably burst with pride anyway, so you'll be saving me from that fate if you turn me down.

What do you think?

See you soon, maybe?
Alexxx

Chapter 3

I'm panicking. *Where on earth is it?* I'm sure I put it in this drawer, but I can't have because it's not there now. 'Shit!' I open the other drawers and rummage around, but I can't find it anywhere. 'Bollocks!'

Julie and Hannah come into my bedroom to see what all the swearing is about. I fill them in. 'But don't tell Alex,' I hiss at them. 'He wants me to wear it tomorrow. He'll be upset.'

I check my jewellery box again before giving up the hunt. With a sigh, I plop down on the bed, feeling a stab of guilt about misplacing his gift.

'We'll look for it later,' Julie says. 'It has to be here somewhere.'

'Yeah, don't worry, sweetie.' Hannah puts one reassuring hand on my arm and pushes her dark frizzy hair away from her face with her other hand. 'Wait until he's out of the house this evening, then we'll ransack it if we need to. We'll find it.'

'OK,' I say. 'Let's get out of here.'

The three of us are keen to escape and do our last-minute shopping in Keswick, a local town, which I know my sister and my best friend will fall in love with, as I have. Before leaving, we pop into the kitchen, where Alex and my dad are talking, to say goodbye. Dad is sitting at the table, smiling and seemingly more carefree than I've seen him in a long time, and Alex is standing at the worktop, his hands covered in flour, making an apple crumble.

A mixture of love and pride suddenly surges inside me. Here are the two men I adore most, in my kitchen, chatting as if they've known each other for more than ten years instead of less than one day. I take six mugs out of the cupboard, stealing a glance at Alex. He looks incredibly attractive, even in an apron. And, evidently, he has made my dad feel welcome. Alex catches me staring at him and winks.

Jet, my dad's black Labrador, is lying on the floor with his nose on his owner's feet.

Alex kisses my cheek as he waits for me to fill up the kettle, and then he washes his hands at the sink.

'All right, fella?' he says, bending down to pat Jet on the head.

I turn away, hiding my grin from Alex, as he pulls out a chair and sits down at the table with Dad. Images flash before my eyes of our walk a few weeks ago and I remember Alex confessing that he was scared of that woman's little dog. Yet here he is, making an effort to get on with my dad by making friends with Jet. A sure way to Dad's heart.

Jet was Julie's idea. A rescue dog, it was in fact Jet that rescued my dad. He was about two years old when we chose him from the RSPCA shelter seven or eight years ago. Julie's sons had given Dad a reason to go on after Mum's death, but although his smile was as permanent a feature on Dad's face as his deep worry lines, it wasn't until he had Jet that Dad's smile reached his eyes.

Watching Alex, who is still stroking the dog, I feel very grateful to him for all he has done for my family since they arrived last night. He has gone to great lengths to impress them all and he has been punctilious in providing every comfort he can think of

24

for our guests. Yesterday, he cooked a delicious dinner, topped up everyone's glasses with wine throughout the meal, and was charming and witty the whole evening. He has even won over my best friend Hannah, who usually takes a while to warm to people she has just met, particularly men.

Julie saunters back into the kitchen after taking a mug of tea into the living room for Daniel, her husband, who is watching a DVD of *Rogue One* with their two sons. 'What are you going to do while we're out, Dad?' she asks.

'We men are all going for a walk,' Alex answers for him. 'I'd like to show everyone around Grasmere and we'll all get some fresh air.'

'Jet could do with some exercise,' Dad adds. 'He was stuck in the car for hours yesterday.'

Julie, Hannah and I finally speed away in my getaway Citroën C3, gravel flying up as I accelerate down the drive. Hannah has made me a playlist with Eighties and Nineties music as, like her, I grew up during those decades. She has plugged her iPod into the car stereo and all three of us are rocking the Casbah at the tops of our respective lungs. I am happy, excited, and, if I'm honest, a little anxious as well.

Twenty minutes later, Julie voices what is still niggling me as I pull into a space in the car park.

'You're certain about getting married, are you?' she asks. I've always admired my elder sister for her frankness. She speaks her mind and sometimes it's not easy to hear, but I appreciate her open honesty. 'I know you want your child to grow up with both parents, but this isn't just a shotgun wedding, is it?'

'I'm nervous about the big day,' I reply, 'but I love Alex so much.'

It's a bit more than pre-wedding nerves. I keep thinking I'm rushing into this marriage blindfolded, even though everything feels so right with Alex. Most of the time.

'Hmm, I can understand why,' my sister says, her eyes sparkling, and I can tell she's satisfied with my answer.

'He's perfect for you,' Hannah agrees. Her words move me because she's always been very fond of Kevin and she gave me a hard time when I left him for Alex. I understood where she was coming from. Kevin is such a loving person; I can't explain – to Hannah or even to myself – why I didn't love him enough.

A lump comes to my throat and I give Hannah's hand a quick squeeze, not trusting myself to speak. We all get out of the car and I head for the Pay & Display machine, putting an end to the conversation.

As I'd predicted, both my sister and my friend adore Keswick. It's a shame they didn't arrive earlier yesterday; they would have loved the market. A chocolate fountain in a shop window catches Hannah's eye and she gives in to temptation and buys a box of chocolate fudge. Julie and I have a facial and get manicures while Hannah chatters away, her mouth full of her recent purchase. Hannah is a hairdresser, and although her hair is usually an unruly mess, her skin is flawless and her nails are always impeccable.

The beauty salon is not far from Alex's shop, and it also happens to be opposite a pub, so we have a late lunch there. Afterwards, we wander around town a bit more, then decide to head back to the Old Vicarage.

As I open the front door, a wonderful smell floats towards us – a mixture of cinnamon and thyme. It's not long before we're sitting at the table eating again. I'm still full from lunch, but Alex has gone to a lot of trouble cooking and I eat as much of the roast dinner and crumble as I can. My round tummy has been protruding very noticeably for a couple of months now, so it's not as if I was trying to keep slim for my wedding day.

After dinner, Alex gets his overnight bag ready and slings his suit, in a protective cover, over his shoulder. He has made arrangements to stay at his best man's house.

'You won't change your mind?' I ask hopefully.

'A groom shouldn't see his bride on the big day before she

walks down the aisle – or, in our case, into the register office,' he says. 'It's bad luck.'

I know he's not superstitious, any more than I am, but I expect he'll go out for a few drinks with his mates and enjoy his last few hours of bachelorhood.

'As long as you don't have too much fun, then,' I say, pretending to pout.

He gives me a tender kiss and now I wish more than ever that he'd sleep next to me tonight. I tell myself that at least this way I'll get some time alone with my family and my best friend. I haven't seen them for about two months, and I've missed them.

As soon as he has gone, Julie and Hannah appear from the living room and usher me upstairs to my bedroom.

'Right, let's get to work,' Hannah says, picking up books from my bedside table and checking under them.

The missing necklace has been crouching in the back of my mind all day, and I'm thankful that Julie and Hannah haven't forgotten about it either.

We've been searching upstairs for a while when Daniel offers to help. He rallies together Oscar and Archie, who were starting to bicker over a board game, but a full hour later we give up. Upstairs, we've checked under the beds, in all the cupboards, drawers and bathroom cabinets. Hannah went as far as to search inside my shoes and in my coat pockets in the wardrobe. And downstairs, Daniel and the boys have looked under the sofas, in the built-in cupboards and on the bookcases. Daniel says he has even checked in the laundry basket, washing machine and tumble dryer.

We've looked everywhere. And at least twice in most places.

Well, nearly everywhere.

'So, do you want to open that box?' Julie asks.

We found a cardboard box in the wardrobe of the bedroom with the peach walls, where my sister and brother-in-law are sleeping. I know Julie wants to open it, not because she thinks the necklace might be in there, but out of simple curiosity about what actually is inside.

'No. I can't imagine where the necklace has got to, but it can't possibly have got into the box,' I say. 'It's all taped up.'

'I wonder what's in there,' Hannah muses.

'Maybe stuff belonging to Alex's daughters,' I say.

'You'd think that would be stored in their room,' Julie says.

My nephews are sleeping in Poppy and Violet's bedroom. Alex wasn't happy about it, but the other guestrooms were going to be taken by Hannah, Dad, and Julie and Daniel. So that only left Alex's daughters' room.

'It's not as if it's used,' I'd pointed out, regretting it instantly as Alex's face clouded over.

For a second I thought he might get angry, although he has never raised his voice at me, but in the end, he said, 'You're right.' And that was that.

Julie goes in there now. The boys are aged twelve and ten, but she still tucks them in. When she has finished, she joins Hannah and me in my bedroom.

'It's a creepy bedroom,' she comments, thumbing over her shoulder towards the door.

'Oh, yeah, those fairies flying around all over the walls would give anyone nightmares,' Hannah quips.

'What do you mean?' I ask Julie, although I realise I'm not at all surprised at her observation.

'Well, for a start, the bookcase has sharp angles and it's shooting poison arrows directly at the bed on the right, which is aligned with the door.'

'Why is that bad?'

'It's like lying in a coffin when you're about to be carried out feet first.'

I shudder, even as I think how ridiculous that all sounds.

'Then the headboards are partially blocking both windows,' Julie continues. 'That creates negative energy. And you sleep badly with your head under a window, anyway. There's an awful lot of clutter in there, which doesn't help. Far too much Sha Chi altogether.'

Until now, I've always been flippant about my sister's firm belief in feng shui. To me, it seems out of character for her as she's usually so sensible and rational. I want to ask her how to remove the negative energy, but Hannah changes the subject.

'So, what are we going to do about the necklace? Have you got another one?'

'The only other one I have was a present from Kevin. I can't possibly wear that.' I bite my lip, pushing away the feeling of guilt that accompanies every thought I have of my ex-boyfriend.

'The one with the letters "K" and "K" entwined?' Julie raises her eyebrows. 'No, you certainly cannot.' She strides out of the room without explanation and I wonder if I've upset her. I look at Hannah, who shrugs.

'Here you are. Wear this,' Julie says, appearing seconds later, holding out a gold chain with a diamond pendant. 'It was Mum's.'

Tears spring to my eyes. 'Are you sure it's OK?'

'Of course I'm sure, Kaitlyn. I brought it here in case you wanted to wear it for your wedding day. I didn't know Alex had given you a heart for the occasion.' She pauses, clearly replaying her sentence in her head. Hannah snorts. 'You know what I mean,' Julie says.

She puts the chain around my neck and does up the clasp. 'There. Now you won't lose this one.'

'Thank you,' I say.

A few minutes later, when Dad, Julie and Daniel have all gone to bed, Hannah and I are both in our pyjamas and Hannah is waltzing around my bedroom trying to talk round the toothbrush in her mouth.

'I can't make out a word you're saying.' I start to giggle.

She goes into my en suite bathroom. I hear her gargle, and then she materialises in the doorway, her eyebrows raised in mock surprise.

'Who do all those bottles belong to?' she says.

'What are you talking about?' I ask, my tired brain conjuring up images of wine bottles, even though I haven't drunk any alcohol for months.

'All those cosmetics. We had to drag you kicking and screaming into the beauty parlour earlier,' she jokes. 'And I know you're not that obsessed about your appearance.'

What she's really referring to, I imagine, is that I wear minimal make-up and don't do enough with my hair for her liking. She has told me several times that people pay a lot of money to dye their hair the same colour as mine, whereas I've inherited this shade naturally from my mum's Irish genes, but I just scrape my hair back into a ponytail most of the time.

'No, I never take two bottles into the shower,' I say, humouring her. 'They're mainly Alex's, actually.'

'Oh dear, someone should have warned you. Never. Ever.' She prods me twice in the chest as she says this. 'Ever.' Another prod. 'Go out with a man who has more beauty products than you!' I burst out laughing. 'Seriously. Take it from me.'

It's hard to imagine that anyone could possibly own more haircare products than Hannah although, to be fair, that goes with the job. Nor do I tell her that I saw Alex pack three washbags in his overnight bag.

'Sebastian, right?'

'Big mistake.' All Hannah's ex-boyfriends are big mistakes. 'I could never get into the bathroom! He smelt good and he looked great, but he was far more in love with himself than he ever was with me.'

'Moron,' I say.

'Yeah. Fuck him. Still, you won't have that problem.' I think she's going to say that Alex is head over heels in love with me, but instead she says, 'You've got about ten bathrooms in this house.' It's a gross exaggeration, and we both laugh.

Hannah sits on the bed next to me. I've known Hannah for a long, long time. We've been inseparable since our first day at primary school. We didn't have the same interests as we grew up: I was athletic whereas Hannah was allergic to sport. I studied hard for my A levels – work was a welcome distraction that year. Hannah, on the other hand, skipped class to concentrate on the practical side of her sex education. I got good results, which was a huge relief as I was able to get away for a while and go to university. Hannah flunked her A levels but couldn't have cared less, even though this meant she had to carry on living with her parents for a few years.

After I lost Louisa, Hannah was my rock. Leaving her behind in Somerset this time was harder in many ways than leaving Kevin. The conversation was a bit strained between us on the phone the first couple of times. Hannah made it very clear that she thought I was making the wrong decision. I'd desperately needed her support, but Hannah had needed a little time to come round. She resented the fact that I'd made her complicit in all this, too. I'm so glad that things are back to normal between us.

'So, what's his family like?' she asks, hugging her knees to her chest and pulling the quilt up around her.

'Well, he doesn't have anything much to do with his dad,' I begin. 'He won't be coming to the wedding. He hasn't been invited. Apparently he was a serial adulterer and Alex's mum threw him out when Alex was little. Nobody actually knows where he is.'

'And his mum?'

'Well, we didn't exactly hit it off the first time I met her, but she's making an effort.'

'Oh? What happened?'

'Well, I was talking about my childhood and growing up with Julie and Louisa, and Dad having his work cut out for him in a house with four women, two of them incorrigible twins. I overheard her whisper to Alex: "Oh, God. You didn't tell me there were two of her." I hadn't told her what had happened to Louisa at that point.'

31

'What a terrible thing to say!' There is a brief silence, which Hannah breaks. 'What about Alex? Does he have any brothers or sisters? I honestly can't remember him from school at all.'

'Well, he was in the same house as Louisa and me, not you. And he was two years ahead of us. He's an only child. I think that's part of the problem between his mum and me. She must think I've trapped her prince into marrying me by getting myself pregnant with his baby.' I become aware that I've been twisting a strand of my hair round my finger. A nervous habit. I sit on my hands, and add, 'Things went a bit smoother last time we met up, though.'

'I'm very jealous of you, you know,' Hannah says.

'Why?' I'm not sure what she means. Surely she doesn't want a difficult mother-in-law.

'I was jealous before. I thought you and Kevin were really good for each other—'

'Hannah,' I say in a warning tone, thinking she's going to tell me again that I've messed up.

'No, let me finish. From what you've told me about Alex, and judging from what I've seen of him since I arrived, I think you've ... Well, let's just say, I hope I find someone I can be as happy with one day.'

'Really?' Hannah has had an endless string of boyfriends, and hasn't stayed with any of them for any length of time. I'm taken aback by her admission.

'Yes. I'd like to settle down one day. Preferably before I'm in my forties.'

'That gives you another three years. That's loads of—'

'I don't want to be left on the shelf. But I don't want to marry someone I'm not absolutely sure about, either.'

I look at Hannah. Her cheeks are even rosier than usual. I'm at a loss for words.

She smiles reassuringly at me, and it occurs to me that I should have found comforting words for her instead of platitudes.

Then her smile drops, and she says, 'You are absolutely sure about Alex, right?'

'Yes, of course,' I reply, my heart skipping a beat at Hannah's perspicacity. 'What do you mean?'

'Just that, oh, I don't know. I like Alex. I like him a lot. But he does seem to be a bit too good to be true.'

I don't answer. I don't know what to say.

'Oh, don't pay any attention to me.' She grins again, but her flippant tone sounds affected. 'I'm just jealous! I'm off to bed now before I say anything else I shouldn't. You need to get some sleep before your big day.'

I've been plucking at the quilt, and realise I've chipped a newly manicured nail. I swear under my breath.

I'm exhausted and sleep comes almost straight away. For once, I don't dream about Louisa. I dream about Kevin, but his face is blurry. He seems to belong to a different world, a different lifetime.

To: kaitlyn.best@newzmail.co.uk
From: alexanderriley9987@premiernet.co.uk
Sent: Thur, 13 Oct 2016 at 00:34
Subject: MY BEST GIRL

Dearest Katie,

Two more sleeps until I see you!

I can hardly believe it! I can't wait.

I hope you're not having second thoughts. I'm having lots of thoughts ... some of them honourable, some of them naughty, and they're all about you!

What's mostly on my mind is that I think I'm falling in love with you. When I see you, I'm confident that I'll *know* I've fallen for you. You are The One. My Best girl.

Now I've made that declaration, I'm worried I'll have scared you off. My promise still stands. I will behave. How is up to you.

It's great that Hannah has agreed to cover for you. I think I remember her from school. Vaguely. She was your best friend then, too, wasn't she?

See you the day after tomorrow, Katie. That sounds so unreal!

All my love,
Alexxx

Chapter 4

I wake up to the noise of an argument and the smell of toast, both coming from downstairs. I close my eyes tight, thinking I'll go back to sleep for a few minutes, and then it hits me. It's my wedding day! I leap out of bed so quickly that the room starts spinning. I sit back down on the bed and wait for it to stop. Grabbing my mobile from the bedside table, I turn it on. It gives the notification sound for an incoming text message. I grin like a loon when I see it's from Alex.

> Good morning, princess!
> See you in church!!!
> (I mean, see you in the register office.)
> I love you, my Best girl.
> Alexxx

My heart skips several beats. I read the text at least four times. Then, as I make my way to the bathroom, I realise his pun won't work for much longer. I'm about to become his wife. A Riley.

After today, 'Best' will be my maiden name.

I shower, singing Depeche Mode's 'Never Let Me Down Again', which has been in my head since I listened to it yesterday on the playlist Hannah created for me. When I'm clean, I pull on my dressing gown and make my way downstairs.

The kitchen is a mess. Oscar and Archie have apparently finished eating – and quarrelling – and have left the table and their dirty plates and glasses on it. My dad and Daniel are still seated, munching toast, Jet is sitting on the floor between their chairs, looking hopefully from one to the other with his huge dark eyes, and, at the far end of the table, Julie is drinking tea while Hannah is standing behind her, drying her hair. She has cut it, too, judging from the clippings on the floor around Julie's chair.

Alex would be appalled. He is rather OCD about tidiness, but seeing my loved ones making themselves at home in the kitchen – *my* kitchen – puts a huge smile on my face.

'Good morning,' they chorus.

'Ready for your big day?' my sister adds loudly to make herself heard over the hairdryer.

'Psychologically, yes,' I say, 'but physically—' I point one hand at my wet hair and the other one at my dressing gown '—not quite.'

Hannah grins. 'Eat some brekky and I'll make you beautiful when I've finished with Julie.'

Daniel jumps up to make a fresh pot of tea. He and Dad fuss with me, forcing me to eat even though I have butterflies and no appetite. I was worried that Daniel would judge me. After all, he and Kevin are good mates and I'm sure he had to pick up the pieces when I left. But Daniel has known me for a long time and has always treated me more like a little sister than a sister-in-law, and to my relief, he's been very supportive. If he thinks badly of me for hurting Kevin, he doesn't show it.

I look at Julie. She is already made up and looks radiant. Julie has fine, blonde hair, which she inherited from Dad, who was blond before he went grey and then bald. Hannah has cut Julie's hair, which was long and a bit lank, into a sleek chin-length bob and, even with my inexpert eye, I can see that this has given Julie's hair a lot more volume.

Hannah, who for the moment is dressed in her usual uniform of skinny jeans and a hoodie, has tamed her own stubborn hair into ringlets. I know she'll look uncomfortable when she has to put her dress on, but for now she looks relaxed and absolutely gorgeous.

At one point, the boys appear in the doorway to show off their outfits to their parents. They're wearing smart trousers and ironed shirts and I'm struck by how grown-up they seem.

But then Julie says, 'Have you brushed your teeth?'

The boys look at each other, turn around and seconds later, we hear them bounding back up the stairs. We all laugh.

The girl staring back at me from the full-length mirror in my bedroom looks like my mum. Hannah has done an amazing job on my hair, and she has given me a hand with my make-up, too. For the first time ever, I love my red hair. We don't have any water-proof mascara, which Hannah says I'll regret as I'm bound to get emotional and cry at some stage today. She has convinced me to go for dark brown mascara instead of the green one I normally use.

It's a bit of a squeeze putting on my ivory maternity wedding dress, my tummy a larger beach ball than I'd anticipated when I bought it. It's supposed to be knee-length, but at the front it now comes down to mid-thigh. I have to breathe in and hold my shoulders back for Hannah to get the zip all the way up.

'You should probably go easy on the wedding cake,' my friend advises as I tie the silk sash loosely above my bump. I'm so nervous that I don't think I'm going to be eating much of anything today, but I don't say that. I just breathe out and smile at Hannah in the mirror.

I realise I've made Dad think of Mum, too, because when he

sees me coming down the stairs, he gasps. 'Your mum would have been so proud of you,' he says, quickly regaining his composure.

This brings tears to my eyes. This is supposed to be the happiest day of my life, but how can it be without Mum and Louisa? My hand goes to my neck and I close my fingers around the pendant of Mum's necklace. Reminding myself that my mascara isn't waterproof, I blink back the tears and we make our way outside and to the bottom of the drive, where the cars that Alex booked are waiting to take us to the register office in Kendal.

The ceremony itself goes by in a bit of a blur. Alex doesn't take his eyes off me throughout the vows. I can feel everyone else's eyes on Alex and me from behind us. He seems to bask in the glow of all the attention, but I shut out everything so there's only him and me.

The Superintendent Registrar conducts the ceremony with the swift aplomb of someone who has married countless couples before and has better things to do on a Saturday. Even so, he is a lot less grumpy than when we met him to give notice of our intention to marry a month ago, although I suppose if Alex had remembered to bring his divorce papers, he might have been more affable.

Sitting at the table, next to Alex, I sign the register as Kaitlyn Best. The last time I'll use this name. Hannah is my witness and I've never met Alex's witness before. He introduced himself as 'Mike from the triathlon club' moments before we entered the register office.

'It's so nice to finally meet you,' I say now, as Alex takes his turn signing the register. He keeps his left hand on my thigh under the table as he does this. 'It's a shame I had to get married in order to meet Alex's best mate!' I'm joking, but Alex removes his hand from my leg and I wonder if I've offended him. I try to catch his eye, but his gaze is focused on the register we've just signed.

For our wedding reception, Alex has reserved a charming hotel at Ambleside with stunning views of the lake. It comprises a country B&B on one side and a historic inn on the other. Alex described it to me, but I haven't seen it before, and as our chauffeur-driven car pulls into the car park, I take in the grounds and the building.

'It's perfect,' I breathe, and Alex squeezes my hand. If he was irritated earlier, all trace of it has gone now.

The hotel is dog-friendly, which means Jet is on the guest list, much to Dad's delight. It's not far from Grasmere, which is convenient as my family is staying at the Old Vicarage again this evening. Alex and I will be staying here, in one of the bedrooms upstairs.

The photographer bustles about and when he's satisfied with his work outside, we all troop through the hotel into a large reception room. I'm rather relieved to be going indoors as it's a cool April day and my arms and legs are bare. Alex and I have to pretend to cut the cake for the final photo, and then the photographer leaves.

I look around the room. There are only a few guests. Alex has more than me, but not that many more. His mum, grandfather, aunt, uncle and cousins are there as well as some of his friends from the triathlon club.

After the food and the speeches, a local band starts playing. Alex was able to book them at short notice because he goes running with the lead singer and one of the guitarists. They're really good, and I'm impressed. As Alex leads me onto the wooden dancefloor, everyone watches from their seats at the tables. I look around at the sea of smiling faces. All the guests look relaxed, including Alex's mother.

Alex holds me tight as we dance to 'All of Me' by John Legend. It was his suggestion. I don't particularly like the song, but he was so pleased when he came up with the idea that I didn't have the heart to say so. And even I have to admit that with the lead singer's voice, it sounds wonderfully romantic.

Then it is my dad's turn to dance with me, and my face feels like it will split from grinning at Alex as he twirls his mum around. My mother-in-law has drunk several glasses of Prosecco and it seems to have agreed with her. Daniel and Julie join us on the dancefloor and out of the corner of my eye, I see one of Alex's cousins ask Hannah to dance.

After a while, the band plays more classic rock and roll songs and I'm enjoying myself in a little group with my sister and Hannah. As one of the musicians plays the opening chords to Chuck Berry's *Johnny B. Goode* on his electric guitar, Alex comes to fetch me.

'Do you know how to rock'n'roll?' he asks me.

'No,' I answer, a little nervously.

Alex shows me a few steps, but I have no sense of rhythm and I feel very self-conscious. I struggle to follow his lead. I bump into him at one point, and I hear him sigh. He gives up before the end of the song.

'You've got two left feet,' he comments, his face as impassive as his voice. 'I'll leave you to bop with the girls.' He nods towards my sister and my best friend. I walk away, but I don't feel like dancing anymore. Instead, I make my way to the toilets.

When Hannah and Julie find me, I am bawling like a baby, trying ineffectually to dab at my mascara with a piece of toilet roll. I can't really see what I'm doing in the mirror – the dim light keeps changing from purple to green to blue.

'What's the matter, Kaitlyn?' Julie asks at the same time as Hannah says, 'What's wrong, sweetie?'

I find myself crying loudly in my sister's arms as Hannah rubs my back. Eventually, even though my breathing is still uneven from my crying fit, I manage to tell them what happened.

'Oh, I'm sure he didn't mean it,' Hannah says, adding, 'although that's not a very nice thing to say, the bit about you having two left feet.'

'Well, it's an accurate assessment,' my sister says jokingly. 'You would have been in the dance-off on the very first round on

Strictly.'

This makes me smile. I used to go round to Julie's to watch *Strictly Come Dancing* on Saturday evenings. Kevin always hated the show and went to the pub with Daniel, but Julie and I are fans.

Hannah opens her handbag and takes out a packet of tissues. She hands me a tissue and takes out another one, which she wets under the tap and uses to wipe away the smudged brown lines running down my cheeks. 'I knew you'd cry on your special day,' she says.

'You probably just got overwhelmed by all the excitement,' Julie says and I feel myself nodding. 'You have a wonderful husband, and you'll have a beautiful baby,' she continues. 'Don't let a throwaway comment get you down.'

'You're right,' I say. It had felt disparaging, that remark about my clumsiness, but now I feel childish and silly. I've overreacted. And, as my sister pointed out, I'm no Ginger Rogers or Darcey Bussell.

'It was probably the Prosecco talking,' Hannah agrees. 'Strange place,' she says, changing the subject completely, for which I'm grateful. She looks around her as if seeing the room for the first time. I follow her gaze. The washbasins are built into what appears to be the outside rock face.

'It's very unusual,' I say.

'Yeah, the toilets really know how to rock,' Julie says.

That makes all three of us laugh.

As we head back to the others, I identify the tune of 'Hound Dog'. I cringe, hoping I won't be called on again to demonstrate how bad I am at dancing.

But as we enter the reception room, I spot Alex dancing with Mike's girlfriend, whose name I don't even know. They're the only two people on the dancefloor, and clearly, she knows how to jive or gyrate, or whatever they're doing, as well as he does. Everyone else has their eyes riveted on them.

I study her. She has quite long, layered blonde hair, which she's

41

flicking about all over the place like a model from a Head & Shoulders advert as Alex guides her through her steps. In my mind, I'd like to describe her as whippet-thin, but if I'm honest with myself, I envy her for her hourglass figure, which her short blue sheath of a dress shows off to perfection. Watching her with Alex, I feel a stab of jealousy.

I scan the room for Mike. He's sitting at a table talking to some of the other triathletes and as I catch sight of him, he throws his head back and releases a hearty guffaw, which even lifts my mood a little. If he's not jealous, then I don't need to be.

As the band finishes their Elvis cover, Mike and his friends start clapping, and everyone else joins in. My new husband and his dancing partner take a little bow. Then Alex comes over to me and kisses me on the lips.

'Where have you been?' he asks. 'I was getting worried.'

'I was talking to Hannah and Julie in the loos.'

'Yeah, they're well worth a visit,' Hannah adds.

Alex puts his arm around me. He squeezes my shoulder a little too hard, or maybe it just seems that way. It occurs to me that he may have drunk a bit too much. Perhaps he's using me to hold himself up after spinning around on the dancefloor. But he's hurting me and I pull away.

After that, Alex stays glued to my side. He's caring towards me, and charming with everyone else. But I can't shake the feeling that there's something else lying beneath his behaviour; that the animated expression on his face is a veneer, stretched thin and about to crack.

I can't say exactly what gives me that impression. Maybe it's as we sit down when I imagine I see a flash of fury in his eyes as they lock onto mine. But if there was any anger there, it's gone in an instant and I wonder if I saw it at all.

At around midnight, Alex and I bundle the guests into taxis. As I give my dad a big hug, I notice Jet licking Alex's hand. He snatches his hand away and wipes it on the trousers of his smart suit. Jet has a habit of licking people's hands and he does it for all sorts of reasons – he seems to sense when you need to be comforted or pacified, and, of course, he licks Dad's hand when he wants to remind him it's dinnertime.

When everyone has gone, Alex grips me firmly by the wrist and leads the way upstairs to a large bedroom with a wooden floor and a four-poster bed. He lets go of me, and I sit on the bed, rubbing my wrist. At first, I think he doesn't know his own strength. But then I see the rage in his eyes again. This time it's etched all over his face, and he makes no effort to hide it. I remember Jet licking his hand a few minutes ago. He was trying to calm him down.

I feel the baby kick hard from inside my tummy, just once. I'm usually overjoyed when I feel our baby move, but this time it's almost as if it's in warning.

'The baby has just kicked,' I tell Alex. 'Come over here and put your hand on my tummy.' I hear my voice quiver, and Alex doesn't move. His eyes are burning into me.

'*Where – is – it*?' he shouts.

'Wh … where's wh … what?'

'The necklace?'

'Is that what's upset you? I'm so sorry, Alex. We couldn't find it anywhere.'

'We?'

'Hannah and Julie helped me look for it.' He raises his eyebrows. 'And Daniel and the boys,' I add, more quietly.

'So everyone knows you've lost my necklace. You've made me into a laughing stock for your entire family.'

'I don't see how, Alex,' I say. I can barely hear my own voice now. 'If anyone looks ridiculous, it's me.'

For a moment, he's silent, and I think it's over. I reach out my arms and he starts to walk towards me.

But instead of allowing me to hold him, he pushes my arms down, leans down towards me and takes hold of the pendant of

43

my mother's necklace.

'So where did you get this? Did some ex-boyfriend give you this?'

'No! Julie lent it to me.'

Alex straightens up, and as he does so, he pulls on the pendant. At the back of my neck, I feel the gold chain break, leaving the necklace in his hand.

Tears prick my eyes. Alex stares at the necklace and then at me. He looks as shocked as I am. Was that an accident? Surely, he didn't mean to break it?

Then he about-turns purposefully, and marches towards the bathroom. I leap up and race after him. The bathroom door slams in my face as I get there.

'Alex, that belonged to my mum,' I shout at the closed door. 'Alex—' I am aware that I'm wailing now '—that was my mother's necklace.'

I fall to the floor, sobbing.

I'm not sure how long I lie there, but when Alex emerges, he's wearing only his boxer shorts. He helps me to my feet. He's gentle now, and the expression on his face is dispassionate.

'I'll get it fixed,' he says, guiding me into the bathroom.

I watch, incredulous, as he opens my washbag, squeezes toothpaste onto my toothbrush and closes my hand around the handle. I see his reflection in the mirror and, catching my eye, he gives me the ghost of a rueful smile. Then he turns and goes back into the bedroom, closing the bathroom door softly and leaving me inside.

I clean my teeth and pee. It can't have taken me long, but when I get back into the bedroom, I can hear Alex's light snoring. He's curled up in bed.

I struggle out of my wedding dress, only just able to reach the zip at the back. I didn't bring any nightclothes – this was to be our wedding night, after all. So I climb into bed in my underwear.

Alex has his back towards me. I lie on my back with my hands on my tummy feeling our baby kick, more softly this time. Tears roll down my cheeks. We've never gone to sleep side by side like this before. We've always kissed and said goodnight, even on the evenings we haven't made love, and then we've fallen asleep either holding hands or with me in Alex's arms.

I don't dream about Louisa that night. Or about Kevin. Or anyone or anything else. I don't sleep at all. All I can think as the tears flow out from behind my closed eyelids is that our marriage hasn't been consummated.

In the middle of the night, I suddenly become aware of heavy breathing. I turn towards the stranger lying next to me, thinking I may have woken him up with my sobbing, but then I realise with shock that I am the one who is panting. I force myself to take deep breaths as my heartbeat races.

Although we went to bed late, the night seems long. And yet I don't want it to end.

To: kaitlyn.best@newzmail.co.uk
From: alexanderriley9987@premiernet.co.uk
Sent: Fri, 11 Nov 2016 at 07:55
Subject: COMMUNI-KATE WITH ME?

Dear Katie,

Clearly, you have taken my last email very badly. I'm sorry if you took offence at what I said. I don't think you interpreted what I wrote in the way I meant it. I didn't bring up my exes in order to make you jealous or to make you feel you have to compete with other women in my life. Firstly, they're not in my life anymore, and secondly, you would win anyway! Hands down! No contest!

I'm happy to discuss this further if you want to, but I think it's just a misunderstanding. Maybe our emotions are spiralling a little out of control after the wonderful night we spent together. We're overreacting and seeing things that simply aren't there.

Shall we ring or FaceTime soon? Far better to communicate that way. That's if you still want to talk to me. Emails are completely devoid of tone, so it's easy to read too much into casual remarks that are really intended only as jokes.

I love you, and I hope to hear from you soon,

Alexxxx

Chapter 5

Alex sleeps soundly until about half past nine the following morning, and when he wakes up, he reaches out for me and puts his arms around me. I feel wooden and cold in his embrace. He kisses the top of my head.

'I'm sorry if I upset you,' he says.

I open my mouth to object to the 'if', but I stop myself in time.

Instead I say, 'I'm sorry, too.'

'I think I had one too many,' he offers by way of an explanation. 'It was an emotional day.'

Hannah's words as I was applying the mascara yesterday echo in my head. She'd predicted – correctly – that I'd cry yesterday. I should have realised then that it would all affect Alex, too.

He gets out of bed and stretches. He's still wearing only his boxers and as I gaze in admiration at his toned body, I can feel myself thawing.

''S'OK,' I mumble.

He pecks my cheek and heads for the bathroom. And just like

that, peace returns. It seems trivial all of a sudden, almost as if we didn't fall out. I'm left feeling I've made last night's disagreement out to be far worse than it really was.

When he has showered, Alex reappears in the doorway, drying his dark curls with a white towel. He has another one around his waist.

'Shall we walk home?' he asks.

'How far is it?'

As soon as the words have left my mouth, I regret asking the question. Alex has discouraged me from doing any sport since I've moved in with him. I like running, swimming and cycling, although, unlike Alex, I've never been tempted to try out any of those activities competitively, but apart from the walk we went on together when I first arrived in the Lake District, I've hardly been out.

Alex even expressed his disapproval a few weeks ago when I walked the short distance into the village of Grasmere. I know he's concerned about me, but lately I've been feeling cooped up.

'About four miles. Part of it is along the same paths we took when we did the Coffin Trail the first weekend you were here.' Alex is standing at the mirror in the bathroom, the door wide open, and I watch him rub moisturising cream into his face. 'We both brought casual clothes,' he continues. 'Have you got some decent shoes?' He doesn't pause for me to answer. 'I could pick up our stuff later. It would certainly help clear my head.'

I'm not sure if he means he's hungover or if he still needs to get our argument out of his system.

'And it would save us paying for a taxi,' he adds, as if he's trying to win me over and that will clinch the deal.

'Alex, I think walking home is a great idea.'

'Hmm. On second thought … it wouldn't be good for the baby.'

'Alex, the baby's fine.'

As if to confirm this, the baby pushes my tummy, ever so faintly, from inside.

'But you lost so much blood.'

'I didn't lose a lot. It was in early pregnancy. It happens some-times, apparently, and it hasn't happened since. The baby is all right. Really.'

'If you're sure. Have a shower and then we'll go downstairs and get some brekky.'

Alex has used both large hotel towels, and he has dropped the one he dried his hair with on the floor in the bathroom. With a little difficulty because of the size of my bump, I bend down and pick it up, resisting the temptation to make a comment – it's only a bit damp after all – and seconds later, the hot water gushing out of the shower jet is washing away the tension from my shoul-ders.

I keep thinking Alex will change his mind. He has been very worried about the baby, and I'm convinced he'll phone for a taxi instead of going through with his suggestion. But after breakfast, we arrange to leave our suitcases at the hotel and set off for home on foot.

As we walk, Alex chats about the weather and about his mum. I'm not sure if he's excited or wired, or merely trying to avoid an awkward silence. He doesn't seem to need much input from me, so I tune out and try to sift through my thoughts.

I wonder if Alex reacts badly to alcohol. Some people lose their temper or their self-control when they've been drinking. At least Alex wasn't violent. I try to imagine everything that happened from his point of view. He'd probably been pleased with himself for buying me that present. Perhaps he'd put a lot of thought into it and the red heart was deliberate rather than a coincidence. If that was the case, then he must have been hurt to see that I wasn't wearing it.

The fact that we didn't make love on our wedding night shouldn't matter to me, should it? It would have seemed inap-propriate after our row and, anyway, the idea that I had in my head all through the night – that our marriage hadn't been consummated – is an old-fashioned concept. It belongs to a time when people didn't have sex before marriage. I glance down at my tummy. We did, and look what happened. And Alex stepped up to the occasion. He asked me to move in with him and marry him so that we could be a family.

'Any ideas?'

His question interrupts my thoughts. I haven't got a clue what he has been talking about. I give him a blank stare. 'Sorry. I was miles—'

'I was thinking "Leo" or "Liam" if it's a boy.'

He wants to discuss baby names. I'm not keen on Leo. 'I like both of those,' I say.

'Liam is an Irish name. It would go well with yours. Kaitlyn and Liam. And mine, come to think of it! Liam Riley!'

I smile, a little wistfully. 'My mum would have liked that. Her Irish heritage passed down to her grandson.'

'Oh God, he might have ginger hair, the poor thing,' he says, elbowing me in jest.

I don't find it funny, but I smile, a little tightly. He's right, though. Louisa and I got teased at school – even bullied a few times – just because of our hair colour.

'What about girls' names?' he asks.

'I love the name "Chloe,"' I say.

'I do, too,' Alex says. He takes my hand.

Well, that was easy. Alex is back to himself this morning. So, why do I feel the need to weigh up every word I say before I speak? Why do I get the impression I'm walking on eggshells with him?

'Do you still want to know if it's a boy or a girl?' Alex asks.

Why is he asking me that? I look at him, trying to second-guess what's going on in his head, but his expression is inscrutable. When I'd gone for the first scan, alone at the Musgrove Park Hospital in Taunton, it had been too early to tell the baby's sex. When Alex and I went together for the second scan at Helme

Chase Maternity Unit in Kendal, Alex was adamant that he didn't want to know. I did. I needed our baby to have an identity. I wanted our baby to have a name. I dreamt of buying suitable baby clothes and not having to settle for neutral greys, yellows and whites.

But Alex said he needed some time. He didn't want to consider a baby girl as a replacement for Poppy and Violet, or as a second chance at happiness when things had gone so badly with his ex-wife Melanie that he could now no longer see his daughters. He argued that as he'd already had two baby girls, he also had to get used to the idea that this baby might be a boy.

We went in for the scan, without having come to an agreement, about a month ago now. In the end, it turned out the baby was in a position that made it difficult for the sonographer to be sure of its sex anyway. And that solved the problem.

'It's too late now,' I say. 'Have you changed your mind?'

'A bit,' he admits. 'I'm ready now. Either way.'

'Well, that's good,' I say, as we stop walking for Alex to tie up his shoelace, 'and now we know we're expecting a Chloe or a Liam.'

Rydal Water stretches along to our left and the views as we walk are so spectacular that any anxiety I'm feeling soon dissipates. Alex holds my hand for most of the way, swinging my arm from time to time or lifting my hand to his lips to kiss it.

When we get home, Alex opens the front door, but Jet bounds towards him, barking and growling with his hairs standing up in a ridge along his back. Alex quickly closes the door again and we wait in the porch until Dad has calmed the dog down.

We find Hannah and Julie in the kitchen making lunch. There are dirty frying pans and utensils stacked up next to the draining board and the tiled floor is filthy. I sneak a peek at Alex, biting my lip. I know how much he likes everything to be tidy, but if the chaos in his kitchen annoys him, he doesn't show it.

Jet, who seconds ago didn't want to let Alex into his own

51

house, is now trying to earn his forgiveness by licking the skin off his hand. Alex pats him on the head.

'What a nice surprise,' he says to Hannah and Julie. 'What can I do to help, ladies?'

Without waiting for a reply, he washes his hands and dries them on the tea towel, which has been draped over the back of a kitchen chair. As he hangs up the tea towel in its place on the hook next to the fridge, he flashes his winning smile at my sister, who is soon issuing him with instructions to chop the onions and set the table.

I sit down at the table next to my dad, who, half-moon glasses at the end of his nose and pen in hand, is doing the crossword in the newspaper. I observe Alex, Hannah and Julie as they chat and laugh amiably while preparing the meal. I wish I could be as cheerful. All morning, I've been feeling as if there's a snake uncoiling in my stomach somewhere behind Chloe or Liam, its writhing eclipsing the baby's kicking. For now at least, the snake is dormant. The baby seems to be asleep, too. I haven't felt it move for a few hours now.

But last night's events are still replaying on a confusing loop in my head. I want to discuss what happened with Hannah and Julie. I get my chance after the meal while Oscar, Archie and Daniel are playing football in the garden and my dad is dozing in an armchair in the living room. Alex has gone to pick up our stuff from the hotel, and Julie, Hannah and I are clearing up in the kitchen.

'So, how was last night?' Hannah asks with an attempt at a lascivious wink.

'Not too much info, please,' Julie says. 'You're my little sister and I'd rather you didn't fill me in on the details!'

When I don't join in their banter, Hannah says, 'Is something the matter?'

'Well, yes. When we got up to our bedroom, Alex had a kind of … meltdown.'

'What do you mean?' Julie asks, the smile vanishing from her face.

'He got really angry about the necklace I lost.'

Only now do I realise I can't tell them the whole story. The necklace Julie lent me is broken. I can't tell her that.

'Maybe that's understandable,' my sister says. She puts the dishcloth down and turns to face me.

'Yeah, I'm sure he was tired after such an emotional day,' Hannah agrees.

If anyone uses the word 'emotional' again, I might throw a tantrum myself. I can feel my head moving up and down automatically like one of those toy dogs on the rear shelf of a car. I sit down on a wooden chair.

'What did he say?' Julie asks.

'I can't remember his exact words,' I say, furrowing my brow. 'He was very upset that I'd lost it and embarrassed that I'd roped you all into searching the house for it. Oh, yeah, then he asked if one my ex-boyfriends had given me Mum's necklace as a present.' I sigh wistfully, reminded of the K&K necklace Kevin gave me long ago. 'Alex fell asleep while I was in the bathroom, so we didn't get to … you know …'

Hannah snorts. 'Sorry! Sorry!' she says, holding up her hands as though I'm about to shoot her.

I know what she's thinking. The same thing occurred to me.

'I'm making a big deal out of this unnecessarily, aren't I?'

Now it's Julie's turn to do the plastic dog nod. Then she turns back to the sink and starts to wash up a saucepan.

'Aww. Don't worry, sweetie,' Hannah says. 'You're bound to have a few teething problems.'

Alex seems to be thinking along similar lines as we get ready for bed that evening. 'You know, I think we're coping pretty well with the situation,' he says. 'Most couples get to know each other, then they move in together, and if that works out they start to think about getting married and finally they start a family. We sort of did all that at once.' He grins at me. 'We'll get there.'

I return his smile. It has been a lovely day. Alex has been a hospitable host to my family, and he has been attentive and affectionate to me. So, why do I still have this uneasy feeling in the pit of my stomach? Is it groundless fear or gut instinct?

It all but disappears as we make love that evening. But when it's over and Alex wraps me in his arms, I realise with a jolt that I haven't felt the baby move for a while. *When was the last time Chloe or Liam kicked?* I try to remember. For a few minutes, I rub my stomach, making circular movements, hoping to stimulate the baby. But nothing happens.

'Alex?'

There's a grunt in response, but he's almost asleep. That's probably just as well. He'd say we shouldn't have walked home. Perhaps he was right.

~

I sleep through the night, which is unusual for me as I've been getting up nearly every night to pee since I found out I was pregnant. I'm surprised I've been able to sleep at all, what with worrying about the baby not moving. I must have been very tired from my sleepless wedding night.

I reach out my hand for Alex, but he's not there. I'm reminded of the very first morning I woke up – alone – in this strange house. I hear voices from downstairs and wonder if he's having breakfast with my family. I get up and put my dressing gown on.

As I am closing the bedroom door behind me, Julie comes out of her room.

'Good morning,' she says. 'Did you sleep well?'

'Yes, I did.' I'm about to ask her the same question, but I hear myself saying, 'Julie, I haven't felt the baby kick for a while now. Is that normal?'

'When was the last time you felt it move?' she asks.

54

I have to think about that. I remember the baby was very active while I lay awake all night in the hotel. Was that the last time? No, it wasn't. My tummy rumbles and it comes to me. It was just before breakfast at the hotel.

'Yesterday morning. It was a very gentle kick, though.'

'Well, that's only twenty-four hours ago,' my sister says. 'The baby could be sleeping or it might have moved into a position that means you can't feel it dancing about so much.'

'OK,' I say, but I don't sound convinced.

'Don't worry.' Julie takes my arm and guides me towards the staircase. 'If you still haven't felt it move this afternoon, go to the hospital. They'll set your mind at rest.' I'm not sure if it's my big sister or the nurse talking. Either way, Julie's words don't put me at ease.

There's no sign of Alex downstairs, either. According to my dad, who got up early to walk Jet, he'd said he had an errand to run.

Alex is gone a long time. I try to call him after breakfast, feeling annoyed, but his phone goes straight to voicemail. Where can he be? He arranged for cover in the shop today and he hasn't scheduled any activities. He wasn't planning to go training this morning. Where on earth is he? Panic eventually overrides my anger.

When Alex does arrive home, my sister and her family, my dad and Hannah have loaded everything into the two cars they drove up here in and they're ready to leave for Somerset. I watch Alex saunter in through the front door. Jet wags his tail and I find myself willing him to growl and bark.

'Where have you been?' It comes out as a hiss. I can feel my sister's eyes on me. Alex either ignores my tone or doesn't pick it up.

'I went back to the hotel. They left a message on my mobile to say you'd forgotten this.' To my astonishment, he holds up my mum's necklace. 'I thought you'd want to give it back to Julie before she left.'

I'm aware my mouth is wide open, but I can't seem to close it. I stare in total disbelief at the necklace. The chain is unbroken.

'Thank you,' I manage.

Alex hands the necklace to Julie, who deftly puts it around her neck and fastens the clasp.

Moments later, as I wave goodbye to my family, I feel confused. I'm grateful to Alex for having the necklace repaired, and at least now I know what he was doing this morning. But he's the one who broke it in the first place. And I'm cross with him for implying that I'd carelessly left it in our hotel room. I turn to face Alex, but he isn't there. He has gone back inside.

I stand outside, alone, watching Oscar close the wooden gate at the bottom of the drive before getting back into the car. Seconds later, both cars round a bend out of my sight. I hope I'll see everyone again soon, although we didn't get round to making any plans as Alex wasn't there this morning.

I find Alex upstairs, kneeling in front of the chest of drawers and wildly turfing out my bras and knickers. I stand in the doorway, rooted to the spot and speechless. He pulls out one of the drawers containing his clothes and tips the socks out on the floor.

Is he having another meltdown?

'Alex.' My heart is beating a tattoo against my ribs. 'Alex.' My voice sounds weak, even to my ears, and I realise I'm frightened of my husband's erratic behaviour.

He looks up. 'It must be here somewhere,' he says. He doesn't sound angry, which I take to be a good sign.

'I'm so sorry I lost it, Alex,' I say. 'It may turn up, but we've … I've already checked in there.'

'Sit down,' Alex says gently.

I do what I'm told and perch on the corner of the bed. Alex tidies everything back into the drawers.

'I can help you if you like?'

'No, no, it's all right. Why should you clear up the mess I've made?' He glances at me over his shoulder. 'Just hang on a sec till I've finished. I've got something for you.'

I study Alex as he puts the pairs of socks away, lining them up in a row. When he has finished, he turns to me, still on his knees, and extracts a box from his back pocket.

'I got you this ...' he says, shuffling towards me on his knees. He looks comical, and I'm relieved that he's not mad at me again. I have a sudden urge to giggle, but although I can feel myself grinning too widely, I succeed in keeping the laughter down.

Alex opens a small square box. Inside there's a necklace. The third necklace in three days. He takes it out and hands it to me.

'... To make up for my inexcusable behaviour,' he continues. 'I had it engraved.'

I look at the wording on the necklace. '"I'm always yours"', I read aloud. It reminds me of the sort of message you get on those sweets. Love Hearts. I find it a little childish and then I scold myself for thinking that. Alex is making an effort after all.

'Look on the back,' he says. 'There's a different inscription.'

I turn the medallion over and read the words on the other side, silently this time. The room feels chilly all of a sudden.

Alex gets to his feet and puts the chain around my neck.

'There,' he says, fastening it. He kisses me on the lips and smiles shyly and I have a fleeting image of him as the diffident pupil I secretly fancied at school.

I'm disturbed by the words on the back of the pendant. It's supposed to be romantic. But I find those words a bit creepy.

You're mine forever.

'Promise me you'll never leave me,' he says.

'Why would I leave you?'

'Just promise me you won't. I don't know what I'd do without you.'

'I promise.'

'We belong together.'

As he takes me into his arms, I feel goose bumps all the way down my own arms. He pulls me to my feet and he holds me as tightly as my bump will allow.

Just as I'm about to protest that he's squashing the baby, Chloe or Liam starts to kick me so hard that Alex feels it, too.

To: kaitlyn.best@newzmail.co.uk
From: alexanderriley9987@premiernet.co.uk
Sent: Wed, 21 Dec 2016 at 23:03
Subject: OUT OF THE BLUE

Dear Katie,

I'm sorry if I've upset you by taking so long to reply to your emails. Your news came as a complete shock, and it took me a while to get used to the idea.

Clearly, I need to zip up the man suit and step up to the occasion, which I'm glad to do. We're both in this together and you can count on me.

Because of my business, I can't work anywhere else but here, as you'll appreciate, and you'll have to stop working at some point anyway (for a while, at least). So, I think the easiest thing would be if you came to live here with me. As you know, I live alone in a gigantic Georgian house – it's been in the family for over a century. You'll love it! And it needs a woman's touch!

Please say you'll come, my Best girl. We belong together.

I expect you'll need some time to sort everything out, but I'm not going anywhere. I'll be right here waiting for you.

You're my world, my life.

Alexxxx

PS: I'm sending you yet another selfie. As you can see (from the huge grin on my face), I'm very excited about your news!

Chapter 6

I don't recognise her the second time I see her. And then I do that thing where you realise someone's face is familiar but they seem out of context, and I can't immediately place her. If she wasn't wearing a swimming hat and goggles, it might help.

She has stopped in the shallow end and, as there are only the two of us in the lane, we've said hello to each other.

'Do I know you?' I feel stupid for asking that question.

'Sorry?' She pulls the silicone hat away from her ears and tips her head from side to side.

'Have we met?' It sounds like a cheesy chat-up line and I cringe inside.

'I don't think so,' she says, moving her goggles up onto her forehead and giving me a quick wide smile. Her teeth stick out a bit, and now I'm sure I've seen her somewhere before.

She rubs the inside of her goggles where they have misted up and puts them back on. Then she pushes off the wall. I watch in admiration as she glides through the water gracefully and tumble-turns at the end. It doesn't look like she's going to stop for a rest any time soon, so that seems to be the end of our little conversation. After my opening gambit, I'm not surprised she sprinted off.

As I'm lathering shampoo into my hair after my swim, she reappears. Whipping off her swimming hat and goggles, she presses the button for the shower opposite mine. Now I can see she has short hair and as she locks her large dark eyes on to mine it comes to me. She's the woman from the lake.

'You have a little white dog,' I say.

'Yes, I do.' She looks at me suspiciously. 'How did you know that?'

'I saw you once a few weeks ago when we were out walking the Coffin Trail.'

Her pencil-thin eyebrows have shot right up and disappeared under her wet soapy hair. 'We?'

'My husband and I.'

'Husband?' she echoes. 'I'm sorry, but I'm afraid I don't remember you. Or your husband.'

'We didn't talk. I probably only remember because Alex – that's my husband – was scared of your dog.'

'Really?'

She introduces herself then. She has a soft melodious voice.

'Hi Vicky. I'm Kaitlyn,' I say. 'Pleased to meet you.' And I am. Apart from a few shopkeepers and some of Alex's friends, I've hardly talked to anyone local since I moved here.

'How far gone are you?' she asks, lowering her gaze to my stomach.

'Seven months.'

'You're looking very good for seven months,' she says, still focusing on my bump.

I'm not. I'm huge. Which is why I wanted to swim today. I'm hoping to come to the leisure centre here in Kendal regularly from now on, but of course Alex mustn't find out. He seems to think any unnecessary movement I make might have an adverse effect on our baby. I find it sweet that he frets so much, but it's stifling spending nearly all day every day in that mansion of his.

'You swim very well,' I say, desperate to keep the conversation going.

'I swam competitively as a kid,' she says. 'I used to train for about three hours a day. I'm bored of doing lengths now, but it keeps me fit.' She grins, revealing her improbably white teeth again, but as she hasn't met my eyes, it's as if she's talking to my tummy.

'I'd like to get fitter,' I tell her. I've put on way too much weight with the pregnancy, but I don't add this out loud.

'You're a pretty good swimmer yourself,' she says, bending down to pick up her shampoo bottle. With a little wave of her hand, she's gone, and I wish we'd chatted more. Perhaps I'll bump into her again if I make a habit of coming here to swim.

But when I've finished getting dressed, she's drying her hair. I fumble in my purse for change for the hairdryer and take the one next to her. I study her in the mirror. I'm tall, but she is a good two inches taller. I consider myself to be a little ungainly, particularly at the moment, whereas she holds herself up straight with an elegant poise. Despite her stark facial features, she's very attractive.

In the shower, I had the impression she was refusing to make eye contact, but now she's staring at me with insistent wide eyes. I look away, feeling a little uncomfortable, as if she's scrutinising me.

To my surprise, when the hairdryers cut out, she says, 'Would you like to go for a coffee in the leisure centre café?'

'I'd love to,' I say, 'but I'm afraid I can't today.'

'Oh. Well, maybe another time,' she says. 'It was nice talking to you, Kaitlyn.'

And with that, she disappears through the swing doors and I'm left alone in the changing rooms. *Damn! I should have made sure there was going to be another time.* Just as this thought enters my head, she's back, rummaging in her handbag. She finds a pen and a receipt. Leaning on the little ledge by the mirror, she scribbles something and then hands the scrap of paper to me.

'Give me a call next week if you come for a swim. Evenings or lunchtimes suit me best. We could grab a coffee afterwards then if you want.'

I look at the paper and see she has noted down a mobile number. She hasn't written her name.

'OK, thanks,' I say, pleased at how eager Vicky seems to meet up with me again. This time she holds the wooden doors open for me and I follow her through the reception area and out into the car park.

As I get into my car, it dawns on me that I know hardly anything about this woman. I don't know what she does for a living or if she's married or single. All I know is she has a dog and she's an excellent swimmer. She knows even less about me. Maybe it's not such a good idea to see her again. I ignore the niggling doubt in my mind, thrilled at the idea I might finally be making a friend.

I fish my mobile phone out of the pocket of my jacket, which I've flung on the passenger's seat, and as I add Vicky to my contacts, the phone beeps and vibrates several times. I have six missed calls, two voice messages and four text messages. They're all from Alex. I read the text messages. Trepidation erases the joy I was feeling. I turn the key in the ignition, opting to get going rather than ring or text him back.

'Hi,' I say, brightly as I make an attempt at breezing through the front door with my large frame about fifteen minutes later. I've left my swimming bag in the boot of my car for now. Alex is sitting on the stairs in the 'vestibule'.

'You're late.' He sounds aggressive.

I wonder how to play this and decide it's best not to snap back at him. I need to placate him before this gets out of hand.

'Where have you been?' he barks before I can say anything.

'Didn't you get my messages? Why didn't you answer your mobile? I was worried.'

'You don't need to worry about me.' I can feel a bead of sweat roll down the side of my face.

'I wasn't worried about *you*.' He looks at me as though I'm unhinged. 'We're supposed to be there at six.'

'Oh, I see. Well, we've got loads of time.' I try to come over as reassuring, but I can hear my voice falter. 'I popped out to buy these.' I thrust the huge bouquet of orange gerberas, lilies and roses, which I bought on the way home, into Alex's arms. 'I didn't want to answer any calls in the car.' It's stretching the truth slightly, but it works. He calms down. I force myself to breathe in and out slowly.

'She'll love them,' he says, holding them up to his face and smelling them.

'Oh, they're not for your mother,' I say, unable to resist winding him up a little to get my own back. His face falls and I burst out laughing. To his credit, he manages a smile. 'Why don't you go and hunt out a bottle of good wine while I put some make-up on and then we'll be off.'

'It's just that she thinks it's bad manners when people arrive late, you know?'

'I know. Oh, and Alex?'

'Yes?'

'I made some brownies. They're on the worktop in the kitchen in a Tupperware box.'

He looks delighted, which gives me such a sense of relief. I turn and run up the stairs as fast as I can, feeling light despite my extra bodyweight. In the bedroom, I apply foundation to conceal the red marks the goggles have left under my eyes. I do a quick job with the mascara, blusher and lipstick and I appraise my reflection. I don't look too bad. I feel good, too, for having done some exercise.

Alex and I arrive ten minutes early at his mother's house and we sit in the car and listen to the news while we wait. As Alex has already told me, my mother-in-law is a stickler for punctuality. She hates tardiness, but she can't bear it when her guests arrive early either.

There is an interesting debate on Radio 4 about the recent French presidential election. I know my colleagues will be discussing this topic amongst themselves as well as with our students and for a moment I miss the world I used to live in.

Just as I'm about to turn up the volume, Alex switches the radio off.

'It's time,' he announces. He comes round to my side of the car, opens the door and helps me out. I carry the flowers and he takes the brownies and the wine.

My mother-in-law opens the door before we can ring the bell. She's a stick-thin petite woman with greying hair and the same hooked nose and blue eyes as Alex. She speaks with an annoyingly loud, shrill voice. She and Alex are very close, and that's an under-statement. She gives me a perfunctory air kiss near my cheek and then she hugs Alex for several seconds while I wait on the doorstep.

She leads us into the living room, which is pristine. Not a speck of dust, nothing out of place. Even the magazines have been positioned dead centre on the coffee table. The first time I came into Mrs Riley's house, I realised Alex must have got his obsessive tidiness from his mother. I hope he won't expect every-thing to always be immaculate when our baby comes along.

'What a lovely picture, Mum,' Alex says.

I look around the walls, before spotting the painting on the floor. It's a striking cityscape, an oil painting in which the hustle and bustle of the centre of London is conveyed by blurred colour highlighting the furious movement of buses and taxis alongside a pavement illuminated by streetlamps. It is indeed lovely.

'I was wondering if you could hang that on the wall behind the sofa for me,' Alex's mum says. It's an order rather than a request.

'Of course. I'll do it right now.'

Alex prides himself on being a dutiful son. He's a bit too devoted to his mum for my liking – he drops everything and rushes round to her house to sort out every little problem the moment it arises, from a squeaky door to a dripping tap. But Alex is an only child and I suppose once his father left, he must have taken on the role of man of the house from an early age.

In truth, I envy their closeness. I miss my own mother when I observe the two of them together. Alex can do no wrong in his mother's eyes. I wonder what my mum would have thought about me getting pregnant after a one-night stand. I know she would never have criticised me. She would have been caring and understanding. I could have done with her support. I could still do with it now.

'Come through with me to the kitchen, Kaitlyn,' my mother-in-law says, breaking into my thoughts just as I'm starting to feel morose.

I follow her as Alex heads for the garage, presumably to fetch the toolkit. She pulls out a kitchen chair for me to sit on, and then she turns away from me to stir the dinner bubbling away in the frying pan on the hob. My gut churns at the aromas drifting towards me.

Since I've been pregnant, I've had a heightened sense of smell. I've become very sensitive to certain odours. I'm suddenly transported from my mother-in-law's kitchen to a lakeside café in Windermere where Alex and I had brunch a few weeks ago. The smell of Alex's bacon sandwich made me so nauseous that in the end I couldn't eat my pancakes. I've stuck to beef, chicken and fish since then.

'I've made your favourite meal,' my mother-in-law trills. 'Sweet and sour pork.'

'Oh.' I can see an open tin of pineapple on the work surface next to the stove.

I frown. I've never told her what my favourite meal is. It certainly isn't sweet and sour pork. When I'm not pregnant, I eat pretty much anything, but I've never liked sugary things mixed with savoury foods, like fruit with meat.

She turns and narrows her eyes as she examines me, no doubt trying to decipher my reaction.

'That's very good of you,' I say. It doesn't sound very sincere, but she looks pleased with herself and goes back to stirring the meal with her wooden spoon. For a fleeting moment, I wonder if she has intentionally made a dish I won't enjoy. But I dismiss the thought. It must be a misunderstanding. She's not that friendly, but she's not so vindictive as to do something like that on purpose. Alex probably told her what I like and what I don't like, and she got confused.

'Shall I set the table?' I say, as the sound of a hand drill starts up in the living room.

Arming myself with plates and cutlery, I make my way into the living room where I dump everything down on the dining table. I go over to Alex to tell him about the mistake so that he can have a word with his mum. But as I reach him, I think the better of it. Resolving to eat up my dinner without making a fuss, I kiss Alex tenderly on the back of his neck as he crouches down to pick up the painting.

At the table, Alex serves me a large helping of the meal before I can ask for a small portion. I can feel my mother-in-law watching me as I take a mouthful.

'It's delicious, Mrs Riley,' I say, trying not to gag.

'Sandy,' she says. 'I kept my husband's surname when he left because it was easier for Alexander but, please, my dear, call me Sandy.'

I give myself a stern talking-to in my head. My mother-in-law has gone to a lot of trouble for me. I should show more appreciation.

'It's delicious, Sandy,' I say, plastering a smile on my face and resolving to keep it unzipped for the duration of the dinner. It gets easier and I manage to swallow down every last morsel.

'Would you like some more?' Alex asks, as I put down my knife and fork. He has already loaded up the spoon, which is hovering over my plate.

'No, thank you,' I say a bit too hastily. Alex serves his mother and himself instead.

He is attentive to both his mum and me during the meal. He hardly takes his eyes off me. He cracks jokes and tells humorous anecdotes. This is the man I fell in love with. And then it sinks in. *This is my husband*. I feel a rush of joy.

~

I muse over the day's events while Alex is in the bathroom that evening. I'm so excited about making a friend. I'd like to tell Alex about Vicky, but that would mean confessing I went for a swim and I can't do that. Alex wouldn't approve. Only two months to go, though. I rub my tummy.

Suddenly, Alex storms out of the bathroom. 'What was that all about?' he demands.

My heart sinks. 'I have no idea what you're talking about,' I say.

'That was delicious, Mrs Riley,' he says in a high-pitched voice, clearly trying to imitate me. 'You *hate* sweet and sour pork.'

'I was being polite, Alex,' I say, not sure yet where he's going with this.

Earlier, when I arrived home from the pool, all I needed to do was cajole Alex and pretend to be light-hearted. Somehow I don't think that's going to work this time. He seems implacable.

The snake residing in my stomach uncoils just as the baby starts to jiggle around, as if they're competing for my attention. I want to sit down, but Alex is standing close to me and I mustn't appear inferior. Instead, I stretch myself to my full height and jut my chin out defiantly.

'You lied!' he shouts. His hot minty breath is like a blow to my face. 'You lied to my mother!'

His words are trapped in the small space between us while I try to interpret them. Even when I do, it takes me a second or two more to find my tongue. 'Would you have preferred me to tell her I couldn't eat the dinner she had made especially for me?'

'Put it this way: at least I'd respect you for being honest. You liar!'

I stare at Alex. He looks like my husband, but he sounds like a stranger. He bores holes into me with his penetrating stare. I have a sudden flash of those piercing blue eyes on me throughout dinner. It strikes me that he may have deliberately set this up.

'Alex, did you tell your mother that was my favourite meal?'

'Are you out of your mind? Why on earth would I tell her that?'

For a split second I think he's going to hit me. But he grabs his pillow and his mobile and storms out of the bedroom.

'I'm going to sleep in one of the guestrooms,' he yells as his parting shot, slamming the door.

In a daze, I drift into the bathroom and go through the motions of my nightly routine. I brush my teeth, hardly aware of what I'm doing. In the mirror, I catch sight of my reflection and I'm stunned by how white my face is.

I don't know how long I sit up in bed, trying to process what just happened. A furious incomprehension has taken hold of me. The more I replay the incident in my mind, the more bewildered I become. My anger is rising inside me, like milk about to boil over in a pan. *How dare he talk to me like that!*

I'm reminded of the necklace incident on our wedding night. On that occasion, Alex acted out of hurt and jealousy, thinking I'd lost his necklace and worn a gift from an ex-boyfriend. But this time, there's no excuse for his behaviour. *I won't put up with it!*

There's no point trying to sort this out with Alex tonight. But

I'd love to talk to someone about it. In the end, I get up and fetch my mobile out of my jacket pocket. My hands are shaking as I scroll down my contacts to find Hannah. Maybe my best friend can help me make sense of all this.

But Hannah's phone goes straight to voicemail. I look at the clock on the bedside table. It's late, so it shouldn't surprise me that I can't get hold of her. But she hasn't returned any of my calls or text messages for about ten days now. Usually, we text each other a lot. Every other day at least. We did even when I lived in Somerset.

I rack my brain, but I can't think of any awkwardness between us since she has come to terms with me moving in with Alex. There has been no sign she has taken something I said badly.

So why haven't I heard from her? This silence isn't like Hannah. I tell myself she's probably busy, but deep down I'm convinced something is wrong. Maybe the problem isn't between Hannah and me, but I know, with unwavering certainty, that there is a problem.

To: kaitlyn.best@newzmail.co.uk
From: alexanderriley9987@premiernet.co.uk
Sent: Sun, 01 Jan 2017 at 00:06
Subject: HAPPY NEW YEAR!!!

Dear Katie,

Happy New Year!!! I can't seem to get through on the phone (perhaps the networks are all saturated), so I'm writing you a quick email until we can talk and I can hear your beautiful voice.

You can't imagine how thrilled I am that you're coming to live with me here in Grasmere.

Just think, we'll be together very soon. What a start to the New Year!

And this time next year when I wish you a happy new year, we'll be face to face. There will be three of us by then, not just you and me.

I understand that you need a while to finalise things with Kevin and put the house on the market. I know you need to sort out your work commitments, too. It sounds like your head of department is being very sympathetic. I'm so glad you can take your annual leave just before the start of your maternity leave. That means you'll be here by the end of March at the latest.

Given that you had a bit of a scare and ended up at the hospital last week, do you think you might be able to finish up at the university even earlier? Perhaps you could get a fit/sick note from your doctor? I've been very worried about you. Did the gynaecologist say why you had lost some blood? The main thing is that you and the baby are fine, but I don't want you to overdo things. The sooner you're up here with me, the better. I'll take care of you.

I'll leave you for now and let you get on with celebrating with your family and friends.

I love you, my soulmate,

Alexxx

CHAPTER 7

I stare at the note in front of me. This seems wrong on so many levels. I reread it.

> Going for a bike ride.
> Back for lunch.
> A.

After storming off last night to sleep in one of the spare rooms, he has gone out training this morning without making up with me first. I'm not one for holding grudges; a cup of tea in bed would have appeased me. Alex knows that.

But it's more than that. The note itself is scrawled. His handwriting is usually very neat. And, I feel pathetic, but this is what's really getting me. He always signs off as "Alexxx." Alex with two kisses. We've been married barely a month and already he has dropped the X's.

Back for lunch. I could make something for us to eat when Alex gets back. Perhaps that would clear the air between us. But apart from a couple of beers, some mouldy cheese and some overripe tomatoes, there's nothing in the fridge. I don't mind doing the shopping, even though it's going to be busy on a Saturday morning, but last time I went to the supermarket, Alex objected to me carrying heavy bags in from the car. I can't win. Is he setting me a trap? Will he get mad whether I do the shopping and make lunch or not?

I'm probably reading far too much into an eight-word-long message.

As I switch my mobile on, I wonder if Hannah has rung me back. But there are no messages. There are no texts either. I put some music on my phone and turn the volume up as high as it will go, but it's not loud enough to drown out the thoughts clamouring for attention in my mind.

In the end, I decide to drive to the local grocery and buy what I need there to whip up a decent meal. It's always chilly in the house, and it's only as I step outside that I realise it's actually quite a warm day. The sky is a clear bright blue; the only clouds are in my head.

As I'm opening the gate at the bottom of the drive, I notice a grey car. I think it's going to stop, but it crawls past and then speeds off into the distance. I stare after the car until it has rounded the bend. It has made me a little jumpy, although I'm not sure why. Maybe because I somehow got the impression that the driver was taking a good look at me, but because the sun was in my eyes, I couldn't make out the person in the car.

I take my time in Grasmere, enjoying the weather and feeling a sense of release at being out of the house. I order a glass of freshly squeezed orange juice in a café near the church and relax, watching the people go by.

Approaching the Old Vicarage on my way home, I pass a grey car going the other way and it reminds me of the one I saw earlier. Was that the same car? It's a similar size, but I've no idea of the make of either of them. Seeing the car drive by so slowly unsettled me before; now I'm determined not to become paranoid. Grey has to be the most common colour for vehicles on English roads. I push the car firmly out of my mind. My little outing has done me good. I'm feeling more serene.

Until I go to turn my key in the front door and realise it's unlocked. Did I forget to lock it? Pushing the door open, I tiptoe into the house, a knot of fear tying itself tighter in my stomach with every step I take.

I creep along the hallway into the kitchen, where I put the shopping bags down on the floor, open a drawer and take out a pair of scissors. Feeling slightly braver now that I'm armed, I make my way stealthily back to the entrance hall, peeking inside the living room and then the study.

I read once that burglars spend on average less than five minutes in your house. I'm not sure how long I've been home for, but I don't think there's anyone still in the house. If there was anyone in it at all. It certainly doesn't look as if we've been burgled.

Scissors in hand, I head upstairs. By the time I get to the top, I've persuaded myself that I simply forgot to lock up and that I'm letting my imagination run amok.

But then I step into the master bedroom. Someone has been in here.

At that moment, the door bangs downstairs. Did I close the front door when I came in? For a few seconds, I'm rooted to the spot. Has someone just left the house? Or have they entered it?

Without making a sound, I walk over to the bedroom window and, half hiding behind the curtain, I look out, through the bars, at the empty driveway. There's no one outside.

I can hear someone walking through the entrance hall downstairs. I can just make out the footsteps over the sound of my own breathing.

'Katie?'

All the fear that was building up inside me is instantly wiped out by a wave of relief.

I concentrate on inhaling and exhaling slowly until I catch my breath enough to shout back.

'Alex! I'm in the bedroom.'

I hear him running up the stairs and then he appears in the doorway, still wearing his cycling jersey and shorts, a hangdog expression on his face and possibly the biggest bouquet of flowers I've ever seen in his arms.

'Are you OK?' he asks. 'You look like you've just seen a ghost!'

'I'm fine,' I say, reaching for the flowers, my trembling hands belying my words. 'These are beautiful. Thank you.'

'To make up for my bad behaviour last night.' The words roll glibly off his tongue and he gives me a blatantly unrepentant grin.

'It's no big deal,' I hear myself saying. I am so pleased to see him right now.

'Can I take you out to lunch to earn your forgiveness?'

'Oh, I've bought some groceries. I was going to make chicken in a creamy mushroom sauce.'

His face clouds over, but as soon as his eyes look into mine the expression disperses. It's gone quickly, but I'm sure I saw it. I'm used to this now. Blink and you miss it.

'But I can always put the shopping away and make that for dinner instead,' I add.

He smiles and I know I've come up with a good answer. The right answer. I attempt to smile back, but it feels alien to my face. His intense blue eyes refuse to look away and I know I'm being examined, but I can't work out why. I can feel the hairs stand up along my arms.

'Are you sure you're all right?' he asks.

Goodness, I am tense! He's only concerned.

'Yes, of course,' I reply.

'I'll go and get a shower and then we'll go out.'

He disappears into the en suite bathroom, leaving me alone with my suspicions. I try to think this over rationally. I want to believe I'm mistaken. No one has been in the bedroom. I got spooked, that's all. The most likely explanation is that Alex arrived home before me, opened the front door and then went to put his bike away in the garage. *Yes, that must be it!* I could go and ask him now. On second thoughts, no, I can't, because if that's not what happened then he'll blame me for leaving the front door unlocked. Surely I locked the door? Didn't I?

Thoughts race around my mind, contradicting each other. I try to shut them out, but I know they won't go away until I think this through.

I look around the room, my heart pounding. A voice in my head taunts me: *who's been sleeping in my bed?* The bed is made, just how I left it. I put the bouquet I'm still holding on the bed and kneel down to look under it, not knowing if I'm checking for something or someone. There's nothing there, *no one* there. I'm starting to feel silly now. I haven't looked under the bed out of fear since I stopped believing in the bogeyman as a little girl. I'm being childish. Nothing is out of place.

I check my jewellery box and my underwear drawer. Nothing is missing. But I'm certain that someone has been in the bedroom. Why am I so sure there was someone here?

Then it comes to me. *It was the smell.* When I walked into the room, I got a whiff of an unfamiliar musky fragrance I didn't recognise. It didn't smell like any of the gels and creams Alex uses and it certainly wasn't from any of my bottles and jars. It smelled like men's cologne. But Alex doesn't wear aftershave.

I inhale deeply through my nostrils, but the air smells of Alex's sweaty body and the pungent scent of the lilies. If there ever was a strange odour, I can't detect it now, even with my currently enhanced sense of smell.

My heartbeat starts to slow down to its normal pace as I visualise Alex's bottles in the bathroom. They are always lined up – whether it's on the shelves or in the shower tray – with the tallest on the right and the smallest on the left. As Hannah pointed out, he does have a lot of body care products. I smile to myself, partly at the thought of Hannah and me laughing together on the night before my wedding, but also at how stupid I've been. Alex must have added another bottle to his collection. That would explain why the smell wasn't familiar.

But Alex didn't sleep in here last night. I shout down the voice in my head with one that sounds a lot more confident and a lot more like mine. *In that case, the smell was already in the room, but I didn't notice it until I came back this morning. End of story.*

I catch sight of myself in the full-length mirror. I'm alarmed at the appearance of the woman staring back at me. Her hair is messy; her face is pale and drawn. No wonder Alex was worried! Only the trousers – low-cut maternity jeans that embrace my rounded tummy – and my favourite green long-sleeved T-shirt look familiar.

The shocking sight of my reflection galvanises me into action. By the time Alex comes out of the bathroom, I've changed into a short cotton skirt and a thin purple and blue jumper, my hair is tied back and my complexion is looking rosier thanks to the copious amounts of make-up I've just applied to my face.

Alex looks me up and down and raises both eyebrows into an approving arch. 'Have you seen my wife?' he says. 'She was here just a few minutes ago.'

I punch him playfully on his arm and he kisses me hungrily, and for a moment I don't think we're going to make it out of the bedroom. But then Alex's stomach rumbles, which seems to be our cue to leave. I take his arm and he takes the flowers to put in a vase downstairs before we leave.

We have lunch at a pub near Grasmere. It has picnic tables in the garden and as it's a lovely day, we opt to sit outside. Alex is ravenous, and shovels the food into his mouth. Over lunch, he talks nonstop about his triathlon season, mostly with his mouth full and waving his fork around for emphasis. His enthusiasm is contagious and I look forward to seeing him compete one day.

When he has finally run out of things to say or stopped talking for me to speak – I'm not sure which – I remain silent. I want to talk about last night. I need to tell Alex that he scares me sometimes and that I don't want to be frightened of the man I married. I'd like to confide in him about Hannah not ringing or texting anymore.

But, inexplicably, I'm struck dumb. I'm aware Alex is looking at my mouth, which is opening and closing repeatedly. I must look like I'm impersonating a goldfish, as I struggle to find the right words, any words. When I do speak, it isn't any of the ideas I was trying to express.

'Does anyone else have a key to the Old Vicarage?'

'My mum does,' he says, scratching his arm where the scars are. 'It used to be her house, you know.'

'That's good to know,' I say, 'in case I lose my keys one day or lock myself out.'

I look at Alex. I think about how kind and sensitive he can be, how caring he is most of the time and I wonder what triggers these mood swings and what I can do to avoid them.

'My father was a violent man,' Alex says, as if reading my thoughts. 'I haven't seen him for many years, not since I was ten, when he left us.'

'Go on.'

'He hit my mother, and from when I learnt to walk and talk, he beat me, too. He used to make me lie over a chair, then he beat me with the belt from his trousers.'

'Oh, God, Alex. How awful.'

'He was cruel and heartless,' he continues. 'I've spent my whole life trying not to become him.'

I notice tears well up in his eyes and I reach across the table and take his hand in mine, but he pulls it away and rubs his neck.

'I don't think you're cruel and heartless, Alex.' He doesn't seem to hear me.

'My father used to encourage me to solve my problems with

my fists,' Alex continues. 'I became a horrible playground bully from the moment I was sent to boarding school. I think I only picked fights in an attempt to seek his approval.'

A solitary tear escapes and races down his cheek. A lump forms in my throat, but I try to stay strong for Alex.

'Oh, Alex.'

'I don't want to be like him.'

'Alex, you're not.'

'I have a quick temper.' He cradles his head in his hands.

'Yes, you do. But you're not violent.' And then I get where this is coming from. 'Are you anxious about becoming a father?'

'Yes.' It's almost a whisper.

'You'll be an excellent dad,' I say, trying to sound reassuring and hoping that it's true.

'D'you think so?' He looks up, into my eyes.

'I know so.' I reach for his hand again. This time he lets me take it, although it feels flaccid in mine.

'I want to be a good husband to you, Katie, and a good father to our child. Or children. Not just good, *great*. The best.'

My heart melts when he says that because that's exactly what I want, too. Alex has grown up without a father and I lost my mother. All we both want is to be the perfect family.

'Come on, let's go.' And as he says this, he squeezes my hand.

~

The rest of the day is perfect. We go for a gentle walk by the lake after lunch; we watch a film on Netflix in the afternoon, snuggled together on the sofa; in the evening we prepare the chicken together for dinner, laughing and chatting. We put music on and Alex dances while I sing.

Alex is back to himself, back to being the man I love. My adorable husband. At the very back of my mind, I've buried the

80

thought that this version, the one that feels genuine, is merely a mask that slips every now and then, revealing underneath it a glimpse of the real man – a damaged soul who is at war with himself and battling against the world. That version of my husband is frightening. But what scares me even more is if that is the real Alex, then I really don't know him at all.

It isn't until the evening that his mood changes. We're in the kitchen. Alex has cleared up the dinner dishes and he's sitting at the table typing away on his mobile while I make us mugs of tea.

'My face is itchy,' Alex complains. He puts his phone down on the table and rubs his face with both hands.

I turn to look at him. His cheeks are red and blotchy. He's wearing a T-shirt and my eyes travel over his biceps. The skin there is irritated and angry, too. Earlier in the day, I'd noticed him scratching his arms and neck.

'Your arms,' I say.

He follows my gaze, then without another word, he gets up and leaves the room. I hear him thundering up the stairs.

I finish packing the dishwasher and then take him up a cup of tea.

When I step into our bedroom, he's looking into the full-length mirror, naked except for his socks. In any other circumstances, I would have cracked a joke, but this isn't funny. I can see all of him; he has his back to me and the front of his body is reflected in the mirror. From behind, he has the appearance of someone who has spent too long on a nudist beach while in the mirror his chest is busy breaking out into blisters.

'Have you ever had chickenpox?' I ask.

'This isn't chickenpox,' he says. 'It's an allergic reaction.'

He whirls round to face me and I force myself not to look down, but I can see out of the corner of my eye that he even has blood-red marks around his genitals. I feel sorry for him, I really do, and I feel utterly helpless.

'To what?'

81

'Chemicals in the shower gel, probably. Allergens. But you know that, don't you?'

His tone is accusatory, but I'm not sure what he's driving at. He stomps into the bathroom, his sock-clad feet and the carpet in the bedroom undermining his physical expression of fury.

Wary, I follow him into the bathroom to find him examining his shower gel. He brandishes the plastic container at me.

I'm about to ask him what he means, but he gets there first.

'You knew I was allergic to certain preservatives in shower gels and shampoos. You did this deliberately, didn't you?'

His face is contorted. He might be wearing socks, but he's taken off the mask.

I don't answer. Now that he mentions it, I did know that. In an email, he once gave me a whole list of chemicals and preservatives that cause him to have dermatitis.

'I thought this morning that this bottle had been topped up. Turns out I was right!' His voice is raised, but he isn't shouting. Not yet. 'Were you trying to punish me for last night?'

Last night? I'm so confused that it takes me a moment to remember what happened last night. We had an argument – I can't even remember what about – when we got home from his mother's house. He ended up sleeping in one of the guestrooms.

'Alex, I haven't touched any of your stuff in the bathroom.'

'Why should I believe you? You lied to my mother's face; how do I know you're not lying to mine?'

That's what the argument was about. My white lie to his mum about enjoying the meal.

I brace myself for him to lose his temper completely and scream at me, but he suddenly stops as if his battery has run out. I watch his blemished hand reach into the bathroom cabinet, as if in slow motion, and take out a large tube of cream. Then he gently pushes me out of the way and goes past me, back into the bedroom.

I pick up the offending body wash. The biggest bottle. The

one on the right. It's nearly full. Alex accused me of topping the bottles up. I flip open the lid and take a sniff. The scent is faint and fruity, nothing like the brand he usually washes himself with, although it's the same bottle. And nothing like the odour I smelled in the bedroom earlier, either.

Stepping back into the bedroom, I see Alex applying cream all over his body. I offer to rub it into his back. He hands me the tube without a word. I hand him the mug of tea I'd made for him. It must be cold by now, but he sips it anyway.

'I promise you, Alex, I haven't tampered with any of your things.' When he doesn't answer, I try again. 'You have to believe me, Alex.'

I can hear my pleading tone of voice and I don't like it. I close my mouth and say no more. Alex doesn't speak either. He doesn't need to. I can see his eyes in the mirror and his look says it all.

Alex doesn't utter a single word for the rest of the evening. He won't look at me and he won't talk to me. By bedtime, I feel as if I've ceased to exist. I'm like a ghost wandering around this soulless shell of a house. I wish Alex goodnight and, when there's no reply, I make my way upstairs.

I expect him to sleep in the other room again tonight, but he climbs into bed some time after me. I'm still awake; I haven't been able to get to sleep. He turns away from me and I put my hand on his waist. He doesn't respond, but he doesn't shake me off either.

I mull over this evening's incident. I feel sorry for Alex and I understand why he got upset. But I wish he hadn't taken it out on me. Alex is tempestuous, but our relationship is full of passion. We never fought, Kevin and I. Well, hardly ever. He never lost his temper. But I'm not sure our relationship could ever have been described as passionate.

I scold myself for comparing my husband with my ex-boyfriend. I don't regret leaving Kevin. But for the first time, I feel a twinge of regret at dashing headlong into this marriage with Alex. At times, I feel like I'm caught. Ensnared in a trap I laid for myself.

I curse myself as silent, self-pitying tears meander their way down my face. I try to focus on the wonderful afternoon Alex and I had. I wonder how to reach Alex, how to get him to talk to me. After opening up to me in the pub earlier, he has now raised an impenetrable wall of silence – resounding silence – around himself and between the two of us.

To: kaitlyn.best@newzmail.co.uk
From: alexanderriley9987@premiernet.co.uk
Sent: Tue, 14 Feb 2017 at 19:35
Subject: HAPPY VALENTINE'S DAY!

Dear Katie,

Happy Valentine's Day, princess! I'm so glad you liked the flowers I sent.

Thank you for your card. It arrived in the post this morning. You're such a romantic!

For Valentine's Day next year, I'll take you out for a candlelit dinner. You deserve to be spoilt rotten. The very best for my Best girl! We'll have to get a babysitter, won't we?! Ooh, there's a thought!

Katie, I have something important to ask you. I wish I could do this over a candlelit dinner this evening, but you're too far away. That said, I don't think I'd feel any more nervous asking you in person than I do right now typing it out on my laptop!

What I want to say is this: Katie, you are the love of my life. What we have feels so special and unique. Would you consider making me the happiest man alive by marrying me? It might seem sudden, but I've never been so sure of anything. I want to spend the rest of my life with you, Katie. You're the one for me. After all, we're going to have a child together! I think it would be the right thing to do for the baby, don't you? I would be very proud to call you my wife. We'll be the perfect family.

You don't need to answer straight away – take as long as you need – but I do hope you'll think about it.

I'll give you a ring later. (See what I did there?!)

Love,
Alexxxx

Chapter 8

When I hear the front door open, I nearly jump out of my skin. I still haven't got over the day I found the door unlocked and thought someone had been in the house, although I've tried to put the whole incident down to my vivid imagination.

I stand there in the kitchen, frozen. I would look like a statue or a sculpture if it wasn't for the rubber gloves.

'Is that you, Alex?' I call out, sounding braver than I feel, appalled at my own jitteriness. There's no one else it could be, but I have no idea why he would come home at this time of day.

The voice comes from behind me and makes me jump again. 'Yes, it's me.' He's leaning on the doorframe, looking at me, an amused expression on his face.

Sexy though he is, I'm still annoyed with him, but I know deep down it will be better for both of us if I can keep that hidden. I don't want him to get stroppy or sulky with me.

'Hello, stranger.' I hear the thinly veiled criticism slip out before my brain-to-mouth filter kicks in.

'Oh, I know,' he says. 'I'll make it up to you, I promise.'

I sigh inwardly with relief. He's in a good mood. I haven't seen any trace of Alex's darker side for a couple of weeks. I've hardly seen Alex this week at all, which is what I'm miffed about. On the one evening he did come home, it was very late.

'It's been a hard week,' Alex continues. 'Meetings, as you know, all over the country. And now the weather and the lakes are warming up, and what with the heatwave last week, I've had lots of bookings for hiking and water sports. Summer's on its way.'

Alex runs an activity centre from his sports shop in Keswick. His words put my mind at rest, although I have no reason to suspect that Alex is anywhere other than where he says he is or doing anything he shouldn't be. He always rings or sends text messages when he's away on business, and this week has been no exception. I realise now that when I arrived in February, it was off-season and so it's only to be expected if he has more on at the moment.

It's rather unexpected, though, for him to come home in the middle of the day.

'To what do I owe this pleasure?' I ask, waving one of my gloved hands at him.

'I thought I'd pop home for a quick lunch and surprise you.'

Briefly, I panic. I've almost finished cleaning the house. Nearly everything is tidied the way Alex likes it. But I haven't been out to the grocery shop yet and there's nothing to make up a lunch.

As if reading my mind, Alex holds up two shopping bags – they look heavy and his biceps flex with the effort. He seems to have come prepared. As I observe him taking out cheese, French bread, pâté and coleslaw, I suddenly become aware of how hungry I am. My eyes follow him as he puts the rest of the food in the fridge and cupboards. I won't have to go out for groceries after all.

As we eat, sitting side by side at the ridiculously large kitchen table, Alex tells me all about his busy week. I listen with half an ear, but I'm distracted by the dark rings under his eyes. He looks exhausted, not to mention dishevelled, which is very unlike Alex, but he seems happy and energetic.

'Perhaps you can relax a bit this weekend,' I suggest. 'Have you got any plans?'

'Nothing much,' he answers, getting up. 'Need to go for a long cycle ride at some point.'

'Leave that if you're in a hurry,' I say as he picks up his plate. 'I'll clear up.'

'OK. Thanks.' He kisses me on the cheek. 'The house is lovely and clean by the way.'

I spot it a few seconds after hearing the front door close. Alex's mobile. He's always tapping away on it. He'll be lost without it. I half-run, half-waddle, after him, but his car is already at the bottom of the drive. I shout and wave my arms around as he gets out to open the gate, but he doesn't hear or see me, so I go back inside the house.

For a few minutes, I remain seated, looking at the mobile I've put down in the middle of the kitchen table. I shouldn't look through it. I shouldn't even be sitting here looking at it, thinking about trying to access it in order to snoop on my husband.

But the truth is, I'm still a little preoccupied and a lot paranoid about his absence nearly all week. One quick peep. I slide the phone towards me. It's on but the screen is locked and I don't know his passcode. It's a four-digit passcode. I put in his year of birth. 1977. The mobile buzzes. Nope. Try again. I enter his date of birth. 2207. The twenty-second of July. That doesn't work either. Probably just as well.

I almost feel glad. I don't want to turn into one of those women who has to check up on her husband every second of every day. Especially when there's no tangible sign that there's anything amiss. I get up and flick the kettle on. I'm going to make myself a proper cup of tea, not that disgusting decaffeinated rubbish Alex insists I drink out of consideration for the baby.

As I sit down again, I sip my tea, staring at the mobile. It seems to be beckoning to me. What could his passcode be? I know I only get one more attempt. And if I get it wrong, Alex will suspect I've been messing around with his phone.

Then it comes to me. *Of course!* The four numbers after his name in his email address: 9987. I have no idea what they denote. They're probably just random digits. I once asked jokingly if there were nearly ten thousand Alexander Rileys. He didn't answer the question. That must be it!

This isn't a good idea, I argue with myself, drumming my fingers on the table. I really don't want to risk unleashing Alex's demons. But then I think: *if I do disable the phone, surely there's a way of restoring it?* I put down my mug.

I'm sorely tempted to have another go. I'm convinced I've guessed the correct passcode this time, but if I *am* mistaken, I could always hide his phone and let him believe he left it somewhere else. That would be lying, but something tells me I've been lied to.

Just as I've made up my mind to give it another shot, the phone rings and startles me. Not Alex's mobile, the landline. It hardly ever rings so it takes me a second to recognise the sound. I wonder if it could be Alex ringing me from work. He probably doesn't know my mobile number by heart but he would know his own home number. I dash out to the hall, supporting my bump with my hands, and snatch up the handset.

'Hello?'

There's no answer. It's the second time this has happened.

'Hello?' I repeat more loudly. 'Alex?'

I slam the phone down, exasperated. Who can it be? The caller ID was hidden so I have no way of telling. I'm assuming, though, it's the same caller as last time. Now I come to think of it, Alex wasn't in on that occasion, either. It must be someone who wants to speak to Alex and won't talk to me.

Feeling more determined than ever to get into Alex's mobile, I go back into the kitchen and pick up his smartphone. I type in the digits with my index finger. *Nine. Nine. Eight. Seven.* The screen unlocks. *Result!*

Now what? I go into Mail. He has two inboxes and I scroll down the emails in one and then the other. I'm not sure what I'm looking for, but nothing strikes me as particularly suspicious. Then I see he has a mailbox sent up for a VIP. My finger hovers over the screen. I'm not sure if I want to see what I'm going see. In the end, I have a look. I smile and sigh at the same time. The VIP sender is me. Lots of the emails we exchanged while I was living in Minehead are still stored in the memory of his phone. And in my own memory, too.

I feel remorseful. But I'm not going to stop there. I may as well go all the way now. I'll only be satisfied once I've checked everything and found nothing. So I look through his contacts. There are businesses that are evidently related to Alex's work, and lots of people whose names I don't recognise. Not for the first time, I'm disappointed by how few of Alex's friends and acquaintances I've met.

Finally, I check the text messages. The most recent text has been sent by Rebecca Brown. *Rebecca Brown.* I say the name aloud. It doesn't sound familiar. She sent a message this morning at 8.30 a.m. I open it. And read it.

Thank you so much, Alex, for going to all that trouble last night. You were amazing.
Bexxx.

I sink down slowly onto the kitchen chair. My mind goes into overdrive. Is this what I was looking for? What happened last night? Does this mean that Alex and Bex – God, even their names go together – are having an affair?

My head suddenly starts to pound. I try to reason with myself, calm myself down. Does the text actually prove anything? All it proves is that Alex must have written to Rebecca, aka "Bex", at some point because she signed off with two kisses, just like he does.

The front door bangs and I want to leap up and put the mobile back on the worktop where I found it, but it's as if I'm glued to the chair.

'Think I forgot my mobile,' Alex says, coming into the kitchen. He stops mid-stride as he sees it in my hands.

My heart is pounding now, too, so frantically that I think Alex must be able to hear it, or even see it through my T-shirt. 'Someone called Rebecca said you were amazing last night,' I say. I mean to confront Alex but it comes out as a question.

'Did she? She sent a text to thank me earlier,' Alex says. 'I pulled a few strings, made a few calls, got her a late entry into a competition.' He takes the mobile from me. 'Cheers. See you later. I'm going training after work, but I won't be home too late tonight, OK?'

Not trusting myself to speak, I nod. He kisses me on the lips and strolls back out of the kitchen, leaving me alone with my thoughts. I realise Alex must have assumed that Rebecca rang and I answered his phone. He didn't seem at all thrown when I mentioned her. I obviously jumped to completely the wrong conclusion. My suspicions were unfounded and now I feel stupid and deeply ashamed of myself.

I grab my own mobile and ring Hannah. Predictably, there's no answer. I could ring Julie, but we've never had the sort of relationship where we unburden ourselves to each other or tell one another secrets, even as kids. I had Louisa for that. Now I have no one. I'm not really alone, but I am really lonely.

Without warning, the kitchen walls start to close in on me and an intense wave of fear consumes me. I can't catch my breath. My heart is now beating so hard and fast that it hurts. I remember a student having a panic attack during one of my lectures once. She was a bit of a drama queen and I showed her very little compassion. Am *I* having a panic attack? I feel as if I'm drowning. I sink down onto the chair and grip the edge of the table, as though my life depends on me not letting go.

Eventually the kitchen stops pitching and tossing, and my pulse slows to a normal rhythm. I'm left feeling a little nauseous and disorientated, with an overwhelming need to get out of the house. So I call the only other person I can call. Vicky.

She meets me in the swimming pool car park. As I hoist my bulky frame out of the car, she perches her sunglasses on top of her head and flashes her pearly white smile at me. She is elegantly dressed in a flowery vintage summer dress and she towers over me in her chunky lime-green platform sandals. She looks like she has just stepped out of the Seventies.

The swim does me a lot of good. I sing songs in my head as I plough up and down the pool. The coffee afterwards in the leisure centre café is even more beneficial, even though this time I've respected what Alex would have wanted and ordered a decaf. At first, Vicky seems unwilling to talk about herself, but once she gets going, she tells me about her family – her father died of lung cancer a few years ago and her brother died in a car accident when they were teenagers. We seem to have a lot in common and I get the impression she is a mirror image of me. She lost her brother and her father; I lost my sister and my mother.

'My parents put a lot of pressure on me to make something of myself to compensate for losing their son, I suppose,' she confides.

'I know what that's like,' I say, and I tell her about how when I lost Louisa – my other half – my mum seemed to expect me to become twice the person I'd been until then. It didn't help, of course, that Julie had just moved in with Daniel. My mum lost two daughters in one go and was left with me.

'What happened to your sister?' Vicky asks. 'If you don't mind me asking.'

I do, really. I don't like to talk about what happened to Louisa, so I keep it short. 'She was attacked.'

'Oh, how awful.' Vicky seems to sense my reluctance to go into detail, so she just asks, 'Did they catch the person responsible?'

'Yes. It was a local man. A known sex offender. He was arrested. He died while he was in police custody.'

'Suicide?'

'So they said.'

'Perhaps that's just as well,' Vicky says.

'Mmm,' I say noncommittally. We didn't think so at the time. We wanted justice. I keep that thought to myself. Instead, I try to steer the conversation back to where we were. 'So, *did* you make something of yourself?' Vicky throws me a blank look. 'You said your parents put a lot of pressure on you to succeed.'

'Ah, I see. Well, no, not really!' She gives a self-deprecating laugh. 'I'm an estate agent.' She chuckles again. She has this wonderful laugh. It's musical and infectious at the same time. 'So I should be able to find a place to live one of these days, at least.'

'Where are you living now?' I wonder if I'm being nosy, but if Vicky minds, she doesn't show it.

'I split up with my boyfriend about five months ago,' she says, 'so I'm at my mum's for the moment. It's not easy, living under the same roof as my mother, I can tell you.' She pauses and then concedes, 'Although she does cook great food and she puts up with all my canine friends.'

'Canine friends?'

'Yes. I have a cocker spaniel called Lady, Scooby who's a Great Dane, obviously, and Shadow an old golden retriever.' She counts them off on her fingers as she introduces them. 'And the latest addition to the family arrived in February. That's Bestie, the Westie – the dog you saw me walking – it might even have been his first walk.' She holds up the fingers of her right hand, her thumb bent into her palm. 'Four altogether.'

'How come you have so many?'

'Well, I adopted Shadow from an animal shelter years ago and they call me every now and then when they have a dog they haven't found a home for. I can't seem to say no. I hate the thought of them being put down. I take them in and rename them, give them a new life.'

In turn, I tell Vicky all about myself, my family, the job I used to do and about Alex and the baby. She's a good listener and when we've drained our mugs of coffee, I feel like I've known her for a while. We're still chatting as we push open the doors to leave the café.

I hear him before I see him. His voice hits me like a well-aimed blow to my stomach just as Vicky and I are coming out of the café into the foyer. Quickly, I turn around and push Vicky back into the café. She's looking over my shoulder and has spotted them, too.

The double doors swing closed, shielding us from their view, and I peer out of the round porthole window, feeling seasick. Vicky remains silent as I watch Alex show the receptionist something – a membership card, maybe – and chat with her. There are four other people with him – two women and two men. I recognise Mike and his girlfriend, who danced with Alex at our wedding. I don't know the others.

'When he said he was going training, I thought he meant cycling or running,' I hiss over my shoulder. Vicky arches what's left of her eyebrows at me. She steps forward and looks out of the window of the other door.

'Who's he?' She asks this in a stage whisper. She's poking fun at me, I realise, and it highlights the absurdity of this situation.

'Alex.'

'Your husband?'

'Yes.'

'And we're hiding from him because …?'

'He disapproves of me swimming. He thinks the baby needs me to rest.'

'I see. I take it he doesn't know about me then?'

'Er … no.'

I expect Vicky to be put out by this, but she grins. I get the

94

impression she likes the idea of being complicit in my deceit, but perhaps she's just amused.

They've gone. I feel my shoulders relax. I push the door open and Vicky follows me into the reception area.

'He's handsome, your husband,' she comments.

It's not until we're in the car park that I wonder how she knew which one was Alex. Vicky asks me something but I'm lost in my thoughts and I don't catch what she says.

'Sorry?'

'When's your due date?' she repeats.

'The eighth of July. A week tomorrow.'

'You're brave, coming swimming today.' Vicky fishes her sunglasses out of her handbag and puts them on.

'Not really. If I'd known Alex was going to be here, though, I wouldn't have come! But I felt like a swim. By the way, how did you know which one was him?'

'One of the men was groping the backside of one of the women, so I assumed that wasn't him.' It's a joke, I think, so I laugh politely. 'And the other two looked to be a couple as well. Plus, Alex's face looked familiar,' she continues. 'I think I vaguely remember him from the day I was out walking my dog after all.'

As I pull down the boot of my car, I promise to text Vicky early next week to meet up for another swim.

'Next time could well be your last session before the baby comes along,' she says, voicing my own thoughts.

When I get home, I have time to put on a load of washing and read some of my book before Alex gets home a couple of hours after me. I'm curled up on the sofa in the sitting room and he sees me through the doorway, but marches straight through to the kitchen.

'Kay-tie!' His voice is imperious and I feel like I'm being summonsed. A little voice in my head begs me not to go to him, not to give in to him, but I ignore it and get up to join him in the kitchen.

He's standing in front of the open fridge with his hands on his hips, his face stormy.

Oh no, what have I done now? 'Is everything all right?' I ask. Stupid question. Clearly something is wrong.

'Have you got the food ready?' His voice is angry with an undertone of world-weariness. It makes my stomach flip. 'They'll be here any second.'

'What food? Who will be here?'

He slams the refrigerator door but it makes very little noise as it closes and I doubt it has had the desired effect.

'Bloody hell, Kaitlyn! Mike and his girlfriend are coming round for a barbecue this evening. I bought all the stuff you needed. The only thing you had to do was get it ready!'

A scowl contorts Alex's tanned face. He takes a step towards me and I take a step back. I wonder if he's going to strike me, and instinctively my hands curl into fists at my sides.

'But this is the first I've heard of it.'

I look over Alex's shoulder out of the window. The sky is dark now and there's not a trace of the earlier sunshine. It's going to rain, rain on Alex's party.

'Bollocks! I told you on the phone earlier this week and then I reminded you at lunchtime.'

Did he? I don't remember.

'I asked you to make a chocolate mousse and some salads.'

I don't believe him. I'm not the one who forgot. I fight the tears that threaten to spill down my face. I'd have remembered if Alex had mentioned this barbecue. I'd have been wildly excited about entertaining and getting to know some of Alex's friends properly at last.

'You watched me put the shopping away!'

Yes, but I also asked him about his plans for the weekend and he said nothing about this.

'For fuck's sake, Kaitlyn!' Alex throws a glass at the wall and it smashes into smithereens. My eyes are drawn to the shards on the floor between Alex and me. The glass is not the only thing that is broken between us, even though I've tried so hard to hold us together.

I want to storm out of the kitchen, but I feel so weak that I doubt my legs will take me. It's all I can do to stay standing. I lean against the worktop for support, an unwelcome and unwilling spectator to Alex's show of anger.

In the end, he doesn't lay a finger on me, but his words hit me hard. He has never called me names before. I listen, speechless, to a string of insults as they stream from his mouth one after the other. Then his words become meaningless muffled sounds as if he's now behind a closed door or underwater and I can no longer make out what he's saying.

I try to think on my unsteady feet.

'Alex,' I say calmly. To my surprise, his mouth stops moving and the noise stops. 'We don't have enough time for the mousse to set, but I can make a chocolate fondant cake in next to no time. And salads are easy. If you get the meat ready for the barbecue, we can do the salads together.'

Alex nods, docile now.

'And I'm quite sure Mike and his girlfriend – what's her name? – won't mind sitting at the table here and having a drink while we finish getting ready,' I say, warming to my theme.

'They might mind a bit. They've just done a two-hour training session. They'll be hungry.'

But the fight has gone out of him. I can breathe again.

'We've got crisps.'

I bend down to get the dustpan and brush from the cupboard under the sink. As I sweep up the fragments of glass, I tell myself that Alex is mistaken. He simply forgot to tell me he'd invited his mates and he thought he'd mentioned it. Then he overreacted when he came home and saw nothing was ready.

But the memory of the dinner at his mother's house resurfaces from where it was lurking in a corner of my mind. Was that an innocent mistake? Or did Alex lie about my favourite meal? Why would he have done that? And why would he lie about this evening? Surely he doesn't want to ridicule me in front of his friends.

These questions stop racing through my mind abruptly. I look down at the floor, aghast. Alex realises what has happened before I do. As I look at him, I can feel the shock etched on my face, and suddenly the roles are reversed. I'm the one who is panicking and it's Alex who takes control of the situation.

'Sit down here for a second, Katie.' He speaks slowly and evenly, almost as if he's thinking out loud. He pulls out a kitchen chair and takes my elbow to guide me, making me feel like I'm an old woman in need of a walking stick. He takes the dustpan and brush out of my hands. 'I'll fetch your suitcase,' he goes on, 'and then I'll help you out to the car.' The smile on his face looks genuine, although I'm not sure whether he's excited or trying to be reassuring. 'We have to get you to hospital, Katie. Your waters have broken.'

To: kaitlyn.best@newzmail.co.uk
From: alexanderriley9987@premiernet.co.uk
Sent: Thur, 23 Feb 2017 at 20:41
Subject: THE LIFE OF RILEY

Dearest Katie,

This is just a quick message to let you know that I'm not going to be able to make it the day after tomorrow, I'm afraid. I know we'd arranged for me travel to Taunton by train so I could share the driving with you up to Grasmere, but I have an important competition I just can't get out of that day. I'd be letting the team down. The good news is that I'll be free by the evening. You don't mind, do you? I remember when I offered to come, you insisted you'd be OK by yourself and I know how independent and capable you are!

I can't make it down to Somerset, but I will make it up to you in Cumbria, I promise! I'll pamper you and make you breakfast in bed and basically let you live the life of Riley now you're going to be my wife!

If you prefer, we could postpone your journey until the following weekend and I can help you out with the driving then. I'd rather you came the day after tomorrow, obvs, because I can't wait to see you! That would be only two more sleeps!

You decide what's best for you, my Best girl, and let me know.

I love you,
Alexxx

Chapter 9

I hear Chloe wailing in the middle of the night. When I roll over, Alex's side of the bed is empty. As usual, he has got there first.

I get out of bed, push my feet into my slippers and grab my dressing gown from the back of the door. Then I make my way along the landing and peep in through the door to Poppy and Violet's bedroom – now Chloe's room – which Alex has left ajar.

He's holding a bottle of milk in one hand and cradling our baby in the other arm and as I watch, he sits down on one of the single beds. The squalling stops as soon as Chloe's mouth finds the teat and she starts to suck hungrily on it.

'It looks like you've got it all under control again,' I say.

Alex has got up twice with Chloe every single night since we brought her home. He hears our daughter before me, gets out of bed to go to her before me, and he feeds her and holds her far more often than I do.

But that's about to change.

Alex looks up. 'Hello there,' he says. 'You go back to bed. Chloe and I can manage.' Looking down again at our daughter, he adds, 'Can't we, petal?'

I wonder if he called Poppy and Violet 'petal', too. Probably, given that they have flowery first names. Maybe he nicknamed his ex-wife "princess" as well.

I feel a strange mixture of gratefulness and helplessness, as I often have since coming home from the maternity hospital. I'm thankful that Alex knows what to do with a newborn baby – he has been amazing – but I feel useless in comparison. He's a great father, but his efficiency makes me feel like a bad mother.

I'm also rather jealous when I witness scenes like this because I'm reminded that Alex has been through all this before – twice – with two other daughters, and, more importantly, another wife.

'You don't need me, then?' I ask, torn between staying here and going back to sleep.

'Nope. We got it.'

As I walk away, my husband starts singing 'Rock-a-bye Baby' to Chloe. How odd. I sing all the time. In the car, in the shower, while I'm cooking. But I've never heard Alex sing before.

The following morning, we're up before Chloe. Alex has been on paternity leave, or so he calls it, although technically he's not an employee, as it's his business. But his two weeks are up and it's back to work. When Chloe wakes up, I bring her down to the kitchen so we can keep Alex company while he eats his breakfast. I get as comfortable as possible on the wooden chair and encourage Chloe to latch on to my nipple, but she's not having it.

'Can't think why she's not mad about your boobs,' Alex says, a cheeky grin on his face. He opens the fridge and takes out a bottle of expressed milk. He runs warm water from the tap over it for a few seconds before handing it to me. Chloe stops protesting mid-scream.

'She has certainly taken to the bottle,' Alex jokes.

I paint a smile on my face, although I wish Chloe would take

101

my breast. Still, with Alex back at work, we'll have time to bond, my baby girl and me.

'Will you cope?' Alex asks.

'Yes, of course,' I say, although I was just asking myself the same question.

'You should get some light exercise. Take Chloe out in the pram for some fresh air.'

'Oh, yes, that's a great idea.' We could walk to the shop in Grasmere and buy some chocolate. Alex has been making me healthy meals so that Chloe gets all the vitamins and nutrients she needs through my maternal milk, but I'm starving all the time. Silver lining: at least the pregnancy weight is falling off me. Perhaps that's the idea.

'Are you feeling up to having that barbecue this weekend?'

I'm keen to meet his friends, but right now I'm permanently tired and I look pretty terrible. 'Yes,' I say. Might be able to sneak a glass of wine. Beer. Punch. Anything with alcohol in it. It's been so long. Ooh. Food. Grilled skewers and kebabs. Rice. Something other than quinoa and lettuce. 'Absolutely.'

'Good. I won't be late home.'

When Alex has left, I carry Chloe upstairs to my bedroom. She falls asleep on her activity playmat on the floor while I shower with the Pet Shop Boys and Dexys Midnight Runners blaring out of my wireless speaker from Hannah's playlist, which I'd put on my phone.

Hannah. Phone Hannah. I sent her a text with a photo when Chloe was born and she wrote back – succinctly – with her congratulations. That was a fortnight ago. And that's the only time I've heard from her for well over a month now.

I stop the music on my mobile, but before I can ring Hannah, the phone rings in my hand. I stare at the caller ID in disbelief. What does *he* want? I'm tempted to let it go to voicemail, but I swipe the screen and take the call.

'Hi, Kevin.'

There's music playing in the background. Placebo, I think. Kevin's favourite band. I can't make out which song.

'Hi, Kaitlyn. I'm just ringing to let you know the sale on the house has gone through. It's all taken care of.'

The familiar sound of his voice and the dulcet tones of his West Country accent – the dropped h's and lengthened a's – instantly transport me to another place, another time. *Home.* I sit down on the bed, still wrapped in my towel, my hair dripping onto my shoulders.

'Oh. Thank you, Kevin, for seeing to all that.'

Kevin always dreamt of building us our own home one day. A place with sea views. That's one of the reasons we stayed in that house so long, even though we could easily have afforded something bigger, something better. That and the fact that with no children, we never really outgrew our place in Minehead. It might have been small, but it was big enough for the two of us.

'There's some paperwork to sign. I'll have it sent to you by post.'

'All right. Thanks.'

'Maybe you could text me your address?'

'Sure.'

'Oh, and, Kaitlyn?'

'Yes?'

An awkward silence. What's that called? *A pregnant pause.* How inappropriate. Kevin breaks it.

'Many congratulations on your wedding and the birth of your daughter. That's wonderful news.'

'Thank you.'

I realise I've thanked him three times and said very little else. I want to say so much more. I want to ask him how he is. Where he's living now. I want to know how he found out about Chloe and if he's OK about that. But it's too late. Kevin has ended the call.

I put on my underwear, which gives me a few seconds to

103

breathe normally again, and then I grab the phone again to try Hannah. I don't expect her to answer, but I can leave her another message. I prepare it in my head as her phone rings on and on.

'Hello, Kaitlyn.'

She sounds out of breath.

'Hannah!' I'm delighted to hear her voice, despite several weeks of confusion and concern. Why hasn't she been in touch?

And then I hear it. This time I can make out the song. *Without You I'm Nothing*. At first I think they must be listening to the same radio station. Kevin listens to the radio all day long while he's at work. So does Hannah. And then the penny drops like a dead weight. It's Monday. Kevin's day off. Hannah doesn't work on Mondays either.

'You're at Kevin's,' I whisper. It's not a question. But I have no idea where he lives now. I correct myself. 'You're with Kevin.' Two possible meanings, both fitting.

'I'm so sorry, Kaitlyn. We didn't want you to know until we were sure it was ... serious. And then I didn't know how to tell you. I feel terrible about avoiding you all this time.'

We don't talk for long – the conversation is stilted. I no longer want to tell her about Chloe. I can't confide in her about Alex. I don't tell her how much I've missed her. At the end of the call, Hannah asks if I think we can still be friends.

'Hannah, you've been my best friend nearly all my life. I'll get used to the idea.' I'm going to need some time. But I don't tell her that. 'You're right for each other, you and Kevin.' As I say it, I realise it's true. Hannah has always needed someone kind and dependable. Someone exactly like Kevin.

I can hear the smile in her voice as she says goodbye. I do my best to keep the tears out of mine.

I don't want to mope around the house all day, so I decide to go for that walk. Thinking about it now, I realise there's no pavement for at least two hundred yards if I walk from home into Grasmere as I planned. I don't relish the idea of pushing Chloe along the road, so I change my mind about setting out by foot and decide to drive into Ambleside instead.

It's a bit of a fiddle, but I manage to fasten the pram into the car and Chloe into the pram and then fold down the pram chassis so I can put it in the boot. I feel ridiculously proud of myself, but it doesn't obliterate my sadness.

As I pull out of the driveway, I reason with myself. I left Kevin. That was my choice. I should be glad he's found someone else. Shouldn't I? Even if that someone else is my best friend. And I should be pleased for Hannah. She deserves to find a man who can make her happy. Perhaps I will be pleased for her, in time.

I start singing 'Molly Malone' to Chloe, even though I'm pretty certain she's asleep and my voice sounds a bit choked. It will get Kevin and Hannah out of my head, anyway. With a jolt, I realise that my mother used to sing that song to Louisa and me. She probably sang it to Julie before us. She could carry a tune, my mum. I stop mid-verse. Oh God, I miss my mum and my twin sister.

I also miss my dad and Julie, Daniel and my nephews. I'd love to see them and for them to meet Chloe. But Alex insists that I should wait until I've fully recovered from giving birth before having to look after guests as well as a newborn baby.

I fight against the lump in my throat. I have to stop wallowing in self-pity. I have to be strong. I'm fine. I'll be fine. I'll talk to Alex again. He only has my best interests at heart, I'm sure, but I'm feeling very cut off from my family, not to mention estranged from my best friend. I'm sure I can make him understand that I need to see someone other than him and Chloe.

And my mother-in-law. Sandy means well and she helps out a lot, but she has been round nearly every day since we brought Chloe home and it's too much. It's probably too much for her, too. I'm looking forward to the barbecue, sort of, but Alex's friends don't count, either. I want to see *my* family and *my* friends. Otherwise I'll go mad.

Then I remember Vicky. She works in Ambleside. Maybe I could pop in to the estate agency and say hello. I sent her a text when Chloe was born with some photos. We've exchanged text messages on a couple of occasions since then.

When I've parked the car and got the pram clipped onto the chassis, I ask a shopper how to get to Swift and Taylor Properties, where Vicky works, and I find it easily enough. There are stone steps leading up to the entrance, only a few of them, but enough to make it impossible to take the pram into the estate agency. I don't want to leave it at the bottom of the steps with Chloe in it, but she's sound asleep and if I lift her out, she's bound to wake up.

I tell myself no one is going to take my baby. If I stand at the top of the steps and don't actually go into the building, I'll be able to keep an eye on her. So, leaving her in the pram outside, I go up the steps. The automatic doors open. I stand in the doorway, turning my head from time to time to check on Chloe, but the doors start to close and then reopen. Close, open, repeat.

'Come in, love,' says a woman in her fifties, who is sitting at one of the four desks and peering at me over the top of her bifocals.

Reluctantly, I step into the room to allow the doors to shut behind me. I shuffle from one foot to the other, uncomfortable at the idea that Chloe is out of my sight now.

'I … um, is Vicky here?' I ask her.

'Vicky?'

'Yes, she's a friend of mine. She works here.'

'Vicky who, love?'

'Er … I don't know her other name, I'm afraid.' Maybe there are two Vickys.

Her phone rings and she picks it up. 'Swift and Taylor Properties. How can I help you?' She covers the mouthpiece and, nodding in my direction, she hisses at her colleague, 'Dennis? Can you look after this lady?'

Her colleague grunts grudgingly from his desk without taking his eyes off his computer screen. He's the only other person in the office. The other desks are unoccupied.

I'm suddenly overcome with panic about leaving Chloe outside. 'You're obviously busy,' I say hurriedly. 'I'll come back another time. Sorry to disturb you.'

How odd. I'm sure Vicky said Swift and Taylor Properties. She even has their name on a sticker plastered along the side of her car. I remember seeing it in the car park at the swimming pool. She said she hated that advert and used her mother's car at weekends.

As I go back outside, it occurs to me that Vicky's colleagues may call her Victoria, supposing that's the unabbreviated form of her first name. Or perhaps they use 'Miss' and her surname. I'm about to turn around and enquire again, but then my heart stops. The pram has gone. I can hear the woman call out to me as I race down the steps shouting.

'Chloe!' I almost lose my footing. 'Chloe!'

My world crumbles around me in slow motion. My chest tightens so that I can't breathe; my eyes mist over so that I can't see.

'My baby!' I cry.

'It's OK. She's here with me.' I know who it is, although she has her back to me and doesn't turn round. I recognise her mellifluous voice. 'I saw you through the window, so I realised this must be Chloe.' She's pushing the pram backwards and forwards as if to calm Chloe, although there's no noise coming from the pram. 'You're so tiny,' she coos, bending over and stroking Chloe's cheek.

'Hi, Vicky. It's great to see you,' I say, feeling stupid and trying to recover. I walk round in front of her and kiss her on the cheek. She's wearing a cornflower blue cotton skirt and a white strappy top and looks lovely, as always. 'You scared me!'

'Did I? I'm sorry.' Vicky focuses her attention back on Chloe. 'Your baby is so beautiful.'

I smile at that. I take a peek at Chloe. Still fast asleep. I can breathe evenly and see clearly again.

'Who does she look like?' Vicky asks.

'Well, she has my mouth and complexion, but the blue eyes are Alex's. She doesn't have his nose, thankfully, or my ginger hair!'

'I assumed you dyed your hair! You're so lucky!'

'Hmm. I didn't use to think so. I'm glad Chloe's fair like her dad when he was little and my dad when he still had hair!'

I look down at Chloe again. She's so pretty when she's sleeping. 'Your colleague didn't seem to want to tell me where to find you.' I nod towards the window of the estate agency.

'Which one?'

'The woman with the glasses. Well, the man – Dennis is it? – wasn't much help, either, actually.'

She rolls her eyes. 'Ruth's a dotty old bat! Harmless, but a bit overprotective. And that Dennis is a waste of space. Have you got time for a coffee?' She pauses long enough for me to nod. 'Wait here a tick.'

And with that she runs up the steps and disappears. For the few seconds she's gone, I wonder if Vicky really does work here. Then I wonder if I'm the one who is dotty. Of course she works here. She's just gone inside. And anyway, why would she say she works here if she doesn't? The misunderstanding with Vicky's colleague Ruth is down to me. Vicky is my friend – the only friend I've made since moving here – and I don't even know her full name.

Vicky re-emerges with a plastic bag in her hand. She waves it at me and I wonder what's in it, but I don't dare ask.

'I haven't got long, I'm afraid,' she tells me. 'I went to a private viewing this morning and my colleagues think I should be pulling my weight this afternoon to make up for it.' She winks conspiratorially, but I've missed the point.

'What? I don't—'

'I think I've found a little house. Well, a garden flat. Near Troutbeck.'

I furrow my brows.

'About three miles north of Windermere,' Vicky informs me. 'It's perfect for me and the dogs. I'm going to put in an offer and avoid showing anyone else around it for the time being.' She grins. 'My mum is paying the deposit. I lost all my money when … well, that's another story.'

'Oh, Vicky, that sounds wonderful!' I ask her loads of questions and she tells me all about the house as we walk along the narrow pavement side by side. Her excitement is palpable and contagious.

As she's talking about how she's going to decorate what to her mind has evidently already become her new home, I think about the house I used to live in with Kevin in Minehead. Some time ago, Alex offered to invest my half of the money from the sale. He mentioned something about a high-interest building society account, but I didn't pay much attention. I'm relieved he's happy to sort that all out for me. I'll have to remember to text Kevin with my postal address and tell Alex the house has been sold.

Vicky stops walking and talking at the same time and I realise I've tuned out. I don't seem to have missed anything important, though.

'This café is quite nice,' she says. 'Will this do?'

'It looks great,' I say and Vicky holds the door open so that I can manoeuvre the pram inside.

Over coffee, she hands me the bag she retrieved from inside the estate agency.

'This is for you,' she says. 'A present for the baby.'

I'm touched by Vicky's thoughtfulness. I'm holding Chloe, and Vicky reaches out to take her so I can open the present. It's beautifully wrapped and as I tear off the paper and ribbons, I can feel Vicky's eyes on me, keen to see what I make of her gift.

It's a baby carrier.

'You haven't got one already, have you? If so, we can exchange it.'

'No. No, I haven't got one.' My family have sent lots of clothes and my mother-in-law bought the activity playmat. Alex and I had already bought the pram and cot. We have no end of baby paraphernalia. But I haven't got one of these.

'You can carry Chloe around like a baby kangaroo in a pouch,' she says, her eyes bright, 'and use your hands to do other things, like read a book or tidy up. A friend of mine had one and couldn't recommend it highly enough when I asked her for advice on what to buy you.'

'Thank you,' I say. I'm very moved by all the trouble Vicky has gone to.

'Also, I've found a sports centre with crèche facilities in Cockermouth. It doesn't have a pool, but it does have a gym. It's a bit of a trek, but I thought when you were feeling up to it, we could go?'

'Oh, Vicky, that's really sweet of you.' I'm tired all the time and the last thing I feel like doing is sport, but I hear myself saying, 'Give me a couple more weeks!'

Then I remember the barbecue.

'Ooh. Alex is having a barbecue this weekend for some of his friends. Would you like to come?' I ask.

Vicky looks shocked, but her tweezed eyebrows do tend to give her that expression. 'I'm not free this weekend, I'm afraid. Sorry,' she says. She finishes her coffee, leans back in her chair and crosses her legs, before adding, 'I thought your husband didn't know about me?'

'He doesn't. But I could tell him about you now. I'm no longer pregnant so I don't need to meet up with you for swimming sessions behind his back.'

Vicky chuckles. 'Oh, you should think twice about that,' she jokes. 'You might need an alibi one day. And anyway, I quite like being a secret.' She winks. I'm a little disappointed she can't come, but I'm not sure how Alex would feel about me inviting a friend round to his party without running it by him first, so it's probably just as well.

As I stifle a yawn, I notice Vicky check her watch. I down the dregs of my coffee. Vicky is apologetic about having to rush off, but I'm feeling much better for seeing her.

By the time I get home, however, I'm utterly exhausted. I feed and change Chloe and when she falls asleep, I put her down gently in the pram, which I'd left in the hall, and wheel it into the sitting room. I lie down on the sofa with my book, planning to read a few chapters before getting the dinner ready for this evening. If I can show Alex I have a handle on everything when he comes home, there's a good chance we'll spend an evening without him losing his temper or me getting upset.

I immediately feel guilty for thinking along those lines. Alex has been terrific recently. In fact, there hasn't been a cross word or a bad mood since the day Chloe came into the world. He seems to be back to his default setting. But at the same time, I'm not going to take that for granted. I'd like things to stay the way they are. Keep on top of things. Keep him happy.

Before long, though, my eyelids get heavy. Slight change of plan. Plenty of time. Right now, I'm going to take a nap.

Chapter 10

It's six o'clock in the evening when Chloe wakes up and wakes me. My neck is stiff from the position I've slept in on the sofa. I carry her upstairs to give her a bath. I cherish this moment with my daughter. Keeping up an endless stream of chatter, I talk to her about Hannah and Kevin, about feeling lonely and home-sick, about my dad, whom I haven't seen since the wedding and who hasn't seen his granddaughter yet, about the things I can't tell Alex. Then I talk to her about her daddy, who should be home soon.

She starts to whimper, so I end my monologue, lift her out of the baby bath and pat her body and fine hair dry. Then I hurry to put on her nappy, body and pyjamas before she gets too vocal in demanding another feed.

Again, Chloe refuses to breastfeed, her face going through every shade on the palette from pink to puce as she howls in objection. It's only as she's guzzling away happily on yet another bottle that I wonder where Alex is. Sitting cross-legged on the sofa, I rotate my head in an attempt to ease my sore neck.

By the time Chloe has finished her milk, it's gone seven and I'm a little annoyed. Alex must have gone training. He could have told me! Then I realise he might actually have told me. I haven't checked my mobile. Holding Chloe so that I can rub her back with one hand – I'm getting good at this – I fetch my handbag from the hall and manage to extract my mobile.

But there's no message from Alex. I try calling him, but it goes to voicemail. OK, now I'm done with annoyed and I'm getting anxious. I put Chloe in the baby carrier and over the top of her head I make the dinner. Shepherd's pie. Alex's favourite. And I might even feel full after this meal. I put it in the oven. If Alex isn't back by the time it's ready, it can easily be heated up later.

By 8 p.m., I'm so worried that I'm contemplating calling my mother-in-law. He said he wouldn't be late. Didn't he? My mind becomes hyperactive. A sudden image of a lorry blindsiding Alex's car forces its way into my head. There will be a knock on the door any minute now when the police arrive to tell me he's dead and I'm a widow. *Calm down. Breathe in. Breathe out.* I'm not sure whose voice is in my head, calming me, but it works for a while.

By nine, though, I'm wondering how long someone has to be AWOL before they're considered a missing person. How long are you supposed to wait before notifying the police about a missing person? Is it twenty-four hours or is that just on TV? I look it up on the internet on my phone. No, you don't have to wait twenty-four hours before contacting the local police. According to the website, they will ask me for details of places he often visits.

Where could he be? Is there somewhere he goes when he's not at home or at work or training?

I text Alex.

Where are you?

Then I add three kisses, send the message and wait. No answer. I try to get hold of my mother-in-law. She isn't answering her mobile or her landline.

For the next hour, Chloe cries. I change her, attempt to feed her again, rub her tummy in case she's colicky, push her dummy in her mouth, sing, coo, croon and beg. Eventually, she falls asleep in my arms. She must be able to sense when I'm on edge. I lay her down in her cot.

It's getting very late now and there's still no sign of Alex. Maybe I'm mistaken. Perhaps he said he wasn't coming home this evening and I forgot. I do feel like I've left half of my brain at the maternity hospital sometimes.

I think about calling the police, but I'm rather embarrassed. I'm sure they'd treat it as an emergency if I reported a missing child. But a missing husband? They'll find me ridiculous. They'll ask questions like do we ever argue? Or has he ever slept away from home before? I ring Alex's mobile again and again, but each time it goes straight to voicemail and I end the calls without leaving a message.

After expressing some more milk, I heat up some of the meal I made and push it around my plate for a while before scraping it into the bin. I decide to go to bed. I make my way upstairs, hoping there is a perfectly good explanation for his disappearance. Maybe he told me he was away on business and I simply didn't register what he said.

I feel worn out, but sleep doesn't come. I toss and turn for a while and then I switch on my lamp and pick up my novel. The words on the page blur and I can't make them out. I try harder to concentrate on my book, but after reading the same paragraph five or six times without taking anything in, I give up.

Twirling a strand of my hair around my index finger, I gaze at the vacant side of the bed where Alex should be. I try to imagine him lying there next to me. Instead, I see him lying in a ditch, bleeding to death, his overturned car hidden from the road, the truck long gone. Shaking my head in an effort to dispel the images, I decide to ring the police in the morning. I notice I've cut off the blood supply to my fingertip so I unravel the strand of hair.

I turn off the lamp and lie in the dark, my eyes staring blindly at the ceiling. When Chloe wakes for the first of her nightly feeds, it comes as a welcome respite from the tangle of alarm and anger that's beginning to overwhelm me.

I do sleep for a couple of hours and I immediately check my mobile when I wake, although I've left it on with the volume right up so I would have heard if it had rung or even beeped with a message. Still no news. I get up, check on Chloe, who is sleeping soundly, and go downstairs to make a cup of tea.

It's early, but I ring Julie. Normally, I would turn to Hannah. But even though I don't often confide in Julie, she does give good advice. Usually when I don't want to hear it. Right now, I do. So, I tell my sister everything. Alex is missing, I'm not one hundred per cent sure he was meant to come home, I don't want to call the police unnecessarily because they'll take me for an idiot.

'Why don't you ring the local hospitals before you call the police?' My pragmatic sister suggests.

Why didn't I think of that? Julie would, though. She's a nurse.

'We get calls at the hospital all the time asking that sort of thing,' she adds.

'Good idea. I'll do that.'

'I'm going to come up there,' Julie says.

'What? When?'

'This weekend. I'll have to discuss it with Daniel, but I don't see why that would be a problem.'

It might not be a problem for her. I'm not sure Alex will be too happy about it, though. 'But Alex thinks—'

'I know what Alex thinks,' Julie says, 'but I think – and so does Daniel – that you need some help. Especially now Alex has gone back to work. He might say you need rest and can do that better without having people around, but I can assure you, a sleepless night does not constitute rest and you could do without that when you've got to look after a newborn baby. Anyway, I'm not people, I'm family.'

'OK.' I sip my tea and make a face. It's cold.

'I'll come up with Daniel and the boys on Friday evening and we'll book a hotel. Then Daniel can take Oscar and Archie home on Sunday and I'll stay with you for a while. I'm due some paid leave.'

'OK,' I repeat. I'm not sure how Alex is going to take this – assuming he has resurfaced by the weekend – but I desperately want Julie with me for a while. I swallow down a lump in my throat as I realise that my sister wouldn't be doing this if our mother were still alive. Mum would.

'And, Kaitlyn?'

'Yes?'

'Don't panic. No news is good news.'

I'm so touched by Julie's kindness that Alex's barbecue this Saturday completely slips my mind.

As soon as I've finished talking to Julie, I look up the nearest hospitals on the internet. I start by phoning the Urgent Care Centre in Kendal, then the A&E in Whitehaven. I get the same result. No patient with that name.

Then I ring the number for the A&E in Barrow-in-Furness.

'Hello,' I begin. I can deliver my spiel fluently now. 'My husband has been missing since yesterday and I'm worried he might have had an accident. I wonder if you could tell me if he was brought in. His name is Alexander Riley.'

'I'm afraid I'm not at liberty to disclose that information,' comes the answer.

This throws me. Who talks like that? Why not? What do I say now?

'I … my … we have a baby girl … I'm worried sick about …' I sigh. 'Please?' I start striding up and down the hallway.

'I'll put you on hold for a second. Don't go away.'

Thinking I'm going to get an earful of some tinny music, I hold the mobile away, but she's back a few seconds later.

'No one called Alexander Riley has been admitted,' she says. I'm going to have to call the police now. But then the receptionist adds, 'But there is a Mrs Sandra Riley.'

My mother-in-law. I stop pacing and end the call. My mother-in-law is in hospital. I'm trying to digest this piece of information, but it seems to raise more questions than it answers.

At that moment, two things happen at the same time. Chloe starts crying and Alex bursts through the front door.

'Are you going to get that?' he demands, nodding his head towards the stairs, as if Chloe is a ringing telephone.

I glare at him as wordlessly I push past him and run up the stairs.

When I come back down with Chloe in my arms, Alex is waiting at the bottom of the stairs. He could have got the bottle ready, but I don't complain. He follows me into the kitchen and watches me while I do it.

As soon as I've sat down with Chloe, I turn to Alex. 'What's happened? I couldn't get through on your mobile.'

'The battery was dead. I had no way of charging it. As if you'd care.'

'Alex. I've barely slept a wink I was that worried.'

'Really? You have a funny way of showing it.'

'What do you mean?'

'You didn't call. You haven't even asked how my mother is.'

'I did call, Alex.'

'You didn't leave any messages.'

No, I didn't, I realise, but Alex's logic seems rather flawed to me. Didn't he just say his phone was out? I decide to let that one go. He's probably a bit short on sleep himself.

'I sent you a text. How's your mum? Is she ill?'

'You didn't bother asking in your text message how she was. After everything she's done for you. Helping with the baby and all.'

'Alex, I'm asking now. What happened? Why is your mum in hospital?'

'She fell. They're keeping her in for a few days for observation and a few more X-rays and until the swelling goes down.'

I should probably be more worried than I am, but Alex is prone to exaggeration, and I'm still mad at him for abandoning Chloe and me. 'What happened?' I sound worried, at least.

'I already told you what happened!'

I'm having trouble following Alex. 'When did you tell me?'

'I left you a message, because unlike you, I'm considerate.'

'What message?' I'm beginning to feel like I've been here before. We just go round and round in circles. Arguing with Alex is like trying to reason with a goldfish.

'I left a Post-it. Here, in the kitchen, in the usual place. I came home yesterday to see if you were OK, but you were out. Then the hospital rang about Mum.'

'I didn't see a Post-it. It's not here now.'

But as I turn my head and glance up at the worktop, I catch sight of a square piece of orange paper next to the kettle. Alex leaps up, grabs the Post-it and waves it triumphantly above his head. Then he slams it down on the table in front of me, making Chloe jump. Her little face twists up as if she's about to start crying again, but then she carries on sucking away at the bottle, apparently more hungry than startled.

'If you didn't see it, how did you know she'd been hospitalised?'

Luckily, he's hissing rather than shouting. I don't want him to scare Chloe. I'm trying hard not to feel scared myself. I don't even answer. I give up.

My eyes are locked with Alex's. I don't want to look away, as if that would make me the loser of some sick game. I need to process this. I'm sure the Post-it wasn't there yesterday evening. I made the dinner and I made several cups of tea. I would have seen it. Definitely. Wouldn't I?

But that could only mean that Alex has just stuck it there.

Which would be a very cruel thing to do. I can't even imagine why he'd do that. To make me doubt myself? Or is he covering up the fact that he forgot to leave me a note in the first place?

Alex breaks our eye contact first, but I don't feel like I've scored a point. Far from it. Once he has turned his back, I glance down and read the note.

Mum has been rushed to
A&E. She is badly injured.
I've gone to the hospital.
Call me later?
Alexxx.

At least the kisses are back. But probably not for long.

Alex is back, too. I should feel relieved. But I feel numb. My husband is home, but I've never felt so far from home in my life.

Chapter 11

As it happens, Alex isn't home for long. He picks Sandy up from hospital the following evening and for the next two nights he sleeps over in his mother's guestroom. It turns out she sprained her ankle when she tripped and fell on her own doorstop – literally. Alex, who was there, took her to hospital. He pops home after work on the Wednesday just long enough to drop off his dirty clothes for the wash and to fetch a freshly ironed shirt.

I seem to have gone from one extreme to the other. Just a few days ago, I resented the fact that Alex and Sandy were around so much that I could hardly pick up my own baby and I was looking forward to having some time to myself with Chloe. Now I'm on my own every minute of the day and night with her. *Be careful what you wish for!*

On the Thursday, Julie calls to confirm that she and her family are coming up to the Lake District this weekend. As it will be late when they arrive, they plan to go straight to the hotel on the Friday evening – tomorrow evening – and come round to the

Old Vicarage on the Saturday morning. Julie intends to stay at the Old Vicarage for a week when everyone else goes home.

'You'd clean forgotten, hadn't you?' she asks when she gets an embarrassing silence in response.

I hadn't forgotten, but it's only sinking in now that it's nearly the weekend. Every day seems to be the same at the moment and I'm losing track of time. As soon as Julie mentions their visit, I panic. I haven't said a word about it to Alex. Then she says they've found a hotel that accepts dogs and they're bringing Dad and Jet, too.

I can't wait to see them all, but I'm dreading Alex's reaction when he finds out my family are going to be here. He has scarcely spoken to me since we rowed about the Post-it. And somehow, I don't think this is going to help matters.

It's not until I've hung up that I remember the barbecue. *Shit!* I feel like slapping my palm on my forehead. I'm just not joining up the dots at the moment. I really did lose part of my brain in childbirth.

Alex comes home again a little later that same evening. My family are going to show up on his doorstep the day after tomorrow. I have to tell him. He's not going to like it! But why shouldn't my family visit? After all, we see a lot of Alex's mother.

Politely, I ask Alex how Sandy is. I'm stalling. I sent my mother-in-law a text message earlier in the day to enquire about her health. I already know from her reply that she's feeling "foolish, but better". I feel a twitch at the corners of my mouth as Alex describes a woman in considerable pain and in a critical condition, but I manage to suppress the smile.

'Mum is more mobile on her crutches now,' Alex admits, 'so she doesn't need me to sleep over at her house anymore.' He sounds a little wounded, as if he would rather tend to his mother's needs than help look after his baby daughter. 'She's a brave trooper,' he continues. 'She'll be hobbling around on her own two feet in no time.'

To my surprise, when I do announce my news to Alex, he takes it really well. So well in fact that I'm suspicious. I narrow my eyes at him.

'What?' he demands. He's holding Chloe while I heat up the shepherd's pie from Monday for tonight's dinner.

'I thought you'd be angry.'

'Why would I be angry?' He combs his fingers through his tousled hair. 'I didn't want them to stay until you'd recovered from childbirth, but if you think you're up for it, that's fine.'

'I'm up for it, Alex,' I say, giving him my warmest smile. 'I'm ready. Really. I coped very well while you were at your mum's.'

'There'll be lots of guests, then. The more the merrier, though, I suppose.' His voice hardens. 'Better make sure everything is perfect.' I can't decide if it's meant as a warning or not. 'For everyone.'

Alex tells me he has invited five friends. 'You already know Mike and his girlfriend Sarah,' he says.

So, Mike's girlfriend is called Sarah. I nod, but I don't say what I'm thinking, that I don't know the first thing about Mike and I've only met Sarah once – at our wedding – but I've just this second learnt her name. The only thing I know about her is that she can jive. Clearly, I really don't know them at all.

That reminds me, I still haven't asked Vicky what her full name is.

'Then there's another three friends from the triathlon club,' Alex continues.

When we've eaten, Alex feeds Chloe while I make out a shopping list. 'Crisps, obviously, and canapés,' he says and I scribble it down.

I have no idea if I'm to buy them or make them, so I ask, 'What do you mean by "canapés"?'

He gives a derisive laugh.

'What?'

'Weren't you a French teacher?' he scoffs.

'I am – still, officially – a senior lecturer in French.'

'Oh, go on. Any excuse to rub it in.'

'What do you mean?' I ask, thinking we're talking at cross-purposes.

'You just can't resist lording it over me because you happen to have a PhD and I've only got a degree.'

'I'm sorry, Alex,' I say, although that hadn't been my intention at all. I had no idea he was sensitive about that. My stomach gives a little lurch in apprehension, but to my relief, Alex seems to accept my apology and he carries on.

'Prosecco or champagne or cava or something similar; sausage rolls, homemade, not that crap from the supermarket shelves; dips, olives, melon with Serrano ham, crostini with goat's cheese …'

I'm not sure what that is, but I know better than to ask this time. As I write down what Alex dictates, I reassure myself. I'll have all day tomorrow to start organising this and I'm sure Julie will help me on Saturday if Alex is busy. I'll make sure everything is perfect. For everyone. But especially for Alex. And I do know why he wants me to get this right. I'm sure he thinks I've forgotten that Saturday is his birthday, but I haven't.

When Chloe falls asleep, Alex takes her upstairs. Then he comes down again to suggest we get an early night.

'Sounds great to me,' I say and clear up our dinner things in the kitchen before following Alex up to our bedroom.

When I come out of the bathroom, Alex is lying on his back in bed, his arms behind his head, his chest exposed above the bedcovers. As I climb into bed beside him, he kicks the quilt off the bed and turns towards me, propping himself up on his elbow.

'How long after giving birth until you … you know?'

I'm a bit slow to cotton on. 'What are you talking about?' Then I notice it's not just his chest that's bare. He's bare from the waist down, too. Completely naked. And he has an erection.

'Until you can have sex, Katie,' Alex says, making no effort to keep the exasperation out of his voice. He stares at me with his piercing blue eyes.

'About six weeks,' I say. 'Another three weeks to go.' I expect him to get up, pull on his boxers, lie down with his back to me and sulk. But he doesn't move. His eyes have a dangerous glint in them.

'Earlier, you said you'd recovered. You seemed so sure you'd healed.' He pouts, but it quickly transforms into a smile. It's an act. 'I'm ready, really,' he mimics. 'I'm up for it, Alex.'

'Alex, this isn't funny.'

'I'm not joking.' He takes my hand and presses it against his erect penis. 'Can you feel that, Katie? Who's up for it now, hey? I'm up for it.'

'Alex—'

'Six weeks?'

'Yes.' I want to stand up to him, but it comes out as a whisper.

'That's how long *you* are supposed to wait,' he says, 'but *I* can't wait that long.'

He's going to force me to have sex with him. I shudder as I think of my episiotomy stitches.

But instead, he rolls onto his back and pushes down hard on my head with both his hands. I have tears in my eyes as I begin to perform oral sex on my husband. Alex wraps my hair around one of his hands and pulls on the makeshift ponytail. Then he pushes down on my head with the other hand. Like a puppeteer controlling the strings, he repeats this pulling and pushing to dictate the rhythm. It gets faster, rougher. He's hurting me.

Thankfully, it doesn't last long. As Alex moans loudly and releases his hold on my hair, I'm left feeling dirty and used. I even get the vague notion I should receive payment for what I've just done. But I'm the one who has paid. That was the price I had to pay for my family gate-crashing his barbecue.

Alex doesn't even look at me. He rolls onto his side and curls up into a ball, facing away from me. I get out of bed and pick up the quilt from the floor, throwing half of it over his naked foetal body.

'Night, Katie,' he murmurs as I get back into bed.

I don't reply.

'Night, Katie,' he repeats, without turning towards me.

This time when I ignore him, he sighs emphatically. I anticipate a stronger reaction and my stomach twists in dread. But before long, his breathing slows and I can tell he's asleep. My breathing slows, too.

A few months ago, before Chloe came along, I would have been staggered and distraught at what has just happened. I'd have found it impossible to get to sleep. I'd have sobbed silently next to Alex in bed.

But now, this sort of incident seems to be par for the course. I'm not indifferent, but I feel detached as if I've just witnessed it instead of experienced it. I feel only a sort of numb apathy, as though I'm becoming immune.

As I lie there, rubbing my sore scalp gently, I think about Alex's moods and behaviour. Sometimes he snaps and shouts at me. On a couple of occasions now he has hurled all sorts of obscenities and insults at me. At other times, I get the feeling he's building up to something but I don't know what until he explodes.

Occasionally, like this time, he metes out a punishment. Evidently, he was not happy about my family coming to Grasmere, but he pretended everything was fine while all evening he must have been plotting his revenge.

Often, when Alex is in one of his moods, he gives me dark looks, which I can handle, or the silent treatment, which, to be honest, I find less frustrating than I used to. When he ignores me now, it still makes me feel worthless and non-existent. But at least it gives him time to calm down and it gives me time to pull myself together.

Tonight is the first time that I'm the one sulking and refusing to answer him. Until now, it has always been the other way around.

Am I giving him a taste of his own medicine? Or am I starting to become like him? One thing's for sure, I don't like who I'm becoming. I don't like who I am when I'm with my husband anymore. But I haven't stopped loving him in spite of everything. In spite of myself.

~

Alex wakes up early. He's happy and energetic. He brings me a mug of tea in bed.

'Thank God it's Friday,' he says. 'I can't wait to spend some quality time with you and Chloe this weekend.' A kiss on the cheek. 'And it'll be great to see your family again.' A kiss on the other cheek.

'Mmm.' That's the only reply I can muster for the moment.

'I'm swimming after work,' he announces, picking up his kit bag as if to make the point.

He leaves shortly after that. He gives me a minty kiss on the lips before he goes. I don't get time to drink the tea as Chloe wakes up.

Chloe cries all morning. I put her in the baby carrier and fire up my laptop. I fetch the shopping list Alex and I made the previous evening and I add a whole load of things to it that he has forgotten or that I've thought of since making the list. Then I do as much of the shopping as possible online and select a delivery time late in the day. That will give me time to go and shop for everything I haven't been able to purchase online, like the bloody canapés. Tomorrow, we'll have plenty of time to make the pies, pastries, sausage rolls and other nibbles.

By the time the shopping has been delivered and tidied away late that afternoon, I'm exhausted, but I wanted this evening to be special, and I'm determined not to let last night's incident in the bedroom deter me.

126

Chloe is fractious, so I put her in the baby carrier while I make a meal for Alex and me. I bake a cake as well – for Alex's birthday. As we're going to be entertaining tomorrow, I'd like to celebrate it with him tonight. I'm going to make meatballs and serve them with the fresh pasta I bought earlier. It's one of Alex's favourite meals. I've also opened a bottle of Segreta Rossa, a Sicilian red wine, to let it breathe. And also to have a little taste. Just to make sure it's not corked. Obviously.

As I get to work in the kitchen, I think about all the presents Alex has bought me. He used to buy me presents all the time. Pretty much every week. He sent them to the university; he sent them to my home address. On one awkward occasion, I had to pretend to Kevin that the huge bouquet of roses, delivered by Interflora, had been sent by a grateful student.

Alex hasn't bought me any gifts for a while. Not even when Chloe was born. Not since the gold medallion he got me to replace the heart pendant and silver chain. I don't think he has forgiven me for losing that necklace.

He put a lot of thought into the presents he bought me, and the gifts I've given him have always seemed lacklustre in comparison. This time, I want to spoil him, particularly as he's celebrating his fortieth tomorrow. I had to rack my brains to come up with something I'm confident he'll love. Then it came to me: he loves whisky. He has a Scotch to unwind most evenings.

Alex is in a jubilant mood when he comes home and after he has fed Chloe and she has fallen fast asleep, it's our turn to eat. Alex compliments me on the meal, on my hair, which is simply tied up in a ponytail as usual, and on getting all the shopping in for tomorrow. His good mood is infectious and it buoys me up and boosts my energy level for a while.

After dinner, we sit down side by side on the sofa in the sitting room and I give Alex his birthday presents. I watch him eagerly as he unpicks the Sellotape and unwraps the bottle of twenty-one-year-old Irish whiskey I ordered online from a distillery in my mother's hometown in Northern Ireland. I let the memory of my family and me visiting that distillery many years ago play out in my head. Louisa held her nose the whole time, including in the gift shop, and complained about the smell. Lost in my thoughts, I smile nostalgically to myself as Alex folds up the wrapping paper painstakingly.

'It's rare,' I say, 'and it's supposed to be the best Irish single malt that exists.' I don't mention how much it cost.

Alex hasn't noticed I've had the glass bottle engraved with his name and date of birth. He's carefully opening the second present. He's so meticulous in his task that I tell him what it is before he gets there.

'It's a crystal whiskey tumbler. So you don't have to drink out of that toothbrush glass anymore.' I chuckle to show I'm teasing and Alex gives a weak smile.

'Very considerate of you, Katie,' he says, and in the same breath he adds, 'You could wear a nice summer dress tomorrow, get togged up a bit. You've lost enough of the pregnancy weight now, surely?'

I'm stunned and I don't know how to answer that, so I say nothing.

'Going to be hot tomorrow,' he adds. 'Scorchio! I'll pour myself a Scotch,' he says, leaving the bottle I gave him on the table. 'It might be unlucky to open this before the day of my birthday.'

I knit my eyebrows, wondering how Alex can think nothing of unwrapping his birthday present before the actual date, but draw the line at opening the bottle itself.

'That glass will have to be washed out before I use it.'

I'm not sure if he expects me to get up and wash the crystal tumbler for him. I stay seated.

Is Alex disappointed with his presents? Or does he just want me to be disappointed by his reaction? Deep down, I think he's gutted I remembered his birthday at all. Last year I remember him doing a countdown in his emails: three more sleeps ... two more sleeps ... one more sleep. We'd only been in touch for a little while and it struck me as touching, albeit childish.

This year he hasn't mentioned his birthday once. Perhaps he was hoping to pick a fight. I used to think Alex couldn't handle difficult situations very well. Now I'm beginning to think he thrives on the drama. He's only really happy when he's angry.

When he has drained his glass of whisky, he yawns and says, 'I'm going to turn in now. You coming?'

I stifle my own yawn. 'I'm just going to read a chapter or two, then I'll be up,' I answer, anxious to avoid a repeat of last night's performance.

I take my novel from the coffee table. I'm too tired to concentrate really, but I read a few pages and hope that will have given him enough time to nod off.

Before making my way upstairs, my eyes are drawn to the bottle I bought Alex, which is still in its box on the coffee table. I study it for a moment, still confused about Alex's nonchalance. Then I pick it up and take it over to the cupboard where Alex keeps his whiskies, to tidy it away.

When I open the cupboard, I look at the bottle labels. I notice he only has Scotch whiskies. My mum's dad wouldn't touch Scotch whisky, although he swore by Irish whiskey. My mum often said "a wee dram" was my grandfather's panacea for every ailment and disease. Maybe it's an acquired taste, or maybe Alex simply prefers Scotch. Perhaps Irish whiskey wasn't a good choice.

While I'm pondering this, a small packet catches my eye. I almost don't see it. It's tucked behind some twelve-year-old Glenfiddich. A box of pills. At first, I'm amused by the thought that Alex would keep paracetamol or aspirin in the same place as his whiskies. The hangover cause next to the hangover cure. Then it strikes me as odd that Alex would keep headache tablets in the whisky cupboard instead of in the bathroom cabinet with all the other medicines.

I open the box and pop one of the pills out of its blister to examine it. It doesn't look like a painkiller to me. It's green for a start. Has Alex hidden these tablets here? I read the name of the drug on the packaging. It doesn't mean anything to me. There's no leaflet inside the packaging. I have no idea what this medicine is for. I decide to Google it, but then I remember I've left my phone charging in the bedroom.

I wonder briefly if Alex is taking performance-enhancing drugs, but I dismiss the idea. He has always been very anti-doping and can't abide cheats. It's more likely this is for a common complaint. Like hay fever. Or an embarrassing one. Like haemorrhoids. I'm making a mystery out of something that's banal.

All the same, I think it might be better if Alex doesn't know I opened this cupboard, so I put the packet of pills back exactly where I found it and I put the bottle of Irish single malt back down on the coffee table where Alex left it. Then I tiptoe upstairs to bed.

Chapter 12

The sun is shining on the morning of the barbecue. Alex is in good spirits and Chloe is gurgling in his arms as he sits in the kitchen, chatting to me. Leaning against the worktop with my arms folded, I watch them together, but somehow I can't quite catch their carefree air.

Observing Alex with Chloe, I wonder, not for the first time, why his ex-wife refuses to let him near their daughters. I understand that it might not have been plain sailing being married to Alex, but he really is a wonderful father. Perhaps I should try and track Melanie down. If I tell her Poppy and Violet have a sister, maybe she'll change her mind about keeping them from seeing their father.

It's as if Chloe knows she's in good hands now her daddy's home. She's so much calmer this morning than she was when Alex was away at his mother's. She cries a lot less and seems happier when it's her daddy who is taking care of her. Either she prefers him to me, or she can sense that he knows what he's doing whereas I still feel like I'm fumbling inexpertly every time I take my baby girl into my arms.

I wish I could say the same for me, that I'm calm when Alex is around, too. But I'm not. Far from it. He's having the opposite effect on me. I seem to be in a permanent state of anxiety. Soon I won't be able to remember what it felt like not to feel anxious. To feel safe and adored, instead of scared and despised.

Alex is going for a long run before checking in on Sandy. He calls me over and gently transfers our daughter, who is now sleeping, into my arms. Then he bends down to tie up his shoelaces. His chair scrapes as he stands up, startling Chloe. Alex pecks me on the cheek and then blows a raspberry on Chloe's hand before he leaves. Chloe starts to wail just as the front door bangs closed. The spell is broken.

I stand up and position Chloe on her tummy across my arm. When she screams even louder, I rock her. I talk to her, but my soothing voice and words are as much for my benefit as hers.

My family arrive at the Old Vicarage before I've had a chance to get dressed. I'm overjoyed to see them again. My father doesn't even look at me; he goes straight for Chloe, who, by now, has cried herself to sleep.

'You'd better get used to it.' Julie laughs. 'Once you have a baby, no one pays attention to you anymore.'

'It's the same when you have a dog,' my dad says, still engrossed in his granddaughter.

'So, what would you like to do today?' Daniel asks me. 'Do you want to go out with Julie while your dad and I look after Chloe and the boys? Or do you need help with something?'

Julie has obviously briefed Daniel on his mission for this weekend.

'Well, actually, we're having a barbecue this evening. There'll be quite a few of us. I could do with a hand. I need to make a lot of food.'

'OK,' says Daniel. 'All hands on deck then.'

'Where's Alex?' Julie asks, as if she has just noticed he's absent.

132

'Oh, he's out training and then he's going round to his mother's. She had a bad fall.'

'Poor Humpty,' says Daniel, who knows I'm not that fond of Sandy.

'And he left you to get everything ready for this evening?' Julie asks incredulously. I see everyone's gaze on me – even Dad has torn his eyes away from his granddaughter – and I feel my cheeks go red.

'Yes, well, no … it's his birthday today.' Seeing disapproval written all over Julie's face, I add, 'The barbecue was sort of a surprise party, really.' The lie comes effortlessly out of my mouth and sounds so convincing I almost believe it myself. 'I invited his friends ages ago.' I'm shocked by my own mendacity. Why am I making up excuses for him? Because I'm embarrassed, I suppose. Or ashamed. Or both.

'How many of us are there?' Julie asks.

'Twelve. The six of us, five of Alex's friends and Alex of course.' I realise I have counted myself with my family instead of with Alex. That seems a bit strange.

'And Jet. That makes thirteen,' Archie says.

'Unlucky for some,' says Daniel.

'Not for us,' I say, sounding more sure of that than I feel. 'This has to be perfect. I think Alex is a bit grumpy about turning forty. I want to cheer him up.'

'Let's get to work, then,' Julie says.

I get showered and dressed while Daniel makes everyone tea and then we all busy ourselves in the kitchen. Oscar and Archie prove to be young chefs in the making and I'm very impressed. Julie informs me they're addicted to *The Great British Bake Off*. Daniel also turns out to be a big help.

Chloe alternates between sleeping very deeply, despite the noise we're making, and squalling. When she cries, nothing seems to pacify her. Dad patiently walks up and down the hallway with her, singing lullabies to her as she screams in accompaniment.

133

I'm worried that she might be sickening for something, but Dad assures me that there's nothing I can do. Babies cry. Fact. Exception: she doesn't cry so much for Alex. I almost wish he were here. I feel oddly comforted that my dad can't do anything to calm Chloe, either.

By mid-afternoon, we've nearly finished the preparations. Daniel offers to see to what's left while Julie and I go into Keswick. Julie wants to buy Alex a birthday present and I want to buy a suitable sundress for this evening. I've lost several pounds since giving birth to Chloe, thanks to Alex's special diet, but I'm still at a stage where my pre-pregnancy clothes are a bit too tight and my maternity clothes are now way too big.

When we get back home, Alex is feeding Chloe while talking to Dad and Daniel in the sitting room. Archie and Oscar are playing electronic games.

When Julie has greeted Alex and asked after his mother, she turns to Daniel. 'Don't we have a rule?' she asks, nodding her head in the direction of her sons.

'We do,' he says, 'but they've been so helpful I thought we could bend it a little.'

'Rules are made to be broken,' Alex says.

'You're quite right, Alex,' Julie agrees. Daniel raises his eyebrows at me in surprise.

I go upstairs to get ready for this evening and when I come back down, only Oscar and Archie are in the sitting room. They're concentrating on their screens and don't notice me.

I make my way out to the garden, where four of Alex's guests are standing with my family while Alex serves everyone drinks. I spot the pram in the shade of the damson tree. Chloe must have fallen asleep.

'You look lovely, darling,' Alex says loudly, admiring my new dress and walking towards me to take his place at my side. 'Come and meet everyone.'

Alex shoots me one of his meaningful looks. Sometimes their

meanings are lost in translation. But not today. Today I've got the message loud and clear. His look says: *We will make the right impression. We'll show everyone that we're the perfect couple.* But to make sure there's no room for misunderstanding, he grips my arm just a little too hard as he steers me towards his friends. Or maybe it's my imagination.

'You already know Mike and Sarah …'

'Hi.' I lean in as Sarah makes a 'mwuaah' sound somewhere near my cheek, leaving me relieved that she won't have left any of her lipstick on my face. Alex has a bright red SWALK mark on his cheek, I notice with amusement. I don't feel the urge to rub it off. Mike gives me a big hug in greeting.

'This is Stacey and—'

'Hello, I'm Tom,' says the man standing next to Stacey.

I've seen Tom and Stacey before. I can't think where. They make a strangely assorted couple, it seems to me. She's about average height, but he's very small and she's probably taller than him even without those wedge-heeled shoes. She has a mane of brown wiry hair, held back by a thick Alice band, whereas he's completely bald. He has a handsome face and she's rather plain. He has lovely eyes; hers are hidden by her sunglasses.

I make polite conversation with Tom, admiring my sister and Daniel, who are chatting away to Mike and Sarah easily. I feel self-conscious and clumsy. I'm out of practice at making small talk. Out of the corner of my eye, I see Stacey making a fuss of Jet.

'You look like you could do with a drink,' Tom says. 'You're the only one who hasn't got one.'

We head over to the kitchen table, which Daniel and the boys carried outside earlier so that we could put all the food on it and let everyone help themselves to the buffet.

Tom and I chat amiably for a while. He claims he's a boring accountant, but he strikes me as interesting and cultivated. I'm only half-listening to what he's saying even so, as I'm still trying

135

to remember where I've seen him before. I almost make the mistake of asking him. But then it comes to me. At the pool. The day I heard Alex's voice and made Vicky hide in the café with me until he'd gone in for his swim. He was with Mike and Sarah, Tom and Stacey.

I eat a couple of canapés and then cram a mini sausage roll into my mouth.

'Stacey wants a dog,' Tom says, watching her playing with Jet and talking to my dad. 'She doesn't want babies yet because she's still competing. She's been on about a dog for a while.' He's smiling fondly. 'I'd better go and make friends with your dad's Lab. Excuse me.'

Realising I haven't touched the drink that Tom poured for me, I bring the glass to my lips and take a sip of the chilled champagne. And then a gulp. The bubbles explode in my mouth, and for a second I feel like I'm in my own blissful bubble.

Until Alex saunters up to me and bursts it.

'Better not eat too many crisps,' he says. The expression on his face belies his jovial tone of voice. When I scowl, he adds, 'Just saying. You've still got some pregnancy weight to lose.'

Julie walks by us at that moment, but she doesn't appear to have heard Alex, who follows her with his eyes.

'If you're not careful, you'll end up with an arse like that sister of yours.' He squeezes my bottom. 'It's the only thing about her you could call generous.'

I think Daniel has overheard, though. He doesn't turn round, but I see him stop in his tracks briefly, ever so briefly, as he walks behind my sister across the lawn.

Oblivious to Daniel, Alex gives a guffaw that, combined with the words he has just uttered, leave me feeling chilled to the bone despite the warm summer evening. He nudges my arm, making me spill some of my champagne. 'Only joking!' he says. 'I know, it was a bit below the belt.' This makes him laugh even more. 'See what I did there?' At that moment, to my relief, his phone goes.

'Oh, I'll come and let you in,' I hear him say before he strides into the house, pushing his phone into the back pocket of his ripped jeans. I reflect bitterly that Alex hasn't really got 'togged up'.

A minute or so later, I hear Alex's voice behind me. I hadn't seen him come back out and I jump.

'Katie, there's someone I'd like you to meet.'

I turn around to see a blonde woman who's a bit younger and a lot smaller than me. She looks like she's dressed for the beach, in denim shorts and silver sandals, showing off legs that are both toned and tanned. She's got a low-cut top on, which matches her baby blue eyes. She smiles sweetly, revealing teeth so white they probably glow in the dark. In short, she looks like a less dainty and more muscular version of Barbie.

'This is Becca,' Alex says.

'Kaitlyn,' I say, holding out my hand formally as my mind races with questions. 'Pleased to meet you.'

'Becca is a top triathlete,' says Alex over his shoulder as he walks away to fetch her a drink.

'Rebecca Brown?' I ask.

'That's right,' she says. 'How did you know that?'

'Oh, Alex has mentioned you once or twice.'

Alex reappears at my side and hands Becca a flute of champagne. She's holding two wrapped gifts in her hands and she hands him one of them in order to take the glass.

'Happy birthday, Alex.'

He rips the gift paper off and scrunches it into a ball. It's a bottle of Scotch. Alex makes such a fuss about it that I have a flash of myself snatching the bottle from his hands and hitting him over the head with it.

He reads the label out loud. 'Highland Single Malt Scotch Whisky. Blair Athol.'

'The distillery's near the Grampian Mountains, where my gramps lives,' Becca informs him with a little giggle.

'I know it, actually. Well, I recognise the name. And the logo with the otter,' Alex says. 'Thank you so much, Becca.'

I can feel myself frowning, but neither Becca nor Alex notice. I look around for an escape route, someone to go and talk to, but I spot Julie and Daniel making their way towards us. I'm trapped.

'And this is for you,' Becca says, thrusting the other present into my hands. 'Well, it's for the baby, really.'

'Oh. Thank you.'

I open the card first. There's a printed message and Becca has written underneath: *To Kaitlyn and Alex, Best Wishes on the birth of your Beautiful Baby. Love, Bexxx.* I suddenly see her text message to Alex in my head. She signed it the same way. I open the present and look at the picture on the box. It's a beautiful handmade wooden mobile with princesses and flowers. I make an appreciative *oooh* sound.

'It's for the baby's bedroom,' Becca says, unnecessarily.

'I'll put that on Chloe's cot tomorrow,' Alex says, taking the box from my hands. 'It looks easy enough to assemble.' Turning to me, he adds, 'It's high time we made a proper bedroom for Chloe, don't you think?'

Each time I've suggested making Chloe's bedroom into a nursery, Alex has come up with excuses. 'We don't know whether it's a boy or a girl.' 'But it's already a perfectly decorated girl's bedroom.' 'We don't have any free time at the moment.'

My breasts suddenly start tingling and I look down. A squeak of horror escapes my mouth. I have two big round wet patches on my dress.

'Oh dear,' I say, feeling Alex's eyes on me. 'Small emergency. Please excuse me.' Embarrassed, I walk briskly towards the house. As I reach the back door, I turn my head and see Alex staring after me. It seems to me he can barely disguise his disgust.

I'm blinking back tears as I go upstairs to my bedroom. With getting everything ready for tonight, I completely forgot to express my milk and now it has leaked all down the front of my brand-new sundress. Now what am I going to wear?

Rummaging around in the chest of drawers, I find a long, colourful T-shirt that I'd forgotten all about among the non-maternity wear. When I've expressed my milk, I wriggle into my black jeans, leaving the button undone and pulling the T-shirt down to hide it. My hands are shaking so much that I don't think I could have done up the button even if I was slim enough.

Feeling strangely disconnected from my body, I walk slowly down the stairs. Julie appears at the bottom.

'Ah, I was just coming to see if you were OK,' she says. 'Now let's go and see if they've left us any food. And champagne.' Taking my arm, she leads me into the garden.

Outside, Alex is handing around plates of food. Everyone seems to be standing in a group around him, drawn to him like a magnet. We walk over to join them.

'You look just as beautiful in that top as in your sundress,' he says, putting his arm around my shoulders, 'and just as beautiful as the day I met you again after all those years.'

Sometimes he says all the right things and I remember why I fell in love with him.

'Aww,' Sarah says.

'I didn't realise you'd known each other before,' Stacey says. I'm glad she ended her sentence there. In my head, though, I finish it. *Before your one-night stand.*

This is all the encouragement Alex needs. He tells his captivated guests about how we fell in love; about the friend request I sent him on Facebook, about our emails and phone calls and FaceTime conversations. He says he had a crush on me at school, which is news to me. I thought it was the other way round. I suspect he's embellishing our story to make our marriage appear unblemished. Or to make our wedding seem less precipitated. He tells everyone how well we get on with each other, how we're made for one another.

He doesn't mention the part where he got me pregnant in a hotel room in Exeter, although I'm sure everyone here knows that bit. In this version of our love story, I moved up here because we could no longer bear to be apart.

Alex is on his best behaviour for the rest of the evening. Apart from the remark he made earlier about my sister, which I've put down to a clumsy joke on Alex's part, and, of course, the glitch with the sundress, the whole barbecue party seems to have been perfect. Perfect for everyone, but especially for Alex.

When all the guests have gone, Alex and I clear up the leftover food and decide to leave everything else until tomorrow. I follow him into the sitting room, where he pours himself a drink from the bottle of Scotch Becca gave him for his birthday. The bottle I gave him is still sitting on the coffee table. I don't say anything; I don't want to ruin the mood. I'm still feeling a little high from the champagne. I sit down on the sofa.

'That was a great evening, wasn't it?' His tone is light, and at first I think he's on the same wavelength as me, thinking the same thoughts as me. He doesn't look angry; he doesn't even sound angry. But then I notice the way he's hunching his shoulders and pursing his lips. I can tell he's mad about something. I can feel it. In my gut. A familiar squeeze, as if by an invisible hand inside me. In the room, as if there's an electric charge. Or an explosive charge.

He starts to pace up and down the room. His fury is a time bomb, set to go off. If I make the wrong move, he'll blow up. If I can find the right thing to say, maybe I can defuse the situation.

'Your friends are lovely, Alex,' I hazard.

For a second or two, he looks at me and I can see recognition in his gaze. But then he disappears behind dead eyes. It's too late.

'My mum said you were a two-faced promiscuous bitch,' he hisses. 'I didn't believe her at the time.'

His words hit me harder than if he'd punched me.

'I wouldn't listen. We had a huge row about it. You came

140

between my mother and me.' He has started to shout. 'I should have known she was right. After all, you slept with me on our first date. And you weren't even bothered about using protection.'

'Alex, that's not how it happened, and you know it!'

'I saw you. I was watching you. You followed Tom around like a dog tonight; your tongue was practically hanging out of your mouth.'

So, that's what this is about.

'I had to stand around and put up with it while everyone saw you making a fool out of me.'

'Alex! Stop!' I screech so loudly that he does stop for a moment. 'You're being ridiculous. I've just given birth – to *your* baby – and the last thing on my mind is sex. With you or anyone else for that matter. How can you possibly imagine that I want to sleep around? I've been unfaithful once in my entire life. *With* you, not *to* you.'

'But you were flirting.'

I open my mouth to argue, but then an image bursts into my head. Me, sitting at the kitchen table, looking through Alex's phone. I suddenly feel hypocritical. I'd been quick to wonder if Alex was cheating on me with Rebecca and he has just accused me of trying to seduce another man under his nose. We were both mistaken. We're both in the wrong.

The big difference is that he got mad and called me names.

Alex has a vacant look on his face. It's over. He's calm again. Until the next time. But I don't want there to be a next time.

'Alex, I can't put up with this anymore,' I say softly. 'I'm going to go back to Somerset with my family tomorrow.' I'm not certain I mean this, but I don't have the strength to go another round. 'For a little while, at least.'

'No, Katie, don't do that,' Alex begs. 'I didn't mean any of it.' He sits down on the sofa next to me and takes my hand. I notice a tear snaking its way down his cheek. 'My ex-wife was a complete nymphomaniac. She slept with many of my friends. I was always the last to find out who she was … seeing.'

141

I want to say something, but I don't know what, so I wait for him to continue.

'I tried so hard, but I simply wasn't good enough for her. I wasn't enough for her.'

His whole body is racked with sobs now. I pull my hand away and put my arm around him. He lies down across my knees. My hand hovers for a second or two, but then I run my fingers through his hair.

'Melanie left me … on my birthday.' I only just make out the words as he spews them into my lap. 'I'm paranoid now. I ask myself every day, if I wasn't good enough for her, how can I possibly be good enough for Katie? I'm terrified of letting you in sometimes because I'm afraid I'm going to lose you. If you ever leave me, I'll lose another daughter, too. I can't go through that again.'

I still can't find anything to say. Alex doesn't truly believe I love him, I realise, not because he doubts me, but because he thinks he's unlovable. He seems so convinced he'll wreck everything between us that he waits for the damage he has caused to prove him right.

'I love you, Katie. I couldn't live without you. I wouldn't want to. I'd rather die.'

I rub his back with one hand and finger the medallion around my neck with the other while I let Alex's words sink in. They instantly bring to my mind his suicide attempt all those years ago after his girlfriend had broken up with him in Australia. I don't think that's what's going through his head, though. I don't believe he'd try to end his life if I left him. In fact, I'm sure that's not what he meant.

'Alex, you can't hurt me just because you've been hurt,' I say. 'It's not an excuse.'

'I know. You're the last person on earth I want to hurt, Katie. I'll do better. It'll get better. I'll get help, see a therapist, whatever it takes. I don't deserve you,' he continues, 'but I want to become

142

worthy of you. You make me a better person most of the time. Please say you'll help me learn to be that person all of the time. All I want is to make you and Chloe as happy as you make me.'

'You were vile tonight,' I say, but I'm caving in.

'I know.' He sits up, sniffing. 'I shouldn't drink so much. It brings out the worst in me.' He lowers his head, looking suitably sheepish. 'I didn't mean what I said about your sister. Julie is one of the most generous people I know. I'm just jealous because I'm an only child and you're so close to her.' He dabs his nose with his bare forearm. 'I'm fucked up, aren't I?'

'Anyone would be with what you've been through, Alex,' I say.

I don't add what I'm thinking. I hope he's not so messed up that he can't be patched up.

I get up and fetch him a tissue. As he blows his nose loudly, I think about what he has said. The one word he should have said, but didn't, was 'sorry'. The words 'I love you' roll off his tongue easily, but he seems to find it almost impossible to apologise. Not that sorry would make it all OK.

I'm well aware Alex uses words to berate me and belittle me. He chooses his words carefully when he wants to cajole or control me. And he invariably finds the right words to inveigle his way back into my heart.

I work with words, or I used to, I reflect. That's my job; that was my career. And yet, I'm falling for this. I'm falling for him all over again. I should know better by now. But I'm letting him talk me into getting back onto this endless rollercoaster ride with him.

As these thoughts chase each other around in my head, Alex kisses me. A slow, tender kiss. I don't stop him. I can't decide if I'm strong or weak.

Chapter 13

On my way back from dropping Julie off at Windermere railway station, I feel a little empty, a little scared and a lot homesick. My sister was a big help and great company while she was staying and now she has left, I'm filled with uncertainty. Can I do this by myself? Can I look after Chloe properly? I was very tempted to get on the train with Julie.

As I pull up in front of the house, I sternly remind myself that I'm not alone. I have Alex. He's such a good father. It all comes naturally to him. I'll get the hang of this parenting thing, too. Eventually. And as for feeling homesick, well that's just ridiculous. My home is here now, at the Old Vicarage. Julie and Daniel brought up everything I'd left at Dad's, and I've unpacked my stuff and tidied it away. It's comforting to see my books on the shelves and photos of my family on the windowsills. It still doesn't feel quite like home, but I'm sure it will. One day.

I get the pram and Chloe out of the car. As I open the front door, Chloe starts to cry at the same time as the phone starts to ring. I rush to pick up the handset and then come back to push the pram to and fro as I answer the call.

'Hello?'

There's no one there. Or rather, if there is someone there, they aren't saying anything.

'Hello?'

This hasn't happened for a while. I hang up, feeling slightly relieved as this leaves my hands free to pick up Chloe. But I also feel flustered. Who is calling? What do they want? Do they only want to speak to Alex? Or are they trying to spook me?

If the caller is trying to unsettle me, it's working. A thought troubles me. Could it possibly be Alex who is behind these calls? He never seems to be at home when I get them. Is he playing some sort of warped mind game? Or just checking up on me to see that I'm home, where he likes me to be? I shake my head, as though to dispel these illogical thoughts.

At least half an hour later, when Alex arrives home after this morning's long run, Chloe is still wailing. Alex barely has time to set foot in the hall before I thrust our baby into his arms.

'I want to take her to the doctor's.'

'Is that really necessary?'

'Something's wrong with Chloe, Alex. She cries too much.'

'All babies cry too much.'

My dad also said something like that, I recall now. He and Alex have both had lots of experience bringing up baby girls. But I'm not convinced. And although Julie seems to agree with nearly everything Alex says, even she was surprised by how distressed Chloe is at times.

'It's probably colic,' Alex says. His firm tone of voice indicates that this is the end of our discussion.

I'm worried about starting an argument with Alex, but I'm more worried about my daughter. 'She's always either in a deep sleep or screaming at the top of her lungs,' I say. 'She's never just awake and contented. I want to take her to see a doctor.'

I'm being demanding, and that's not the best way to talk Alex into doing anything. He has been lovely since the barbecue. The whole week Julie stayed at the Old Vicarage, he was wonderful to both of us. I think he really believed I might go back to Somerset with her, so he has been making an effort to keep his bad moods at bay. Now she's gone, there's less risk of me going home. Alex knows that. I need to tread carefully. I look at him with what I hope are pleading eyes.

'OK. If it will make you feel better, we'll make an appointment with Dr Irving.'

Dr Irving has been Alex's GP for years. Since Alex was little. He's also a close friend of my mother-in-law's. He's getting on a bit, and on the two occasions I've been to see him, the word 'doddery' sprang to mind, but he'll do nicely.

'Thank you,' I breathe.

My relief is short-lived.

'But he won't be able to see us so late in the morning and the surgery is closed on Saturday afternoons,' Alex adds. 'We'll have to wait till Monday.'

Alex gets a bottle ready and feeds Chloe, and she calms down and falls asleep. He flashes me a smile that's only slightly smug.

'I'll put her in the cot and then I'd better take a quick shower,' he whispers, leaning forward to kiss me on the cheek. I'm still not feeling reassured, but Alex has everything under control.

I follow him into the hallway. As we walk past the locked door next to the cupboard under the stairs, I realise I've never asked Alex where it leads.

'Alex, what's through that door?' I ask, pointing.

'It' the cellar.' I'm slightly behind him now and I can't see his face, but it sounds as if his voice is strained.

'Why don't we use it?'

He pauses a beat too long and I know I won't believe his answer even before he gives it. 'I lost the key some time ago and didn't see the point in calling in a locksmith.' Then he mutters a few sentences I don't quite catch. Something about 'unnecessary expense' and 'a room that serves no useful purpose', I think.

He doesn't turn around as he heads upstairs with Chloe in his arms. I'm not sure how long I stand there, at the bottom of the staircase. I'm not sure what's going through my mind. Everything is misting over.

I sense it coming. I am suddenly swamped by a fear so intense I can hardly move. My legs buckle under me and I sink down onto the stairs. I can't think straight, but instinct tells me to put my head between my legs. Suddenly two hands are around my throat, strangling me, choking me. I know they're imaginary, but they feel so real that I claw at my neck, trying to loosen the vice-like grip. *I'm losing my grip. I'm losing my head.*

Just when I think I'm going to black out, I manage to catch a breath. My heart is still thumping way too fast, but it feels now as though it will stay inside my chest instead of hammering its way out of my body.

I break into uncontrollable sobs and after a few seconds I hear Alex's voice. He's right behind me on the staircase. I didn't hear him come down. How long has he been there? He sits down behind me with his legs either side of me. He wraps his arms around me and holds me against him. I pull his arms down from my neck so that his embrace is around my chest instead. I can feel the rise and fall of his chest against my back and my heartbeat gradually slows down. We stay like that until I stop crying and start breathing normally again.

'Stay there. I'll be back,' he instructs. He gets up and squeezes past me on the stairs. I watch him take his mobile out of his jeans pocket as he makes his way into the kitchen. He closes the door behind him. I can hear him talking, but I can't make out what he's saying.

He isn't gone more than a minute. 'Doctor Irving has made an exception,' he says, coming back into the hallway. 'He'll see us at one o' clock.' His tummy rumbles. 'We'll have to eat lunch afterwards.' He directs this sentence at his stomach and when he looks up, grinning, I manage a weak smile in return.

Alex goes upstairs to fetch Chloe. I get up and walk gently towards the kitchen to get a glass of water.

Just as we're leaving, the landline phone goes. I look at Alex. 'Leave it,' he shrugs. 'Probably some telesales bollocks.'

'Alex, someone rang earlier.' I grab his arm. 'But they wouldn't speak to me. It wasn't the first time.'

'Don't worry about it. We hardly use the home phone anyway. Don't answer it. Or unplug it altogether if it bothers you.'

Alex is right. I'd more or less dismissed the calls myself until I got worked up over them today. And even so, I wouldn't have given them another thought if the phone hadn't just rung now. It's not as if there have been that many calls. Three at most.

Something else occurs to me on the way to the health centre in Grasmere. Alex can't be the one making these calls as he was with me when the phone went just now. He could feasibly have rung from his mobile without me seeing, I suppose, but that thought is just too far-fetched.

When we arrive at the doctor's surgery, Dr Irving leads the way into his consulting room. He slides into his black leather chair and Alex and I sit down in uncomfortable metal chairs opposite him.

The GP peers at me with watery blue eyes through rimless glasses. 'Let's start with you,' he says, leaning across his desk towards me. I can smell garlic on his breath. I sit back, trying not to wrinkle my nose. 'Alexander tells me you had a panic attack.'

I wish Alex hadn't told him that. It's humiliating and it makes me sound weak. 'Oh, no. We didn't ask for an appointment—'

'Can you describe the symptoms you had when you experienced it?' His voice is flat, soporific.

I look at Alex. It's meant as a reproach, but he takes it as a prompt and answers for me.

'She has difficulty breathing,' he says, 'and she feels dizzy. That's right, Katie, isn't it?'

I nod.

Dr Irving hasn't taken his eyes off me. 'Go on please, Mrs Riley,' he says.

'I get frightened. My pulse races and I feel the need to escape, sort of, to get out of the house, I suppose, but my legs won't hold me up.'

The doctor swivels in his chair so he's facing the computer screen, and jiggles and clicks his mouse. 'Uh-huh. Anything else?'

'I feel sick.'

'Nausea,' he says, typing slowly, using mainly his index fingers. 'Insomnia?' There's no rising intonation and it takes me a second or two to realise that this is a question.

'No. I find it hard to get to sleep sometimes, but I've been tired since ... well, you know, with Chloe, so once I fall asleep at night, I don't wake up until she does.'

'I see. Any chest pain?'

'No. Just a pain in my stomach. Like bad nerves.'

'OK. How long did this panic attack last?'

'I'm not sure.'

'Less than five minutes, I'd say,' Alex offers. 'Three or four minutes, tops.'

Again, I wonder how long Alex was behind me on the staircase before he came to my aid. Did he just stand there while I was struggling to catch my breath? Did he watch me panic for three or four minutes without intervening?

'Have you had an anxiety attack like this before, Mrs Riley?'

I'm staring at Alex, lost in my thoughts, and the doctor has to repeat his question before I hear it.

'Yes.' I can't find it in me to elaborate.

'Any crying episodes?'

I remember sobbing earlier as Alex held me against him on the stairs.

149

Again, Alex answers for me. 'She did cry earlier. And she cries sometimes in the evenings or at bedtime.'

I look at Alex, but he seems to be avoiding my gaze. Surely he's not referring to our wedding night when I sobbed next to him in bed? Or the evening he accused me of tampering with his shower gel and made me cry?

Doctor Irving rolls his office chair round to my side of the desk and unwinds the stethoscope from around his neck.

'I'll just check your heart and lungs,' he says, 'and then I'll take your blood pressure.'

When he has finished examining me, the doctor types up a few more notes. Then, without further comment to me, he starts talking to Alex about Chloe. I hear them talking, but I can't decipher what they're saying. I'm in a daze. I allow myself to zone out for a while.

Recently, I'm the one who has been looking after Chloe the most, and yet the doctor doesn't ask me a single question about my baby. The two men seem to have forgotten I am there. I don't feel like I'm there myself. I'm removed from all of this, as though it's all happening to someone else.

I vaguely register that Chloe wakes up when Doctor Irving starts to examine her. Although she cries, it is not the high-pitched screeching that I'm used to hearing. It's a cry that I find less disturbing and normal.

'I'm going to prescribe you some low-dose anti-depressants, Mrs Riley,' the doctor is telling me when I tune back in. 'The anxiety, bouts of crying and tiredness you've described indicate to me that you have post-natal depression.'

'I'm not depressed,' I protest. But I think my words might have stayed in my head.

'Your family live far away and so it's hardly surprising,' the GP continues. 'I understand that you were worried about bonding with your daughter when Alexander went back to work—'

'Well, I was looking forward—'

'And, of course, I know about your mother-in-law's bad fall, but now she's on the mend, I think it would be a good idea if she could help you out with Chloe,' he says. 'Alexander seems to think that Sandy would relish the chance to see more of her granddaughter.'

Alex takes my hand. I resist the urge to snatch it back.

'Can I continue to give Chloe my breast milk on this medication?' I hear the words coming out of my mouth even though I'm not aware of the thought going through my mind. I have no intention of taking anti-depressants anyway.

'Yes, you can. It's very mild.'

'Perhaps we should switch to formula,' Alex says. 'Chloe prefers feeding from the bottle anyway.'

'That's up to the two of you,' Doctor Irving drones, 'but it could be a good way of monitoring how much milk Chloe is taking.'

'Monitoring?'

'As I was saying to your husband, Mrs Riley, I don't think there's anything wrong with your baby girl except for the fact that she's a little underweight.'

I say nothing all the way home. I'm confused. I close my eyes and pretend to be asleep so that I can begin to unravel what's going through my mind.

I replay my conversation with Doctor Irving in my head. I'm not depressed. I feel misunderstood by the GP. I feel betrayed by my husband, as if he didn't stick up for me when Doctor Irving made his diagnosis. I even feel let down by Chloe, although I know this is irrational. But it's as though she was on her best behaviour at the health centre so that the doctor would think I was the one with a problem.

I do fall asleep for a few minutes and when I open my eyes, we're home. I see it before Alex does. There's a cardboard box in the porch. With his easy stride, Alex is wheeling Chloe in her pram towards the entrance when he notices it. He stops dead in his tracks and I nearly walk into him. He turns to look at me, a quizzical expression on his face.

The parcel doesn't have a name on it or an address. It's the size of a large shoebox. I pick it up and notice it's quite light. I shake it and something moves around inside the box. I hand it to Alex. He doesn't even open the door and take it into the house. Instead, he tears off the parcel tape, ripping the box open right there on the doorstep. I stay behind him, as though he's shielding me.

An unmarked parcel. Someone has come up the drive and left this here. I'm reluctant to find out what this is. I cling to the hope that this could be a benign present, but my senses are telling me otherwise.

Looking over Alex's shoulder, I smell it at the same time as I see what it is. This is no gift. There are flowers in this box, about a dozen of them, but it's not a bouquet from a friend, that's for sure. The flowers are dead and their heads are separate from their stems.

To begin with, I'm more puzzled than frightened. Is this supposed to be scary? A warning? A threat?

I look at Alex. If I had any doubt about the phone calls, this time I know it's not him. He was with me when this was delivered. He has fear written all over his face, which has drained of colour. I notice he's biting his bottom lip. I'm missing the point, I think, taking the box gently from his hands.

'I don't get it,' I tell him.

I peer into the box again. There are purple flowers and red flowers. There's a lot of soil, which appears to have been scattered over the flowers. Tentatively, I touch them. The purple flowers are artificial rather than dead, I realise now, but their heads have been snipped off their stems just as for the red ones. I count them, pushing each dead bloom to the side of the box in turn. Thirteen flowers altogether.

My fingers feel something else, under the flowers. It's a small card. I pull it out and read the words written on it in small, neat letters. How ironic. But I'm not sure I've grasped the meaning. I read the words again. *Wake up and smell the dead flowers.*

Alex is leaning against the stone wall and hasn't seen me take the card out. Quickly, I stuff it into my handbag. He doesn't look like he can take much more for now.

'The flowers,' Alex says. 'They're … they're …' He doesn't seem to have the force to finish his sentence.

It takes me several seconds, but then it hits me. *Oh, no!* I feel my eyes widen as I meet Alex's gaze.

'Poppies and violets,' I whisper.

Chapter 14

In the end, I have to drop it. I bring it up several times that day, but Alex either changes the subject or walks out of the room. He refuses categorically to call the police and I can't get him to tell me why.

But I can't stop thinking about the box. Questions whirl round and round in my head. Who would do this? Why? What does it mean? All this has rattled me. And I am scared now.

It's clear in my mind that the parcel is linked to Alex's older daughters Poppy and Violet. Poppies are in season right now, a quick internet search has informed me, but violets are springtime flowers. Perhaps that's why the violets were artificial. I think the number of flowers – thirteen in total – is supposed to be unlucky. Is someone cursing us?

I think Alex should contact his ex-wife, but I know there's no point suggesting that. Maybe I should try to find her myself. I'm also tempted to go to the police tomorrow when Alex goes back to work, but he has burnt the box and everything in it, so there's no evidence now anyway. Except for the card. It's still in my handbag.

I haven't been able to tell Alex about the card. I'm not sure if I should. He's obviously shutting this out and that seems to be his way of dealing with it. But every time I close my eyes, I see the words. *Wake up and smell the dead flowers.* It's as if they're stamped on the inside of my eyelids.

I can't explain why, but I get the impression that the message is intended for me. Someone is warning me, telling me to open my eyes. I have to be more aware of what's going on around me. Or more wary. I think that's what it means. But I have no idea what I'm not seeing.

I need to keep my wits about me, which is another reason why there's no way I'm taking the medication Doctor Irving has prescribed for me. The main reason, of course, is that there's nothing wrong with me. I'm not depressed. Freaked out at times, yes. Sad, homesick and lonely, yes. But depressed, certainly not. And I know what depression is. I've seen it. I know what it can do. They've got it wrong.

I don't protest, though, when Alex goes to the chemist late that afternoon to pick up my prescription. And that evening, when he opens the bottle of pills and hands me one, I take it compliantly and put it on my tongue. Then I take a sip from the toothbrush glass, which Alex has filled with water from the tap.

I don't want to make Alex angry by refusing to take the tablet. So, under his watchful eye, I pretend to swallow it. I can tell from the look on his face he's very concerned about me.

'I'm worried about you,' Alex says, as if reading my thoughts, 'so I've asked my mum to come round next week. She'll help out with Chloe, give you a chance to rest.'

In my head, I swear. In the mirror, I smile at Alex. Then, on second thoughts, I decide it might be a good thing if my mother-in-law spends some time with Chloe. Perhaps I could go out on my own for a while and shop for some clothes that actually fit. Or I could meet up with Vicky at that gym she mentioned or go for a swim. I like the idea of a change of scenery. And I think a bit of sport would do me good now.

On the Monday, Sandy arrives before Alex leaves for work. I can hear them talking in the kitchen as I pad down the stairs and along the hallway in my slippers.

'She's suffering from post-natal depression,' Alex says. 'Can you keep an eye on her?'

I don't like the idea of my mother-in-law watching over me.

'Do you think Chloe's safe when Kaitlyn's on her own with her?'

'I don't know, Mum,' Alex says, in a solemn voice I haven't heard before. 'Just keep an eye on her.'

This time I think he's instructing her to look out for Chloe rather than spy on me.

'You certainly know how to pick them, Alexander.'

I clear my throat loudly as I come into the kitchen. Then, as my mother-in-law's words sink in, I wish I'd eavesdropped a little longer. What did Sandy mean by that?

'Good morning, Sandy,' I say. My tone is cool and I glare at her. I can't help it.

Alex leaps up from his seat to make me some tea, and once he has done that, he makes a speedy departure for work.

By mid-morning, I'm fed up with making cups of tea and polite conversation. By mid-afternoon, I'm starting to go mad.

'Why don't I take Chloe out for a long walk and you can have a nap?' Sandy asks when I sigh for at least the tenth time in five minutes.

I'm about to snap that I'm not tired, but then I think the better of it. It will do me good to have some 'me time', as Julie calls it. When she was staying, she kept saying how important it is for mothers of young children to pamper themselves now and then so they don't lose their minds.

'Are you sure, Sandy? I'll come with you if you like.' I don't sound very enthusiastic.

Luckily, my mother-in-law insists, so I get the baby bag ready and a few minutes later I watch Sandy pushing the pram down the driveway in her impracticable heels.

I don't know what to do with myself once Sandy and Chloe have left. I don't feel like taking a nap – I'm wired, not tired. I consider doing some cleaning, but I can't be bothered. The house isn't quite as spotless as Alex would like, but it's spick and span by anyone else's standards.

As I'm sitting on the sofa cradling a mug of tea in my hands, my mind inevitably wanders to the box again. The dead flowers covered in dirt. The card with its confusing message. I remember the cardboard box in the guestroom and I picture Julie's curious face when she asked months ago if we should open it. I rejected the idea at the time – we were looking for the necklace and it couldn't possibly have found its way by accident into a sealed box, but ever since it cropped up in my dream the other day, I'm as keen to know what's in there as Julie was.

Do I dare? How would I feel if Alex went through my things? My eyes are drawn to the whiskey I gave Alex for his birthday. The bottle is still in its box, unopened, on the coffee table. The sight of it and the memory it carries spur me into action. I set down my half-full mug of tea on the coffee table next to it and then I make my way into the kitchen and grab a pair of scissors before heading upstairs. My movements feel automatic and unconscious, as if I'm sleepwalking or being pulled along by my hand. I don't resist.

Moments later, I find myself kneeling in front of the open box, hesitating. Last time I didn't trust Alex, I made things worse by going through his phone and jumping to the wrong conclusion about a text message that turned out to be perfectly innocuous.

You really don't trust me at all, do you? It's so like his voice, I almost believe my husband is on his knees next to me. I shudder.

He's the one who accused me of chatting up Tom.

But I'm the one snooping on my spouse.

I've no inkling of what could be in there. What if I discover something I don't want to know? I might be better off not going through with this. But that parcel has reminded me of this box and now I have to find out what's inside.

I feel bad about not trusting Alex, but he has told me so many lies that I can no longer see the truth. I've been blind, or blinded. I need to open my eyes – and therefore this box. Inside there might just be one more piece that's missing from the puzzle my life is becoming. If I don't open it, I may not ever see the bigger picture.

All this wavering is getting my adrenalin going, but it's also giving me pins and needles in my calves. I'm not really in two minds about opening this box; deep down I know I'm going to open it. I also know it will probably turn out to be nothing. I'm building this up out of all proportion, but I'm in for a huge anticlimax. At least, I hope I am.

The very first thing I pull out of the box is a book entitled *First to the Finish Line: My Incredible Journey from Injury to Ironman*. It has a photo of a triathlete in action on the cover. Thumbing through it, I notice there's a handwritten dedication at the front of the book.

To Alex.
With all my love,
always. Nicola. X

My heart misses a beat or two. Then I reason with myself. The spine of the book is quite worn and I'm pretty sure this box was taped up long before I got here. I've never heard of Nicola. She must be one of Alex's ex-girlfriends from before he married me.

Under the book are lots of trophies. I inspect each of them in turn. Unsurprisingly, they're all for triathlons. Under the cups are medals with pictures of swimmers, cyclists and runners embossed on them. I'm surprised Alex doesn't have them on display. He likes to extol his athletic prowess at every opportunity, and I think he's quite right to be proud of his sporting results.

But then, on closer examination, I notice the athletes on the medals are female. Do these belong to Nicola? Or to another of Alex's ex-girlfriends? The jealous thoughts just keep coming. He must have lived with this woman at one point if he still has her trophies. I imagine he packed them away when they split up. Whoever she was. It can't have been Melanie. I've heard him criticise his ex-wife many times for being 'intellectual rather than athletic'. His words.

Wondering if the whole box contains mementos of Alex's past flames, or belongings one of them has left behind, I breathe in deeply and exhale slowly before carrying on. The next thing I take out is a pair of handcuffs. With black fur. For fuck's sake! I'm starting to feel sick now. I need to stop now. I don't want to know any more.

But I push my hand into the box again and rummage around to see what else it contains. There's nothing else. I peer into the empty box and then I do a double take. There is something left – a large white envelope at the bottom of the box. Opening it, I find a photo, its colour faded with age.

I turn the photo around so it's the right way up. I feel my mouth and my eyes opening wider and wider as I take in the picture. It shows a young boy, aged eight or nine, lying across a wooden chair, his jeans and his pants around his ankles. Next to him, a man stands over him, a belt in his hand.

The boy is Alex. Tears spring to my eyes. He told me his father used to beat him with the belt from his trousers. Even as my heart thuds against my ribcage, I force myself to look at the photo. The room isn't furnished. It's not inside a house but more like inside a garage. I can make out shelves in the background, but the quality has suffered over time and it probably wasn't a good photo to begin with. It looks as if the photographer took this without a flash.

The photographer. A disturbing thought strikes me. Who took the photo? It couldn't have been Alex's own mother, could it? Was she complicit in this with her husband? And then an even more unsettling thought. She's alone with Chloe. Oh, dear God, she may have physically abused her own son and now she's with my daughter.

I try to get hold of Sandy, but she isn't answering her mobile. I ring again. Then, throwing my phone onto the bed, I hear a growl escape my mouth. It sounds like a mixture of frustration and fear.

My hands shaking, I start throwing everything back into the box. Book, trophies, medals, handcuffs, the works. Well, nearly everything. As I go to put the photo back into the envelope, I look at it again. My attention is drawn to the orange digital date stamp in the bottom right-hand corner: 08.09.1987. The eighth of September 1987. Ten. Alex had just turned ten years old when this photo was taken. I decide to keep it and I close up the box with everything else in it.

You can tell the box has been opened. The parcel tape won't stick back down properly. I'll have to buy some tape and do a better job later. As I'm pushing the box back into the wardrobe, I scan the room for my phone. There it is, on the bed, where I tossed it. Sitting down on the edge of the bed, I call my mother-in-law's mobile once more. But there's still no reply.

Making my way back downstairs, I look at my watch. Sandy and Chloe have been gone for three hours now. Three hours is a long time. What if Sandy has a quick temper like Alex? Chloe cries all the time. What if my mother-in-law can't handle that?

To fight my rising panic, I try to think things through. I don't know if Sandy took the photo. And even if she did, it doesn't mean Chloe is in danger. I tell myself Chloe will be fine and no harm will come to her with Sandy.

All I can do now is wait. And try not to fret. But by the time another hour has gone by, I've chewed off all my fingernails and twirled my hair into knots. I'm not sure what to make of the photo I've just discovered.

Have I opened up a can of worms? Or Pandora's box? When all the evils flew out of Pandora's box, only Hope was left inside.

I hope to God Chloe is OK.

Chapter 15

I need to know more about the photo. I have to find out who took it and why. I need to know, if only so I can be sure that my mother-in-law won't harm my daughter and that Chloe isn't in any danger. But I can't ask Alex. Apart from the fact that it might open up old wounds if I show him the photo, he'll be furious that I've been prying. I feel a stab of guilt for firstly looking through his phone and then opening the box.

It occurs to me that once upon a time Alex and I used to talk about everything. There was no topic we couldn't bring up. Now, there are so many tricky subjects I avoid for fear of setting him off. Countless things we would once have confided in each other have become taboos. Instead of telling my husband secrets, I keep secrets from him. Most of what I do tell him is only half the truth. And often, anything I say seems to be weighted with the echo of every argument we've ever had.

Not knowing what to do, I pick up the mug of tea I didn't finish earlier from the coffee table and take it into the kitchen, where I make myself a fresh cup. Then, sitting on the sofa, my hands shaking visibly every time I lift the mug to my lips, I try to convince myself that my daughter is in safe hands with my mother-in-law. *Sandy won't hurt Chloe. Sandy wouldn't hurt Chloe.* I repeat the words over and over in my head, like a mantra.

It certainly doesn't cross my mind to tell my mother-in-law what I stumbled across in the box. But when she arrives home with Chloe, I'm in the living room with the photo on the coffee table, poring over it. I hear her come in, banging the front door against the wall as she tries to get the pram into the house, but my instinct is to run and check on Chloe rather than hide the snapshot.

Chloe is sleeping, her thumb in her mouth. Kissing her gently so as not to wake her, I decide to leave her in the pram in the hallway. I hear myself offering to make Sandy a mug of tea. I expect her to follow me into the kitchen, but she kicks off her heels before going into the sitting room and flopping down onto the sofa.

I can feel the look of horror on my face as I peer through the doorway and see my mother-in-law pick up the photo to examine it. I hesitate, but then I continue to walk towards the kitchen. I can't ask Alex about this, but I might be able to get his mother to shed some light on it all.

In the end, Sandy needs no prompting. Putting the mugs on the table, I sit down next to her, trying to read her expression, but she won't meet my eye. She's still staring at the photo in her hands.

'Alex was so young. No child should have to go through that,' she begins. 'His father used to take him down to the cellar and "discipline" him.' She spits the word out vehemently, her husband's word.

So, the photo was taken in the cellar. No wonder Alex keeps it locked and won't go down there.

'Did you take this picture?'

'Yes.'

163

I'm about to ask her why, but she repeats, 'No child should have to go through that.' She pauses, then adds, 'And no child should have to witness one of his parents … hurting the other one. Physically, I mean.'

'Your husband hit *you*?'

It comes out no louder than a whisper and at first I think she hasn't heard, but then she nods. 'He beat both of us.'

I remember Alex said his father left when he was ten. 'Why did you … what made you stay so long?'

'I don't know, really.' Her voice becomes distant. 'I still ask myself that question every day. The good times were very good. I loved them. I loved him. He was genuinely sorry after each of the bad times. He kept saying he wanted to get better and that things would improve between us.'

Her words bring to my mind what Alex said after our row on the night of the barbecue. *I'll do better. It'll get better.*

'He said he needed me to help him,' she continues.

You make me a better person most of the time. Please say you'll help me learn to be that person all of the time.

'I believed him. I also thought a lot of the time that it was partly my fault. I wound him up. Then when he lost his temper and lashed out, I retaliated. I shouted obscenities at him, too. I even hit him back or threw things at him sometimes. I thought I was being strong to stand up to him. Then, afterwards, I would tell myself I was as bad as he was.' She sighs. 'The truth is, I felt too weak to leave. I hoped he would sort himself out, but deep down I knew that was never going to happen. Things could only get worse.'

I want her to carry on, but she seems as surprised as I am that she has said so much.

'So how did it end?' I remember Alex's description of his father as a serial adulterer, so I ask, 'Did he leave you for someone else?'

'What? No!' Her voice is back to its usual shrillness again. She turns on the sofa to face me, her eyes narrowing. She waves the

164

photo at me. 'Did Alexander give you this?' Sandy is questioning me with the same piercing eyes my husband has.

'No. I found it.'

'Oh, I see.' Thankfully, she doesn't ask where. She removes an imaginary thread from the leg of her neatly ironed trousers. 'Well, perhaps it would be best if he doesn't find out you've seen this. I didn't know he had it.'

I can tell she doesn't want to discuss this anymore, but I can't let it go. 'Alex said you'd … separated from his father. He told me no one knew where he was. Weren't you afraid he would come back?'

'No. I showed him that photo. It was the only one of Alexander. But there were others of me. My bruises. I had the film developed the following day.' She brandishes the photo again. 'And that evening, when he came home, I told him to get out. I said if he came back, I would go to the police and the press.'

So that's why she took the photo. And that probably explains why she didn't use a flash. She didn't want her husband to realise she was there.

Sandy scoops up the envelope from the table and puts the photo inside. Then she picks her handbag up from the floor.

'May I?'

I nod. Slipping the envelope into her bag, she gets up to leave. This conversation is over.

After she has left, snatches of her story run through my head. *The good times were very good … I loved him …* Some of the things my mother-in-law has said are resonating with me. *He was genuinely sorry …* There are similarities between her marriage and mine. *Things could only get worse.*

Then the voice of reason pipes up in my head. It's Alex's voice again. *Not everything is always about you. My mother was abused. I've never laid a finger on you. My father didn't love her. I do love you.* It's what he would say, or a watered-down version of what I imagine his reaction would be, anyway.

I feel bad about comparing Alex's father to Alex. After all, Alex is trying so hard not to be like him. And I feel terrible for imagining that Sandy could have been complicit in her husband's abuse of Alex and for worrying about leaving my daughter alone with her.

For a few minutes, I stay sitting on the sofa, my head in my hands and my eyes shut. I can visualise the photo. Alex's father standing over him, about to beat him with a belt. I can see the detail as clearly as if the photo were in front of me. The shelves, the chair, Alex's trousers around his ankles, the date stamped in the bottom right-hand corner.

There's something about the date: 8th September 1987. The next day, according to Sandy, she threw Alex's father out. That would have been the 9th of September. The 9th of the 9th. Numbers start swirling around in my mind. At first, I can hardly visualise them, but then they spin more slowly. The passcode for Alex's mobile. The numbers after his name in his email address: 9987. It can't be a coincidence. Perhaps Alex considered it was a new start. The first day of the rest of his life.

I resolve not to breathe a word about the photo to Alex. When he comes home, he finds me upstairs, giving Chloe a bath.

'Hello, my two loves,' he says, kissing me on the back of my neck. 'How was your day?'

'Fine,' I say, just as my mobile phone starts to ring.

'Where is it?' he asks.

'In my back pocket.'

I've lifted Chloe out of the bath, and she's in my arms. Alex slides his hand into my pocket, gives my backside a little squeeze, and pulls out my phone. I lay Chloe on the changing mat, cooing to her and drying my hands in her towel. I assume Alex will take over with Chloe and enable me to take my call.

But he leaves the room and then I hear his voice booming from the upstairs landing.

'Hello, Julie. How are you?'

I feel irritation spark up inside me. We've never answered each other's phones. Not only has he taken my call, but he has also taken my mobile out of the bathroom. I have nothing to hide, but that's not the point. Then I remember accessing Alex's phone to check up on him and the spark of irritation is replaced by a pang of guilt.

'No, she's busy with Chloe right now ... I don't think that will be possible ... You do know that she's been ...' He either lowers his voice or goes into another room and I can't make out any more of his side of the conversation.

I see Alex before I hear him. I catch sight of him in the bathroom mirror. He hasn't got my phone, so he's not going to put me on to Julie.

'What did Julie want?' I ask. I make an effort to sound curious rather than demanding.

'Oh, she just wanted us to go down to Somerset to visit,' Alex says. 'I had to tell her that we really can't get away at the moment.'

I'm still watching him in the mirror. He seems to be avoiding eye contact. *He's lying*. When he looks up, he misinterprets my expression of disbelief for disappointment.

'Oh, don't worry, Katie,' he says. 'We can go down at the end of the summer if you like. You understand, don't you? There's so much going on at work in August.'

I notice my reflection nodding.

I want to call my sister back, but Alex doesn't give me a chance. He follows me around, talking nineteen to the dozen about inconsequential things. After a while, I find it so exhausting trying to follow him that I switch off.

I think about texting Julie, but it would only cause an argument with Alex. I could do it discreetly from the toilet, I suppose. But I have no idea where Alex put my mobile after he spoke to my sister. Presumably he left it in our bedroom. Just as I'm trying to come up with an excuse to go upstairs, Alex suggests we go to bed. I sigh. I'll ring Julie tomorrow. It can't have been urgent or Alex would have handed me the mobile when she called.

167

I find my mobile on the bedside table before I go to bed. But the next morning, my heart sinks as, for the second day running, Sandy arrives before Alex leaves. I'll have to wait until she goes homes before I can ring my sister back. Discreetly, I send Julie a text message while Sandy is fussing over Chloe.

Hi.
    Sorry I didn't get to talk to you last night. My mother-in-law is here right now but I'll ring you later. Hope you're all well.
    Love, Kaitlyn. X

The reply comes back a few minutes later.

Hello Kaitlyn.
    The rest of us are fine. We're worried about you!
Call me when you get a mo.
    xoxo

I puzzle over Julie's message all day. What does she mean, *the rest of us are fine*? And why would she be worried about me?

When I'm not trying to work out what her text message means, I'm wondering how I can subtly steer Sandy back to yesterday's conversation. I'm desperate to find out more, but she seems determined to stay on safer ground with mundane matters.

I catch Sandy looking at me expectantly and realise she has said something that I haven't taken in. I have one of those moments where you wonder whether to say 'yes' or 'no', or just grunt noncommittally. I stare at her blankly.

'I'm going to get going.'

'Oh.' Inside, I sigh with relief, both that she has helped me out by repeating herself and that she's leaving.

I pick up her handbag and hand it to her and I just about refrain from physically pushing her out of the front door. As soon as she has left, I call Julie. I actually cross my fingers, hoping she's not at work – I don't know what shifts she's on – but she answers after two rings.

'Julie, what was your message about?' I burst out, dispensing with formalities. 'I've been thinking about it all day.'

'Hello, Kaitlyn. How are you?' Thinking this is her big-sister way of reminding me of my manners, I don't immediately pick up on the concern in her voice.

'Oh, I'm sorry, Julie. It's just I was a bit confused by your message. I'm fine. How are you?' There's a pause and that's when I realise I've misinterpreted. 'Why do you ask?'

'Well, Alex told me … you know, but he said not to tell you he'd said anything.'

Another pause. Then I say, 'Julie, I have no idea what you're talking about.'

'About your post-partum depression,' she says.

'Oh. That. I'm not depressed, Julie. Alex has got it into his head that I am, but I'm absolutely fine. I'd be even less miserable if his mother gave me some space!' I give a hollow laugh at my feeble attempt at a joke.

'Are you sure you're OK?'

'Yes. Chloe cries a lot, as you know. We took her to the health centre. Alex's GP said there was nothing wrong with *her*, but he put *me* on anti-depressants.' When Julie says nothing, I add, 'I'm not taking them.'

She still doesn't respond.

'What's this about asking us to come down to Somerset?'

'Is that wh … What did Alex say to you exactly, the other night? Obviously, he told you I'd called?'

'Yes. He said you rang because you wanted us to visit. He said he told you he's really tied down at the moment.' I'm about to back Alex up, explain to Julie how busy he is at work during the summer season, but then I remember thinking at the time that Alex was lying about something. He wouldn't look me in the eyes in the mirror.

'You make it sound like we invited you for the weekend or something,' Julie says.

'That's sort of how *he* made it sound.' A feeling of unease washes over me. 'What's going on?'

'I expect Alex is trying not to burden you, you know, if he thinks you're depressed. He sounded very worried about you on the phone.'

'I'm not depressed!' I spurt out. 'Why did you ring yesterday?' I ask. What didn't he tell me? What has he kept from me?

She doesn't answer straight away. I can almost hear her asking herself if I really am able to cope with what she rang to tell me. I think the best way to convince her I'm stable, strong and of sound mind is to remain silent.

After several seconds, I hear her take a deep breath. 'Kaitlyn, I'm afraid I've got some bad news,' she says.

Chapter 16

By the time Alex gets home from work, my bags are packed. He arrives just as I'm throwing the last of them onto the back seat of my car. Bad timing. I was hoping to have this discussion as calmly as possible inside the house before leaving.

He has a clear view of the chassis of Chloe's pram and the suitcase in the open boot of my car as he storms up to me. Imagining the scene through his eyes, it does look a bit like I'm baiting him. His face is a picture of indignation tinged with confusion and I realise I've misjudged the situation. I should have made sure I'd be gone before he got home. I can see my own anger reflected in him, but he takes a step closer to me and my fury is jostled away by fear. I want to step away from him, but I stand my ground.

I've been practising what I want to say to Alex since speaking to Julie earlier. And yet not a single word of my well-prepared speech comes to me now. I'm going to have to wing it, knowing that if I don't say the right thing, I'll provoke him into a rage.

'Are you … you're not leaving me, are you?' I wasn't expecting this. He looks like he's about to cry. He has suddenly become weak and I have the upper hand.

'No, Alex, of course not.'

'You promised you'd never leave me.'

I reach for his hand, but it's clenched tightly into a fist and I let go quickly, as if touching him has burnt me. 'Alex, my father is ill, as you know.' Damn! I shouldn't have said that last bit. It sounds like a dig. 'He's had a stroke, as Julie told you on the phone ...' I've done it again. He'll think I'm criticising him.

I pause. I need to do better than this. I need to avoid anything that might come over as reproachful. Alex is an explosive obstacle to be circumvented gingerly, like a land mine.

'I know you wanted to protect me, Alex,' I resume. The lines I rehearsed are coming back to me now. 'But I do need to be there for my dad. I'm sure you understand. You're always there for your mum.'

I pause again, hoping he's thinking about how he looked after Sandy when she fell. 'I'm going to Somerset for a few days,' I continue. 'I'm taking Chloe. I'll ring or text every evening, like you do when you're away.'

For a while, Alex looks at me and I get the impression he's looking through me. His face is still contorted and I have no idea what he's thinking or even if he has taken in anything I've just said.

Then he runs his hand through his curls and says, 'OK, but on one condition.'

I bite my tongue to stop myself from protesting that this is unconditional. I need to hear him out.

'Stay here tonight and leave tomorrow morning. It's a long drive. If you set off now, you'll arrive in the wee hours.' It's one of my mother's expressions that Alex must have picked up from me. I don't say that was the idea. I wanted to avoid traffic. I wanted to avoid drama and confrontation. I hoped Chloe would sleep for the whole journey this way.

Not leaving until tomorrow will mean not being there when Dad comes out of hospital in the morning. Staying at the Old Vicarage tonight will mean unpacking one of my bags and all of Chloe's stuff. It may mean traffic jams. But as Julie often reminds me, marriage is about compromise.

'OK,' I agree, hoping that Alex isn't using this to buy time. Maybe by tomorrow morning he'll have come up with something to stop me going at all.

It's not until I come off the M5 the next day that I relax. I really thought, right up to the last minute, that Alex would pull out some trick so that I couldn't go. Instead, we had a lovely evening and Alex held me in his arms all night long. Glancing at the lush green hills rolling away from me towards Bridgwater, I wonder how I could have suspected that he would try to prevent me from returning here.

Before Chloe came along, I wanted to come back for a week or so to put in some KIT days – Keeping in Touch days – at university. I wanted to see some of my PhD students and stay in close contact with my head of department during my maternity leave. It would also have been a good excuse to visit my family and friends in Somerset.

Alex wouldn't hear of it. I tried to argue that I could defer my return to work after the baby was born if I put in a few days at the university, but it wasn't negotiable.

Somehow I got it into my head that Alex didn't want me to see my family and friends. But now, reflecting on all that as I drive along the Bristol Road, past Minehead where I used to live, I think I've got it wrong. I feel bad for underestimating Alex. While I was pregnant, he didn't want me to work or travel, by train or by car, and at the moment he thinks I need his help – and his mother's help, too, clearly. I don't, but I can see that he's only looking out for me.

A few miles further along the A39, I drive past the ornate sign at the side of the road, welcoming me to Porlock, where my dad still lives in the house Julie, Louisa and I grew up in. For once, the sky is almost as blue as it is on the sign. My heart starts to thump in excitement, even though I haven't come here in ideal circumstances.

I take a turning just after The Lorna Doone Hotel and, opening my window, I inhale the fresh salty air through my nose. I drive through a labyrinth of lanes, each one narrower than the previous one, and then up a steep hill. At the top of it, checking there is no one behind me, I stop the car for a minute to admire the sea view.

I took the beauty of this area for granted, I realise. I never appreciated how beautiful this village was when I was growing up here, feeling at times walled in by the hills of Exmoor on three sides and the sea on the other. I feel so small and unimportant in such a vast expanse of beauty that now I wonder how I ever felt enclosed here.

Now I've moved away and come back everything around me seems at once familiar and different. I know this view; I've seen it so many times that I can visualise almost every detail, even with my eyes closed. I know this place; I know these roads like the back of my hand. But I don't feel I belong here. I'd like to, but it's no longer my home and I don't think you can ever find again exactly what you've left behind.

I feel nostalgic and homesick, but my longing is for the past, a time when my mother and my sister were part of my life, and not reduced to painful memories. There's a word for this in Irish Gaelic, my mother once told me. *Uaigneas*. Melancholy and wistfulness for the past. The picturesque setting somehow only serves to accentuate my grief. I put the car into gear and drive down the hill. The very last leg of the journey now.

I park in the road in front of my dad's house and behind my sister's car, deciding to leave my bags in the car for now. Before I even undo my seatbelt, I send a text to Alex, as promised, letting him know we've arrived safely. Best to do that before I forget.

As I push Chloe in her pram towards the front door, I notice how unkempt the front garden looks. My dad used to mow the lawn regularly. The petunias in the hanging baskets either side of the door are wilting, too. That's not like Dad. Any trace of my earlier excitement is now replaced with concern about my father's health. I feel guilty for not ringing Dad more often since I've been living in Grasmere. I never really know what to say when I call, but that's no excuse.

Opening the door without knocking, I hear Julie's voice from inside the house.

'Hello,' I call, lifting Chloe out of the pram and leaving it in the porch. I nearly shout, *I'm home*, but instead I add, 'It's Chloe and me.'

'We're in the lounge,' my sister calls back.

My father is sitting in his favourite armchair with a rug over his lap despite the warm weather. He looks just the same as the last time I saw him, which wasn't long ago, but I expected to be shocked by his appearance and I'm so glad I'm not. A smile fixed on his face as ever, he reaches for his granddaughter. I'll have to wait my turn. In the meantime, Jet greets me, although his welcome is less enthusiastic than usual. He thumps his tail on the floor and rolls over lazily for me to tickle his belly instead of jumping up and attempting to lick me to death.

I leave Chloe with Dad, as Julie leads the way into the kitchen, ostensibly to make tea, but really to give the two of us some privacy.

'When did Dad have his stroke?' I ask.

'The day I got back from the Lake District. I didn't tell you at first because he begged me not to.' That's typical of Dad. 'He thought you had enough on your plate with Chloe being fractious and all. But I thought you should know and, well, I hoped you could help out a bit. I used up nearly all my leave coming to see you, unfortunately.'

'Oh, Julie, I do wish you'd told me before.'

175

'Listen, it's no big deal. It was a minor stroke. Dad's had an MRI scan and he's taking anticoagulants. The main thing is there's no permanent damage. You know Dad, he insisted on being discharged as soon as possible.'

'So he's on the mend?'

'Yes, but there's still a slight risk of him having another stroke. It's only been four days. It's way too soon for him to come home, really.'

Julie, in full nurse mode, then proceeds to outline all the symptoms and tells me exactly what to do if Dad should have a stroke while I'm caring for him. I can feel the panic written on my face and Julie must see it because she reassures me that it's very unlikely to come to that.

The first few days go by in a blur. I walk Jet, look after Chloe, look after Dad, eat, sleep, repeat. Dad says he feels well, and indeed he looks on form, but Julie has insisted he must rest and so I make sure he does.

Every day, I send a text to Alex, as promised, and every evening I phone him and leave him a message when he doesn't answer. The few replies he does send to my text messages are laconic. They leave me with the impression that he's determined not to strike up a conversation. 'Hope your dad is better soon' rather than 'How's your dad doing?' for example. Or 'Love to Chloe' and no mention of me. To begin with, I'm annoyed. But then I just feel sad. It's his busy season and life is getting in our way.

Each time I think about our emails and texts when we fell in love last year, my eyes threaten to brim over with tears. I miss Alex so badly. I have a visceral craving for him, a basic need for him to make me feel whole. Everything was fine when I left the Old Vicarage, or so I'd thought, but I can't reach Alex from here. He's not nasty; he's not even rude. He's just not there. But I realise I've been missing the Alex I fell for even when I'm with him. He's not always there then, either, and he's certainly not there for me.

One morning, after texting Alex and getting no answer, I go

on Facebook. I posted some photos of Chloe just after we brought her home, but I hardly go on Facebook anymore. I rarely have my computer on these days for one thing, and I can't usually be bothered to do it from my phone.

I used to spend a lot of time on here, though, checking out Alex's wall, hungry for every single titbit of information about him I could come by. I would spend ages looking at his photos, zooming in on his handsome face. I would try to find out all about his friends. I needed to know who had commented on his posts, who these people were who shared in his everyday life while, unable to be by his side, I could only watch from the sidelines.

Out of habit, I check to see if Alex is on Facebook, too. We would sometimes send each other messages via Facebook, batting words back and forth like a tennis ball. The green light by his name is on. I fire off a quick 'I miss you', but he doesn't reply. Instead, the green light next to his name disappears. I frown, wondering if he's trying to avoid me.

I haven't looked at his wall for ages. He seems to post every day, as he did before, and sometimes more than once. Alex is very concerned with his appearance. That's immediately clear from the number of photos of himself he has published and the look-at-me captions. He has always done this. But looking at this now, it bothers me.

Nowadays, when the internet comes with any number of free disguises, you can promote any image of yourself you like; you can create a false persona and pretend to be someone you're not. And yet so many people choose to share the most humdrum things about their lives, like photos of their dinner or their pets. That baffles me, but I also find it reassuring. Most people's lives aren't any more or less exciting than my own.

At the other end of the scale, are people like Alex, who culti-vate their images with numerous selfies and other photos of themselves as well as with carefully worded posts. At first sight, Alex comes over as brilliant, beautiful and enviable.

But on closer examination, he appears to look down his nose at a lot of things and a lot of people. He also seems to be an expert on a wide range of topics. Is this recent, or did I just not notice it before? For a moment, I wonder if I'm on someone else's Facebook page, but I take another look at the profile picture – a fit suntanned man wearing a short, tight-fitting wetsuit. Despite the hat and goggles, I can see it's definitely Alex.

I start to read his posts. Some of it would be amusing if he wasn't being so scathing, but he seems to criticise everyone and everything. We've never discussed politics, and yet he's censorious of both Theresa May and Jeremy Corbyn, not to mention Diane Abbott. He has no end of things to say about Brexit and its aftermath. He can't abide breaststrokers in *his* lane at the swimming pool any more than 'runtards' at his marathons. He also has it in for Ed Sheeran, the French, *The Guardian*, *The Voice*, and vegetarians and vegans. And that list is far from exhaustive.

I scroll down Alex's posts to the time when I first got in touch with him after a gap of twenty years. He kept cropping up, making comments on mutual friends' posts and in my 'People You May Know' notifications, and so, curious to know what my school crush had become, I sent him a friend request. I reread some of my comments on his posts, seemingly innocent remarks with an in-joke that only he would get, or congratulations on his competitions. I remember how proud I felt.

There are no photos of the two of us, not even on our wedding day. In fact, Alex hasn't added any information about his relationship status. Not for the first time, I feel insignificant, as if I don't exist for Alex. But then I reason that there are no photos of Chloe either. Or of Poppy and Violet, come to think of it. Alex just likes to keep his private life private.

I scroll back a few months before we were together. There were fewer rants at that time. Fewer posts altogether. And then I see her name. Nicola Todd. My heart stops dead for a beat or two, just as it did when I read the dedication in the book about the triathlete that she gave Alex. I can still see the words in my mind. *To Alex. With all my love, always. Nicola. X.* It has to be her. She must be an ex-girlfriend, but he has never mentioned her by name. He may well have talked about her, though – he talked about his exes a lot until I got upset.

I click on her name. But her privacy settings are on 'Friends Only'. I can only see her profile picture, which is a picture of her from the side, taken when she wasn't looking at the camera. She has long dark hair and she is gazing at something only she can see behind the photographer. It's not a great photo – it's a little blurred when I zoom in – but it's good enough for me to see that I've never met her.

Something about it disturbs me, but I can't put my finger on exactly what it is. I stare at it, trying to pinpoint what has stirred some hazy memory, but even the memory itself is out of my reach.

As I try to work out what's troubling me, Julie, Daniel and the boys burst in. I didn't know they were coming and the noise they bring with them, the boys bickering and Julie shouting at them, makes me jump.

'Shhh,' I urge, putting my phone down on the arm of the sofa, 'Dad's having a nap.'

I stand up and hold my arms out to catch my nephews as they run to greet me, nearly bowling me over in the process.

'We thought seeing as you've been caring for Dad for the last few days, you might like a break,' Julie says, pecking me on the cheek. 'Do you want to get out for a bit while we take over?'

Daniel suggests I leave Chloe with them, but she has got noticeably calmer as the week as gone on, and I'm enjoying her company.

'Oscar and Archie will be cooking dinner this evening if you'd like to join us,' Daniel says, holding up a shopping bag, 'but if you have other plans, that's OK, too.'

'No, I'll be back in time,' I say, smiling. 'That sounds great!'

I fetch my handbag and a cardigan and I get Chloe's stuff together. Jet wags his tail, thinking he's going for walkies.

I haven't made any plans. But there is something I need to do while I'm here.

Chapter 17

It's usually a fifteen-minute drive from my dad's house to Minehead, but it's the weekend, and the good weather and Butlins have attracted families in their droves, so it takes me a bit longer. I find a space to leave the car in a side street and I walk to The Parks with Chloe in the pram, past a playground where a boy is pushing a younger girl, his little sister, perhaps, on a swing. There are children on the merry-go-round, too. I can hear their squeals from here.

'Higher!'

'Faster!'

'Stop! I wanna get off!'

I stand still for a moment and watch. The boy has stopped pushing the girl now. The swing still goes up and down, but the highs are becoming ever lower. The merry-go-round continues to spin, though, going round and round at a sickening pace. Up and down, round and round. *The story of my married life so far*, I think, walking on.

When I get there, I stand on the pavement opposite for several minutes, trying to pluck up the courage to cross the road and go in. I think I'm going to bottle out and go back to the car, but then I take a deep breath and press the button at the pelican crossing. It's now or never.

I push open the narrow door and walk in backwards, pulling the pram in behind me. When I turn round, she looks shocked to see me, but she quickly recovers her composure. Her hair is unusually tidy and she's beautifully made-up. I'm amused to see she's still wearing a hoodie and her Doctor Marten boots as always, her only concession to summer being that she has swapped her jeans for a short skirt.

She puts down her scissors and comb, saying something into the ear of the middle-aged lady whose hair she was doing, and then she comes towards me. There's a moment's hesitation before Hannah gives me a big hug and for a second or two it's as if nothing happened, as if I never left, as if we're still best friends.

'How are you?' She doesn't pause for me to answer. 'Ooh, let me see Chloe!' She peers into the pram, where my daughter is sleeping.

I watch Hannah as she gently strokes Chloe's cheek. She frowns and I wonder why. Perhaps she's worried Kevin can't have kids. There was nothing wrong with either of us, the doctors said; it was just one of those things. I hope the chemistry works better for them.

'I have a break for lunch in half an hour if you'd like to join me,' she says, studying the floor as if it needs attention. I almost follow her gaze, but then I understand her body language. She expects me to refuse.

'Actually, I was hoping you'd cut my hair,' I say.

She smiles. 'OK.'

Thirty minutes later, the back of my neck aching from the sink and my scalp smarting from Hannah's massage, I'm sitting in front of the mirror.

'So, shall I just take off a couple of inches, get rid of these split ends?' Hannah asks, inspecting the strand of long ginger hair she's holding between two of her fingers.

'No, cut it short,' I instruct her.

I catch Hannah's surprised face in the mirror. I'm as taken aback as she is; I was only going to ask her for a trim and a blow-dry, just as an excuse to see her, really.

Hannah gets to work. I study her in the mirror as she cuts my hair. Every now and then, she glances at Chloe, next to us in the pram, and each time she does, I'm struck by the strange expression on her face. At one point, the hand holding the scissors shakes. Whatever is going through her mind, I can't ask her. We're nowhere near that place now.

By unspoken agreement, we don't talk about Kevin. I know from Julie and Daniel that the company he works for has been contracted to build the new sports centre in Minehead, but I don't ask after him, and Hannah doesn't mention his name. He's the elephant in the hair salon.

When it's over, I admire my reflection and then turn and beam at Hannah. She has transformed me. Having my red hair around my face, instead of tied back in a ponytail, brings out the emerald colour of my eyes. The same eyes as my mother and Louisa. It also suits the shape of my face, which is a bit long for my liking.

'You look beautiful,' Hannah says, 'though I say it myself.'

As I dig into my handbag for my purse, insisting on paying Hannah even though she protests, Chloe makes herself heard. She's awake, but she's not screaming. She's not even crying. Dad says the sea air suits her.

'Can I hold her?'

'Sure, no problem.' I'm delighted Hannah has asked. Red hair falls to the floor all around me as I get up to lift Chloe out of the pram, but Hannah is already walking around the room with Chloe in her arms, supporting her head and talking to her gently. After stripping off the protective cape, I carry on hunting in my handbag.

183

Suddenly, Chloe screeches, sharply, and then starts crying, as she does sometimes when she has been frightened or hurt.

I look up. Hannah walks towards me and gives Chloe to me. 'I don't know what happened,' she says. 'I'm sorry.'

'It's all right. She cries a lot,' I say. But she hasn't cried much for the last couple of days.

In the end, Hannah won't let me pay and I leave. We promise to keep in touch.

When I get home, Daniel is deadheading Dad's petunias in the hanging baskets. Seeing the scissors in Daniel's hand, I think of Hannah snipping away at my locks just a few hours ago. But at the smell and the sight of the decaying blooms, another memory soon superimposes itself. The box left on the doorstep of the Old Vicarage with the handwritten message, *Wake up and smell the dead flowers.* I shudder.

'Wow! You look stunning,' Daniel says as I push Chloe in her pram up Dad's drive. He looks a little embarrassed and turns back to the petunias. I notice a small balding patch on the back of his head as he tips it back to look up at the flowers. I've never noticed it before. His dark hair is greying, pepper and salt. And his kind face has quite a few wrinkles that weren't there when he first started going out with Julie.

'Just trying to sort out your dad's plants,' he says unnecessarily. 'He seems a lot better, by the way. Julie's very relieved. I expect you're keen to get back to that man of yours, aren't you?'

'Oh, there's no hurry. I'll stay another week, I expect.'

Daniel turns round again to face me. 'You know, Kaitlyn,' he begins, 'if it doesn't work out and you want to come home, no one here would think any less of you.'

Like Julie, my brother-in-law is straightforward. He tends to speak his mind, no matter what's on it. Pretending not to understand, I pull a puzzled face.

'I mean, you were very brave and made a go of it. But if it goes tits up …' He breaks off, sighs and waves the scissors around.

It's not so much what he says as what I can't say. All the thoughts and feelings that I can't put into words, and wouldn't express even if I could, form a large lump in my throat, and in that moment I don't know if I'm going to cry or suffocate.

'Sorry, I didn't mean to sound patronising,' Daniel continues. 'I just wanted to say, I know Julie thinks Alex can do no wrong, but if you need to talk about anything at any time, I'm here, too.'

I can feel my cheeks burning, and I can see Daniel's are as well. He overheard Alex's demeaning remarks at our barbecue, I remember, first about my weight and then about my sister's 'generous' backside. I wonder if that's going through Daniel's head, too.

'Thanks, Daniel,' I say, kissing him on the cheek. 'I appreciate it.' I mean it when I say it. After all, I walked out on Kevin, who is Daniel's friend, and yet my brother-in-law has remained protective of me. But then something in me rises and makes me want to race to my husband's defence. What does Daniel know? He isn't aware that Alex was abused as a boy; he hasn't allowed for Alex's ex-wife taking away his children. 'But everything is fine,' I add, turning my back on Daniel to take Chloe inside.

The rest of the evening goes by uneventfully. Oscar and Archie have made a lovely meal – gazpacho, followed by grilled pork and ratatouille, and to top it all off, a lemon meringue pie. Then Julie and I play the board game Rummikub with the boys. When I go to bed that evening, I'm still feeling full from the meal.

At 3 a.m., I give up. I know I'm not going to get any more sleep tonight. I've been fretting about why Alex isn't talking to me. I'm not just worried; I'm angry. I play over in my mind all the rows we've had and all the ups and downs, and deep down I know I'm putting up with more than I should. There will be a reason for his lack of communication. He has an excuse for everything. But does that mean I should excuse him?

I want to be understanding – Alex is bound to be mentally scarred by his upbringing, but his moods are too much for me.

I feel weaker each time I give in to him and allow him to get his way, like I'm becoming a fainter, sepia version of my former self. I often question my judgement. Perhaps that's what you're supposed to do in a marriage. But it seems to me that I do this, but Alex doesn't.

Sighing, I get up and go downstairs to make a cup of tea. Jet, curled up on his bed, opens his eyes as I pass him, but he doesn't get up to follow me into the kitchen. I bend down to stroke him, but he's not as responsive as usual.

'I bet you're wondering what I'm doing up at this hour, Jet, aren't you?' I whisper, caressing his ears. 'You think I'm mad, don't you?' I straighten up, adding, 'You're right, Jet. Absolutely right.' I'm not going mad so much as hopping mad.

I spend the rest of the night sitting on the sofa with Dad's rug over my lap. I drink tea, flick through TV channels and read my novel without taking much of it in. There's a confused jumble of thoughts piling up in my head, but I can't sort them out just yet. I don't know what to think about this. I don't want to think about it at all. But the TV and my book don't hold my attention for long and I'm desperate to find something to take my mind off this. I play *Words With Friends* in French on my mobile for a while, but after taking a few turns I have only consonants and no vowels, so I resign.

I look forward to Chloe waking up for her feed, for her company and for something to do. And I want to be able to hold her. But for the first time ever, she sleeps all the way through the night. I creep upstairs and check on her several times, but she doesn't wake up until nearly seven o'clock.

When my dad gets up, he fusses around me, asking me every five minutes if I'm all right. He seems to sense that something is wrong so I try my best to put on an act and sound carefree and happy. After all, I'm the one who is supposed to be looking after him.

Over the next week, I do look after my dad, even though he's a lot better and doesn't really need me to stay on much longer. Alex has texted me a couple of times to ask after my dad's health, more to find out when I intend to come home, I think, than out of genuine concern. I've been evasive in my replies. I haven't made up my mind when I'm going back to the Old Vicarage.

A part of me doesn't want to go home at all, but it's only a small part. I miss Alex; I love him. Most of me wants to run to him, but at night I lie awake, thinking I should be running from him.

The following Saturday, Julie, Daniel and the boys come round again and I decide to get out and get some fresh air. I'm hoping I can go alone. Well, with Jet. It will help clear my head and wake me up a bit, and hopefully tire me out at the same time so that I sleep better tonight. I want to go for a long walk along the paths my twin sister's feet took her.

I can't tell Dad where I'm going. He wouldn't understand why I need to go there sometimes. He hasn't been to Hurlstone Point since the day we lost Louisa. He certainly wouldn't want me anywhere near those windswept clifftops.

But just after Julie and her clan have arrived, the doorbell goes.

'Kaitlyn!' he exclaims when I open the door. 'It's so nice to see you after so long.'

'Hi,' I say, trying to remember his name. I haven't seen him since he left school, a year before me. Then it comes to me. His name is Edward, but no one called him that. 'Good to see you too, Teddy.'

Although he was slightly tubby back then, he looks very lean and fit now. A bit pale. He's not short, but he's only an inch or so taller than me. Receding hairline, but what hair he does have is still dark brown; there's not a hint of grey.

'What are you doing here?'

'I'm your dad's physiotherapist,' he says.

'But ...' My sleep-deprived brain tries to remember the name of the physio who has been coming to see Dad.

'Joe's away on holiday for two weeks. I think this is your dad's last session. It'll be with me today.'

I step back to let Teddy into the house. We chat for ages, reminiscing about school and laughing about some of the teachers we both had. The school we went to, East Exmoor School, is in the middle of nowhere. It's a private boarding school where Julie, Louisa and I were day pupils, like Teddy. Because Alex's parents lived up north, he was a termly boarder. Alex has since told me he was there on a sports scholarship and he often spent the weekends at his aunt and uncle's in the nearby town of Exford.

In the end, instead of going out alone to Hurlstone Point, I wait until Teddy has finished with Dad's physio and the two of us walk down the road to The Whortleberry Tearoom, where we sit outside and have a cream tea. I listen as he tells me about his work and about his ten-year-old daughter, Olivia. He giggles nervously sometimes in the middle of a sentence, which I find charming, and I notice that he twists his wedding band around his finger.

I observe Teddy as he eats the last of his scone and wipes his mouth with a paper napkin. Then he takes an electronic cigarette out of his pocket.

'I've given up smoking,' he says, waving it at me. 'I'll need to give this up next.'

As he draws on his e-cig and exhales the vapour, I get a very faint whiff of a pleasant lemony smell, a bit like air freshener, but when I try to breathe in the smell, it has already gone.

'So, does Olivia go to our old school?' I ask.

'Oh no, I couldn't afford it!'

'What does your wife do?' I ask, clamping my hand over my mouth just after the words escape from my mouth and I hear how they sound. 'Forgive me. That was clumsy of me.'

'Not at all,' Teddy says. 'Actually, she died three years ago.'

Now I'm mortified. 'I'm so sorry, Teddy.'

'Brain aneurysm.'

'Oh, how awful.'

'Her parents help out a lot with Olivia, as do mine, and we get by, but she won't be going to East Exmoor, that's for sure!'

He stops turning his ring and picks up his teacup. We both remain silent, sipping our teas for a while. I feel bad for causing the awkwardness when we were chatting effortlessly before.

'I heard you married Alexander Riley,' Teddy says after a while.

'Yes.'

'Do you both still live around here then?'

'Oh, no. We live in the Lake District. In Grasmere.'

I don't know what else to say. I remember the rose-tinted version of our story that Alex told everyone at the barbecue, but I can't tell it like that. And I don't want to tell the true story, either.

'I've never been further north than Birmingham.' Teddy says.

'No, I hadn't either before I moved up there.'

Teddy walks me back and we say goodbye at the front gate of my dad's house. He says he'll look me up on Facebook. He waves out of the window of his car as he drives away.

'Who was that?'

I whirl round. He's sitting on the doorstep.

'Alex! What a lovely surprise!' Then I notice what he's wearing. 'Did you ... you didn't ...? How did you get here?'

'Train to Tiverton Parkway. The guy sitting next to me on the train gave me a lift as far as Dulverton. Ran the rest.'

'But that's miles! I would have picked you up from the station if you'd told me you were coming.'

'Nah. I needed a longish run, and it's only about fifteen miles. Thought we could drive back home together tomorrow in your car.'

'Did you ring the doorbell?'

'No, I've just got here. So, who was that?'

'Teddy Edwards. Remember him? From school?'

'How could I forget someone with a name like Edward

Edwards? He's lost a lot of weight since he was at East Exmoor, hasn't he? Edward Edwards.' He whistles through his teeth, although I'm not sure what he means by it.

'Hmm. I suppose that's why everyone called him Teddy,' I say, choosing to ignore Alex's last comment. I don't tell Alex I used to think it was because he looked cuddly.

Alex does his stretching exercises while I announce his arrival – and my departure for the following day. When Alex steps into the hall, dumping his rucksack on the ground and smiling at me, my heart thumps wildly. I'm pleased to see him, but I'm nervous now he's here.

'I've got a surprise for you,' Alex says, bending down to unzip a side pocket on his rucksack.

I watch as he pulls out a white envelope and hands it to me. For a second, I look at it in horror, thinking Alex's mother has given him the photo I found in the cellar. But then I realise this envelope is far smaller. I open it, my eyes on Alex. It's my red heart crystal necklace. The one I was supposed to wear on my wedding day.

'Where did you find it?' I manage at last.

'In the laundry basket,' he says, without missing a beat. 'It must have fallen out of one of your pockets.'

I know he's watching me, trying to gauge my reaction. I try to stretch my mouth into a smile, but the effect feels more like a rictus frozen across my lips.

I lead Alex into the sitting room, where he greets my family. As Julie and Dad make everyone a cup of tea, Alex flops down next to me on the sofa. I catch him glancing sideways at me, as if studying my new look, but although he must have noticed, he doesn't mention my haircut. First I think, better no comment than a disparaging one. Then I bristle inside, thinking that even if he didn't like it, he could have said he did. What's one little fib when he has fed me several huge ones, not to mention a few lies of omission? After all, he has just told a little white lie about the necklace.

190

Then a thought worms its way into my head. What if that wasn't a little white lie? What if it was a big black lie? What if he had the necklace all along? But why would he do that? It makes no sense. Unless he wants me to doubt myself. No. That can't be it. That would be a very sick game to play.

Alex manipulates the truth, like he manipulates me. He twists and bends it in any way that enables him to get *his* way. So, there's no point in confronting him about the necklace. I'll only become bogged down deeper in this morass of lies with no hope of untangling them.

But I know he's lying. At the time, Daniel looked in the laundry basket and Hannah went through all my pockets. And I'm absolutely certain that I put the necklace in my drawer. As soon as I get home, I'll put it back in the drawer. I don't want to wear it. I'm not superstitious, far from it, but it's as if the red heart necklace is jinxed.

Chapter 18

I was sort of looking forward to going back to Grasmere; at least I was until Alex turned up in Porlock. But now I'm back here, a heaviness lines my stomach, a foreboding that trouble is just ahead and I can't avoid it.

On my second day back, I desperately want to get out of the house for a while, get some fresh air. So when Alex has left, I decide to ring Vicky and ask her if she's free after work.

'I need to pop home and get my sports kit, but I can do that during my lunch break,' she says, assuming I want to go with her to the gym she mentioned in Cockermouth.

'Actually, I was wondering … would you like to go out for a walk? We could take your dogs.'

'OK. We could go up Wansfell Pike if you like. It's quite steep, but it's not a long walk.'

'That sounds like a great plan.' I inject as much enthusiasm as I can into my voice.

I think about taking Chloe in the baby carrier, but in the end, I ring my mother-in-law and ask her to look after her granddaughter. Chloe has been so calm recently. I'm worried she'll get irritable if she senses I'm a bit on edge. She'll be much happier with Sandy.

My mother-in-law must hear tension in my voice. 'Is anything wrong, Kaitlyn?' she asks over the phone.

'No. Everything's fine,' I tell her. 'I just thought I'd go out and meet up with a friend. Someone I met at the pool.' I'm past caring if this gets back to Alex. Anyway, he seems to sense that I haven't settled in since I've been back and I think he's worried I'm not going to stay. He's being very careful about what he says and does at the moment. I don't think he'll make a song and dance about me going out with a friend.

When Sandy arrives, she takes one look at me and says, 'You're looking a bit peaky. I expect it's your baby blues.'

I'm about to protest, tell her I'm not depressed, when she adds, 'Go out and have some fun. I'll look after Chloe.'

I pull on trainers and a light jacket, pushing my purse into the jacket pocket. I park my car in Ambleside and meet Vicky outside the estate agency. Then she drives her company car – the one with the *Swift and Taylor Properties* stickers on each side – as far as her mother's house.

'More room in this one,' says Vicky, after she has loaded two of the dogs – the Great Dane and the golden retriever – into her mum's silver hatchback. 'And no dreadful adverts on the doors.' As we set off for Troutbeck, Vicky is in high spirits. Her happiness rubs off on me a little, although it doesn't completely lift my mood.

'I've got some good news,' Vicky says. 'My offer has been accepted on the place I told you about! I can't wait to move in!' She describes the ground-floor flat, part of a converted church, which Vicky says has views of the fells beyond the garden. She's so excited that for a moment I feel envious. I haven't grown to love the Old Vicarage as I'd hoped, but I love the sound of Vicky's cosy new home. 'A new start,' Vicky continues. 'On my own. With the dogs.'

'Do you think you'll feel a bit lonely?'

'No,' she says. 'My mother is kind and caring, but she's hard to live with. And my fiancé treated me very badly. And yet, I stayed until *he* finished with *me*. Afterwards I realised how much happier I could be without him. I'm looking forward to being by myself for a while.'

Vicky flashes that wide smile of hers at me as she parks in the pub car park. We let the dogs out and begin our ascent of Wansfell Pike. When we get to the top, we sit down on the ground side by side and I hug my knees to my chest. Vicky says the views are breathtaking on a clear day. I look out across the water at a stretch of land in the distance, barely visible through the veil of cloud. I have no sense of direction, but it occurs to me that this expanse of water might be the Irish Sea.

'Could that be Northern Ireland, do you think?' I ask Vicky, thinking of my mum. I like the idea that from where I'm sitting, I can see where she came from.

'No. Those are the Coniston Fells over there.' Vicky points. 'And that's Lake Windermere.'

'Oh.'

I got that wrong. I feel a quick stab of almost physical pain. It leaves me short of breath. I feel a long way from home. Further than ever right now. I wish my mum were here to hold my hand and tell me that everything will be OK. Because I'm no longer sure that it will be.

'What on earth's the matter, Kaitlyn?'

It's only when I hear Vicky's words and clock her worried tone that I realise a tear has made its way down my cheek. Followed by another one. And then a torrent of tears. It's a while before I can tell her what's wrong.

And then, like the tears, it all gushes out. I start at the end with the red heart necklace. Then I let things unravel backwards. I tell Vicky about the parcel; I tell her about Hannah and Kevin. I explain that I met up with Alex in Exeter, which resulted in us conceiving Chloe. I tell her I'm feeling cut off from my family and friends. I describe the knot in my stomach that just won't go away. And I finish with Alex's moods and controlling behaviours.

'Even when he's telling the truth now, I think he's lying to me. I'm getting paranoid,' I say.

It's cathartic, putting all of this into words, but at the same time I feel disloyal. I usually jump to Alex's defence instead of criticising him. I justify his actions in my head all the time by finding fault within me. Now I'm admitting out loud what I really think deep down, I realise I won't be able to deny any of this to myself anymore.

Vicky listens to it all without interrupting. She puts her arm around me and I lean against her.

'It sounds like a rather abusive relationship,' Vicky says.

'But he doesn't hit me,' I argue, 'and he's an excellent father.' Here I go, sticking up for Alex. It's second nature. 'And we have some really good times.' Now I sound a bit like my mother-in-law.

'Sometimes psychological abuse can be much more insidious than physical abuse.'

She pauses. I say nothing, but I think: she's an estate agent, not a psychologist. How would she know? Then I feel angry with myself because I realise she's probably right.

'If you ever need to talk about it or if there's anything I can do to help …'

'Thank you.'

'I don't know about you, but I'm starving,' Vicky says, getting up and taking my hand to pull me to my feet.'

I'm about to say that I have no appetite whatsoever, but then my tummy rumbles faintly. It's loud enough for Vicky to hear and she persuades me to have a pub dinner with her in The Mortal Man, where we started out on our walk.

As we begin our descent, the sun breaks through the cloud and

195

I realise I've forgotten my sunglasses. When we're at the foot of the fell, I ring my mother-in-law, who tells me Alex is home and puts him on. I haven't had time to think up a story, and there have been more than enough secrets and lies, so I say I'm having dinner with a friend. I half-expect him to be brusque, but he sounds upbeat.

'I understand. You have a lovely time,' he says. 'Chloe and I will be fine.'

I'm still not that hungry, so I order a bowl of soup. Vicky wants me to try a local beer, Black Sail, which turns out to be a meal in itself. A liquid dinner. I don't usually like stout, but this one tastes a bit chocolatey and I think I could get used to it. We sit outside in the beer garden, soaking up the last rays of sun and taking in the panoramic views. Out here, I can breathe again. Fill my lungs with fresh air. Out here, I can tackle the thoughts crowding my head, with the green hills stretching away from me, and Scooby and Shadow stretched out at my feet.

As I watch the sun go down, I resolve to talk to Alex. He seems repentant after his 'radio silence', as he calls it, when I was in Porlock, and I think he's scared that I might go back to Somerset for good, so I don't think he'll sulk or pick a fight any time soon. I should be able to make a few demands while he's making amends. Nothing unreasonable. Nothing much. Just a few hours of childcare a week – from a professional rather than from his mother – and the opportunity to do some sport with Vicky without Alex guilt-tripping me about it. I need to have some sort of life outside the walls of the Old Vicarage.

~

I can feel the onset of a headache as I drive back from Ambleside, and when I get home, Alex is in the garden with Tom and Stacey, Mike and Sarah, and Rebecca. I won't be able to discuss my plans with Alex this evening.

I watch them all for a few seconds through the kitchen window, Alex's friends apparently drinking in his every word as they drink their beers. Then, baring my teeth into a wide smile that feels both foreign and fraudulent, I join them. For a few minutes, I attempt to make small talk with everyone, careful not to speak to Tom in any way that could be misconstrued as flirting. But I don't feel like socialising right now. In fact, I'm starting to feel quite sick. I regret drinking that pint in the sun now.

'I've got a headache,' I say. 'I'm going to go and lie down.'

Alex looks concerned and asks what he can do.

'Nothing, thank you. Just look after Chloe.'

When I get upstairs, I hunt for aspirin, ibuprofen or paracetamol, but there is none in the bathroom cabinet. I tip the contents of my handbag onto the bed. There's none there either. Then I remember Alex's tablets next to his whisky in the cupboard in the sitting room.

A minute later, I'm sitting on the bed examining the packet of pills. The migraine has blurred my vision and I struggle to read the label on the packaging. Fluni ... something. I don't know whether it's a painkiller or not. I want to Google it on my phone, but there's no way I can look at the backlit screen now. I can't stand the light anymore.

The throbbing has become intense; the pain in the right side of my head and behind my right eye is excruciating. It feels like someone is drilling into my skull. A wave of nausea submerges me. I decide not to take the medicine. I can't be sure what it's for and I doubt I can keep it down anyway. It's all I can do to draw the curtains, strip off my clothes and clamber into bed.

The next thing I know, Alex is waking me up the following morning to hand me Chloe. 'Good morning,' he says. 'Have to skedaddle. I've fed Chloe and changed her nappy. I'll bring you a cuppa before I go.'

Plumping up the pillows, I sit up in bed. My head is a lot better. Seeing the contents of my handbag still spilled on the sheets on Alex's side of the bed, I realise he hasn't slept next to me.

'I didn't want to disturb you last night,' he says, as if reading my mind, 'so I slept in the guestroom.'

As I sit in bed, holding the mug of tea Alex has brought me in one hand and tickling Chloe's tummy with the other, I'm astonished once again at how calm she has been since we went to Somerset. Before, she only seemed to stop screeching when she fell into a deep sleep. Now she smiles and gurgles, and because she's happier, I feel like I'm a better mummy, like I'm finally doing something right with this parenting business.

I decide to have a relaxing day with my baby girl. I can sing her nursery rhymes and read her children's stories. I want to go for a long walk with her in the baby carrier. And while I'm waiting for her to wake up from her nap later, I'll lose myself in my novel.

My thoughts are interrupted by a tapping noise, as if someone is drumming their fingernails on the windowpane impatiently to give me my cue to get up. Then the sound becomes more urgent. A pummelling with fists. I freeze as Chloe's mouth forms a startled "O". It takes me several seconds to realise it's raining.

'It's all right,' I soothe. 'It's just the rain. We won't be going for a walk today after all.' I sigh. 'Daddy may come home early though. He won't want to go for a run in this weather.'

That thought would usually have prompted me to write all sorts of housework chores on my to-do list to get everything clean and tidy for Alex coming home. But today a rebellious streak prevents me from even making the bed. I don't want things to go back to the way they were. I'm no longer going to give in to the pressure he puts on me to be perfect.

Chloe falls asleep. I leave her on the bed and go into the bathroom. In all the baby books Alex encouraged me to read, that's a big no-no. But Chloe is only seven weeks old. She's not going to wake up and roll onto the floor. And perhaps I'm not quite as good a mother as I prided myself I'd become after all.

Coming out of the shower, I catch sight of all the junk I tipped out of my handbag. I have slept next to an array of pens, lipsticks, tissues and papers. For a second I panic, wondering where my purse is, but then I remember it's in the pocket of the jacket I wore to walk the dogs with Vicky.

I may have decided against doing any housework, but I should clear up this mess. So, after getting dressed, I start sifting through my stuff. I throw out the used tissues – yuk! – and put the rest of the packet back in my handbag along with half a packet of Polos, two pens, one lipstick ... And then I see it. The card that was in the parcel. I pick it up and turn it over and read the message even though I know the words by heart. *Wake up and smell the dead flowers.*

These words seem even more sinister this morning, although I'm not sure why. Dead poppies and violets. Poppy and Violet. Maybe the message was intended for Alex. But I still don't get it. Why would anyone write that to him?

I get a strange feeling in my gut. I've had this impression before. I feel like I'm missing something. A piece of the puzzle. No, that's not quite it. I've got the piece that fits right here with this card, but somehow I'm not making the connection.

Then it comes to me. I jump up from where I was sitting on the bed and race into Chloe's room. The wooden mobile Becca bought for Chloe is dangling over the cot. In a rage, I tear it down and stamp on it. *Now where is it?* I hunt around until I find it on the bookcase. The card Becca wrote to congratulate us on the birth of Chloe. I open it and read the words she wrote. *To Kaitlyn and Alex, Best Wishes on the birth of your Beautiful Baby. Love, Bexxx.* Her handwriting is a spidery scrawl. That's not it. That's not what I'm after. False alarm.

I tear Becca's card into tiny pieces and let them fall to the floor. For some reason, I was convinced it was her. I could already see myself slapping her pretty little face and kicking her tanned toned legs. *Dammit!* And now I've broken Chloe's mobile. I kick the bits of wood under the cot. I need to calm down and think.

Then an image bursts into my head. This time I know I'm right. I walk slowly into the peach guestroom, knowing what I'm going to find, but scared of confirming it all the same. Kneeling in front of the wardrobe, I pull the cardboard box out and tear at the Sellotape, but I have sealed up the box thoroughly and I can't get it off, so I go downstairs and into the kitchen and grab a knife. A sense of urgency seizes me and I bound back up the stairs.

I cut the tape and open the flaps of the box. I start pulling things out. The handcuffs, the medals, the trophies ... the photo's not there anymore, of course; my mother-in-law has it now.

Then I find what I'm looking for. The book, the one about the injured ironman's comeback. Opening it, I stare at the neatly penned dedication inside the cover. *To Alex. With all my love, always. Nicola. X.*

Holding the card next to the wording of the dedication, my eyes flit from one message to the other. But even without close inspection, I can see that I was right. The capital W gives it away. It's the same loopy letter for the 'With' inside the cover of the book as for the 'Wake' on the card that was underneath the dead flowers in the box.

I think my heart has been thumping fast for a few minutes, but I only register it now. I also become aware that my calf muscles have become numb, so I sit on the floor with my back against the bed and kick my legs out in front of me. Still clutching the book in one hand and the card in the other, I ask myself what this means.

Nicola. I try to remember her surname. Todd, that's it. Nicola Todd. A friend of Alex's on Facebook, and clearly one of his exes. She's the one who gave Alex this book. And it's her handwriting on the card. So, she's the one who sent the poppies and violets with their heads snapped off. No, she didn't *send* them. She *delivered* the flowers to our door. She knows where we live. She probably even lived here once herself.

A voice inside my head warns me not to say anything about this to Alex. He'll know I've opened Pandora's box in the guestroom if I tell him I know who has been trying to scare us. Then I reason that I don't know Nicola or how to find her. She could be dangerous. But Alex knows who she is and he'll know where she is. I have to tell him.

I get up and throw everything back into the box, including the book, and send a text message to Alex.

Hi Alex. Please can you come home early? I need to talk to you.
XXX.

I go back into the bedroom, where Chloe is still sleeping peacefully, and I check out Nicola Todd on Facebook. But there's no more to see than there was the other day, and I'm certain I've never seen her before. There's no reason for me to have met her if she's Alex's ex-girlfriend. I zoom in on her face. Her long hair partly covers her face, but I can see that she's very attractive, although I think she'd probably be prettier still if she smiled. She looks very serious in this photo. Maybe even a little sad.

Alex doesn't reply to my text, but he arrives home at five. I'm getting dinner ready, with Chloe in the baby carrier. Alex sits down at the kitchen table, so I hand Chloe to him and she babbles blissfully on her daddy's lap.

'Got your message,' Alex says. 'What's up?'

'Alex, remember the day we received that parcel with the dead flowers inside?'

'How could I forget?'

'Well, there's something I didn't tell you at the time, because, well ... you didn't look like you could take any more and I've only just realised you might know who it is.'

Alex says nothing, but he furrows his brows.

'You see, under the flowers there was a card. Written by

201

someone called Nicola.' I haven't actually lied although it strikes me that I'm getting really good at twisting the truth when I need to. 'Anyway, today I was looking at the profiles of some of your Facebook friends and I noticed you're friends with someone called Nicola Todd.'

Alex's eyes widen.

'So I was wondering who she is and if she would have any reason to … intimidate us.'

'She was my girlfriend once, a long time ago now. Maybe she has heard about you, or she's heard I've got married and she's jealous.'

'She'd have to be insanely jealous to pull a stunt like that, Alex. The dead poppies and violets looked like a warning or a threat.'

Alex nods. 'You're right. I'm not in touch with her anymore. I didn't even realise we were still connected via Facebook. But I'll sort this out. I'll sort *her* out. Leave it to me.'

Alex and I have dinner and watch *Top of the Lake* on TV even though we've missed all of the previous episodes and neither of us has a clue what's going on.

Alex chooses this evening to open the bottle of Irish whiskey I bought him for his birthday. He even uses the glass I gave him. He fetches me some wine. With Nicola Todd on my mind, I don't feel like bringing up my childcare plans. Instead, we talk and laugh for hours. The later it gets, the more the whiskey and wine slur our words.

When we finally go to bed, I don't feel tired. The bedside light doesn't seem to disturb Alex and I read a bit as he sleeps soundly next to me. After that, I waste some time on my mobile, looking through my photos and deleting some of my old emails, mainly from university. I check my Calendar and I'm surprised by how few dates have an entry for the weeks to come. That has to change.

After a while, I tiptoe downstairs to make a cup of tea. I catch sight of myself in the full-length mirror as I come back into the bedroom with my mug in my hand. I do a double take. I still haven't got used to having short hair. I smile at myself and see my grin in the mirror.

It's my reflection that gives me the jolt. It suddenly hits me and my amusement turns to shock. I jump and spill some tea, scalding myself. My breathing becomes erratic and I have to concentrate on it to ward off a panic attack.

You lied to me! I think, sitting down on the bed. *How could you?*

I'm overwhelmed by a sense of betrayal. *I trusted you!*

Feeling absolutely murderous, I close my eyes and concentrate on breathing in and out. I force myself to sip my tea. I'm no calmer, but my thoughts are lucid as I ask myself what I should do about this.

I take my time and compose the words in my head until they sound right. Then, careful not to wake Alex, I pick up my mobile again and I tap it out. My finger hovers over the screen, but I don't hesitate for long before sending the text message. I don't think I'm wrong. But if I am, I'll put it down to a slip of the tongue. Or a typo.

Chapter 19

I know I'm going to burst into tears again. I've spent most of the night crying. I think I even cried in my sleep as each time I woke up, my eyes were sore. I don't think I woke up Alex, luckily, and I pretended to be asleep when he got up to get ready for work. I want to get up, too, but I can't quite find it in me, so I sit on the edge of the bed for a while, hugging myself with my arms and rocking backwards and forwards until I'm strong enough to swing myself to my feet.

In the shower, I tilt my head back and let the water from the jet mingle with my tears and wash them away. I don't know how long I stand there, but when I get out, the mirror is steamed up, which, I think, is a good thing. I can imagine how I look. Puffy-faced and red-eyed. I don't need to see it.

My mobile is ringing as I step into the bedroom. It's Julie.

'Hi. How are things with you?' she asks. She doesn't sound very happy.

I don't answer straight away. I don't know what to say. 'Mustn't grumble,' I say in the end. Isn't that what you're supposed to say when your world is falling apart? 'I've been thinking, I'd like to come home again sometime soon,' I add. 'For a weekend. It did Chloe and me a lot of good to stay at Dad's.'

Then my heart skips a beat when Julie doesn't respond.

'Is everything all right? Is everyone OK?'

'Well, Dad could probably do with you coming home for a while, too,' she says. 'That's why I'm ringing really. Jet might have to be put down.'

'Oh, no! Why? Has he had an accident?'

Dad must be devastated.

'No, he has lymphoma. He—'

'What?'

'He has cancer. Of the lymphocytes. Dad was worried because Jet wasn't eating. So he took him to the vet's.'

'I should have known something was wrong. Jet didn't seem to want to go out for walks and didn't even jump up to greet me in the mornings when I stayed at Dad's.'

'Yes, Dad said that, too,' Julie says.

'So, Jet has to be put down?'

'Maybe. The cancer is quite widespread, apparently. He can have chemo, but it will only give him a bit longer. He won't get better.'

I'm crying. Again. Julie sounds choked up, too. This is an awful thing to happen to Dad. Mum died of cancer, although Dad always says she died because she lost her will to live the day she lost Louisa.

'Poor Dad. Poor Jet.'

'I know.' Julie pauses and for a moment I think we've lost the connection. Then I hear her voice again. 'Dad is worried that Jet's suffering too much despite the painkillers. Jet is ten now. And I don't think Dad wants to watch him get weaker and weaker until he … you know.'

'Yes, I do.' I know exactly what Julie is thinking. Dad will relive the loss of his wife through the loss of his dog. 'I'll have a word with Alex and see how soon we can come.'

205

'OK. I need to get going. I've got to get to work. Are you sure *you*'re OK?'

'Don't worry about me. I'll be fine.'

'I do worry about you. You're my little sister. I'm in a rush right now. I'll call you again soon.'

As I put the phone down on the bedside table, lost in my thoughts, I knock something to the floor. It's the medicine I nearly took when I had a headache. I pick up the packet and put it back next to the phone. I could have asked Julie what it is, although it doesn't seem at all important right now. Everything is paling into insignificance next to my friend's treachery and my sister's bad news.

I get dressed, see to Chloe and then have breakfast before calling Alex to let him know about Jet. He says he'd like to drive down to Porlock with me, but he has a competition this weekend and as it's Friday today, it's too late to scratch from the race.

'At the end of next week, I'm away on business for a few days,' he continues. 'How about the weekend after that? The first weekend in September?'

His voice is fainter and I imagine him holding his smartphone in front of him to examine the events in his Calendar. I already know I have nothing on.

'Sounds good,' I say, wishing we could go sooner, but grateful for Alex's support. 'I'll tell Julie when she rings back.'

The weather is good, much brighter than yesterday, although dark clouds loom ominously on the horizon. I decide to get out and go for a walk. As well as his shop, Alex runs a water sports centre at the Derwent Water Marina, near Keswick, so I park there. I lift Chloe out of the car and into the baby carrier, strapped to my chest. Then I text Alex to see if he's at the centre, thinking we could pop by and say hello, but he texts back to say he's at the shop today.

It's ten miles if you go the whole way round the lake, according to Alex, who sometimes runs around it during his lunch break.

He says it's relatively flat and wonderfully scenic. I slip my mobile into the front pocket of my rucksack, which has a bottle of water and a sandwich in it for me, and everything I need to feed and change Chloe. Then I set off clockwise to do the Derwentwater Walk.

There are a lot of people out walking, and the happy faces of the people we pass cheer me up a little. About halfway round, I find a nice stretch of stony shore to sit on and eat my lunch. I take a towel out of my rucksack to lay Chloe on and I gaze at the hills on the far side of the lake, their purplish tops standing out against the cloudy sky, the whole colourful scene reflected in the water.

There are lots of people on the lake, too, in the distance, in rowing boats, on paddleboards, swimming or windsurfing. Sometimes their shrieks of excitement reach my ears, or the splashes they make when they fall into the water, but mostly it's calm and almost deathly quiet. Until a stick lands in the water just in front of me, and a golden retriever bounds in after it, breaking up the stillness of the water as well as the silence. I turn my head, half-expecting to see Vicky, but instead an elderly man shouts encouragement to his dog from the lakeshore.

I'm instantly reminded of Dad and Jet, and an immense wave of sadness crashes over me. I remember I'd planned to take Jet out to Hurlstone Point with me when I was down in Porlock. It occurs to me that I may never get to go on a walk with Jet again. I also think how much Shadow, Vicky's golden retriever, would love it here. But I don't suppose I'll be going on a walk with them again, either.

The goldie comes running out of the water, up to its owner, but refuses to let go of the stick. The man tugs at it, but the dog shakes its head, turning the stick from side to side, as if to emphasise its refusal. Then it lets go suddenly and the old man stumbles backwards, catching his step and laughing as his dog shakes its whole body and sprays him with drops of water. I should find the scene amusing, but I feel low. I've been reminded of the very things I wanted to forget for a while.

The sky gets more and more menacing as I continue on my walk, and I speed up my pace, hoping to make it back to the car before it starts to rain. But in the end, the rain doesn't come, although daylight seems to be struggling by early evening as I arrive home.

As I unpack my rucksack and pull out my mobile, I notice I have two text messages. Both from her. I have no intention of replying, but I read the messages anyway. The first one says, *I'm so sorry. I can explain. Can we talk?* What catches my eye is her name underneath. It's the first time she has ever signed her texts. It's not the same spelling as I used – I only changed the first letter – but she has obviously realised from the text I sent her last night that I know. I know who she is and what she did.

If the first message makes me sad, the second makes me angry. And a little scared. *Please call me, for your sake. You're in danger.* And, again, underneath, her name: *Nikki.* Is there a subtext that I'm not getting? I can't tell if it's a threat or a warning, just as when I read the words she'd written on the card with the dead flowers.

I don't want to reply. I don't want to talk to her. I'm stung by her duplicity. She lied to me. Then I realise, she didn't actually, not really. Not technically. She must have told me her name was Nikki the day I met her in the swimming pool. I misheard and she didn't correct me. She probably thought she could use that to her advantage. If I told Alex I'd met someone called Vicky, he wouldn't cotton on that I'd befriended his ex-girlfriend. Or that she'd befriended me, because I suspect now that she orchestrated our first meeting at the pool.

I remember her colleague, Ruth, who seemed confused when I asked for Vicky at the estate agency in Ambleside. Her other colleague, Dennis, hadn't been very forthcoming, either. No wonder. They know her as Nicola. Nicola Todd. I remember, too, she declined my invitation to Alex's barbecue, saying she quite liked the idea of being kept a secret.

But far worse than all of that is that she pretended to be my friend. It's not just what she didn't say; it's what she did. She held me while I cried, and she comforted me, and yet she'd caused some of my pain. She listened when I told her about the box of dead flowers with its disturbing message when she'd been behind that all along. And then she offered to help me. *Why?*

I wonder if she was taking revenge somehow. I replay some of our conversations in my head and try to read between the lines. If she was telling the truth, it seems more than likely that the fiancé she told me about, who treated her badly and split up with her, was Alex. Did he throw her out so I could move in? That would certainly explain why she'd have it in for me. And yet, I really did think we were becoming friends. And if she'd wanted to make me pay, she'd had ample opportunity to do a better job of it. I sigh.

Unbidden, the image of Nicola Todd's face from her Facebook profile picture forces its way into my head. I close my eyes, but I can still see her behind my eyelids. Her long hair in the photo. The serious look on her face. It was when I was surprised at my reflection in the mirror last night that I realised. I'd forgotten Hannah had cut my hair. It made me smile. And then I saw her. The Vicky I know, or thought I knew, with her short hair and wide grin.

Next, I visualise Alex's face the day we were walking along The Coffin Trail. He pretended to be scared of the little white dog, but in fact he was reeling with the shock of seeing Vicky. No, *Nikki*. He must have been terrified she would say something to me – or to him – as we passed her.

I suddenly realise I've dropped Nikki in it. I implied to Alex that the card with the flowers was signed 'Nicola'. He said he would 'sort her out'. What did he mean by that? And she thinks I'm in danger. Does she think that Alex might harm me? In that case, Nikki may be in danger herself.

But then I reason, Alex has been an utter bastard to both of us, but he's not dangerous. I've been giving my imagination free rein and blowing this up out of all proportion. I'll have to talk to Nikki at some point, I suppose, if only to understand her motives and intentions. I decide to call her after all. But not today. I'm not ready yet. I'll do it tomorrow.

Chapter 20

I've switched the ringer to silent, but I can feel my phone vibrating in my back pocket again as I walk past The Moot Hall. It's bound to be her. I know I resolved to talk to Nikki today, but I still can't face it.

It's always heaving in town on Saturdays, but today Keswick seems to be even more packed than usual. There are groups of tourists spilling out from the Information Centre or milling around in front of it. And I'd completely forgotten it was market day. I regret coming here now. Everyone seems to be walking in the opposite direction to me and as I weave Chloe's pram in and out of the multitudes of people making their way down Keswick High Street, it's as if I'm trying to swim upstream.

After a while, I feel as though I'm struggling to keep my head above water and I wonder if it's possible to drown on dry land. It's hard to breathe; I'm choking. I stop and bend forwards, using the pram to support me and forcing myself to take deep breaths. What am I doing here?

The plan was to buy a present for Dad to cheer him up a bit.

When Julie and Hannah came here just before my wedding, Julie spotted a waterproof wax jacket she said Dad would love in the window of a sports shop.

It's a bad idea, I realise. Firstly, Alex will go mental if I buy something in a sports shop that's not his. And secondly, I expect Dad would have worn it to go out for walks, and as Jet isn't likely to be around for much longer, it's a stupid idea for a gift. Moreover, it's unlikely, six months on, that it's still in the shop window or even available in the same shop.

Why on earth did I come here? And I don't just mean Keswick. I don't belong here and I never will. I don't know why it's taken me so long to realise this, but it's crystal clear now.

A woman barges into me and walks on without apologising. I don't know whether to yell at her or cry. I turn around and head back to the car, feeling both angry with myself and disappointed.

I should drive back to the Old Vicarage, but I don't find the thought of going home very appealing right now, either. I pull out of the car park, functioning on automatic pilot. After a while, it dawns on me that I've passed the turning I should have taken for Grasmere. I don't know where I am. I've been driving around aimlessly. I start to read the signposts. At a junction, I realise I'm somewhere between Ambleside and Troutbeck.

And then I recognise the road I'm on. It takes me a while to find it, but finally I pull up outside the right house. Her mum's silver car is in the driveway, but Vicky's black company car isn't there. Vicky – *Nikki* – works every other Saturday. I stare at the front door for a few minutes, wondering what I would do if it opened or if Nikki did arrive home. Then my eyes fix on the car.

I don't know why the thought didn't cross my mind before. I'd forgotten all about the grey car in front of the Old Vicarage that day. The one that crawled by as I was closing the gate at the bottom of the driveway. It spooked me because I thought I saw the same car a little later when I came back from doing the shopping. Of course, I can't be sure. I'm hopeless with car makes and models. And grey is such a nondescript colour. But I have a feeling my suspicions are right. I have a feeling Nikki was spying on me that day.

As I turn the key in the ignition, it occurs to me that I'm now sitting in my car peering at her house, just as I imagine she was driving past that day, in her mum's car, trying to get a good look at the Old Vicarage. The roles have been reversed. Is this what I've stooped to? Spying on my husband's ex-girlfriend? I type Grasmere into the satnav and see that I'm facing the wrong way. Turning the car round, I start heading for home.

'Alex,' I call, as I step over the threshold into the entrance hall. I try not to shout too loudly since Chloe is sleeping. Leaving the pram in the hall, I go into the kitchen to make a cup of tea. There's a Post-it next to the kettle, a yellow one this time, but it still reminds me of the orange Post-it I didn't get. Sighing, I read it.

In Bassenthwaite with my teammates.
Checking out the course for the triathlon
tomorrow. Back in a bit. I'll make us spag bol for
dinner. Alexxx

Flicking on the kettle, I decide to curl up with my book in the sitting room until Chloe wakes up. It will take my mind off Nikki. I run upstairs to fetch my book from the bedside table. As I pick it up, I catch sight of Alex's pills. I didn't put them back in the cupboard with his whisky, but if he noticed, he hasn't said anything. I grab the box of tablets, too.

Moments later, I'm sitting on the sofa with my tea steaming on the coffee table in front of me. Taking my mobile out of my handbag, I see that I've had two missed calls, but I want to relax right now. I'll ring Nikki later. Holding the packet out in front of me, I read the name of the drug out aloud, syllable by syllable.

Flu - ni - tra - ze - pam and I type it into the search engine of my mobile.

I glance at the results and a few keywords stand out. At first I think there must be a mistake. As I stare at them, the words seem to come away from the screen towards me. And then they blur. But I saw them. *Rohypnol*. And *date rape drug*.

Why on earth would Alex have kept that drug in his whisky cupboard?

Just then, the phone vibrates in my hand with an incoming call, making me jump and drop the packet of pills. It's Julie. I swipe the screen to take the call.

'Hi, Kaitlyn,' she says. 'I was beginning to think I'd never get hold of you!'

I can hear the overtone of criticism in her voice. I realise the missed calls must have been from Julie, not Nikki as I'd assumed.

'I'm so sorry, Julie. I went out to buy Dad a present to let him know I was thinking of him. But there were hordes of people in town and in the end I gave up and came home.'

I'm gushing. The words are coming out of my mouth without me thinking about what I'm saying. The words in my head, though, are clear: 'Rohypnol' and 'date rape drug'.

'I thought I'd ring you back,' Julie is saying when I manage to tune in again, 'seeing as I didn't have time to chat before work the other day.'

We talk for a while about Dad, my brief sentences punctuated with thoughts that have nothing to do with our conversation.

There must be an explanation.

I tell Julie that Alex and I will come down the first weekend in September.

'The weekend of the 2nd and 3rd of September or the weekend after that?' Julie asks.

Isn't it mixed with alcohol when it's used in sexual assaults?

'The weekend of the 2nd, I think,' I say, twisting around on

214

the sofa and looking at the cupboard where Alex stocks his whisky. 'I'll check with Alex and send you a text.'

It must be prescribed for something. It must have a therapeutic effect.

'You sound distracted.'

It doesn't look like it was prescribed, though. There's no patient information leaflet for one thing, although that might have been discarded. But there's hardly anything written on the box, either. No laboratory name. Just the name of the drug.

'Julie, can I ask you a question?'

'Sure. Fire away.'

'What would Flunitrazepam be taken for?'

'Well, it's better known as Rohypnol or the Date Rape Drug.'

Those words again. 'I know that.' There's a pointed silence on the other end of the phone. 'Sorry, Julie. I didn't mean to snap. Could it be used in doping … for athletes, I mean?'

'It might be a banned substance in sport, I don't know about that, but it wouldn't improve your performance if you took it, put it that way. No. It used to be prescribed for patients having difficulty sleeping.'

'Used to be?'

'Well, for all I know, it still is, but I expect there's far better medication for insomnia. Flunitrazepam is horribly addictive and the withdrawal symptoms can be very unpleasant.'

'I see,' I say, although I'm still none the wiser as to what these tablets were doing in the drinks cupboard.

'Why do you ask?'

'Um …' I can't come up with anything plausible off the top of my head. Why should I lie, anyway? 'I found a packet of tablets in a cupboard and wondered if it was OK to take them for a headache.' Not the full truth, but at least it's true.

'Well, I wouldn't take them if I were you,' Julie chuckles, 'unless you want to knock yourself out.'

Julie and I say our goodbyes, and I promise to confirm the

dates for our visit to Somerset. After I end the call, I think over everything my sister has told me about Flunitrazepam. Addictive. Withdrawal symptoms. She seemed certain it wouldn't enhance an athlete's performance. Prescribed for insomnia. Though the more I look at this discreet packaging, the more I'm convinced Alex didn't get this from the doctor's. I think he ordered this online. But the question remains: *What for?*

Surely not for insomnia. Alex has never had difficulty sleeping. He always sleeps like a baby. Even when we argue, he rolls over and he's sound asleep in mere minutes. It doesn't make sense.

I can hear Chloe making funny sighing and cooing noises in the hallway. She has woken up. I pick the tablets up from the floor where I dropped them when Julie rang. I put them away in the cupboard, pushing them out of sight behind Alex's bottle of Glenfiddich, where I found them in the first place. Hopefully, Alex never noticed they were gone.

Making my way out to the hall, I decide to leave this for now. I need to have a think. I'm not sure why the Flunitrazepam seems important. But I don't want to confront Alex just yet. I need answers, but I won't get them from him.

It's as I'm picking up Chloe that it suddenly comes to me. At first, I don't believe it. Then I feel so dizzy that I have to put Chloe back in the pram and let myself sink down to the floor. My earlier thoughts echo in my head. *Alex always sleeps like a baby*. The linguist in me ponders that expression as I sit on the floor. I suppose the idea is a baby has no real worries and can rest easy.

But it always seemed to me that Chloe slept deeply rather than peacefully. I thought she must be exhausted from the wailing she kept up for most of her waking hours and that she just conked out. She used to wake up screaming again. She wouldn't breast-feed and we had to give her the bottle.

Chloe was calm for Alex. She wasn't calm for me until I took her to Somerset. And she has been calm ever since.

I make a vain effort to push my thoughts out of my head before they are fully formulated. Alex is an excellent father. He wouldn't hurt Chloe, would he? But the more I tell myself I'm jumping to conclusions, the more I convince myself that I'm right.

Alex has been drugging our baby.

Did Chloe refuse to breastfeed because she was addicted to the drug Alex was spiking her milk with? Did she get distressed because she was experiencing withdrawal symptoms?

She's been calm ever since we went to Somerset. How odd she didn't start wailing again when we got back. But as that goes through my mind, I realise I already have the counterargument. Since we've been back at the Old Vicarage, the tablets have been on my bedside table.

Why would Alex do that? Why would he drug Chloe?

Chloe starts to whimper in the pram. I leave her there while I go to make up a bottle, not trusting myself to stay upright. My legs are heavy and unresponsive as I walk through the hallway, as if they're sinking in quicksand. In the kitchen, I lean over the sink, feeling both dizzy and sick.

As I straighten up again, I look through the barred windows and fix my gaze on the damson tree. I marvel that it's still standing there, not because it's leaning at such an improbable angle, but because my world is falling down and my marriage is falling apart, and somehow it seems like the house, the tree and the swing should all collapse, too. I can't quite comprehend how everything looks the same when everything has changed.

While I feed and bath Chloe, I turn the radio on to try and drown out the voices in my head. But then I think I should pay attention to them, so I switch off the meaningless background noise. The silence in the large house unnerves me, however, and I find myself pacing up and down the hallway with Chloe in my arms as I wait for Alex to come home. I feel as if my world has been twisted inside out. I've never wanted to be wrong so much in my life.

After a while, I bring down Chloe's playmat and leave her lying on it in the living room while I go into the kitchen and pour myself a large glass of white wine. I down it without tasting it, as if I were parched and the wine were water. Without thinking, I pour myself another glass and take several huge gulps of that before topping up the glass and taking it and the bottle into the living room. Watching over Chloe, I force myself to take sips, although the temptation to knock it all back is very strong.

I've just drained the last drop of wine when I hear Alex's car on the gravel outside. My heart pounding, I pick Chloe up and carry her upstairs. It's not her bedtime, but I lay her in her cot, drawing the curtains and leaving on a light. I put some toys in her cot and admonish myself for breaking her mobile the other day. She seems happy enough, though.

When I turn around, Alex is standing in the doorway of Chloe's bedroom. I didn't hear him come up the stairs and he startles me.

'Is she asleep already?' he asks.

'No,' I answer curtly, brushing past him. He follows me down the stairs and into the living room.

'Something wrong?'

I whirl round, my fists clenching and unclenching at my sides. 'Alex, did you …? Alex, why did you drug Chloe?'

I expect him to deny it, but he says, 'You won't be able to prove it.' His mouth twists into an ugly snarl. 'I'll say you did it. I'll say you needed to sleep because of your post-natal depression.'

His words render me speechless. It's several seconds before I find my tongue. 'Alex, I'm not suffering from depression and I never have been,' I hiss at him.

'Ah, but everyone thinks you are. Doctor Irving, your sister, my mother.' He counts them off on his fingers and laughs cruelly.

'You bastard, Alex. Why? Why did you give our daughter sleeping tablets?'

He plops down onto the sofa and runs his hands through his

hair. The fact he has sat down enrages me. He's not fazed by this in the slightest.

'Well, initially so she'd sleep,' he says.

I wait for Alex to say more, but he seems to have clammed up. I've worked it out for myself though. When I fed her, the milk wasn't spiked. It made him look like a great father when she was calm for him, and it made me feel like an incompetent mother when she was agitated with me. I had no confidence in myself and I felt worthless. This made me dependent on Alex. Alex needs to feel needed. He has to be idealised and idolised.

Feeling as though I will explode with rage, I turn on my heels and make my way upstairs. I expect him to follow me again, but he doesn't. I'm not really aware of what I'm doing as I pull my bags and suitcases down from the top of the wardrobe and out from under the bed and start to pack my clothes. Blinded by tears, I keep throwing in underwear, T-shirts, pairs of jeans and cardigans. I'm feeling a little unsteady and very sick and I'm not sure if it's the shock or the alcohol.

I realise I haven't planned my next move at all. I know I need to be one step ahead of Alex at all times, but I haven't thought this through. Deep down I was hoping so hard that I was wrong. I didn't think further than confronting Alex. Here I am, packing my bags, but I can't go anywhere. Not tonight. I scold myself for being so stupid. I've drunk almost a whole bottle of wine. I'm well over the limit and I have nowhere to go unless I drive all the way to Somerset. I'll have to wait until tomorrow.

But that doesn't stop me. When I've filled one suitcase and a big holdall, I tiptoe into Chloe's bedroom. She has fallen asleep. I look around the room, at the two single beds that Poppy and Violet used to sleep in. Alex promised to make this into a nursery and take out those beds to let in some light. But he never got round to it. There won't be any point now.

I take some clothes out of Chloe's chest of drawers and carry them back into my bedroom. As I'm zipping up the second case, the hairs on the back of my neck stand up. I haven't heard a sound, but I can sense Alex behind me. Standing up, I turn round to face him.

'Don't go,' he says. He's pleading. 'I fucked up. I only wanted to look good in your eyes.'

'Alex, I can't stay. Not after this.'

'You promised you'd never leave me. You can't leave me.' This time his voice has hardened. It's not a plea. It's an order. An interdiction.

I should have taken that as a warning sign. At the very least, I should have moved away from him. But when he does it, I'm caught completely off-guard. Ironically, I've often thought he was about to hit me but he never did. And this time, he does strike me and I didn't see it coming.

His blow has knocked me to the floor. I can taste blood and realise that my lip is split. It's the first time he has ever hit me and I think he's as shocked as I am.

'I'm so sorry,' he says, kneeling on the carpet next to me. 'Oh, Kaitlyn, I'm sorry. I promise you, it won't ever happen again.'

On that at least, we agree, but we're not on the same page. Not by any stretch of the imagination. I think this might be the first time he has ever apologised properly, and apart from on the day of our wedding, when he pronounced his vows, it's the first time I've ever heard him call me by my full first name. I hated his abbreviation. Katie. It sounded truncated, as if he were belittling me by undermining my identity. But now he has used my full first name, I don't want that either. I no longer want that intimacy.

I'm in a daze, my head spinning from the pain. I let him help me to my feet and sit me down on the bed, where I wait for him as he runs downstairs and comes back with frozen peas wrapped in a tea towel. Gently, he presses the ice to my face. All trace of the angry monster he turned into a few minutes ago has gone.

'Stay here tonight,' he says. 'We can discuss this tomorrow.'

I nod. I have no choice but to stay. But I have no intention of discussing this with him. I'll be gone first thing tomorrow morning with Chloe. I don't feel in any immediate danger anymore. The storm in Alex has blown over. Knowing Alex, he'll be contrite and loving now.

'As soon as I get back from Bassenthwaite tomorrow, we'll work this out.'

He's still planning on doing his bloody race. Unbelievable! Some people climb mountains to see the world. Alex runs and cycles up hills so the world can see him.

I try hard not to shudder as he pulls my sweater off over my head and tugs at my jeans. My heart starts thumping inside my chest. Surely he doesn't expect me to make love to him? He wouldn't rape me, would he? But he leaves my underwear on and dresses me in my pyjamas, then helps me into bed and tucks me in like a little girl before leaving the room.

I lie there, wide awake, for a few hours. It's strange to think that this is my last night here. The last time I will sleep in this bed, in this house. This is the second time I've decided to walk out on my life, but I haven't really been living it. Instead, I've been trapped in a life that has never felt like my own.

There's no way I can stay now. My husband has drugged my daughter and struck me. There's no getting past that. But Alex must realise this, and that troubles me. So, I think about trying to get away now, in the middle of the night. If Chloe wakes up when I take her from her cot, she might wake Alex. I have no idea how he'll react if he catches me leaving. But I don't want to wait until the morning. I have to get out of here.

At 3 a.m., when I'm pretty sure Alex is asleep in the guestroom, I get up and get dressed. I've never felt so sober in my life. The pain in my face from Alex's punch is excruciating, but I already know I have no painkillers in the house.

I hear a noise coming from a bedroom along the landing. Alex is awake. At first I can't identify the noise. I open my bedroom door just a crack, enough to peep into the corridor and see that the light is on in the peach bedroom. Now I know what he's doing. He's ripping the tape off the cardboard box he keeps in the wardrobe.

I close the door and lean against it. My breaths are shallow. What is he looking for in the box? What should I do?

Suddenly, he bursts through the door into the bedroom and I'm sent sprawling across the room.

'You can't ever go,' he says. His voice makes my blood run cold. 'You won't get custody of Chloe if you do. Not if they think you were the one who drugged her.'

His words have much the same effect on me as his punch earlier.

Then I see what he's holding in his hand.

'No, Alex, no,' I beg. 'We'll talk this over tomorrow, like you said.'

But I can tell from the gleam in his cruel blue eyes and the object dangling from his hand that we're beyond words now.

Chapter 21

I wake from one nightmare into another, shivering in a pool of sweat. My heart is pounding relentlessly just like the rain outside, which I can hear rather than see from my supine position. I feel every fibre in my being screaming out, but the sound is trapped deep inside me. The sock he has stuffed in my mouth and taped over doesn't help. Why he felt it was necessary to gag me, I can't imagine. I could scream myself hoarse and no one would hear me from here.

Alex has left me lying here. I've been here for three nights and three days. He comes in three times a day. And when he does, he doesn't utter a single word. Over the last twenty-four hours, I've tried several times to remember the last words he has spoken to me. In case they turn out to be the last words I ever hear.

I can't remember the words Louisa's rapist said, either. It's always the same. It's a recurrent dream of mine, her nightmare, and every time I re-create it as if the whole incident happened to me and not to her. But, when it's over, I can never recall the words her attacker whispered in her ear before he walked away.

The words my twin sister told me would be etched in her mind forever.

Usually, when I wake up from this, my first thought is the realisation that this was Louisa's ordeal, not mine. I'm just a helpless spectator, reliving her experience by proxy. While Louisa's life was destroyed forever that day, I can get up, walk away and live my life. Usually.

But not today. Today I'm stuck in my own nightmare. Handcuffed to a bed. One of the single beds in the nursery. The bed on the right, the one my sister compared to a coffin targeted by poison arrows. I'm a prisoner in my own home. *Breathe in. Breathe out.* Easy to think, not so easy to do when I'm on the verge of another panic attack with a gag in my mouth. I can't get enough air through my nostrils.

I turn towards Chloe. I can just make out her sleeping form through the bars of the cot. I watch her until she wakes up too, then listen to her as she chatters away in her baby language for a while, surprising herself with the new sounds she can make. After a few minutes, hunger sets in and she starts to whimper and then cry. Bound and gagged, I can't get to her. I can't even sing to her. Feeling utterly helpless, I start to whimper myself.

It seems like several hours pass before I hear the front door slam. Just as for the previous two evenings, it's a while before Alex comes upstairs to the nursery. I imagine him pouring himself a whisky and making the meal first. Taking his time. I'm not going anywhere.

Every day, it's the same routine. I wake up handcuffed to the bed. He feeds and changes Chloe here in the nursery and lays her back down in the cot before fetching me breakfast. I'm allowed to use the bathroom while he watches. He ties me to the bed again before leaving for work. At lunchtime, he pops home from work, but he doesn't stay long. I don't get fed, but Chloe does, thankfully. I do, however, get to go to the toilet and drink some water from the tap. In the evenings, he takes Chloe downstairs for a while and when it's her bedtime, he brings her back to the nursery. Then he brings me dinner and finally he lets me take a shower and clean my teeth.

I'm trapped in a time loop. It feels like the film *Groundhog Day* I watched with Louisa when we were thirteen or fourteen. Except that I wonder if I'll ever escape it or if I'm doomed to live the same day for the rest of my life. I'm not sure if I'll ever work out what I need to do to escape.

Ironically, I can't wait for him to come. Not because I'm hungry. I have no appetite. No, I'm looking forward to his visit because time goes so slowly here. Although he won't speak to me, his presence is a welcome distraction. And I can take a shower and feel ever so slightly human again. And above all, as I'm unable to hold my own baby, feed her, change her and comfort her, Chloe needs Alex to do that.

There must be a way to get round him. I replay the evening drill over in my head to see if there's a moment when this opportunity arises. I have to make a move when he's least expecting it. I close my eyes to try and see more clearly. But it's hard to see a way out when there isn't one and when I open them again, everything is just as muddled and murky. If I do manage to grab Chloe and make a dive out of the door, how far am I going to get before he catches up with me? If I'm fast, I might just about make it down the stairs and as far as the front door. And even if I did make it as far as the drive, I'd be barefoot, with Chloe in my arms. Alex is a runner. I wouldn't stand a chance.

My mind wanders back to Louisa. She was a runner, but she didn't manage to get away from her attacker. She used to win all the school cross-country races. She won the day she was raped. I'd skived off school because I didn't want to compete. I should have been with her, walking by her side as she took the short cut through the woods on her way home that day. If I'd gone to school, Louisa would still be alive. She wouldn't have been raped and she wouldn't have committed suicide.

The door opens and Alex comes in. He picks up Chloe, who is screaming now, and leaves the room again, cradling our baby in his arms. I'm left in the nursery, alone apart from the fairies frozen mid-flight on the walls, observing me.

When Alex comes back, I need to be alert. Anything that he does or doesn't do that differs from the usual routine could be my chance. In the meantime, I need to keep building up his trust. That way, he might lower his guard.

More time ticks by. When Alex has laid Chloe, clean and calm once more, in her cot, he fetches my tray. He puts it down on the bed next to me and puts his index finger against his lips. When I nod, he rips off my duct tape, making me wince from the sting. Then he removes my gag and I gulp in the air, greedily.

I decide to talk. Alex has decided, for reasons known only to him, not to speak to me. He doesn't even speak to Chloe, at least, not in front of me. But it doesn't mean I have to be mute.

'Thank you,' I say.

He looks a little surprised. But he's not about to break his silence, apparently.

He takes the key to the handcuffs out of his pocket and releases my wrists. I sit up, rubbing my sore wrists. Not for the first time over the last few days, I scold myself for not taking the key to the handcuffs when I opened that box. Or not taking the handcuffs themselves.

I eat the dinner. Slowly. Partly because it's an effort to keep each mouthful down but also because the longer Alex is here, the more chance I have of coming up with a way to get out of here.

'It's delicious.'

This time he looks at me suspiciously. Time to change tack.

'Alex, is it really necessary to keep me tied up? You could put a lock on the bedroom door and keep me prisoner here without having to attach me to the bed. I could look after Chloe. She needs me.'

I look behind me where the handcuffs are lying on the pillow.

226

I have picked off most of the black fur. I had the idea that the cuffs might be a little larger that way, enabling me to pull my wrists out of them. It didn't work. I merely succeeded in pulling off the skin around my wrists.

He has a smirk on his face and I think he's amused by my one-sided conversation. He sits on the bed, close to me, so close I can smell him, his smell mixed with a tinge of sweat from working all day in warm weather. That familiar scent that once turned me on. Right now, it's making me feel sick. I turn my head away from him and load another forkful of food into my mouth. I have to eat. I need to keep strong for Chloe.

'Do you have to gag me? No one would hear me if I shouted anyway.' If he has taken in a word I'm saying, he gives no sign of it. 'I won't shout, Alex, I promise. But I can't breathe properly with that sock in my mouth. And I'd like to be able to comfort Chloe when she cries.'

I'm not getting anywhere. *Think, Kaitlyn! Think!* He isn't armed. I look around me discreetly for something – anything – I could use as a weapon. He brings me my food with a plastic fork and no knife. I don't think hitting him over the head with the tray will stun him enough. I could make a dive for the bookcase, grab a storybook, but I doubt that will be of any more use than the tray. *Christ, I'm desperate.*

When I've finished eating, Alex nods towards the door. This is my cue to make my way to our en suite bathroom. While Alex stands in the doorway, keeping an eye on me, I strip off and pee and then get into the shower.

I stay for as long as I think I can get away with under the jet. Can I use the hot water somehow? Alex's bottles are lined up the way they always are with the tallest on the right and the smallest on the left. I pick up the bottles and rearrange them. Then I turn a couple of them upside down. I feel a strange sense of satisfaction at this small act of defiance, although it's short-lived. I contemplate hurling the bottles at Alex, but I've always been a terrible shot and even if I hit him with one of them, it wouldn't buy me enough time to get Chloe and myself out of here.

After a few minutes, Alex pulls back the shower curtain and turns off the taps. I stand there, shivering and dripping, hugging myself as Alex looks me up and down. I'm sure he's dying to say something, some vicious remark, but he can't break his self-imposed vow of silence.

Eventually, he hands me my towel. I dry myself slowly and scan the bathroom frantically. A little bird settles on the window-sill, a wren or a sparrow maybe, looking in at me, emphasising just how helpless I am. It's probably sheltering from the rain, but I get the feeling it's taunting me. It can fly away.

There must be something I can use. Then it comes to me. The toothbrush glasses. I could seize one and throw it against the wall, then use a shard as a weapon. Why didn't I think of it before? Alex is holding out my toothbrush for me to clean my teeth. I'll have to act quickly. I walk over to him. Then my heart sinks. Alex has already anticipated this. I hadn't noticed until now, but the glasses have been replaced by plastic beakers.

I catch sight of my face in the mirror on the bathroom cabinet above the sink. My eyes are as red as my bloodied lip and my cheekbone looks sore and bruised. I wince and continue to scan the room in the mirror. Could I smash the mirror? What with? Nothing. There's nothing.

When I'm dry and I've pulled on some pyjamas, he leads me back into the nursery and cuffs me to the bed again. Then, pocketing the key, he pulls the curtains. This signals the end for tonight.

'Talk to me,' I plead. 'Say something. Don't go. Stay here and let's discuss this.'

As Alex turns to go, I scream it. 'TALK TO ME!'

But still he says nothing. Not a word. He leaves the room, leaving me feeling like a failure. I've failed to escape. I've failed my daughter. I start crying and I scold myself for breaking down. *Keep strong, Kaitlyn!*

It takes me several minutes to realise that this time he hasn't gagged me. I have my voice. I'm not sure how that will help me get out of here, but it feels like a start.

I haven't slept much since I've been bound to the bed. But this evening, my body is screaming out for rest. Sleep promises me temporary relief and oblivion. I do like the idea of escaping from all this for a while, although I'm afraid of what I might dream. I'm also afraid of that moment when I wake up, that moment when reality kicks in and reminds me my world has been spun upside down.

I think of Chloe. I must sleep. When my chance of escape comes, I'll need all the strength I can muster. I can breathe more easily now that my airway isn't obstructed and I do sleep for a few hours.

I wake up with a jolt. I don't know what woke me. I have no idea what time it is. The curtains are still drawn and there's not much light in the bedroom. I'd guess it's early in the morning. Too early.

'Alex?'

Something is very wrong, but I'm not sure what it is. My breath comes in short, sharp gasps and they seem to echo in the room. My laboured breathing is the only noise. Everything else is quiet. Too quiet.

I turn my head to the right towards the cot, my eyes becoming accustomed to the dim light. A sudden spike of terror slices through me. *Chloe!* But the sound doesn't leave my lips. My breath has been snatched away. *Chloe!* This time it comes out, a sound somewhere between a yowl and a scream.

Despite the semi-darkness of the room, I can see quite clearly through the bars of the cot. My baby has gone.

229

Chapter 22

I've never experienced a panic like the one that takes hold of me now. It spreads through my whole body as if I've just plunged into a lake of icy-cold water. My baby! He's taken my baby!

I force myself to concentrate on my breathing. I don't know where Chloe is, but I do know that Alex would never harm her. I block out the voice that reminds me he drugged her. I have to believe he wouldn't hurt her, even to hurt me. I have to get out of here. I have to find my baby!

I hear the landline ring. I recall the phone calls to the house when the caller remained silent. On one occasion Alex was there, but he could have rung using his mobile without me noticing. I'd rejected that idea at the time. Now I'm not so sure. Is he messing with my head?

Hearing the phone reminds me that I was supposed to ring Julie back. She'll leave me messages on my mobile to ask why I haven't confirmed dates, but she's more likely to be annoyed than worried. And I haven't replied to any of Nikki's messages. That in itself sends a message. But not the one I want her to get. She'll think I'm ignoring her and give up on me. I need to send her an SOS. As for Hannah, she and I have barely been in touch since she cut my hair. If she does contact me and I don't answer, she might be disappointed, but she won't find it strange. And Dad has other things on his mind. *I* should call *him*, not the other way round.

No one will miss me. Not anytime soon, anyway.

Crying out in frustration, I pull against my restraints. At first I think it's my imagination. Or wishful thinking. But then I twist my left hand. No, it's definitely loose. The cuff on my left hand is loose! Alex hasn't tightened it as much as usual. Trying in vain to shut out the pain and pulling hard, I attempt to free my hand.

In the end, with my wrist and hand throbbing, I'm ready to admit defeat. One last try – I pull with all my might. It hurts so much that I howl. But it works! I've managed to pull my left hand out of the handcuffs.

Immediately, I roll over and start to work on my right hand. But this time I really do have to give up. I can't undo the cuff. I can't even loosen it.

Even though the curtains are drawn, it has got a little lighter, and from my position on my right side, I'm facing the cot. I stare at the empty mattress. My eyes fill with tears. Then my gaze is drawn to something underneath the cot. I'm not sure what it is at first. I blink away the tears and look again. It's the broken mobile.

With my right hand still handcuffed, I roll off the bed onto the floor. Stretching out as far as I can, I can almost reach the broken bits of wood with my feet. Almost. I stretch further, my wrist pulling against its metal restraint. Using my toes, I manage to roll a stick of wood towards me. Then I grab it with my feet. When I'm holding it in my left hand, I allow myself a few seconds to catch my breath.

Getting back on the bed is harder than rolling off. When I'm lying back in position, I hide the stick under my bottom. Now

231

all I have to do is wait. I practise my movements. When I hear Alex, I'll put my left hand back up above my head so that it looks like I'm still cuffed to the bed. I'll have to wait until he has taken out the key to the handcuffs before I make a move. If he goes for my right hand first, I can wait until he frees it. If he goes for my left hand, I'll have to go for the stick and hope I can get the key off him and unlock the right cuff myself.

I'm going to aim for his eye. I'm hoping that I can hurt him enough so that I can get past him and down the stairs. My car keys are on the hook by the front door.

I try to stay focused and replay my escape plan through my mind. But something is troubling me. I turn my head towards the empty cot. Why did he take Chloe away? For the past few days, he has fed her and changed her in here in the morning. He hasn't given me any breakfast this morning. He hasn't even pulled back the curtains. Why the change in routine?

And then I remember Alex's words when I wanted to go to Somerset to be with Dad. *At the end of next week, I'm away on business for a few days.*

He's not coming back. He's going to leave me here. How many days? The reality of my situation soon sinks in. I'm going to die. I'm going to starve to death. Tears flow down my face as images of my daughter stream through my head.

Then I hear it. Footsteps coming up the stairs. I assumed Alex had left. Has he been in the house all this time? I push the fingers of my left hand through the cuff.

I'm ready. As ready as I'll ever be.

I hear the door to the master bedroom close and then footsteps going back down the stairs.

'No!' I scream. 'No! No! Alex! Don't leave me! Come back!'

I'm hysterical, banging my head against the pillow repeatedly and pulling at the cuffs. When I see the handle of the door turn downwards, it takes all the mental and physical strength I can muster to refocus on my plan.

I stare in disbelief as the door opens. It's not Alex. It's Nikki.

Initially, I'm overcome with relief, but then a thought strikes me. What is she doing here? Is she in cahoots with Alex?

'Kaitlyn!' She looks horrified. 'Oh dear God!' She comes over to the bed and sits down next to me. 'Let's get you out of here,' she says. 'Any idea where the key is?'

I can't seem to say anything. I shake my head.

'OK. Well, it looks like a novelty toy,' she says. 'It shouldn't be too difficult.' She's trying to be reassuring, but I can hear the panic in her voice. 'I'll be right back.'

She comes back a minute or so later with bolt cutters without having needed to ask where Alex's toolkit is. In seconds, I'm free. I can't quite believe it and at first I don't move from the bed. Then sitting up, I fling my arms around Nikki, all traces of animosity and mistrust towards her gone.

Nikki studies my face. 'What has he done to you? He hit you, didn't he?'

'Yes, but I'm OK. Chloe! He's taken Chloe!' I shout, leaping up. 'I have to fetch her!'

'Any idea where she might be?'

Yes, but I can't seem to get the message from my brain to my mouth in order to answer. Nikki is still talking and her voice becomes deafening. It's as if she's standing right next to me, shouting at me through a loudspeaker turned up to full volume. And yet I can't make sense of a single word she's saying. She's speaking a foreign language, one I don't understand. The ground starts to shake and I'm thrown off-balance. Nikki catches me and helps me sit down. Her perfume is heady and it's making me dizzy. The light in this room is too bright and I can't see.

Everything comes rushing at me at once, bombarding my body with a sensory overload. I want to cover my ears with my hands, but I can't move. The screaming, the sound of Nikki's voice and the lights all blur into each other and I feel as if I'm stuck on a sickening rollercoaster ride or inside a pinball machine. I want to press pause, stop the world and get off or get out.

When the floor becomes stable underneath me and the room stops spinning, Nikki is sitting next to me, holding me. The screaming stops, too, and I realise it was me all along.

Now when Nikki speaks, it's softer. 'Are you all right?'

I nod. She gets up and disappears along the landing. Then she's back, holding out a plastic beaker of water from the bathroom. My hands are shaking so badly that I need both of them to take it.

'I'm going to call the police,' Nikki says.

'No, don't do that,' I plead. 'Not yet. I have to find Chloe first. And then I need to get out of here. I want to be with my family.'

'In that case, can you stand up?' she asks when I've taken a sip of water. I nod and she helps me to my feet. 'I think we should get out of here,' she says, 'before he comes back.'

'He said he'd be gone for a few days,' I say. My voice is almost inaudible, even to me.

'Let's not take any chances. Where should we look for Chloe?'

'At my mother-in-law's.' My brain is thinking with a lot more lucidity now. 'It's the only place I can think of. There's nowhere else she can be.' I sound more certain than I feel.

My suitcases and bags are on the floor of the master bedroom where I left them, with Chloe's and my clothes still packed inside, ready for us to leave Alex. Nikki and I haul the luggage down the stairs. I take my car keys off the hook in the hall, but Nikki holds out her hand.

'Leave the keys,' she says. 'We'll go in my car. You're in no state to drive.'

'But I was hoping to drive to my dad's once I've got Chloe.' *If I get Chloe.*

'I still think you should go to the police afterwards,' Nikki says, raising an over-pruned eyebrow at me.

Nikki's right, but I really need to be with my family. 'Listen, if Chloe isn't at Sandy's house …' I trail off and swallow. That eventuality doesn't bear thinking about. '… We'll call the police immediately. Otherwise, I'll go to the police station in Minehead as soon as I get to my dad's. I promise.'

'OK. I'll take you to your dad's house, then.'

'You can't drive to Somerset.'

'Why not?'

'It's too far. You can't drive all that way.'

'On the contrary,' says Nikki, 'It's the very least I can do.'

She wriggles the fingers of her outstretched hand and I put my car keys in her palm. She hangs them back on the hook. Nikki has parked her mum's grey hatchback in the driveway and we load the cases and bags into it.

While we're doing this, Nikki fires questions at me and I answer them, filling her in on how I ended up confined to the nursery with a swollen face.

'Why did you come here?' I ask Nikki as we're getting into the car, suddenly suspicious. 'Did you know Alex was keeping me captive?'

'No. I had no idea,' she replies. 'I wanted to see you and I've – well, I've driven past a number of times, but I hadn't seen you leave the house for a few days. I thought you were away, actually, but I wanted to make sure.'

I'm not sure I believe her, and I'm more convinced than ever that it was Nikki driving past in her mum's car that day. She was spying on Alex and me, I know that now, but I'm very glad she was. Otherwise I'd still be stuck in the nursery.

'How did you get into the house?'

She slides her hips forwards in her seat, pushes her hand into the pocket of her black pencil skirt and takes out a key. 'He never asked me to give it back,' she says. I look into the palm of her hand. The front door key. 'I let myself in.'

As Nikki turns the car round, I take one last look at the Old Vicarage. This remote, desolate house that has sadness and despair

235

seeping out of every wall inside. Ironically, from the outside it looks less austere than when I arrived. The creeper, which appeared barren in February, now bears leaves that lend it the illusion of life and hope. This house was the setting for my dreams of a happy family but it became the setting for my nightmares as my home turned into my prison. That was a gradual process. I was trapped long before Alex handcuffed me to the bed.

Nikki pulls out of the driveway. She has left the gate open and she doesn't stop to close it. As I get another whiff of her perfume, a memory stirs. Alex breaking out in hives from head to toe the day I was convinced someone had been in the house.

'You switched Alex's shampoo in the bottles in the shower,' I say, giving her a sidelong glance.

'I knew he was allergic,' she admits, keeping her eyes on the road.

'It made him blotchy all over his body.'

I imagine in other circumstances, we might laugh about this as two scorned women whose man has had a taste of comeuppance. But Nikki shows no sign of amusement. In fact, she doesn't react at all, and I know she's thinking of Chloe right now, as I am. She turns left without asking for directions. She knows the way. She must have been to Sandy's house several times before now. After all, Sandy almost became her mother-in-law instead of mine.

'How did you know?' she asks.

'Your perfume. I smelt it in the house that day.'

For a moment, Nikki doesn't speak. Then she says, 'It's aftershave, actually. I bought it for Alex. He wore it once. That's how I know he's allergic. I really like the fragrance, so I wear it sometimes. It sort of reminded me of him at first, after ... well, after he ended our relationship.'

'When was that exactly?' I ask.

She takes her eyes off the road for a second and looks me in the eye. 'At the end of January. I came home from work one day to discover he'd packed up my things. He broke off our engagement, demanded I give him the ring back and then asked me to leave.' For once, her voice contains no hint of honey; it is flat and cold. 'I didn't see it coming and I didn't get an explanation.'

She takes a deep breath and then continues, 'I lost all our mutual friends. I've no idea what he told them, but they wouldn't speak to me. I had to pack in the triathlon club.'

So those are her medals in the box in the peach room. And that's why she's such a good swimmer. She was a triathlete. It's probably how she met Alex, too, through sport. For the first time, I see Nikki's point of view. I understand what I did to her. I stole her fiancé. She was engaged to Alex, who discarded her and threw her out of the house when I came up to the Lake District to live with him.

I also realise Alex waited until the very last minute before he got Nikki out of the picture. He'd known for several weeks I was pregnant, and yet it sounds like Nikki lived at the Old Vicarage until a few days before I moved in. Perhaps he was boxing up her stuff the very weekend I arrived. I drove all the way up here by myself, as he'd offered to come down by train and share the driving with me, but he let me down at the last minute.

'And you found out about me the day you saw us out walking?'

Nikki nods. 'I could see you were pregnant and I put two and two together.'

This time she doesn't look at me, but I can see that her eyes are glistening with tears.

Talking to Nikki has kept me from going out of my mind with panic about Chloe. But when neither of us speaks, my baby spills into my thoughts and heart again. I've been telling myself that she's in good hands at her grandmother's. Now, though, as Nikki pulls up in front of Sandy's house, I can feel my anxiety levels soaring. What if she's not here?

I've leapt out of the car and raced up the path to Sandy's front door before Nikki has even parked. I hammer on the door. When there's no answer, I pound my fists against the frosted glass. But the door remains closed.

I hear Nikki behind me.

'She's not here,' I say.

'That doesn't mean Chloe's not with Sandy,' Nikki points out. 'Is there a play area or a park near here they could have gone to? Have you got her mobile number?'

Sandy's phone number is in the memory of my mobile. I didn't think to look for my phone before we left. I've got my handbag with my purse in it, hopefully, but no phone. I shake my head.

'Have *you* got her number by any chance?'

'No. I deleted it.'

Just then, I catch sight of Sandy over Nikki's shoulder. She's pushing Chloe's pram towards us, but she hasn't seen us yet. I push past Nikki, and sprint towards my mother-in-law. She stops in her tracks. I can see I've startled her.

'What on earth is wrong, my dear?' she asks, recovering from her shock. 'What has happened to your face?'

'Is Chloe OK? Let me see Chloe!'

Without answering either of her questions, I push her out of the way more roughly than I mean to and she wobbles on her inappropriate shoes as I reach into the pram. As I take Chloe into my arms, I feel myself smile. It hurts, not just because of the split lip and the bruise on my cheek, but because my muscles are no longer used to stretching my mouth upwards. But a split second later, hunched around Chloe's tiny frame, my body starts shaking with long, racking sobs. Tears of relief.

'What's wrong?' Sandy repeats, her strident voice faltering this time. I glance at my mother-in-law and see she has spotted Nikki, who is walking towards her. 'Nicola,' Sandy says, nodding at her. If she's puzzled, she's hiding it well. She sounds curt rather than confused.

'How's your father?' Sandy tries again, turning to me.

This is a question I can answer. I try to get a grip, and politely,

I reply. 'He's, well … he's been better, I suppose. I think he's devastated at the idea of having his dog put down.' I see Nikki flinch out of the corner of my eye. She would hate that idea too, of course, being a dog lover.

'I meant, has he recovered from his stroke?'

'Oh, yes.' I frown. 'A while ago now.'

'But I thought …' Sandy breaks off. It's clear to me that she's not going to say any more.

'Did Alex tell you that's where I was? At my dad's house?'

Sandy pushes a strand of grey hair behind her ears. 'Alex … Did Alex …?'

She's looking at my face, but she can't bring herself to ask. I feel inexplicably angry with her all of a sudden as if she's somehow responsible for what her son has done to me.

'Your son kept me prisoner – for several days – after beating me and threatening to take Chloe away from me,' I inform her. My mother-in-law casts her eyes downwards. My words have hit her like a slap in the face.

'Alexander asked me to look after Chloe until his return,' she says, and for a moment I think she's going to refuse to give me my daughter. But then she adds, 'He's due back on Friday.' Friday! That's three days! I would have spent another three days and nights in that nursery with no food!

'Do you know where he's gone?' Nikki asks.

'No,' she says. 'He doesn't like me to pry. I only know he's away on business.' She pauses, then asks, 'Are you going to the police?'

I scrutinise her, trying to work out if she's going to plead with me not to. 'Yes, I have to.'

My mother-in-law nods. 'He rings me every day,' she says. 'I'll pretend Chloe is still here, to make sure he does come back on Friday.'

For a few seconds, I'm stunned. Then holding Chloe in one arm, I place my other arm on Sandy's shoulder. 'Why would you do that?'

She lets out a weary sigh, the lament of a mother who suffered for years in a marriage to someone evil and who knows she didn't manage to eradicate his evil from her own child.

'He pushed me,' she says.

At first I think she means that Alex has made her do something she didn't want to.

'Pushed you to do what?' I breathe, not sure that I really want to know.

She shakes her head almost imperceptibly and just when I think she isn't going to say another word, she continues. 'We had an argument. Over something inconsequential.' She waves her hand dismissively. 'He was angry with me. So he pushed me and I fell down my own front doorstep. That's how I sprained my ankle.'

'I'm so sorry, Sandy,' I say.

'It was deliberate,' my mother-in-law continues. 'He had this malevolent gleam in his eyes.'

Sandy reaches out and gently touches my face. 'Go now, both of you.' She lowers her voice and I only just make out her words. 'Kaitlyn, make sure the police find him before he finds you.'

Chapter 23

As Nikki drives away, the enormity of what I've lost and of what I'm leaving behind hits me with as much force as Alex's blow. I've lost my dignity, my self-respect and my confidence. I'm not just abandoning my dream, my home and my husband, but also part of my identity. Not for the first time in my life, I feel as if half of myself has gone. I've spent all my adult life coping with being a 'twinless' twin. And now I'm a wife with no husband.

I can hardly breathe or speak until we turn onto the M6. Then the knot in my stomach loosens a little. *I have Chloe*, I keep saying to myself, over and over again. I can feel the tension lift ever so slightly from my stiff shoulders and at the same time my eyelids become heavy. There's a lot I want to talk to Nikki about, but I'm mentally and physically exhausted. I allow my eyes to close, intending to rest for a moment. I don't want to sleep. It wouldn't be fair to Nikki. Besides, I don't know if I can trust her completely. She's put my dad's address into the satnav, but I want to check she stays on the right road.

The next thing I know, Nikki is calling out to me.

'Kaitlyn? Wake up, Kaitlyn.'

'Where are we?' I ask just as my sleepy eyes spot a sign for Gloucester Services. Then, reading the time on the digital clock on the dashboard, I add, 'How long have you been driving?'

'We've done a good three hours of the journey now,' Nikki says. 'I could do with some coffee to wake me up a bit. Otherwise, I'll fall asleep, too.'

Her words chill me.

'Wake up and smell the coffee,' I whisper. 'Or wake up and smell the dead flowers.'

Biting her lip, Nikki pulls into a parking space. I can see she has heard me. She wraps her arms around the steering wheel, and resting her cheek on her hands, she fixes me with her large chocolate eyes.

'Were you responsible for that parcel?' I ask.

'Yes.' It's no more than a whisper.

'And you delivered it yourself?'

'Yes,' she repeats.

'But weren't you scared you'd get caught? We could have seen you!' Without meaning to, I've raised my voice and Chloe starts to stir in the carrycot on the back seat of the car.

'I always rang the house first. To make sure no one was in.'

At first, I think she means the doorbell. Then I get it. The calls to the landline. They were from Nikki. When I answered, she didn't say anything. She was hoping no one would pick up, checking there was no one home. I remember hearing the phone ring while I was imprisoned in the nursery. She called today before coming out to the Old Vicarage, I realise.

'But why did you deliver poppies and violets? I don't get it. And that message? What the hell was that supposed to mean?'

'It was just to … I wanted to … I suppose my aim was to freak Alex out. I didn't want him to do the same thing to you and your daughter.'

I take a few seconds to process this. Then I ask, 'The same thing? Are you talking about Melanie, Alex's ex-wife?'

'Yes. Melanie and the girls.'

'What happened to them?'

'I have no proof,' she says, 'but I think he killed them.'

I inhale sharply. Chloe begins to whimper. 'What makes you think that?' I ask.

'He planted poppies and violets under the damson tree in the back garden. They didn't grow. So then he planted daffodils. They died, too.'

Smell the dead flowers.

A series of images plays through my head, like in the trailer of a film. St Oswald's church. William Wordsworth's gravestone. Alex. Dora's field. The Coffin Trail. I remember that day as clearly as if it were yesterday. The day we saw Nikki walking her little white dog.

'Wordsworth planted daffodils as a memorial to his favourite daughter when she died,' I say.

Nikki nods gravely. 'It's just a theory,' she says, 'but once I'd come up with that scenario, I couldn't get it out of my head.' She shrugs, seemingly less sure of herself all of a sudden. 'Maybe I wanted to make Alex into more of a monster than he really is so I could get over him. I don't know. But I figured something bad had happened to Poppy and Violet, so I cut up thirteen flowers—'

'Why thirteen? To bring bad luck?'

'No! That's how old they would be now.'

'And you added dirt,' I say. 'What was that about?'

'It was earth.' I narrow my eyes at Nikki. I'm not sure if she's telling the truth. None of this makes sense. 'To let Alex know someone was on to him in case I was right and he had buried them all under that wonky damson tree.'

'But Alex isn't capable of ... murder!' As I utter these words, I wonder if I'm conditioned to stand up for Alex, even when he commits the most atrocious acts. 'Is he?' I add weakly. Would he kill someone? Could he kill someone? His own family?

I can feel Nikki shrug next to me as I shudder. Chloe starts to cry. She must be hungry. Her evening feed is long overdue. I look at Nikki. She sits up straight and avoids my gaze. I don't believe her.

Then I remember a day about a month before the wedding, the day Alex and I met the Superintendent Registrar to give notice of our intention to marry. The officer was irritable because Alex had forgotten his divorce papers. Alex went back with them later. Is it possible he handed in a death certificate instead? Would he have a death certificate if no body had been found because his wife is buried under the damson tree? Maybe he provided false documents. I wouldn't put it past him.

I open the car door and get out on shaky legs. Leaning against the car, I'm vaguely aware of Nikki getting out of the car and taking Chloe out of her carrycot. I hear her soothing Chloe and her words soothe me a little, too.

I desperately need a pee and this primal need enables me to function in spite of the state I'm in. I take the baby bag and Nikki carries Chloe and we walk towards the entrance of the motorway services side by side in silence.

Inside, I make up a bottle of formula and Nikki starts to feed Chloe while I race off to the loos. When I get back, I suggest we have something to eat. For the first time in several days, I'm famished.

'Good idea,' Nikki agrees. 'Anything. As long as it comes with a double espresso.'

I order two plates of spaghetti bolognaise and two double espressos, but my card is declined. It's a debit card. I haven't spent any money recently, so I should have more than sufficient funds in my account. I have another card, a credit card, the one for our joint account, so I try that. But to my dismay, it doesn't work either.

Leaving my tray by the cash desk, I have to ask Nikki to lend me the money. She gets up immediately and, handing me Chloe, she pays for our dinners.

'I'm so sorry, Nikki,' I say as soon as she comes back. I'm mortified. 'You've driven all this way, I didn't keep you company on the journey and I can't even buy you a meal.'

I burst into tears. I'm aware that people are staring at me, but right now I just don't care. I've shed so many tears recently, I should be all cried out by now, but I've got a feeling there's a lot more to come.

Nikki places her hand on my arm. 'Think nothing of it,' she says. 'I've deceived you terribly and I'm trying to make it up to you. You mustn't feel you owe me anything. Not even dinner.' She gives me a quick toothy grin and it makes me feel a bit better.

When I've calmed down and we've nearly finished eating, Nikki asks me, 'Have you got any idea why your cards might have been refused?'

I shake my head. 'It's odd that neither of them work, though.'

'They haven't expired?'

'Nope.'

'You've definitely got money in your account?'

'Funnily enough, I've been a bit too tied up to go on any spending sprees recently,' I say, my voice dripping with sarcasm. I bite my lip. 'God, I'm sorry, Nikki. I'm tired and frustrated. I didn't mean to take it out on you.'

'No, that's fine. You've been through a lot. Don't worry about *that*.'

The way she says that seems to imply I should be worrying about something else entirely.

'What? What is it?'

'Do you remember I told you my mum paid the deposit for my house because I'd lost my money?'

A vague memory stirs in a recess of my mind.

'Well, Alex stole all my money. I had a savings account but he said he had a high-interest account in some building society and persuaded me to transfer my money.'

My stomach lurches. The money from the sale of the house

245

in Minehead. The house I used to live in with Kevin. I let Alex handle the money. He said he'd pay it into a building society.

'Stupid of me, really,' Nikki continues, 'but we were engaged and I trusted him.'

'Oh God.'

A wave of nausea suddenly rises inside me and I leap up, thrusting Chloe into Nikki's arms. I dash to the toilets. There, I retch and retch until I've brought up everything I've just swallowed. When I've finished, Nikki appears juggling Chloe, two handbags and the baby bag in her arms.

'How are you feeling now?' she asks as I splash cold water on my face.

I look at her in the mirror, trying to keep my eyes on her and avoid looking at my own bruised ashen face. 'Not great,' I say.

'It's the shock, I expect.'

A plump middle-aged lady emerges from a toilet cubicle, accompanied by the noise of the flush, and washes her hands at the sink next to mine. She glances nervously at me in the mirror and when I glare at her, she looks away. I wait until she's at the hand dryer before I turn to Nikki and tell her what I suspect happened to the money from the sale of my house.

'You really must go to the police as soon as possible,' she says as we make our way out of the loos and towards the exit. 'Tell them that Alex beat you up, locked you up and emptied your bank accounts. They'll protect you and Chloe.'

Alex is the father of my child. Somehow it seems wrong to report him to the police. But I suppose sometimes doing the right thing feels wrong and it has to be done anyway.

'I will.'

We pass the chairs we were sitting in a few minutes ago. There's a couple there now, holding hands across the table while steam rises from their styrofoam cups. They look happy and carefree. Nikki strides on towards the sliding doors and I almost have to run to keep pace with her even though she's the one carrying Chloe and all the bags.

Once we're back on the motorway, Nikki picks up the conversation from where we left off. 'I didn't report Alex for taking my money. I should have gone to the police, but … I don't know, at first I was stupid enough to hope he might come back to me. That was what I wanted. I was completely … in love.' Her voice cracks a little and a lump forms in my own throat.

'Then I was ashamed,' she continues. 'I imagined telling the police, seeing them roll their eyes at each other, thinking how gullible and naive I'd been. We hadn't even been together that long before we got engaged. It was a bit of a whirlwind romance.'

Now why doesn't that surprise me?

In the half-light, I notice Nikki's knuckles whitening as she tightens her grip on the steering wheel.

'Then I thought maybe he'd threaten me,' she continues, 'although he'd never been violent when we were … together. Controlling, yes. Violent, no. Perhaps we simply hadn't got to that stage.'

She pauses for a second, lost in her thoughts, maybe playing out a scene further along the road she'd have taken in a parallel universe. I wait without prompting her.

'In the end, my mum said to leave it, that it was best to put it all behind me. She said it was a small price to pay for … for escaping from the bastard before it was too late. Sorry, Kaitlyn.'

'No! Don't be!'

We say nothing for a second or two. Then something occurs to me. I don't like to ask Nikki how much money Alex took from her. But I know how much my half of the sale of the house in Minehead amounted to, and that in itself is already quite a large sum.

'What the hell has he done with all that money? He's not particularly materialistic. He inherited the Old Vicarage. He owns a successful shop. He earns a good living. What does he spend it on?'

Nikki turns and looks at me. 'He doesn't earn much. It's not his shop,' she says. 'He just works there. And he didn't inherit the Old Vicarage.' Nikki pauses, her eyes fixed on the road as she pulls into the middle lane to overtake a van. When she has finished this manoeuvre, she resumes speaking. 'Alex's parents rented the Old Vicarage when they married. About fifteen years ago, when the owners decided to sell it, Alex bought it, but I think he's always had difficulty paying the mortgage.'

'He told me it had been in his family for years!' I realise now Alex lied about the Old Vicarage and his job so there would be no question of him leaving the Lake District. I had to come to him. 'How do you know all this?' I ask Nikki.

'His mother told me.'

I realise that I've never really talked to Sandy – apart from when she told me about Alex's father. I've never tried to get to know her. I was put off by her obsession with cleanliness and jealous of her close relationship with Alex. She tried to help me with Chloe and I resented her for meddling. I should feel bad about that now, particularly given the support she showed me earlier today, but instead a solitary tear for my own mother rolls down my cheek.

'I just wanted to say, if it helps, you can mention me,' Nikki says, 'to the police, I mean.'

I'm so choked up now I don't trust myself to speak. I reach out and touch her shoulder.

Staring out of the window a few minutes later, I see a sign for Gordano Services. We're near Bristol. Poor Nikki has done all the driving so far, I realise.

'Stop at the services, Nikki, if you like,' I say. 'I'll take the wheel from here.'

Nikki indicates and pulls off the motorway. As we get out of the car and swap sides, I ask her to lend me her mobile so I can ring my dad.

The home number for the house in Porlock, the house I grew

up in, is one of the few I know by heart. I keep the call short. I don't want to alarm Dad, but I can tell from his voice he's worried. He must be wondering what our unexpected visit is all about. I promise Dad I'll fill him in when we get there – or in the morning as we're going to arrive very late.

Gripping my phone against my ear with my shoulder while I fasten my seatbelt, I glance at the satnav. If everything runs smoothly, I tell my dad, we'll be there in a couple of hours' time.

Chapter 24

As we pull up in front of Dad's house, I feel like a teenager again. Although it's well past midnight when we arrive, there are lights on inside and I know he's waiting up for me, just as he did when I first started staying out late at parties.

Dad opens the door before we reach it and when he sees me, I see his smile vanish for the first time in years. He kisses me on my good cheek and then helps us in with all the bags and suitcases.

'The cot's in Julie's room for now,' he says, 'and I've made up a bed for Nikki in the boys' room.'

Chloe slept in the boys' room last time I came down. It used to be my bedroom. Mine and Louisa's. When we lost Louisa, Mum wouldn't allow anyone to touch it. She made me move into Julie's room as soon as Julie had moved out to live with Daniel. Mum would sleep in Louisa's bed for days and nights on end and I was no longer allowed to go in there. Even Dad was only permitted occasionally when he'd made her tea or soup.

After Mum died and Oscar and Archie came along, Dad and

I moved my things into Julie's room and redecorated my mum's shrine to my twin sister, transforming it into 'the boys' room'. Julie hasn't slept at Dad's house for years – she doesn't live far away and she says the Si Chi energy vibes are too strong – but the room I sleep in at Dad's is still 'Julie's room', even though there is hardly anything of hers anywhere in our childhood home.

Dad goes into the kitchen to make tea, cradling his sleepy granddaughter in his arms, while Nikki and I trundle upstairs with the luggage. It's only as we're coming back downstairs that I realise Jet hasn't come to greet us. He usually comes rushing to jump up on me, his tail wagging so hard that it's a wonder he doesn't put his back out.

Jet's bed is still in the hall, though, near the kitchen door. I look closely at it as we walk past because it's black, like Jet, and when he's asleep, you don't always realise he's there, as if the bed provides him with camouflage.

But his bed is empty.

'Dad, where's Jet?' I ask, entering the kitchen.

Still holding Chloe in one arm, Dad hands me my tea with a little shake of his head.

'Oh, no. When?'

'This morning. I left you a message on your mobile.'

'I haven't … I didn't get it. I'm so sorry, Dad.'

We all carry our mugs through to the sitting room and Dad changes the subject to focus on me. He wants to know what's going on.

'Did Alex do that to you?' His eyes are looking over the top of his glasses at my face.

'Yes.'

'The bastard.'

Out of the corner of my eye, I can see Nikki vigorously nodding her agreement at this description of my husband, having used the same word herself only a few hours earlier. I'm struck by the realisation that I've never heard my father swear before. Not once.

251

'Did he … treat you badly often?'

'It was the first time he'd hit me, if that's what you mean,' I say, 'but he could be manipulative and mean.'

I don't want to tell Dad that Alex kept me captive and handcuffed me to the bed. I don't want him to worry more than necessary. Nikki seems to understand this. She sips at her tea silently, sitting next to me on the sofa.

Dad gazes at Chloe, who has now fallen asleep on his chest. He strokes her blonde head. 'What are you going to do?' he asks without looking up.

'I'm going to go to the police station in Minehead first thing tomorrow morning and report him.'

'I'll drive you,' my Dad offers. 'Chloe and I can go for a walk along the promenade while you're talking to the police.'

As I'm getting ready for bed, there's a knock at the bedroom door. It's Nikki.

'I thought it would be a good idea to take some photos of your face,' she says. 'You can give them to the police.'

I remember my mother-in-law using her photos to make sure her husband wouldn't come back. I can use mine as evidence to make sure my husband doesn't get away with what he has done.

'I'll email them to you seeing as you haven't got your mobile,' she continues, waving her mobile at me as she waltzes barefoot into Julie's room wearing a nightdress with the logo *Don't judge my dogs and I won't judge your kids* on it.

'OK,' I agree, my lips twitching. It's the closest I've come to a genuine smile for a while.

'I think you should look a bit more serious,' she says, aiming the camera of her phone at me.

'Sorry. It's your nightie. It's great.'

She smiles at that while I keep a straight face as she snaps a few shots.

When I wake up the next morning, I'm glad she came up with

that idea as the bruising on my face has gone down and it's not nearly so noticeable. For which I'm also glad.

Nikki leaves at around nine o'clock with a large packed lunch that my dad made her for the journey. When she has gone, I boot up my dad's desk computer to check my bank accounts. I always use the same password for everything, which I know is a mistake. I'm sure Alex knows it, too. It would have given him easy access to my money. But it turns out my password is no longer valid for our joint account.

I try my current account and discover to my horror that the balance totals only £3.20. I was expecting something like that, but it still makes me feel sick from the pit of my stomach up to my chest. Scrolling down through the most recent transactions, I can see that several fairly large sums of money have been transferred out of that account into Alex's. I print out the online statements.

Next I use Dad's landline to ring the emergency number and cancel my bankcards. I'm not sure why as they're useless anyway. At some stage I'll close down my current account and open another one here and inform the university so that I continue to get my maternity pay.

Finally, I access my emails and print out a couple of the photos Nikki took of my face.

Dad pops his head around the door to see how I'm getting on. 'I've just rung the police station,' he says, waving his mobile. 'I've made an appointment for ten-thirty this morning. You were on the phone, so I just told them what I knew and they said to come in then. We need to get going.'

Just before half past ten, Dad drops me at the police station in Townsend Road. I've been past this building before, of course – I used to live in Minehead. But this is the first time I've noticed the white wooden bars on all the windows. It's a building built of reddish brick, nothing like the cold grey stone of the Old Vicarage, but for a moment I'm reluctant to go in.

'Here's my mobile number,' my dad says, pushing a scrap of paper into the palm of my hand. 'Ask to use their phone and give me a ring when you've finished. There's no hurry. Chloe and I will find a café along the Esplanade.'

I give my dad a kiss and watch him as he walks back to his car. Then I examine the piece of paper in my hand. My heart skips a beat as the coincidence strikes me. He has written his number – very neatly – on an orange Post-it. Just like the one Alex pretended to have written a message on. The message I didn't get. About his mum's accident, which I know now was no accident.

My legs are weak and heavy as I go up the steps to the entrance.

A few minutes later, I find myself face to face with a stocky man with dark hair gelled to one side. I'm not sure if it's the uniform, or the hairstyle or his stance with his arms by his sides, but he reminds me of one of the Playmobil figures Oscar and Archie used to play with. I'd assumed I would be talking to a female officer and I'm thrown for a second. I also find the fact that he's smaller than me disconcerting, even though a lot of men are. But he has a firm handshake and a friendly face and I warm to him instantly.

'Kaitlyn Best? I'm Detective Constable Nigel Bryant.' He has a surprisingly deep voice for his build, I notice. 'Would you like to follow me?'

I don't know whether Dad did that deliberately when he rang the police station this morning or if it was a slip, but I feel bolstered by the officer's use of my maiden name, as if, by assuming my old identity, I've taken a baby step towards mending myself.

I follow him into a small office and he sits down, gesturing for me to take the seat opposite him. He asks me to tell him what happened in my own words and he types on his computer as I do, prompting me or asking specific questions from time to time. He rephrases some of what I say, translating my words into his jargon.

'Domestic abuse … coercive behaviour … false imprisonment …'

I don't know how much time goes by. I'm exhausted by the time we've finished. DC Bryant reads back what he has typed up and I elaborate on a few things or try to clarify others. Then he amends a few sentences and prints out my statement for me to sign.

Reading it over, I realise I've mentioned Nikki, but only for her role in helping me escape. What happened to her and the nature of her relationship with Alex just didn't come up. DC Bryant asked me if Alex had hit *me* before, not if I knew whether he had a history of controlling behaviour or previous relationship problems.

I wonder now if I should add that, but decide against it. Nikki didn't want to report it when it happened to her after all. And I don't want to come over as a bitter wife intent on discrediting her husband. The last thing I need is for the police to think my statement is defamatory. So I stick to the facts as I know them. The rest may come out later.

I haven't brought up Alex's ex-wife and daughters, either. I can't get Nikki's belief – that they're buried underneath the damson tree – out of my head, but she has no proof of that. Although I think I would have starved to death if Nikki hadn't come to my rescue, I don't truly believe Alex is capable of killing in cold blood.

I have told DC Bryant that Alex drugged our daughter. I'm scared that Alex will claim I was the one who drugged her, as he threatened to, and turn the tables on me. His word against mine. But this is part of my story, so I've told it, although I realise it will be impossible to prove.

But I can prove that Alex took my money. DC Bryant takes my bank statements and he also keeps Nikki's pictures of my face that I printed out this morning.

'What happens next?' I ask him, signing my statement.

'The Avon and Somerset Police take domestic abuse very seriously,' he says, 'and we do everything in our power to protect victims from this crime. We can involve a specialist Domestic Violence team to place you somewhere where you'll be safe, until—'

'No,' I say firmly. DC Bryant tries to insist, but I'm not having it. I've been kept prisoner for several days and I was cooped up in the Old Vicarage for far too long. I don't want to feel confined to a women's refuge.

'I don't think I'm in any immediate danger,' I say. 'I'd much rather be with my family. Anyway, my husband won't know I've got away until he gets back on Friday.'

'Well, we'll be doing everything we can to locate your husband before then, obviously. But if somehow he does find out you've left, he may contact you because you've taken his baby.' DC Bryant's choice of possessive adjective makes me wince, but he doesn't seem to notice. 'If you hear from him, you must let us know. Immediately.'

'Yes, of course.'

'Unlawful imprisonment is a very serious offence.' His voice conveys the gravity of Alex's actions. 'We'll liaise with the Cumbria Constabulary on this matter. I'll be in touch with them today and I fully expect them to check out your house as part of their investigation. They'll be looking for evidence that you were detained by force by your husband in your home. That will be the first step. This, I'm confident, will lead to his arrest.' He sits forward in his seat, signalling the end of my appointment. 'And we'll be in touch to take it from there. In the meantime, I'll be checking in with you on a daily basis.'

Coming out of the police station, I tilt my head back and allow the sun to warm my face for a few seconds before I walk down the steps. I haven't rung Dad and I don't want to just yet. I wander around for a while before realising where I'm going.

'I would have rung,' I say, seeing Hannah's eyes widen as I enter the salon, 'but I don't have a mobile at the moment.'

She looks startled to see me, and almost scared, although I can't imagine why. I was going to give her a hug but this stops me. I watch her as she hands a customer's credit card back to him and goes to open the door for him. As soon as we're alone, Hannah asks, 'What happened?'

It takes me a second to realise she means my face. I sigh.

'I left him, Hannah,' I say. 'You were right. He was too good to be true. He was cruel and calculating. And in the end, he was violent.' My brief marriage summed up in a few short sentences.

Hannah says nothing; she just stares at me. The pity exuding from her is almost tangible, and in her eyes it's legible. It makes me feel inexplicably angry with her. I don't want her to feel sorry for me, but I don't know what reaction I was hoping for.

A bell chimes as an elderly lady enters the hairdressing salon. I hardly acknowledge her.

'Are you home for a while?' Hannah asks after fetching a protective cape for her next customer and getting her seated.

'I'm not going back to the Lake District, if that's what you're asking.'

'No, it wasn't. I just meant, will we see you around?'

I don't answer. The 'we' bothers me. Hannah locks eyes with me. She has realised this.

'You need to go and see Kevin,' she says.

I wasn't expecting that. 'Why?'

'You just … do. That's all.' She turns away from me, perches on her stool, and looking in the mirror, she tucks a wayward ringlet back into the messy bun on the top of her head.

'I don't want to … I've nothing against … Can't you and I meet up, just the two of us?'

'No. Yes! Listen, Kaitlyn. Kevin has something important to tell you.' She's still studying her own reflection above her customer's head, avoiding eye contact with me for some reason. 'I think you should know. It might … change things. I'd rather you talked to him. It's not really my place to tell you.'

'Tell me what?'

Hannah shakes her head. 'Why don't you come round to dinner on Saturday evening?'

I hear myself accepting the invitation, ignoring my brain telling me that this is a very bad idea.

'Here's our address,' Hannah says, getting up to fetch a business card for her salon and jotting the address down on the back of it. 'We're renting,' she adds.

Our address. This is where Hannah is living with Kevin. My ex-boyfriend and my ex-best friend.

I read Hannah's familiar handwriting upside down. *Hopcott Terrace. Minehead.*

'You can't miss it. It's the redbrick one on the end.'

While Hannah focuses her attention on her customer, I borrow her mobile to ring Dad. I have no intention of going to Hannah and Kevin's place for dinner. I'll call her on Saturday morning and tell her I'm ill.

Chapter 25

Porlock is a long way from Grasmere and I feel safe here. For a while. But by Friday afternoon, the familiar knot in my stomach is back. The police still haven't located Alex. DC Bryant has informed me that according to Alex's colleagues, Alex had taken a few days off work and wasn't away on business at all. No one seems to know where he is.

I tell myself that he's due home today and he'll be arrested then.

The phone rings and interrupts my thoughts. I hold my breath while Dad answers it.

'It's the police,' Dad says, and I breathe out. For a second, I thought it might be Alex.

'Nigel Bryant here,' the detective constable says. 'Nothing to tell you, really, but I wanted to touch base. As you know, we're working with the Cumbria Constabulary and they found evidence of unlawful imprisonment at your house when they went there the day before yesterday.'

'The handcuffs,' I offer.

'Yes. Obviously, there will be a full investigation now. My colleagues in the Lake District will continue to drive by both Mrs Riley's house and Mr Riley's house until your husband shows up. Then he'll be taken into police custody.'

This is nothing new, but the uneasiness in my tummy begins to lift.

'He's supposed to come home sometime today,' I say, although we've already been over this, too. 'He'll probably go to his mother's first. That's where he thinks Chloe is.'

'Mrs Riley is cooperating with us, Ms Best.'

DC Bryant continues to talk to me, but I listen with only half an ear, thinking about Sandy, and hoping this will all be over soon. Then the police officer mentions something that grabs my attention.

'My colleague in Cumbria also said that a friend of yours was at the house today.'

'Which house?'

'The Old Vicarage. A Nicola Todd? You mentioned her in your statement.'

'Yes. What was she doing there?'

'She said she was picking up a few things.'

'What things?'

'I don't know. Apparently she said that would be OK with you?'

'Um … yes.' I clear my throat and try to sound more convincing. 'Yes, that's fine.'

'I think my colleague only brought it up because, well … I don't know why he told me, actually. I think they've done what they need to do inside, but they weren't expecting anyone to enter the house except your husband. She was just leaving with her mother when my colleagues arrived.'

'Her mother?'

'Apparently,' Bryant repeats.

When the police officer ends the call, I'm left feeling confused.

260

I have no idea why Nikki would go round to my house with her mother or what she would take. The only things that belong to her, as far as I can see, are some of the medals and the book she gave Alex that I found in the cardboard box.

I try to calm myself down. I'm sure Nikki would have a perfectly good explanation for this if I asked her. I would call her, but of course I haven't got her number – it's in my mobile. I decide to email her. I have her email address thanks to the photos she sent me of my face.

By the next morning, I'm consumed with paranoia. Nikki hasn't replied to my email and I don't know why. I can't imagine what she was doing at the Old Vicarage.

But, more importantly, the police haven't arrested Alex. They still don't know where he is. I'm convinced he found out somehow that I escaped from my prison in the nursery. His mother might have warned him after all, or maybe he drove by the Old Vicarage and saw something that raised his suspicions – Nikki and I left the gate open, I remember, although it may have been closed since then, or perhaps he spotted a police car or Nikki's car.

Alex will come after me now, I'm certain of that. He won't let me get away. I don't know where he is, but he'll know where I am. Where else would I be? This is the very first place he'll look. My mother-in-law's words echo in my mind: *Make sure the police find him before he finds you.*

DC Bryant has promised to let me know as soon as he hears anything. He says he will send a patrol car round periodically to check on Dad's house as a precaution. Dad has also tried to reassure me, saying that the police in Cumbria have probably got him and if we haven't heard anything yet, it's simply because it's the weekend.

I try to relax under the hot jet of the shower, savouring the homely mess of Dad's bathroom. It's quite a contrast with the showroom neatness of the sparkling en suite bathroom at the

Old Vicarage, where Alex lines up his bottles according to size and keeps everything in its place.

It's as I'm looking among the bottles on the windowsill for the shower gel that I spot it. I gasp. It's the make Alex always buys because it contains no parabens or allergens. A memory replays in my head – Alex waving an identical bottle to this one in my face, accusing me of switching his body wash deliberately to bring him out in a rash.

Alex has been in the house. He has been in the bathroom. He's playing tricks on me.

I don't remember getting out of the shower or getting dressed. The next thing I know, my dad is holding me as I sit on the floor in Julie's room, shaking and gulping for air.

'Breathe in,' he says, rubbing my back. 'Breathe out.'

I realise that it was my father's voice in my head, helping me control my breathing, every time I was overcome with anxiety. *Breathe in, breathe out.* These are the words I've been repeating to myself whenever it has felt like my lungs are shrinking. A mantra I'd stored in my memory, but that wasn't meant for me to begin with.

This is how my dad used to calm my mum down, I remember now, when she had panic attacks after losing Louisa. I recall peeping round the bedroom door and seeing him sitting on his daughter's bed as his wife lay in it, unable to face life for a while, but ready to embrace death. The cancer didn't grant her that wish until a few years later.

Damn! I thought I was done with the panic attacks. The memory of my mother doesn't help. But I'm determined not to let Alex beat me and I focus on my breathing and shut out everything except my dad's voice.

When I've finally recovered, I ask him about the shower gel.

'I probably bought it when I did the shopping,' he says. 'There was some shampoo and stuff I don't usually buy on special offer at Tesco's last week.'

A false alarm, then. All that for nothing. Feeling annoyed with myself, I let out a huge sigh of relief.

'Speaking of which,' my father says, 'we need to get some shopping in. Do you want to come with me?'

I don't, but I don't want to be alone, so the three of us go to Tesco's, then come back and make lunch. I appreciate spending time with Dad and I can see Chloe loves being around him, too. I think having us around is taking Dad's mind off Jet a bit.

It's mid-afternoon by the time I remember I wanted to ring Hannah to tell her I can't make it for dinner. I realise I don't have her mobile number and I don't think I ever learnt Kevin's by heart. Looking at my watch, I think I should still be able to get hold of Hannah at the salon, but it seems a bit late now and a bit rude. Both she and Kevin work on Saturdays so they will have got organised before now for this evening. I'm going to have to go.

So later that evening, I borrow Dad's car and drive to Hannah and Kevin's. After strapping Chloe in her carrycot in the back seat, I follow the satnav instructions to Hopcott Terrace, stopping just outside Minehead to buy chocolates and flowers from a petrol station.

The whole way there, I wonder what Kevin wants to tell me. The only thing I can come up with is that he must have asked Hannah to marry him, but I don't know why she couldn't have told me that herself.

I find their house easily enough. Hannah opens the door.

'Hi, come in. We're so glad you could make it.'

Her delighted tone is affected. I know Hannah well, or I used to, and I can tell she's feeling as awkward as I am. I follow her into the kitchen and sit down to tend to Chloe while Hannah opens the oven, peers inside and then closes it again. I watch as she undoes her bun, winds up her hair and pins it up again. It doesn't look any different to me.

'I'll show you around in a minute if you like.'

Fortunately, she seems to forget about this idea, or maybe she just thinks the better of it. I don't get the guided tour in the end anyway. I look around the kitchen. Kevin collects those rectangular magnets you can buy in tourist traps all over the world and clearly he still uses them to stick important notes and business cards to the fridge. Whenever we went abroad, he bought one. Paris, Lyon, Rome, Florence, Madrid … So many memories. There's a new one, I notice. Prague. We always talked of going there. He must have gone with Hannah.

Kevin appears in the kitchen doorway. Chloe is on my lap, and I'm grateful for that as it saves me from having to get up and greet him. I don't know what the correct etiquette is for greeting your ex in his home when you've been invited for a meal. His damp fair hair tells me he has just taken a shower, the first thing he always did when he got in from work.

'Hi, Kaitlyn. I was a bit later than I'd hoped getting home,' he says, by way of an apology. 'We're having problems with the foundations for that new sports complex up the road because of the sloping site and bad drainage. It's all turning out to be more complicated than we'd anticipated.'

He's babbling and I can see he's not at ease with me being here. I try to show an interest in his work, though, as that's a topic we're safe with. But there are lots of uncomfortable silences even before we take our seats in the dining area at the table Kevin and I chose a lifetime ago in a furniture shop in Taunton.

Throughout the meal, I find myself stealing glances at Hannah's tummy, trying to work out if she could be pregnant. Hannah and I only have one glass of wine each. If Hannah had got drunk, I'd have known she wasn't pregnant, but with one glass I can't be sure. The fact she hasn't drunk much doesn't mean anything, either, as she rarely overdoes it on the alcohol.

I would certainly have downed more wine this evening if I hadn't been driving. A lot more. If nothing else, to help the conversation flow more easily. After all, what is there to talk about?

We seem to have the choice between Hannah and Kevin's plans for the future or the events leading up to me leaving Alex and coming back down to Somerset.

Chloe is on the floor in her car seat next to the dining table, studying a toy that Dad bought in Tesco's that stretches across the handles of her seat. I notice Kevin gaze at her several times while we're eating. He has what I can only interpret as a longing expression on his face. Perhaps he's broody.

When Hannah has polished off the last of her dinner, she asks if she can hold Chloe. Maybe I'm right and they are expecting a baby. Hannah coos away to her while Kevin clears the plates and I sit watching Hannah with Chloe, keen to get away and head back to Dad's.

Kevin and Hannah wait until we're having coffee after the meal before they drop their bombshell.

'Kaitlyn, Hannah and I have something to tell you,' Kevin begins with his broad Somerset inflections. Kevin went to the local comp whereas at my school we all spoke with plummy accents. Even now his voice is like music to my ears.

He pauses and I can hear a drum roll in my head. I get ready to offer my sincerest congratulations with a contrived look of joy.

But when he says it, I'm dumbfounded.

'What?'

He repeats, but I can't take it in. To say this gives me pause for thought would be a huge understatement. It takes me a few seconds, but the first thing that springs to my mind is, *I have no connection whatsoever to Alex now*. The shock becomes infused with a rush of relief.

'But how do you know? Are you sure?' I try to think back to October, when Alex came to Exeter and I slept over at his hotel. It's possible, I suppose.

'Do you remember when you came to see me at work a few weeks ago?' Hannah says. She doesn't wait for me to reply. 'I pulled a hair from Chloe's head.'

265

I remember Hannah holding Chloe after cutting my hair. Chloe suddenly started screaming for no reason. Well, for no reason I could see at the time. It was the first time she'd screamed like that since we left Grasmere and she wasn't being drugged by Alex anymore. Now I know the reason. Hannah pulled some of her hair out.

'I got the hair tested,' Hannah continues. 'You know, DNA? You can send it off—'

'There's no doubt,' Kevin interrupts. 'Chloe is mine.'

'Oh God. Oh, Kevin, I am so sorry.' I put my head in my hands with my elbows on the dining room table. 'It's just that you and I had been trying to have a baby for so long with no result, I just assumed … It never occurred to me …'

The next half an hour or so goes by in a daze. I think it's Hannah who suggests I should go home and let it sink in. I'm homeless at the moment, but I don't say that.

As I'm leaving, I try to ask Hannah something. 'But how did you …?' What I really want to know is how it crossed Hannah's mind that Chloe might be Kevin's when it didn't cross mine. I can't finish the question, but Hannah has understood.

'Kevin said he never saw it coming. You leaving him, I mean. He confided in me before we … as a friend. At the time he said he hadn't stopped loving you and it wasn't like you were no longer sleeping together or anything. I don't think he meant to open up as much as he did. We'd been drinking wine that evening. But it was something I couldn't forget afterwards. And then, well, Kaitlyn, Chloe's got blonde hair. Like Kevin's.'

'Yes, but Alex was fair when he was a baby.'

She shrugs. 'I didn't know that,' she says.

'And my dad was fair-haired. Before he went bald.'

'I know. I remember.' She shrugs again. 'I wasn't sure. It was a hunch, I suppose. But I needed to know.'

Hannah and I are standing on the doorstep. Kevin has stayed inside, ostensibly to finish clearing the table. I've never known him not to see any of our guests off as they were leaving. He would always wave until they'd driven off and were out of sight. But I expect he's as confused as I am.

'And Kevin? Was he the one who—?'

'No. It never entered his head. I didn't tell him until the results came back.'

'How long have you known?'

'A couple of days,' she says.

That explains the strange look she gave me when I turned up at the salon. And it explains why Kevin needs to be alone with his thoughts right now.

'Will you call us in a few days' time?' Hannah says. My cue to leave. 'When you've had a chance to get your head round this?'

I can feel myself nodding.

She gives me a brief hug, then, and I can smell the fruity scent of her hair. *I've missed you*, I think, but there's a lot to be sorted out and, although I'm going to be linked to Hannah through Kevin and Chloe now, I'm not sure if we'll ever be friends again. I'd like us to be, though. One day.

I drive to the promenade and fit Chloe's car seat onto the chassis. Then I walk. When the Esplanade becomes a path that leads round the clifftop, it becomes too tricky for the buggy, so I turn around and walk the other way. Then, sitting down on a bench on the Esplanade, I close my eyes and inhale the salt air.

I'm not sure what to make of this. Opening my eyes, I look out across the Bristol Channel at the lights along the Welsh coast and I let my feelings churn every which way in my mind before trying to identify them.

Relief. I'm relieved that Chloe no longer connects me to Alex. I'm married to him, but that can be undone. When we're divorced, there will be no reason whatsoever for him and me to stay in touch. I'll be free.

Guilty. I have messed up – badly. And I'm going to have to put this right. I can't turn back time or rewrite the past. I can't erase what I've done. But I can use a fresh page to write my future. And Chloe's future.

Nostalgic. I sigh, thinking of Kevin. Our relationship was one of missed chances and broken dreams. We were always in the wrong place at the wrong time. Or maybe in the right place at the wrong time. After all, we made Chloe, and I wouldn't change that. Not for the world. But Kevin and I had run our course. There's no going back for us, either. Only forwards.

Stupid. I can't believe Hannah worked out that Kevin could be Chloe's father when I had no inkling of that myself.

I'm wrenched from my thoughts, suddenly aware of the little hairs on the back of my neck prickling. Someone is watching me. I whip my head round and look behind me, but although there are a few people about, no one seems to be paying any attention to me.

I can't shake that impression, though, the feeling I'm being observed, so I get up and hurriedly wheel Chloe's pushchair along the Esplanade, past Butlins on the opposite side of the road and on towards the car park.

It takes me less than five minutes to reach Dad's car and strap in Chloe's infant seat. I whirl around every few steps, convinced I'm being followed. As soon as I've folded the chassis down and shut it in the boot, I jump in the car and press the button for the central locking.

It takes me less than fifteen minutes to drive back to Dad's. Despite my grip on the steering wheel, my hands are still shaking as I drive past the sign for Porlock. I keep looking in the rear-view mirror, but there are no headlights behind me. Another false alarm.

As I pull into Dad's road, I can see there's a car in front of his drive, where he usually parks. Because it's dark and the streetlights are dim, it takes me a few seconds to recognise it. When I do, I feel like my world has tipped on its side. I can't see straight or think straight. For a while, time seems to stand still, at an odd angle. Then my brain kicks in.

It should be in the driveway of the Old Vicarage. What's it doing here? Who drove it here from Grasmere? These questions tear through my head, but the answer is already racing after them. Alex is here. My first instinct is to drive off. Not used to the clutch on Dad's car, I stall it as I turn it around in the road. Then panic takes hold of me as though someone is gripping my throat. Dad! I can't leave Dad!

I park behind the red Citroën. There doesn't seem to be anyone in it. He's in the house. Getting out of Dad's car on wobbly legs, I check the registration plate on the red car. It's definitely my car. Clutching the handle of Chloe's car seat with a sleeping Chloe strapped in it, I creep up the drive to Dad's house. My eyes dart all over the place. I feel utterly terrified and yet faintly ridiculous at the same time. I open the front door as quietly as I can, but, as always, it sticks a little and I know I'll have been heard.

'Kaitlyn, is that you?' My dad's voice sounds muffled. I picture him in the sitting room, bound to a chair. 'We've got visitors.'

'Kaitlyn! Chloe!' a familiar voice calls out. 'There's someone here to meet you! Come and see!'

Chapter 26

Even though I recognise her silky voice, I'm mistrustful as I walk towards the living room. What's she doing here? What does she mean, there's someone here to meet me? Standing in the doorway, I stare at the sight that greets me. My wariness evaporates, and so does some of the tension that has been building up over the previous hours with Hannah and Kevin's bombshell.

Nikki's here. In my dad's living room. And she has brought a furry friend, by the look of it. My dad is holding the puppy, his face buried in its fur, and Nikki is watching, all wide smiles.

'Hi there,' she says to me. 'Allow me to introduce you to Marley. He's a goldador. His mum's a golden retriever and his dad's a yellow Lab. Marley's twelve weeks old.'

In spite of everything, I find myself mirroring her smile. Dad has put the puppy on the floor now and he's bounding around, his tail going, the spit of the Andrex dog without the toilet roll. I put Chloe's infant seat on the floor in the corner of the room to keep her safely out of the way of this fluffy ball of energy.

Then I go up to Nikki and give her a hug. She's wearing socks and I'm in my heeled boots and for once we're the same height.

'What are you doing here?' I ask, still bewildered.

'I drove down in your car with as much of your stuff as I could get in it along with Marley and all his equipment.' Her eyes flit from the puppy to me and back again. 'Your dad knew I was coming. I rang him.'

Briefly, I wonder how she had Dad's number. Then I remember I called Dad from Nikki's mobile on the way down to Somerset in the car.

'I thought it would make a nice surprise for you,' my dad says.

'It's a lovely surprise,' I say, adding to myself, *especially after the shock I've just had.*

I understand now why Nikki went round to the Old Vicarage with her mother. She picked up my things for me and loaded them into my Citroën. She knew where the keys were. She'd hung them on the hook when we left the house together. But Nikki couldn't have known for sure that she wasn't in danger. I hate to think how Alex would have reacted if he'd come home while she was there. Her selfless gesture brings a lump to my throat.

'Nikki surprised me, too,' my dad says. 'She asked if she could bring a canine companion and I assumed she was bringing one of her dogs.'

I'm confused again. 'Whose dog is this, then?'

'He's mine,' Dad says, his face lighting up, like my nephews' faces at Christmas. 'Nikki says the shelter had some puppies. She couldn't say no when they asked her, but she already has four dogs, so she thought maybe I could give him a home.'

Nikki winks at me. She must have been moved when she found out Dad had had to put his dog down, even though she'd never met Jet. And this is her way of making him happier. She has obviously chosen the puppy's name, just as for the four dogs she adopted. Marley. I remember watching the film with Archie and Oscar.

Nikki has brought a crate for the puppy and before we go to bed, we make him comfortable in it with toys and a cushion. But Marley howls all night and we all look the worse for wear the following morning. Except for Chloe. She slept through it.

I'm not sure I would have slept anyway. I spent most of the time lying awake, staring blindly at the ceiling, trying to banish all thoughts of Alex from my head. I've also been absorbing the fact that Kevin is Chloe's father.

At breakfast, I announce this news to Dad and Nikki.

There is a long silence that seems to reverberate around the kitchen.

Then Dad says, 'That's probably a blessing in disguise.' He asks how I found out and so I fill him in.

Nikki hasn't said a word. I study her face, but her expression is blank. I wonder what's going through her mind. Maybe she's thinking if I hadn't made such a stupid mistake, she would still be with Alex. Or, at the very least, that she wouldn't have been kicked out so unceremoniously. I feel the need for her moral support. But perhaps she needs mine, I don't know. I just wish she'd say something.

I'm the one who brings it up as I'm driving her to the train station in Tiverton later that day. Dad and I invited her to stay for a while, but she said she had to get back to work.

'Nikki, I feel I owe you an apology.'

'What on earth for? I'm the one who deceived you.'

'That's all good, Nikki. You've more than made up for it.' As I say it, I realise I really mean it. Nikki has been an absolute godsend. I would probably be dead if she hadn't helped me. 'I meant, you know, with Alex. I made a terrible mistake. I assumed Chloe was Alex's. And, well, he left you because of me, didn't he?'

'He threw me out, you mean? Kaitlyn, I'm sure your situation was just a catalyst for causing Alex to break off our engagement. But you know what? I had a lucky escape.'

'I think I'm the one who had the lucky escape,' I say.

I turn towards her and she flashes me one of her contagious grins.

For a while neither of us speaks. Then, as I'm turning off the link road at the exit for Tiverton Parkway, Nikki says, 'Kaitlyn, are you sure you're not in danger?'

Her question throws me. I know she thinks I should have listened to DC Bryant about the women's refuge. Am I in danger? I've been thinking about that, or rather, I've been trying not to think about that. I'll feel a lot safer when Alex is behind bars, that's for sure.

'If he comes after you, he will find you. This is the first place he'll look.'

'The police are going to arrest him,' I say. I've already told Nikki about DC Bryant and she bumped into the police officers from the Cumbria Constabulary at the Old Vicarage.

'If he shows up.'

'They're keeping an eye on the Old Vicarage and his mother's house. They've been driving by regularly and keeping a lookout for him.'

'Yeah, me too,' she says. This doesn't surprise me.

I've been telling myself that Dad is right, that Alex has arrived home since I last spoke to DC Bryant. I'm hoping DC Bryant will call, the moment the police station in Minehead opens on Monday morning, to tell me Alex has been arrested.

But I'm not convinced. I suddenly feel jumpy. I look all around me as I pull into a space in the station car park.

'Do you think Sandy tipped him off?' I ask.

'Maybe,' Nikki says. 'She's his mother. Who knows how far she would go for her son?'

My hands are trembling as I unclip my seatbelt and open my car door. Nikki puts her hand on my arm.

'No need to come in,' she says. 'Get back home to Chloe and your dad. And Marley.'

'Are you sure?'

273

She nods. 'Keep in touch.'

And with that, she pecks my cheek, grabs her rucksack and heads towards the steps of the block of brown bricks that is Tiverton Parkway Railway Station.

Before she disappears through the doors, I realise I don't have her phone number. I get out of the car and, calling her name, I run after her.

I don't think to lock the car.

Nikki turns round and waits for me to catch up with her. 'I need you to give me your number again,' I say. 'I don't have my mobile anymore.'

'Yes you do,' she says as I catch up with her at the top of the steps. 'I put it and the charger in one of the bags. You'll find it when you unpack.'

As I drive away from the station, I get the feeling again that someone is following me. I look in the rear-view mirror, but there's no one behind me. I drive a little further, still checking behind me every few seconds.

Then I remember I didn't lock the car. I only realised when I went to unlock the car, pressed the button and locked it instead. I slam on the brakes and pull over to the side of the road. Then I leap out of the car and run a few steps away from it. He's in the back of the car.

Slowly, I approach the car and look through the back window. Then I open the boot. Then I get back in the car, put on the hazards and give myself a severe telling-off. Aloud. I can't allow him to do this to me. I can't let him win. He's not here. This is all in my head. *Get a grip, Kaitlyn.* My anger has kicked out my fear. I'm furious with myself. I keep up the scolding all the way back to Dad's.

Dad has been looking after Chloe and when I get back, we decide to take Marley out for a walk.

'We'll just go up the road and back,' Dad says. 'Marley will have to build up some strength, won't you, Puppy? It will be a while before I can take you to Watersmeet or Tarr Steps.' He ruffles Marley's fur. 'We might make it as far as the harbour.'

Dad used to take Jet to Watersmeet and Tarr Steps, local heavens for dogs. He avoided Worthy Woods, though.

As we reach Porlock Weir, Dad says, 'The Ship Inn's dog-friendly. Perhaps we should give Marley a bit of a rest before we head back.' I suspect he knew we'd wind up here when we set out.

I offer to buy Dad a pint while the dog is recharging his batteries. I end up ordering dinner to go with our pints. I have to pay with Dad's money, of course, as I still have none of my own. It's a warm evening and we sit at the wooden pub benches outside.

'Hi, Kaitlyn. What a lovely surprise! And Mr Best. How are you? On the mend, I hope? You're looking well anyway.'

It's Teddy. Edward Edwards. Dad's physiotherapist who was in the year above me – and Louisa – at East Exmoor School. He's wearing a short-sleeved shirt that shows off his toned biceps, but also reveals how white his skin is. I remember noticing how pale he was last time I bumped into him, but now I find myself wondering if he has worked all through the summer without taking a holiday.

He introduces me to his daughter, Olivia. He also introduces Chloe to Olivia. I'm impressed. He remembered my daughter's name. I'd forgotten Olivia's, but I know he told me last time.

'What are you doing here? Just down for the weekend?'

'Um, no. I think I might be coming back permanently,' I say.

I exchange pleasantries with Teddy while Olivia fusses over Marley and then Teddy offers to give me his mobile number. ('In case you want to go for another cream tea one day'). I haven't had a chance to dig out my mobile yet and I don't have a pen in my handbag, so I give Teddy my number instead. He and Olivia sit at the table next to ours.

'You could have asked them to sit with us,' my dad hisses.

'Shhh. I hardly know him,' I say. 'I've only seen him once since he left school, when he came round to your house.'

As Dad and I tuck into our Sunday roasts, I can't help glancing at Teddy from time to time. He catches my eye once and grins at me. But other than that, his gaze is glued to his daughter.

As Dad and I leave with Chloe and Marley, we stop by Teddy and Olivia's table to say goodbye. They've finished their meal, too, and Teddy is vaping while Olivia is playing with her phone. When Teddy and I went for our cream teas, I remember, his e-cig smelled faintly of lemon. This time I detect a trace of vanilla.

'I'll call you,' he promises as we walk away.

I don't mind if he does. He seems like a lovely guy, but I hope he's only looking for a friend. I'm not ready for anything else and I doubt I will be for a long time.

When I get home, I go through the bags Nikki packed and brought down for me until I find my mobile. The battery is dead. I plug it into the charger before I go to bed. I want to keep in touch with Nikki and the phone will help me to feel a bit more connected again. Plus, I'll feel safer with my mobile on me. Tomorrow I'll go to the bank, I decide as I climb into bed. I need some money of my own so I can be more independent. At least I have my car now. Thanks to Nikki.

I ring Nikki the following day to check she got back all right. She hasn't heard anything about Alex.

'I'll swing by this evening and take a look,' she says.

It's on the tip of my tongue to tell her she would have made an excellent spy, but I check myself and instead I say, 'Be careful, Nikki.' I want to add that Alex may be dangerous, but I can't bring myself to say it. Partly because I don't want to scare Nikki but mainly because this is still my husband I'm talking about. He has drilled screws into my speech over the months I've known him and even though he's no longer around, I continue to filter and censure anything I want to say.

Every day DC Bryant either calls me on Dad's phone or calls

round in person. But it's Wednesday before he gives me any news of Alex.

'We're doing all we can. My colleagues have been questioning his friends. It turns out one of them saw Alex last Friday night.'

But the detective constable knows nothing more than that. He can't tell me who saw him or if he met up with this friend or was just spotted by chance.

Two days later, Nikki sends me a text containing an internet link. I open up the page on my phone. It's an article in the *Westmorland Gazette*. I read it, reread it and then read it aloud to Dad.

1st September
Cumbrian police launch search for forty-year-old local man

Investigating officers would like to speak to Alexander Riley, 40, in connection with an alleged assault.

The victim, a woman in her thirties, is believed to have been beaten and then unlawfully detained.

Mr Riley, who was last seen on the evening of Friday 25th August at his home in Grasmere, is described as a person of interest in relation to these accusations.

If you recognise the man pictured above or have any information that may assist with the investigation, please contact the police on the number below.

Dad looks over my shoulder at the photo of Alex. I can't stop staring at it myself. It's as if Alex is holding my gaze. I recognise the picture. It has been taken from his Facebook page. It's a selfie Alex took before a triathlon event about a year ago. The photo has been cropped so that only Alex's face is shown, but in the original, he is holding his swimming hat and goggles by his side.

'They'll find him,' Dad says, squeezing my shoulder.

It's a gesture that is meant to reassure me, but although this article has given me no new information, the feelings of apprehension and terror I've been trying to quell this last week are stronger now than ever.

Where the hell is he? The police are searching for him in the Lake District, but I'm convinced he's in Somerset. I just know it. He's not far away from me. I can feel it.

Chapter 27

It's not even seven o'clock when I wake up from my troubled sleep. It takes me a moment to work out where I am. *In Julie's room. At Dad's.* It takes me another second or two to realise I can move my arms and get up. I'm disorientated from my nightmare, in which I was back in the nursery at the Old Vicarage, handcuffed to the bed, and my mouth feels dry and scratchy, as though I've been eating something salty coated in sand.

I roll over, swallow several sips of water from the glass on the bedside table and get out of bed to peel off my sweat-sodden pyjamas. I can hear my dad talking downstairs. At first I think he has a visitor but then I realise he's talking to Marley.

I get showered and dressed, then go down to join them.

'You're up early,' Dad says. 'Couldn't sleep?'

'Bad dreams.'

'Oh dear. Try not to worry. This will all be over soon. Listen, Julie sent a text message late last night. She wants to know if we'd like to go to hers for lunch.' He peers at me over the top of his glasses. 'She says she'll do a Sunday roast with all the trimmings.'

'Why not?'

Julie lives in Exford, which isn't far away. In fact it takes us far longer to get my car loaded up with the baby and puppy paraphernalia than it does to actually drive there. As I pass the Exford village green, I remember Alex said he used to stay here with his aunt and uncle to avoid spending all his weekends boarding at school. I don't know exactly where their house is. I think they still live here.

My sister lives in a four-bedroomed detached house, just up the hill from the church. It has a thatched roof and the outside walls are pale pink. Daniel jokingly calls this particular shade 'nipple pink', although it is more the colour of bubble gum or strawberry ice cream. He has been meaning to paint the house since they bought it nearly ten years ago, when Archie was a baby, but he seems to do more DIY at Dad's place in Porlock than at his own home.

Julie, of course, is far more concerned with the interior design. She has had extra windows put in downstairs but there are no curtains or blinds. Although the rooms have a lot of natural light, there are always lamps on or candles lit.

After taking our shoes off and tidying them away in the cupboard under the stairs, Dad and I are ushered into the 'lounge' where the sofa and chairs are positioned in a circle around the coffee table.

Daniel asks if I've had any news about Alex and we discuss my situation for a while before focusing the conversation on Oscar and Archie, which is a subject everyone is more at ease with.

After the meal, while the boys – Dad, Daniel, Oscar, Archie and Marley – are outside playing ball, Julie and I find ourselves alone. We flop down onto the sofa in the lounge.

'I wanted to apologise, Kaitlyn,' she says.

'What on earth for?'

'Well, I think you were trying to explain that you were having problems with Alex and I didn't see how serious it all was. Anyway, Daniel and I want you to know that we're both here for you, if you need us.'

Julie gives me a big hug. When she pulls away again, her hair is caught in my necklace. It's only as we're freeing her fine hair that I realise this is the necklace Alex gave me to replace the heart pendant and silver chain he blamed me for losing. I remember him rifling through the drawers in my bedroom, pretending to look for it when he must have known where it was all along. I drop my hands to my sides.

I can't believe I've been wearing his gold medallion all this time. I suddenly feel as if it is burning me, the metal chain branding my neck. When Julie has untangled her hair and sits up straight, I clench the medallion in my hand and yank it downwards so that the chain breaks.

My gesture transports me back to my wedding night. Alex had a meltdown because I wasn't wearing his heart necklace and then he broke my mother's necklace by pulling the pendant so that the chain snapped at the back of my neck.

At the memory, a lump comes to my throat, but I refuse to let myself break down. I don't want to cry over him anymore. He doesn't deserve my tears. I toss the medallion onto the coffee table.

'You want me to get rid of this for you?' Julie asks, picking up the necklace.

I nod.

She toys with it, and then looks down, spotting the inscription. '"I'm always yours"', she reads aloud.

'It's engraved with different words on the other side,' I say.

She flips it over. '"You're mine" …'

I look at her. She's studying the necklace. The colour has drained from her face.

'"Forever"', she finishes in a voice that is barely audible.

'It's creepy, isn't it? I think Alex meant it to be romantic.'

My sister's mouth is wide open, and so are her eyes. I notice the hand holding the necklace start to tremble.

'Julie? What's the matter?'

But she seems far away. I don't think she has heard me. I'm not sure what to do. Something is very wrong. Julie's hand goes to her mouth. Her movements are sluggish, as if the message isn't getting through from her brain to her body. It's as if I'm watching her actions in slow motion.

'Do you want a drink of water?'

'These are the words … Louisa … Oh, God, Kaitlyn.'

For a fleeting moment I think she has called me by my twin's name by accident. And then I understand. I feel sick with anger and weak with sadness.

'In Worthy Wood.'

Julie nods.

The words Louisa could never get out of her head. She said she could hear his voice saying them over and over again.

'You belong to me,' Julie begins.

'You're mine forever.'

As I say the words, I know this is no coincidence. Alex told me we belonged together when he gave me the necklace. There's no doubt in my mind that Alex was Louisa's rapist. After raping her, as she lay helpless on the ground, he whispered in her ear, 'You belong to me. You're mine forever.' Those were the last words he said to her.

I get through the rest of the afternoon on automatic pilot. I clear up Marley's pee on the kitchen floor; I ask the boys to go and play their electronic games upstairs. I feel oddly detached, as if this is happening to someone else and I'm observing the scene. My dad weeps. Daniel swears he'll find Alex and kill him.

While I force myself to go through the motions, Julie stays sitting on the sofa, unable to speak or move. Her face is pallid and the expression in her eyes is blank. I realise I've never considered Julie's grief. She lost a sister the day Louisa committed suicide, too, but because she'd moved in with Daniel, and Louisa was my twin, it never occurred to my teenage self that Julie could be feeling as broken as I was.

I bring Julie a glass of water, and as I place the glass in front of her on the coffee table, I grab the necklace and stuff it into the pocket of my jeans. I know what I'm going to do with it.

~

The following morning, leaving Chloe with Dad, I drive as far as Bossington, a nearby coastal hamlet, where I park the car. Then I set out by foot to Hurlstone Point. This is a walk I've intended to do since the last time I was down visiting. It's a sort of pilgrimage, I suppose, that I make from time to time in memory of my twin, retracing her steps to the place she chose to end her life.

Taking the South West Coast Path, I pass the old coastguard station and then I start to climb the steep hill. The views are great from the top, but I haven't appreciated them for a long time. I stand for a while, gazing blindly out to sea, allowing my thoughts to turn to Louisa.

Not for the first time, I wonder if she was scared when she threw herself off this cliff. Did she have time to regret her decision in the short seconds it took her to fall to her death? The coastal path can be treacherous in places. The weather was sunny the day Louisa died, just like today, and there was little wind. It couldn't have been an accident.

She didn't leave a note. She hadn't said much to anyone in the weeks leading up to her suicide, anyway. She'd become more and more withdrawn. Mum blamed herself. She said she should have seen it coming.

I take the gold medallion out of my pocket and with a growl, I throw it as far as I can over the cliff. I want Alex dead. I'm overcome by the hatred I feel towards him. My sister died because of what he did to her. Because of him, she no longer wanted to live.

I don't hear him approaching, I sense him. The hairs at the back of my neck prickle and my heart beats faster. I whirl round. This time it's not paranoia – he really is there. Alexander Riley. My husband. My jailor. He's standing a few feet away from me.

'Alex, get away from me,' I shout. My voice is shaky. 'I'm leaving.'

I take a few quick steps, but he comes towards me, ready to cut me off. When I stop, he stops. He's nearer to me now. Too near. The breeze carries his smell to me and I almost retch.

I try to move to my right, but he moves in the same direction. I take hurried steps the other way, but he imitates me. He's playing with me. It's a game of cat and mouse for him. It's no game for me, though. It's a question of life or death. He means to kill me.

'How fitting you should choose this place. Everyone will think you committed suicide. Just like Lou. The depressed Best twins. Although your sister went over a bit further round there.' He points. 'It slopes a bit too much here. There's a sheer drop just around the corner.'

I feel my legs start to buckle underneath me. It takes a lot of willpower to stay standing. I can hear the sea behind me and I know I'm only a few steps away from the edge. How does he know the precise spot where Louisa committed suicide? Even I don't know exactly. Alex had left school by then. He wasn't even in Somerset.

Fury rushes through my veins. I can feel my nostrils flare. Without letting my eyes stray too far from Alex, I look around for something I can use to protect myself, some sort of weapon, but there is nothing. The path is a dirt track. There are no pebbles. There are no trees this close to the edge and so there are no sticks or branches.

'I know you raped her, you bastard.' I don't recognise the voice as mine. It sounds ferocious. I need to keep him talking. Play for time.

'She was a feisty one, your sister. My lovely Lou.'

I almost want him to run at me. I am ready to gouge his eyes out with my fingers. No one ever called my sister 'Lou'. And she was never his. How dare he!

'Why Louisa?'

'She turned me down. She didn't want me. She was the only one.'

I'm not sure what he means by that last sentence, but Alex continues before I can ask.

'When I came back from my gap year, I spent a fortnight or so at my aunt and uncle's in Exford,' he continues. 'That's when I saw Lou again. It was months after I'd held her and told her we belonged together. She was out walking alone. Not far from here. I followed her. She walked all the way out here. To Hurlstone Point. She stood on the clifftop for ages.'

I want to argue. *You didn't hold her. You raped her.* I want to shut my eyes to the vivid image Alex is painting in my mind of my twin sister just minutes before her death. But I can't afford to take my eyes off him. Not even for a split second.

'She wasn't going to jump. She didn't have it in her. So I talked to her for a while. Tried to save her. Lou recognised me, of course, from school – we were on the school cross-country team together. But she didn't realise it was me behind the mask at first.'

'The mask?'

'I was wearing a balaclava that day in Worthy Woods. Anyway, it didn't take her long. She said my voice gave me away. She got angry. Very angry. She tried to scratch my face.'

He stops. I wonder if he's about to make a move, try and catch me off guard, but he stays where he is. He seems lost in his memory.

'What happened next?'

'I pushed her away from me. But she pounced on me again and carried on clawing at my cheeks. So I pushed her over the edge.' For a moment, Alex looks almost remorseful. 'I shouldn't have done it. I'm not like my father. I'm not a violent man.' At these words, I touch my face. 'I thought I'd got away with it when they arrested the wrong man. I swore never to do it again. And I didn't. I never … loved anyone the way I'd loved Lou.' His jaw sets in determination and any hint of regret has vanished. His voice is cold as he says, 'I didn't want her to die. But she realised it was me. I couldn't let her live.'

I can feel my body betraying me. I am shaking, shivering in the wind as well as from the brutal shock of Alex's confession. I want to make a dash for it, but my legs won't move.

'Then you sent me that friend request,' Alex continues. 'It was like being given a second chance. But now you've found me out, too.'

My vision is blurred with tears. But my mind is focused. Alex makes a terrifying noise just before he rushes at me. It's like a war cry. It gives me a fraction of a second's warning and I manage to dive to one side. He's on me now and the edge of the cliff is perilously close. We could easily roll right over it. He grabs my wrists and yanks me to my feet.

'Think about Chloe,' I beg.

He doesn't know she's not his baby, but my plea falls on deaf ears anyway. Alex is thinking of no one but himself. Still gripping my wrists, he pulls me towards the edge of the cliff. I feel doomed. Alex is strong, far stronger than me. I have no chance. But Chloe gives me mental strength. I'm thinking straight.

Then it comes to me. It goes against my instinct, but I suddenly stop resisting. Alex stumbles backwards and I use all my force to push my hands downwards so that my wrists bend back his thumbs. He releases his grasp.

For a split second he sways and I think he's going to recover his balance. His blue eyes are vacant – in denial or disbelief, I can't tell which. I don't know if I reach out to push him again or to pull him to safety, but as I do, he tries to grab my hand. Before he can take hold of me to regain his footing – or make me lose mine – gravity claims him and he tumbles backwards.

I don't remember hearing any sound at all. If he screams, I don't register it. If there's a crack or a thud as he lands on the rocks below or a splash as he hits the water, I'm not aware of it. The next half an hour or so is a complete blank.

Chapter 28

I wanted him dead. I should feel relieved or pleased or some sense of closure. Perhaps I could be forgiven for feeling elated or devastated. But I feel none of this. Instead, I'm restless.

I ring Sandy. It seems like the decent thing to do. The police have already notified her of her son's death. She asks me a lot of questions. I skip the part where Alex turned out to be Louisa's rapist and killer. But I tell her what happened to me on the clifftop. I don't think she has any difficulty believing her son would try to push me to my death. And I get the impression, that through her tears, she accepts that he's dead. She seems to have expected it, as if fatality was always his fate.

But I don't accept it. I don't believe he's dead.

Dad's house has been teeming with people since it happened. My family, of course, Hannah and Kevin, the dog walkers who arrived on the scene just as Alex went over the edge and who came to my aid. Teddy has been round a couple of times, too. And the police.

'It's not uncommon for no corpse to wash up,' DC Bryant repeats. We have the same conversation every day, either over the phone or face to face, and each time I'm struck by the number of negative forms he packs into that single sentence.

'It may well wash up further round the coast,' he continues. 'It can take several days. Or we may never find any remains. It happens.'

But just last year, on the local news there was a story about a hiker who slipped and went over the edge. She was rescued by the Minehead RNLI the following morning, having spent the night in a cave. There have been stories like this in the local papers for as long as I can remember.

I've told all this to the detective constable a few times now. And I wasn't telling him anything he didn't already know the first time. But as DC Bryant has told me, there have been news items about people who weren't so lucky, too.

'Ms Best … Kaitlyn, the police dogs spent two days out there with their handlers. The lifeboats were launched as soon as this incident was called in, and they were out again at first light the next day. They didn't find anything. If your husband had fallen onto a ledge, he couldn't have got off it by himself. The most likely scenario is that he lost consciousness as he hit the water and then sank like a stone.'

He sounds convincing. But I'm not convinced. Alex is a great swimmer. If he fell into the water, he'll have landed correctly and he won't have drowned. He's strong. I've no doubt he could have climbed up or down the cliff face, even injured, if he'd landed on a ledge.

I wonder if this is the first time DC Bryant has had the job of reassuring the spouse of a missing person that she's definitely a widow. Wouldn't he normally be promising that there's still hope the police will find that person alive? But Alex is not your run-of-the-mill missing person. He's 'missing, presumed dead'.

'I just need to know for sure that he's dead,' I say in a low voice to Nikki over the phone late one evening. 'I've never wanted his body as much as I do now!'

Nikki roars with laughter and I almost manage a smile.

I'm sitting on the sofa next to Dad, who is prising his slipper out of Marley's jaws. The TV is on, but neither Dad nor I are watching it.

'You can apply to have Alex declared dead even without a corpse,' Nikki says. 'I Googled it. You'll need a death certificate so you can inherit his property and get your money back and also if you want to remarry one day.'

'There's no risk—'

'The process is quite short and simple if the circumstances surrounding his disappearance leave little doubt about his death. When there's no body, they rely on police evidence.'

I shudder. This is a bit morbid for me this evening. I'm too tired. But after ending the call with Nikki, I start to read 'declared death in absentia' on Wikipedia while Dad puts his slipper back on and gets Marley ready for bed.

As I'm scrolling through the article on my mobile, there's a notification sound for an incoming text. I read the message, staring at the phone in disbelief. I check the sender. No, I haven't made a mistake. It feels as if the temperature in the room has dropped by at least five degrees all of a sudden.

I pick up the phone and read the text again. I've been waiting for proof that Alex is dead, but now I have proof that he's still alive. Just as I feared.

It's definitely from him. The message has been sent from his mobile. I close my eyes, as if that will make it go away. But I can still see the screen of my phone behind my eyelids. And I can see his signature. Alexxx.

I don't want Dad to worry. I try to act normal while I say goodnight. I check that the doors are locked and then I go upstairs, where I check on Chloe. She's sound asleep in her cot, back in the boys' bedroom. In Julie's room – my bedroom for now – I catch my leg on the flap of one of the cardboard boxes that Nikki brought down containing my stuff. I've unpacked, but I still haven't taken out the boxes. I certainly couldn't have left them lying around for several days in the Old Vicarage. Alex wouldn't have stood for such untidiness.

Climbing into bed, I call Julie. I know she and Daniel both leave their mobiles on for me at the moment. Just in case. I can tell by Julie's sleepy voice that I've just woken her up. I tell her I've received a text from Alex.

'Are you absolutely sure it's from him? I mean, wouldn't he have had his mobile on him when he went over the cliff? Is there any chance someone might have found it on the rocks below?'

'No, they would have needed his passcode. It's definitely from him. He signed it the way he always does.'

'What did he say in his text?'

'He said, "I'll never regret falling for you", I tell her. I hear her inhale sharply.

'Oh, God. It really is from him, isn't it? He's a sick prick!' she exclaims. 'Have you rung the police?' For once, I appreciate her big sister tone.

'I'll do it now,' I say. 'I didn't want to alarm Dad.'

'Do you want Daniel and me to come round?'

'No, you go back to sleep. I'll ring the police. Anyway, Alex will be lying low, lying in wait. I doubt he'll do anything tonight. It would be too risky after sending the text. Wouldn't it?' I'm not sure if I'm trying to convince Julie or myself. She promises me that they'll be there first thing in the morning.

I call DC Bryant on the mobile number he gave me. It's a quarter past eleven now and his phone rings for a while before going to voicemail. Despite the late hour, this surprises me. I leave a message. I contemplate calling 999. I know I should, but in the end, I decide not to. I have a half-formed idea in my head and I need to think it through. I even wonder if I've made a mistake leaving a message for DC Bryant.

I'm jittery and tense and I don't expect to sleep, but after a while, I can feel myself starting to drift off.

I don't know what has woken me. It feels like I've only been asleep for a few minutes, but daylight is forcing its way resolutely through the curtains. I get a strange sense of déjà vu, an unsettling flashback to the morning I woke up handcuffed to the bed in the nursery to discover that Chloe was no longer in the cot. I hear the front door close downstairs and realise my dad must be taking Marley out for an early morning walk.

It takes me a couple of seconds to make out the shape. I sense him more than see him to begin with. I'm not alone. Someone is sitting on the bed, watching me. I gasp.

Alex.

Before I can move, he seizes my arm and pulls me out of bed.

'You're coming with me,' he says. 'You and Chloe. You belong to me.'

As Alex starts to drag me by the wrist across the room, I realise he is injured. He's limping. He must have hurt himself when he fell from Hurlstone Point. I try to keep my breathing even and calm myself down enough to use my head. Easier to think than to do, but I can see my daughter's face in my mind and it spurs me on.

Then I spot them on the floor. The scissors I used to open the cardboard boxes. They're half-hidden from view by the flap. Bending down, I grab them with my free hand. Alex hasn't seen. He seems to think I've stumbled. He pulls me to him, then pushes me roughly in front of him, pinning me against his chest with his left arm.

His mouth is next to my ear. 'Don't try anything. For Chloe's sake.'

I notice he has difficulty opening the bedroom door with his right hand. He seems to have hurt his arm, too. I grip the scissors tightly by my side. Then, as he opens the door, I turn around, pushing against his grasp and raising my arm quickly. In that moment, I remember the movement I practised over and over again as I lay bound to that bed, holding the piece of wood from the broken mobile. I use all my strength as I bring my hand down.

I feel him slump against me and then he falls to the floor. He tries to say something – I can see his lips moving – but if he does manage to get any words out, they are drowned out by all the noises that start up at the same time. My mobile rings on the nightstand. The doorbell goes. Chloe starts to cry.

Ignoring the phone, I make my way along the landing to the boys' room and pick up my daughter. Then I go downstairs and open the door. It's Julie, Daniel and the boys. Julie takes one look at me and takes Chloe out of my arms.

'What's happened?' she asks.

I can't seem to answer, or perhaps some instinct prevents me from doing so in front of the boys and I nod towards the stairs. Julie hands Chloe to Daniel and follows me upstairs.

Seconds later, Julie is feeling for a pulse on the side of the neck that doesn't have the scissors sticking out of it. She shakes her head.

'We need to ring for an ambulance,' she says.

'But he's dead.'

'And the police,' she adds.

'The police already think he's dead.'

Just then, my mobile rings again. Almost automatically, I walk round the bed and pick it up from the bedside table.

'It's DC Bryant,' I tell Julie.

'Don't say anything,' she says hastily just as I swipe the screen to take the call.

DC Bryant apologises profusely for not answering his mobile last night. He says he had the ringer on silent. 'I'm on my way over now, Kaitlyn,' he says. 'Is everything all right?'

'Everything's fine,' I say, my eyes locked on Julie's.

'Have you had any more messages?'

'No. It's not a good time to come round right now,' I say. Some part of my brain is kicking in and taking over and I'm not aware of meaning to say any of the words that are spilling out of my mouth. 'I'm not at home. I made a mistake about the text,' I continue. 'It wasn't from Alex after all. It was someone's idea of a joke.'

When I end the call, Julie is nodding. I start to giggle uncontrollably; out of nerves, maybe, or just at how surreal all this seems. But the gravity of the situation soon hits me. My sister and I discuss succinctly what needs to be done.

We go downstairs and find Daniel and the boys in the kitchen. Daniel has made up a bottle of formula and he's feeding Chloe.

Julie starts issuing orders. 'Oscar, Archie. Granddad has gone out with Marley. I want you to find them, tell Granddad you haven't had anything to eat and get him to take you to that little café near the harbour that does English breakfasts on Sunday mornings.' She hands Oscar three ten-pound notes. 'Here. In case Granddad hasn't got his wallet on him. Keep him away for as long as you possibly can. Auntie Kaitlyn and I are going to clean the house and if he comes back too early, it'll ruin the surprise.'

As soon as the boys have left, Julie and I bring Daniel up to speed. 'I'll ring Kevin,' he says. At first I don't want him to. I don't want Kevin involved in this. But then I reason, Chloe is his daughter.

An hour or two later, Julie and I have finished cleaning upstairs and I've finally taken the boxes out to the garage. The bedroom will need a new carpet, but for now an old rug that used to be kept in the wardrobe is hiding the bloodstains.

Stepping out of the shower, I hear voices in the hallway. I quickly get dressed and go downstairs to find out how Daniel and Kevin have got on. But it looks like they've arrived back at the same time as my dad, Oscar and Archie.

The boys ask their dad if they can play on their electronic games in their bedroom upstairs.

'Of course you can,' Julie answers for Daniel. 'Up you go.' The boys look at each other, astonished, and then race off before she can change her mind.

Dad makes everyone a cup of tea and Julie, Daniel and I sit down in the living room. Kevin stays standing. No one speaks, each of us, I imagine, lost in our thoughts and still reeling with shock. We're all tainted by what we've just done, all bound together in Alex's destructive web and tarnished with Alex's blood. The silence says it all. It's a tacit promise never to tell anyone about this, an unspoken pact never to mention it, not even among ourselves.

'It's good to see you again, Kevin,' my dad says. 'To what do we owe this pleasure?'

'I … um … had to sort out a problem. Daniel gave me a hand and then I came here to see Chloe … and Kaitlyn.'

'Building problem was it?' Dad has noticed their clothes. Kevin and Daniel are both filthy and have stains – dirt and blood, I imagine, on their jeans and tops. And a grey stain that Kevin's work clothes have always had from the cement.

I need to change the subject quickly. Kevin is a terrible liar. But he answers before I can think of anything to say. 'An urgent problem with the foundations for the leisure centre in Minehead.'

'We had to pour some concrete,' Daniel chimes in. I watch as he exchanges a glance with Kevin. Its meaning is lost on me.

'The new leisure centre that's under construction? The one named after that Somerset athlete?'

'Mary Rand. Yes, that's right.'

'On a Sunday?'

'Yes,' Kevin repeats. He sounds credible and I'm surprised, but then it occurs to me he probably isn't lying. Not really.

'Ah,' Dad says, as if that explains everything.

Kevin catches my eye and without a word, I get up from the sofa and hand him his daughter. He fixes his gaze on Chloe.

'You're safe now, Chloe,' he says, his voice loud enough only for Chloe and me.

'Are you OK?' I whisper.

'I'll be fine,' he whispers back. 'And so will you and Chloe.'

295

Julie, Daniel and the boys and Kevin leave soon after that and I decide to get out of the house and clear my cluttered mind. Dad looks after Chloe and I drive aimlessly for miles until I see a sign for Nether Stowey. I pass the place where Wordsworth lived until he felt homesick and moved back to the Lake District. How ironic that I've left the Lake District and now I've come back here to Somerset, to my roots.

In the village, I park the car and order a pub meal in The Rose and Crown. I'm ravenous, I realise, washing my burger and chips down with half a pint of beer.

It's only as I'm parking the car in front of Dad's house that I realise I haven't checked in the rear-view mirror. Not once the whole way back to Porlock.

And as I'm getting ready for bed that night, I realise something else. I'm pretty sure I haven't locked the front door. But I can't be bothered to go downstairs. I clamber into bed. I've got a feeling I'm going to sleep well tonight.

Epilogue

2019

Chloe marches up the drive. Kevin opens the front door before we reach it and scoops her up into his arms.

'Daddy,' she coos, giving him one of her slobbery kisses.

'I like your dress,' he says. She insisted on wearing her Elsa from *Frozen* costume, complete with blue gloves and tiara. 'And who's this?' He points at the teddy bear tucked under her arm.

'It's Sorbet,' she announces.

'Sorbet, huh? That's a good name for a bear.'

'I don't know how she came up with that one,' I say, although I suspect her granddad has been spoiling her with ice cream and sweets behind my back. He looks after her on Mondays and Thursdays, the two days I've been working at the university since I went back, part-time, a few months ago.

'Have a nice time, Kaitlyn,' Kevin says.

I grunt. I'm dreading this. I don't know why I agreed to do it.

'Yeah, try not to tread on too many people's toes,' says Hannah, who has appeared behind Kevin and is ruffling Chloe's hair.

I'm a few minutes early when I pull into the car park of the new Mary Rand Sports and Fitness Centre just down the road from Kevin and Hannah's terrace house, but Teddy is already there. I spot him standing on the steps, exhaling vapour from his electronic cigarette as he waits for me.

My heart skips a beat, but I remind myself that I'm not ready for romance. For the moment, I just need a friend. And Teddy and I have become very good friends over the past eighteen months or so. His daughter, Olivia, dotes on Chloe, who adores her, and the four of us spend a lot of time together.

Just before I get out of the car to join Teddy, my phone pings with an incoming text. I read it.

> May have found a buyer for The Old Vic. Watch this space ...
> Nikki. X
>

I smile at the three 'fingers crossed' emojis at the end of Nikki's message as well as at the news. I'll be relieved to be shot of that house and all the bad memories it holds. When the High Court officially declared Alex presumed dead, as Alex's widow, I inherited the Old Vicarage. For that, I'm glad, although I have no intention of ever setting foot in that place again.

The official date on Alex's death certificate is Monday 4th September 2017, the day he fell from Hurlstone Point. On Tuesday 4th September 2018, a year later to the day, Nikki and I had the ground under and around the damson tree dug up. Just to check. No bones were found, no human remains, nothing. This hasn't shaken Nikki's belief that Alex killed Melanie, Poppy and Violet, but I harbour the hope that they got away. Sometimes I wonder if they ever existed at all. I'll probably never know for certain. Just one of the many secrets the Old Vicarage keeps within its walls.

Then Nikki put the house on the market and once it has been

sold, I'll pay off the rest of the mortgage. There are surprisingly few monthly payments left. And, although Nikki doesn't know this yet, I'll not only pay her estate agent's fees, but I'll also pay her back every single penny that Alex stole from her. With interest.

If my calculations are correct, I should have enough money for a deposit on a property in the Porlock area. At the moment, I'm still living at Dad's, and he has been wonderful to Chloe and me. But I'm looking forward to being fully independent again soon.

I'm still smiling as I walk towards Teddy, despite the butterflies flapping around in my stomach. I'm not sure if all that fluttering is because I'm in Teddy's company or if it's nerves about this first lesson.

'I was worried you'd change your mind,' Teddy says, kissing me on the cheek.

'I'm not sure about it, but this is a free trial lesson, right? If one of us decides we don't like it, we don't have to sign up.'

'Exactly. We can just go out for a meal every Friday night instead.'

'OK. I'll give it a go. But I've warned you, I've got two left feet.'

That's not quite how I phrased it last time and I grimace at my choice of words. *Two left feet.* That's the exact phrase Alex used at our wedding to describe my lack of coordination on the dancefloor. I'm well aware that part of the reason I let Teddy persuade me to take ballroom dancing classes is to spite Alex. He'll never know about this, so he won't feel at all peeved, but I feel a wonderfully perverse sense of satisfaction.

Before we get started, I look around at the other dancers in the group. Most of them are wearing jeans, like Teddy and me, but one older woman has a sequined dress on and a younger woman is sporting a grey T-shirt with 'I carried a watermelon' on it over Lycra leggings.

As the instructor takes us through the basic steps for the waltz,

I relax and realise I'm enjoying myself. We start to move on the dancefloor, clumsily at first and then more smoothly.

Suddenly, I freeze. I feel cold fingers running up my spine and then an icy hand on the back of my neck. I shiver. A pang of guilt stabs my conscience. And then the feeling dissipates.

He would have killed me, I remind myself, continuing my steps. I was never going to get away. Not if Alex lived. It was always going to be him or me. In the end, I'm the one who has survived. I'm the one who, quite literally, gets to dance on his grave.

Acknowledgements

A huge thank you to...

...Clio Cornish, my bubbly, brilliant editor. Your advice is always incredibly insightful and you have helped me to shape this book into the best novel I can make it. (I wish I had come up with your beautiful name for one of my characters!)

...the whole talented team at HQ Digital for all your hard work and in particular Anna Sikorska for another fantastic cover and Helena Newton for the copy edits.

...my lovely agent, Sam Copeland, at Rogers Coleridge & White. I appreciate your quick replies to my messages as well as your excellent sense of humour! You've been terrific. Thanks also to Max and Eliza at RCW.

...my husband and our children for putting up with me writing and believing in me as well as to my Labrador, Cookie, who takes me out for walks so that I can talk aloud to my characters.

...my beta readers: my mother Caroline Maud, my friends Emmeline Blairon and Bella Henry, and my cousin Anne Nietzel-Schneider. Thank you for wading through the early drafts and spotting the glaring errors, and for your encouragement and positive feedback.

...the talented Caroline Frear, author of *Sweet Little Lies*. Thank you, Caz, for your help with police procedures in the case of domestic abuse.

...my fellow authors, particularly the members of the Facebook support and advice groups I belong to, and the amazing bloggers I'm in touch with on social media. You're incredibly supportive and friendly folk!

I am indebted to all of you.

A special mention for Paul, the owner of the Glen Rothay Hotel/Badger Bar, which features as the venue for the wedding reception in *He Will Find You*. Although I have eaten (the delicious pub food) here, I had to email Paul for a few details. Paul asked me to mention the badgers, great beer and the lovely hotel rooms with a lake view.

And finally, thank you from the bottom of my heart to all my readers, whoever and where ever you are, for taking the time to read my books. I hope you enjoyed them.

Dear Reader,

I had so much fun creating *He Will Find You*. The inspiration came from a summer holiday I spent in the Lake District with my family. While running with my dog around Derwentwater (the lake my main character, Kaitlyn, walks around), I saw a huge ugly grey house, which looked so out of place with the incredibly beautiful surroundings. And the idea sprang from there. Kaitlyn has difficulty settling into her new home, but the Lake District is the most amazing place with kind, friendly people and I'm desperate to go back there one day soon!

I hope you enjoyed reading *He Will Find You* as much as I enjoyed writing it. Writing can be a solitary occupation at times and so hearing from readers is one of the many highlights. I can be contacted through Twitter @dianefjeffrey and I can be found on my Facebook author page @dianejeffreyauthor/facebook.com. I would love to hear from you!

Finally, I'd really appreciate it if you could leave a review. It doesn't have to be very long. Your feedback is very useful for me and your review could help other readers to make up their minds about whether or not this book is for them.

I'm currently writing my third psychological thriller, which will be published next year. So, stay tuned…

Love,
Diane xxx

Dear Reader,

Thank you so much for taking the time to read this book – we hope you enjoyed it! If you did, we'd be so appreciative if you left a review.

Here at HQ Digital we are dedicated to publishing fiction that will keep you turning the pages into the early hours. We publish a variety of genres, from heartwarming romance, to thrilling crime and sweeping historical fiction.

To find out more about our books, enter competitions and discover exclusive content, please join our community of readers by following us at:

🐦 @HQDigitalUK

f facebook.com/HQDigitalUK

Are you a budding writer? We're also looking for authors to join the HQ Digital family! Please submit your manuscript to:

HQDigital@harpercollins.co.uk.

Hope to hear from you soon!

If you loved *He Will Find You*, check out these other twisty thrillers from HQ Digital!

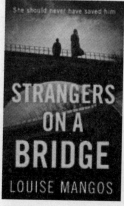